I0824643

Also by Maria Adelmann

How to Be Eaten

Girls of a Certain Age: Stories

THE ADJUNCT

A Novel

MARIA ADELMANN

SCRIBNER

New York Amsterdam/Antwerp London
Toronto Sydney/Melbourne New Delhi

Scribner
An Imprint of Simon & Schuster, LLC
1230 Avenue of the Americas
New York, NY 10020

First Scribner hardcover edition March 2026

Interior design by Kathryn A. Kenney-Peterson

Manufactured in the United States of America

1 3 5 7 9 10 8 6 4 2

Library of Congress Cataloging-in-Publication Data is available.

ISBN 978-1-6680-8997-2
ISBN 978-1-6680-8995-8 (ebook)

for Derek, who lived it,
and for everyone who deserves more

THE ADJUNCT

DISPATCH FROM THE END OF THE SEMESTER

I'm writing from under a desk. I'm writing from on the floor. I'm writing at two a.m. from the adjunct office in the literature wing of Henri Bowen B. Not my office, not anymore or not really or not ever. A lot of nots I will try to untie.

A cold December midnight in an underheated humanities building where anything could be afoot: creepy custodians, serial-killer professors, ghosts of dead adjuncts haunting the halls. The ideal setting for an Agatha Christie novel in which the ensemble cast gets knocked off one by one. The disappointing big reveal is that, actually, *capitalism did it,* and suddenly you realize that you aren't in a mystery novel at all but just another *Jacobin* article, but no, no, it's not even that, there is a twist beyond the twist: It's just real life.

The "desk" is actually a wood laminate table with metal legs, and I am under it because my phone charger is only a foot and a half long. My phone battery drains from 60 percent to 1 percent in mere minutes, then completely shuts off one to five minutes later. I keep it plugged in like a landline and use the screen as a light, since the overhead would give me away.

I'm lying prone and propped up on my arms, so both my lower back and elbows hurt. Also my shoulders. Also my fingers, which are stiff from the cold. Most demoralizing of all, I'm writing on wide-ruled paper. My handwriting fills up all available line height, so my letters are bloated and unwieldy, and I worry it will affect the prose. I never thought of my love of college-ruled paper as a love of containment, but maybe it is.

I use my puffer coat as a blanket. The first few nights, I tried wearing it arms-in-sleeves, like a regular person, if a regular person were sleeping in an empty adjunct office, but I prefer the illusion of a blanket, plus the chunky zipper left such a deep impression on my stomach that it looked like I could unzip myself.

I don't sleep much or well. Instead, I swipe. I pod. I Reddit and I Wikipedia and I worry. I tongue the sharp, craggy remains of tooth number five. I google. The other day I googled Henri Bowen, the building's namesake and one of the college's founding fathers. After fifteen years of dedicated service, he left both the school and Baltimore, citing the relentless heat, the oppressive humidity, and the college's decision to admit women, which, he thought, would ruin the institution's reputation and distract the male students.

I scroll through local job listings, writing up cover letters that attempt to cheerfully frame a career shift from academic to custodian, to cashier, but it's right before Christmas, and not even retail replies.

I lose hours staring at the tiled floor. It's the color of lightly beaten egg, white with yellow strung in. I search for images or patterns, a close reading of swirls. In the dark, now, barely lit by the glow of my secondhand iPhone, the floor is just a hard, cold plane of gray.

When the novelty of nothing wears off and I'm tired of the endless scroll, I write. Don't mistake this for ambition. Maybe I read too many deserted-island-diary chapter books as a kid. Or maybe it's something deeper—a desire for catharsis and revenge but mostly the latter. Maybe I want to figure out how I got here.

Shouts from the quad cut through the building's hum, the last of the undergrads who haven't disappeared for winter break tripping their way dormward. I imagine them back in those cozy rusticated stone buildings, stomachs full from the dining hall's hibachi grill, tucked into their real, warm beds under extra-long jersey-knit sheets, and I pity them, the ones whose dreams are as immense as their student loans. Protected in college's chrysalis, they believe that transforming into a butterfly is enough, that being capable of flying means flying.

I imagine the others, too, the ones planning their spring breaks abroad, whose ears are studded in AirPods, who are watching their parents' HBO on their sleek, charged MacBook Pros. Then jealousy rises like stomach acid, the kind that you just end up swallowing back down.

I curl up under my puffer, enter sleep's anteroom, sleep's purgatory, sleep's joke's-on-you. Images flash in the cold dark. A flexing Zeus. The apparition of Gabe in the dark woods where my face was plastered to his car. Sophie in her Victorian catering blouse, her eighties blazer, her fuchsia backless dress, her long-lasting lipstick. Tom's—that is, Dr. Sternberg's—hands cupping mine at a bar, many years ago, his face cast in a dim yellow light.

To empty my head, to get rid of these people, I turn on a podcast where a guy theoretically helps you sleep by speaking in gibberish. I try to follow senseless sentences, the thread disappearing each time. It's like reading a John Ashbery poem while high, like swinging from rope to rope to oblivion, like dropping something on the ground and picking it up, over and over again, but each time you pick the thing up, it's a different thing, and yet you keep doing it, ad nauseam, as if, eventually, you'll have something you can keep, something real you can hold in your hand.

A LIVE BODY

It was 9:58 a.m. on a hot August day that marked the beginning of the fall semester, and I was late, apparently.

The shadowy bumps of heads turned toward me as I stepped into the dim lecture hall where an IT guy paced in front of the projector, his huge and ominous silhouette appearing and disappearing over a slide that said OCCUPATIONAL HEALTH.

"This started like an hour ago," reported the undergrad manning the table of name tags at the back of the room. The tags hung from red lanyards that said WORK PLAY LEARN ROSEDALE WORK PLAY LEARN ROSEDALE.

"But Dr. Brighton said ten for new-teacher orientation?" I offered, the questioning lilt so I wouldn't seem rude.

The student's fingers flew across her phone. Black sunglasses were pushed into her hair—Ray-Bans, à la Tom Cruise in *Risky Business,* a movie she probably had never seen, but to be fair, neither had I. The glasses, I knew, cost almost two hundred bucks. My roommate, Brianna, had ordered a pair for herself, and by the law of proximity and the internet, I was now getting ads for them, too.

I scanned the tags while gathering my hair into a ponytail with both hands to cool off the nape of my neck and surreptitiously get some air to my sweaty underarms. "I can't find my name," I said.

"Oh, wait, are you one of those"—she looked up at me—"whatevers?"

"Part-time lecturer," I said.

"No, that's not it," she said. "Oh, yeah, like an *adjunct*?"

The word sounded new in her mouth. *Add-junk*. I, too, had been unaware of the weird institutional hierarchies at her age. Adjunct, postdoc, visiting professor, assistant professor, associate, full—they all taught my classes, graded my papers. It was hard to fathom a salary range of less than $10,000 to more than $300,000.

Part-time lecturers—or, less eloquently, adjuncts—didn't fit with the academia of books and movies. There, professors were a protected class whose jobs were perhaps *too* cushy—a professor could teach as an afterthought, write a book every ten years, and never be fired! But adjuncts were hired on semester-long contracts, teaching whatever classes at whatever colleges, making a few thousand dollars per course. Such roles were originally designed to be temporary, a way for colleges to fill teaching gaps and for newly minted PhDs to buy time while applying to permanent positions that would come with a salary, benefits, paid time to research and write.

But fewer and fewer faculty received tenure, and when these professors retired—sometimes in their seventies or eighties—institutions often didn't rehire for tenure-track positions. Instead, they used adjuncts or other contract labor—full-time lecturers, visiting assistant professors, postdocs—to cover the retirees' former teaching duties.

Still, there were *some* good jobs left. There was hope. Or at least, at that point, I had spent two years adjuncting while on the academic job market and hadn't lost it yet.

"Adjunct, part-time lecturer, same thing," I said.

"Oh," she said. "But, like, you don't get name tags, and you're not supposed to be here."

"What?"

"Yeah, I guess this session isn't for you."

The projector screen glowed with the empty outline of an employee sitting in an ergonomic office chair: his shoulders back, his feet resting on a foot stand, his eyes level with the upper part of his desktop monitor, as evidenced by dashed lines that shot out from his eyes like lasers.

"It's an absolute necessity to consider ergonomics in your workspace," the IT guy said. "Your working conditions have vast consequences for your overall health." He looked out at the audience. "Both knowable and unknowable."

A double bind is when you can't win. A child advances toward her mother, arms extended. The mother crosses her own arms over her chest, looks out the window, notes the mailbox is in disrepair. The child stops, drops her arms. "Why don't you come here and hug me?" the mother scolds. The mother is my mother, but that's not the point of the story. The point is: The adjunct office, I would come to learn, had an absurdly tall table and two broken chairs.

"So, where am I supposed to be, then?" I asked.

"Shouldn't you know?" she said, back on her phone.

I left to track down Dr. Brighton, head of the Department of Literature at Rosedale, who had hired me the day before during a three-minute phone call. One of her professors—"a somewhat high-profile academic in his younger days"—had broken his hip disembarking from a plane at BWI on his way home from a vacation in Greece, and she needed a last-minute replacement. "The classes are The Campus Novel and"—a tiny pause—"The Masculine Voice."

I didn't hesitate, just launched into my spiel: "I've taught a range of undergraduate classes in rhetoric, English, and comparative literature, with a focus on modern American—"

"It's fine," she said.

"I'd be happy to elaborate on my research interests," I offered, trying not to sound frantic. My budgeting spreadsheet had haunted me for months, its oppressive little cells, its endless columns stacked with late bills and upcoming bills, groceries and gas. I had ninety-six dollars in my bank account and was approaching four months overdue on rent.

Rosedale was a private college known for its picnics on Preakness—the post–Kentucky Derby jewel of the Triple Crown. The women wore sundresses and flying-saucer straw hats, and everybody got wasted on Black-Eyed Susans garnished with orange wheels and maraschino cherries. Which is all to say, Rosedale's adjunct rate—$4,400 per class—was higher than any college I'd taught at over the past two years, and $1,400 more than at Lewis, the public college where I'd be teaching three classes that semester.

"My dissertation was on the embodied experience—"

"Sam," she interrupted, "to be perfectly honest, I just need a live body. Are you a live body?"

"I am," I said. I pressed two fingers below my jaw, felt my beating heart. "I've got a pulse and everything."

She didn't laugh.

⁓

After twenty-five minutes scouring a maze of unnamed buildings in the scorching summer sun, I finally found Dr. Brighton's office in Henri Bowen A. It was a kind of institutional hazing ritual, figuring out where the hell you were. No one answered when I knocked, so I waited against the opposite wall, my skin prickling to goose bumps as my sweat evaporated in the overpowering AC.

The door next to Dr. Brighton's was ajar. Through the crack, I could see floor-to-ceiling books, perfectly aligned on heavy wooden shelves. On an oak desk sat a giant retina display and a man's hand on a Magic Mouse.

"Hello?" I said with a knuckle tap, leaning in, hoping he might have an ETA on Dr. Brighton.

When his head appeared from behind the monitor, I sucked in my breath and stepped backward. A little "Oh" escaped my mouth.

I knew the head. I had seen that head many times before, too many, in fact, and stupidly thought I'd never see it again. Pale face, pink lips, boyish cheeks on a face attached to a lithe runner's body. Attractive but not too attractive, which was disarming in its own way. Even now the haircut was a vague nineties punk-rock/prep-school hybrid, but also out of time, a signature look: a side part with carefully tousled bangs that curled on their own, designed partly to cover a large forehead, partly to offset an otherwise buttoned-up look, like the cool youth-group pastor who always wants to discuss premarital sex.

Did his eyes flash fear? Or did I imagine it?

"Hi, Sam," he said as he stood up and walked to the door. Tom—or Dr. Sternberg, as I'd never called him—didn't want me in his office, though I'd already been in plenty of offices with him, and other places, too: coffee shops, bars, his home with his dog, Cheever, napping at my feet.

The sleeves of his button-down were rolled up in such a way that it seemed he could just as easily fix a car as fist a woman as teach a class. Behind him, the bottom row of his bookshelf consisted entirely of hardcover copies of *Ten Four,* the novel he'd published at twenty-nine, which had been nominated for a major award that was always mentioned in the first line of his bio.

He had yet to produce a second book—year after year for what, twenty years now?—and I knew it weighed on him, but the premise never changed: Because he'd written his first book so well and so early, he was a genius, and because he hadn't written a second, he was a *tortured genius,* an even more revered designation. The only thing that could've improved his status was if he'd died young, and it was too late for that.

Tom had to be around fifty. The thought shocked me. The version of him I'd met in grad school was a transparent overlay on the man he'd become, though I had seen him in the intervening decade—or had it been longer?

"If you wanted to talk to me," he said, crisp and polite, "we could have set up a meeting." I was in the middle of the hall. He had walked me out here by walking toward me.

The more I looked, the older he seemed. His hair was graying, his bangs partially obscured three sharp wrinkles that cut through his forehead, his face was round to match a softening body. Everything had loosened—his eyelids, his cheeks, his neck—save his lips, which had thinned. And next to his left eye was an archipelago of age spots.

"I didn't want to talk to you," I said. He flickered between hims, the younger and the old.

"You *did* just knock on my door," he said with a half smile. He was full of half smiles, generous laughs; even now, when he was being cautious, he was also being casual, making my own stiffness feel ridiculous.

When I used to appear in his doorway at Samuel Hudson, he would turn his head to the side and say "Come in" or "Come on," the latter accompanied by a nod, and already I was following him, wherever he was going, possibly to the photocopier, possibly to an ATM, possibly to grab coffee for the both of us, on his dime. And when he said "Come in," it was even better, especially if he rolled his chair close, sitting forward with his elbows on his knees, holding my work in his hand, shaking it, saying, "This could be very, very good," and even if the coming monologue concerned generalities about talent and potential and not specifics about the writing, that little bud of pride and hope still bloomed idiotically in my chest.

"I thought you were in France," I said.

"One comes back from sabbaticals," he said. He had been a guest professor, I knew, but he had always preferred quips to facts.

"What about SHU?" I asked, pronouncing it *shoe,* like we all did. SHU, my grad school alma mater, where his position had awaited him, just a few miles away.

"You really didn't know I was here?" he asked.

Why would I ever guess he'd leave SHU? Tom thrived on prestige. I couldn't imagine a salary offer that would convince him to switch from a top-ten university to a relatively obscure liberal arts college like Rosedale.

"I was looking for Dr. Brighton," I said. Was my voice shaking? I felt desperate to explain that my presence had nothing to do with him. "I thought you might know where she was. But I didn't know *you* would be, well . . . you."

"Are you teaching here?" he asked, assimilating the information, perhaps relieved that I hadn't hunted him down, or distressed that I would be wandering around the department all semester.

"Part-time lecturer," I said. "As of yesterday."

"Ah," he said.

"Orientation is—"

"Shit, is that today?" he said. I nodded. "All right, let's find Dr. Brighton." *Let's.* I felt something pull inside me, that old feeling.

"You must be one of us," Tom had said the first time we met, flashing a big boyish smile. I looked behind me, and he laughed. *One of us.* I'd never belonged to anything so quickly.

I'd walked into grad school orientation way too early, still sweaty from buying a used window AC unit and lugging it to my new apartment, and found him at the front of the room, wiping his bangs off his face, trying to get the projector to work.

There was an energy to his physicality that his author photo didn't capture, and I was nervous standing in front of him, as if I'd just met my celebrity crush.

There were two tracks in SHU's English and Comparative Literature program. On the academic track, your dissertation would be the traditional scholarly research project. On the creative track—which Tom led—your dissertation could be a novel. That's the track I'd entered on—the whole point, originally, had been to find a way to support myself while writing a book.

During my first workshop with Tom, he told the class, "I've never read a story so delightful and gruesome, have you?" I'd written about a serial killer and the would-be victim he decides not to kill. The would-be victim goes through her whole life not knowing how brutally she was almost murdered and how lovingly she was spared. "This really charms you with gore from the very first page," Tom said. I scribbled down his words in my notebook, and after class I rewrote them in precise print, so I wouldn't forget, like a girl taping a love note into her diary. I was twenty-two—a young twenty-two.

"You're a real writer," he told me over coffee when we met off campus to discuss my work. In retrospect, such a statement is ridiculous—a cliché, a come-on—but at the time, I believed every word from his mouth. Everything he said must have at least two meanings, I thought, one deeper than I could comprehend. I had to pin my arms to my sides to keep the nervous sweat contained, which made it difficult to drink my latte. "Not everyone is cut out for it," he added. Did he mean I *was* cut out for it? Or that I could be a "real writer" and *not* be cut out for it? It seemed stupid to ask. I picked up my little spoon to stir the foam around.

"Hey, Sam?" he said gently.

"Yes?"

"You can just be yourself around me, okay?"

During the second week of classes, Tom handed me a signed copy of *Ten Four*. When I returned it a few days later, he laughed and said he'd meant I could keep it.

The book is about a young man—a thinly veiled version of Tom—who feels pressured by his family to become a lawyer. On his first day of Harvard Law, he has a panic attack that he thinks is a heart attack. He leaves the university and heads straight into a job as a long-haul trucker. While driving back and forth across the country, he feels a freedom he has never felt before. He meets all kinds of people—gas station attendants, other truckers, sex workers, rest stop custodians, waitresses, coal miners, car accident victims (one of whom he saves), and even a charming family of undocumented immigrants traveling north. At the end of the book, he considers returning to law school, realizing he can use the privileges of his own life to help those in need.

The first time I read it, I loved *Ten Four,* caught up in the deceptively easy language, the descriptions of the open road, the grittiness of the truck stops. Tom had been compared to both David Foster Wallace and Denis Johnson in separate reviews, and somehow neither seemed wrong.

But on a second read, years later, I saw something completely different: a rich person's fantasy of the lower class. The people on pseudo Tom's road trip were half stupid, half sage, occasionally almost magical. The problem with poverty, it seemed, was not crushing debt or lack of access to health care but that people like the narrator failed to see the poor for who they really were—smart and useful in their own pure and charming ways. Most ridiculous of all, they taught him that poverty was freedom, that money didn't matter.

The literary establishment was, of course, blind to the condescension. They loved *Ten Four* because it confirmed their worldview and made them feel generous at the same time, to think about poor people in such a positive light. What was my excuse? My mom had been a secretary, and my father had worked endless overtime as a gas station attendant, a car mechanic, a delivery driver.

We weren't destitute, but there were thin times and even thinner times, and I knew well that lack of money wasn't some secret key to wisdom you could slip in your pocket. It was heavy; it pinned you down.

Ten Four was the right book at the right time, written by the right kind of person. Hemingway gave way to Cheever gave way to David Foster Wallace gave way to Jonathan Franzen. Tom Sternberg was an obvious heir. But then he never wrote that second book, and the moment—I thought, I hoped—had passed.

I fast walked a half pace behind Tom as we hunted down Dr. Brighton. He thought she might be in a meeting near the auditorium, the place he now realized he was supposed to be, too.

"Working on anything new and interesting?" he asked, as if he had stayed abreast otherwise. For many years of grad school, we'd barely spoken.

"Doing a revise-and-resubmit on embodiment for *Critical Inquiry*," I said, hoping to impress him.

"Really? *Critical Inquiry*? Was that your dissertation, embodiment?"

"It was."

"Thematic thread makes sense; this sort of stuff follows you through the years."

"Sure."

"Your stories were about disconnection, if I remember. You seemed to be struggling with an almost overdetermined *lack* of embodiment."

Years ago, I'd admired Tom's ability to nail down the heart of my work. I'd felt heard, known. But this was a power play—had it always been? The offhandedness of his comment made it feel dismissive, like: It's been a while and I can't really remember anything about you, except maybe this problem with your psyche, which I see you still have not resolved.

"What about you? Are you working on something new?" I asked, hoping the question would be as painful as always. But just then we stopped in the doorway to a classroom of chatting professors.

"Here we are," Tom said.

Soon Dr. Brighton—who now thought I wasn't supposed to be at orientation after all—was leading me back to the adjunct office in the Department of Literature, rattling off information about keys, computers, and campus values while I wondered what the fuck Tom was doing at Rosedale.

She paused in the middle of a skybridge in a light-bathed atrium that connected New Bowen (Bowen A) to Old Bowen (Bowen B), looking proudly out of the massive windows as if she were the very god who had created this scene. The lawn was bright green despite the dry summer. I could see part of Old Bowen's facade, a neoclassical behemoth with three entryways flanked by columns and, out front, a marble statue of Zeus, pure white and flexing, sparkling in the sun. I always imagined Zeus as a CrossFit guy, throwing lightning bolts from a throne of clouds, occasionally recalling that time he'd turned into a swan and banged Leda, an action described by scholars variously as seduction and rape.

Below us, students were eating meals, which, according to the café sign, were only SNACKS! Small boxes of sushi, Old Bay chicken wings, bubble tea. My stomach growled. A man in line looked up, caught my eye, and offered a kind but self-conscious smile, breaking the fourth wall of a scene where I had been mere spectator. He was older than the students, maybe a professor or a guidance counselor, and had a kind of earnest fifties-crooner look—mostly it was the jet-black hair slicked with gel—except he was Asian. He glanced up at me again as he advanced toward the register. We both smiled, averted our gazes.

"Come," said Dr. Brighton.

The view from the adjunct office was epic, overlooking the main quad's long green lawn bordered by colonnades that ran to meet a grand stone library. The office itself was empty save two tables and two chairs. The walls were an almost frantic white, like bad veneers.

"We cleared this out when we got rid of all the paper and desktops on campus," said Dr. Brighton almost apologetically.

"Excuse me?"

"We're a fully mobile campus."

"Oh." Was paper not mobile?

"This was made very clear on our website," she said in a chastising tone. "We were named *Computer* magazine's Number One Mobile Campus of the Year. It's one of our most exciting green initiatives. We're hoping to eliminate paper as much as possible, make everything portable. The students and professors are all issued MacBooks."

"Will I be issued—"

"Well," she said with a smile, as if, by interrupting, she could pretend I hadn't tried to speak. "I'll leave you to it."

~

I first noticed Sophie—eraser-pink lipstick, skin glimmering in a glaze of sweat—jogging away from the adjunct office at Lewis as I was walking toward it. She wore black pants and a vaguely Victorian button-down, stiff and white with slightly puffed shoulders, scalloped piping at the neck and cuffs. It didn't match her black high-tops, her wrinkled tote that said SHOP LOCAL. She seemed to be about my age, early thirties, tall, with the straight, boyish figure I've always envied, the kind of woman who wears a T-shirt and her arm doesn't fill out the sleeve. Her brown hair was up in a ponytail, and her bangs were at that awkward midpoint—too long to fan evenly across the forehead, too short to be pushed behind the ears.

She slowed to a fast walk, tucked a hooked pointer finger into her collar, and slid it back and forth. "Hot one," she said to me. I hadn't realized she'd registered my existence.

I noticed her again a few hours later, while I was getting some air outside of Russell Memorial Hall, a beige square building with all the no-frills practicality of public funding. With no awnings or overhangs nearby, I'd opted for the splotchy shade of a parking-lot tree and was peeling open a cheese stick when she emerged from the backseat of a beat-up black Mazda wearing an oversize green blazer and matching wide-legged pants. "Ta-da," she said upon noticing me. "Sophie," she said. "Adjunct."

"Sam," I said. "How did you get a sticker for Lot A?" I'd had to park in Lot D, which was a parking garage so far from the main campus that a shuttle ran during the semester.

"Got hit by a car," she said.

"Is that all it takes?"

"It was more like a very hard bump, though my back was

pretty fucked up," she said. "I went through this whole rigamarole for the disability sticker last spring, so for three weeks I had to take the shuttle, basically a nightmare when you have a bruised tailbone. In retribution, every semester, I peel back the sticker and scrape off the date and write in a new one."

"Amazing," I said. I gestured to her ensemble. "Wardrobe change?"

"I was catering," she said. "Up at fucking Pimlico. Some bride and a gaggle of extras getting their hair done for a wedding, eating French toast on toothpicks and drinking mimosas since four a.m."

"Extras?"

"Bridesmaids, whatever," she said, waving her hand.

Sophie was teaching two sections of English Composition—a required undergrad humanities course taught by adjuncts and TAs across disciplines—along with two Intro to Poli Sci courses. I was also teaching English Composition, along with Survey of American Literature I and II. She warned me that if I didn't pass the mind-numbing series of IT and sexual-harassment modules, they would eventually hold my paycheck. "You have to do it *every* semester," she said. Because adjuncts weren't continuously on payroll—we were basically hired and then rehired as temps from semester to semester—we had to keep doing it as if we were new.

"I'm not planning to get used to this place," I said.

"So far they've kept reupping my contract."

"But, just, adjuncting generally."

"Yeah? How long have you been adjuncting?"

"Four semesters," I said, thinking it might sound shorter than two years.

In my first postdefense academic year, I'd taught a single class each semester, at BCMU and then Montoya, at a rate of $3,000 and $3,300 per class, respectively. My income didn't even cover the $500 per month I owed on my undergraduate student loans, so I'd burned through most of what I'd managed to save during grad school as I worked on rewriting one of my dissertation chapters, which I submitted to *Critical Inquiry* at the end of the academic year.

The following year I scored three classes each semester at MBMU. The $18,000 (before taxes) didn't cover my expenses—rent and student loans alone came to $15,000. Even as I couldn't quite pay my credit-card bill each month and got behind on rent, I assumed it was only temporary; the department head at MBMU told me they planned to hire a lecturer to teach my classes, the implication being that I was a shoo-in. It wasn't a tenure-track job, but it paid more than adjuncting, and the yearlong contract was theoretically renewable.

They ended up hiring someone five years younger than I was, straight out of a slightly more impressive grad school, reinforcing a percolating worry—that it had taken me too long to finish my PhD, that at thirty-three, with no other experience under my belt, I was already too old to get a full-time job in a tight academic market brimming with fresh meat.

When I'd started grad school straight out of college, the advice was to go slow. At the time, eight years to complete a PhD (with a master's degree along the way) wasn't just realistic, it was encouraged. But it took me even longer—ten years—because I'd switched tracks two years in and basically had to start over. By the time I was done, the advice had changed, and students were wrapping up PhD programs in just six years.

The same day I learned that they'd hired someone else at MBMU—which meant that I both hadn't gotten the job and was out of a job—I received a revise-and-resubmit from *Critical Inquiry,* one year after I'd submitted the paper. This was big news. A publication like that could change the entire job search, and I knew my main goal had to be rewriting it, but first I had to pay the rent—past and future—and all the other bills, and to do that, I had to find some work.

I simultaneously celebrated the win and drowned my sorrows by eating a Hershey bar, rectangle by rectangle, while carpet-bombing the inboxes of every department chair in Baltimore, asking if they had classes up for grabs. By the end of that academic year, I'd applied to thirteen tenure-track jobs, seven postdocs and lectureships, and five one-year visiting assistant professorships, while also floating around in the adjunct hiring pools for most of Baltimore City and County's thirteen institutions of higher ed.

I gave Sophie the CliffsNotes version of this.

"So what now?" she said. "You have some secret escape plan?"

"Well, I'm still hoping to get something more permanent."

"I've found that hope isn't a very good strategy."

"What other strategy is there?"

"Insurrection," she said, straight-faced before she laughed.

I told her about Rosedale, how I'd been uninvited to an unpaid orientation which I'd then had to go to on another day because their system had failed to generate adjuncts on the attendance sheet and, actually, it was mandatory.

"Ugh, Rosedale," she said. "Probably don't want the riffraff associating with the professorial class."

"At least it's work," I said.

"Speaking of, I'm getting a meeting together, trying to unionize. Interested?" She handed me her phone to type in my name and number.

A few days later, Sophie and I converged on a post–faculty meeting classroom bursting with abandoned bagels. Other than the students, I hadn't talked to anyone all week. At Rosedale, familiar colleagues reappeared only in slivers or blurs. Dr. Brighton rushing down the hall, not even noticing my pathetic wave. The guy I'd locked eyes with across the atrium always seemed to be crossing the quad just as I looked out the adjunct office window before leaving to teach The Campus Novel. And Tom, of course, whom I avoided, not even glancing at his doorway if I had to walk past. Somehow this only made his presence more acute, like a numbed body part tingling its way back to life.

Sophie was wearing bloodred lipstick and stuffing a bagel into the interior pocket of her oversize dark purple blazer, part of an eighties business suit that made me wonder which job she'd come from, though later I realized this was just what she wore to teach. It was a bold choice—I tried to neutralize myself in the academic setting, stuck to the boring professionalism of grays.

I glanced around to make sure no one other than Sophie was watching, then wrapped two bagels in a napkin that I slid into the padded laptop compartment of my duffel bag before slathering cream cheese on a third. I'd learned the art of foraging as an undergrad. The goal was not to look too desperate, to act like you just happened to be there and were only trying to minimize food waste. Ludicrously, my first paychecks wouldn't drop until the last day of September.

Sophie either didn't notice the duffel or didn't feel the need to comment. It was a three-hundred-dollar cream-colored canvas cylinder with brown leather accents. Classy but out of place, like I was about to take a road trip to Nantucket. The bottom was already tinged lightly in dirt. What kind of psychopath would buy cream-colored luggage?

I had gotten the duffel for free from my side gig writing fifteen-hundred-word product reviews for a travel website I didn't entirely trust. The reviews were supposed to be "cheerfully honest personal takes," and I got the sense pretty quickly that, while I was supposed to highlight a limited number of flaws, full-on panning was frowned upon.

I got $250 per review, plus I could keep whatever items they sent, and write under a pseudonym. Mostly they sent cheap stuff like eye masks or power adapters, so this duffel was a bit of a boon, especially since my navy backpack had kicked the bucket over the summer, along with my laptop, as if by suicide pact. The duffel was enormous, thankfully fitting all five Lit classes' worth of books and papers.

I had started the product-review job during my fifth year at SHU. We were discouraged from taking "side gigs" other than odd jobs for professors or teaching the undergrad classes that paid our stipend, which was only $14,000 the first year. "Grad school isn't the real world," Tom had told me. "That's exactly the point. It's a nest. It's nurturing. Do whatever you can to focus on your real work."

I took his advice, working only a part-time summer job at the library and using the allowable four-year deferment on the $64,000 of private student loans I'd taken out as an undergrad. By the time I had to start repaying the loans, they had collected so much interest that the balance had ballooned to over $80,000, and I was chained to payments of $500 a month for the next twenty-six years. That's when I started taking in piecemeal work writing SEO-optimized product copy, tutoring in the writing center, and reviewing products.

"Fucking ridiculous, so much food," Sophie said, mouth full of bagel. "Some of us are on food stamps." I took a bite of my bagel and noticed, for the first time, a dull ache in one of my teeth. "Wanna grab coffee in the faculty lounge?" she asked. "I've got fifteen minutes before class."

The tenured professors who swung in and out of the lounge were mostly cordial, but one woman side-eyed us, intruders. The look was enough to make Sophie want to keep coming back, which we planned to do Mondays, Wednesdays, and Fridays, a friendship that would be made in fifteen-minute intervals, my only socializing time of the week.

The rest was work. I had to teach thirteen classes each week, and my schedule was absurd:

```
Lewis, 8:00-8:50 MWF, Survey of American Literature II
Rosedale, 10:10-11:00 MWF, The Campus Novel
Lewis, 1:25-2:15 MWF, Survey of American Literature I
Lewis, 8:00-9:15 T/Th, English Composition
Rosedale, 2:30-3:45 T/Th, The Masculine Voice
```

They say that for every hour of teaching, you need two to four hours of prep. Because I'd never taught any of the classes, and the somewhat high-profile academic's syllabi included six novels that

I'd never read, prep for me was at least four. That was sixty-five hours of work up front and didn't include office hours or printing lecture notes or running back and forth from campus to campus or grading, one of the most time-consuming tasks. I had more than a hundred students who, over the course of the semester, were meant to turn in a combined total of over two thousand pages of written work, and I felt a particular obligation to provide good feedback because it's so important in literature and writing courses. As for my own research, I'd aspirationally taken a few books out of the library for the *Critical Inquiry* rewrite but had yet to open them. The academic job season was in full swing, with new postings appearing each week, and I spent every spare minute writing applications.

The pockets of time with Sophie in the lounge were a release valve, a chance to blow off steam. She talked with purposeful volume about contract labor, the plight of the adjunct, the labor movement, CIA-backed coups, the ice loss in Greenland, the burning of the Amazon, the pro-democracy protests in Hong Kong, our fascist reality-TV president, and the MeToo movement, which still hung ripe in the air after the Harvey Weinstein bombshell two years before.

Sophie supported the movement broadly but criticized its inevitable ties to the capitalist structure—i.e., the commodification of trauma. I was impressed by how easily she'd synthesized this argument, which she seemed to be making off the top of her head, and how willing she was to criticize aspects of a popular movement so recently at its peak. As she ranted, her face ignited with passion, gleamed with it, the hazel of her eyes almost disappearing into her shining pupils.

I told her, with a dash of theatrics, about teaching at Rosedale. She was offended by its private school preppiness and relished the ridiculousness of certain details—the mere fact of an equestrian team, for example, or the college's commitment to being a "fully mobile campus" and the associated undertone of environmental sustainability.

She listened with an expression of deep camaraderie, her lips parted enough to frame a portion of her two front teeth, bright white against the dark lipstick, lipstick that remained despite whatever we were consuming. I had never learned the secret to long-lasting lipstick.

I considered mentioning Tom. His surprise appearance at Rosedale seemed more absurd to me than an equestrian team, but I didn't know how to frame it, what the story was, what to say.

Chapter 2

CASUALTY

Outside, the temperature was scorching for two days, then cooler for a day, then blazing again, and we started reading the modernist poets in American Lit II, the red wheelbarrow and the cold plums, and my car was towed from Lewis's Lot D.

Apparently, you needed a sticker to park there, but to get a sticker you needed to work at the university, and to prove you "worked at the university" you needed a pay stub, which, as I've noted, I wouldn't get until the end of September. I explained this to the guy at the tow lot, to a woman at the registrar, to the director of Parking and Transportation Services. I was always doing this, trying to prove the breakdown in logic, but no one was ever responsible for that crack in the system where I fell through.

I would eventually put the $215 towing and storage fee on my credit card, but not before I burned $15 on an Uber to get to Rosedale in time to teach *Pictures from an Institution*, which was full of quaint scenes, like a professor getting hired for a full-time job on the spot after a single, casual interview.

After The Campus Novel, despite the humid, misty rain, I decided to walk back to Lewis for American Lit I, where we were chasing Native American trickster tales with sobering explorer narratives of the New World.

There was a strange dissonance to teaching five classes in the same field at once, like church bells and alarms announcing noon at slightly different milliseconds, at different pitches and cadences, for different lengths of time, so your brain is forced to search for a pattern or go crazy.

American Lit I ran forward through time and would catch up with the beginning of American Lit II only at the end of the semester, by which time American Lit II would jump off the diving board of now, ready to swim into the future. The Masculine Voice essentially expanded the timeline of the second half of American Lit II, while The Campus Novel was mostly a magnification of weeks nine to twelve, but in no particular order, and English Composition was an all-encompassing meta experience about what, exactly, one was supposed to do with words at all.

Sometimes the contradictions were satisfying (like teaching the Puritans and the Jazz Age the same week), but other times (Faulkner and *The Federalist Papers*) the combinations were harder to make sense of. Certain authors appeared in multiple classes, advancing through the semester in a crescendo of Hemingway, Hemingway, Hemingway.

I walked down the long driveway wearing my duffel bag like a backpack, the straps cutting into my skin, later evidenced by a bright red slash under each armpit. So far, I had used this duffel in no way that was appropriate to talk about in a review. I cinched the hood of my raincoat tight, hoping no one would recognize me, as the plastic lining of the coat, which wasn't even that old, flaked off behind me.

The twenty-three-minute walk, according to Google Maps, didn't account for Rosedale's estate-like, winding driveway, which had no shoulder. Either it had never occurred to anyone that someone would walk here, or it was active retaliation against people without cars, which seemed to be misaligned with the environmentally friendly values spouted on digital signage around campus. It was on brand for Baltimore, though, that these two schools were so physically close, a mile and a world apart, with no public transit between.

At the sound of a car coming down the road, I stepped off into the wet grass, but instead of driving past, the car slowed. A window whirred down, the deep tones of a good speaker system pouring out, Childish Gambino singing about America. I hoped it wasn't one of my students. Or Dr. Brighton. Or that guy from the atrium. Or anyone. I felt a split-second charge, like the pulse when a coin toss reveals a true desire: I wanted it to be Tom. Get in, get in, he might have said years ago. Sam, this is dangerous, you can't walk on the side of the road. You need to take care of yourself. I hated myself for wanting it, the same stupid comfort I'd already bought into, then deemed defective.

Instead, it was another ghost from my past: Aliana Williams, dressed like she'd walked out of a J.Crew catalog and into a car commercial about a woman who could have it all. The cap sleeves on her baby-blue top, a style that typically accented the worst part of the arm, only seemed to show off how thin and hot she was. "Sam?" she said. "What are you doing?"

"Car problems," I said.

"Where are you headed?"

"Lewis."

"Hop in. I can swing past."

I set my duffel in the back footwell. The beige leather seat held a cardboard box of hardcover books with bubblegum-pink spines repeating the title, *Rolex,* and Aliana's name in all caps.

"Nice duffel," she said as I buckled up. "I have the same one."

"In cream?"

"Yeah, exactly the same."

I congratulated her on the book, which I understood was doing well.

"Oh my God, thanks," she said, shaking her head in a show of disbelief as we made our way down the drive.

I'd met Aliana at SHU over a decade before. She was six years older than I was and had worked for a talent agency in L.A. before quitting to attend grad school. *Rolex* referred to both the luxury watch and a type of ecstasy. The pink cover featured a giant blue pill, the same shade of blue as Aliana's shirt. (Not a coincidence, I later deduced after stalking the Instagram pictures of her whistle-stop tour of local bookstores.) The pill was imprinted with a pattern akin to the Rolex logo, a crown with spikes so long it looked like a Photoshop stretching error.

The book was "autofiction"—that is, a memoir with fewer potential legal issues and more clout—about the pressures of attending a private high school in Hollywood with the children of celebrities. It was also about how she'd always been bullied for being naturally skinny and about how much E she'd done while nonetheless maintaining an A average and getting into Yale.

I had read some of the book in first-draft form, many eons ago in workshop. It had a faint literary edge but mostly bridged the gap between pop lit and straight-up gossip, and I had to admit it sucked me in.

"What brings you here?" I asked her.

"Oh, you know, just signing some copies around town," she said. "Local shops, campus bookstores."

"But I thought you'd gone westward," I said. Westward? Aliana made me feel so inferior that I behaved like a robot poorly programmed to act like myself.

"Moved back east, D.C.," she said lightly, because she knew that I'd immediately understand why. We'd all applied for that job. I focused on the raw slits of skin under my armpits and the emerging dull throb in one of my teeth, pain easier to manage than seething jealousy. "The whole racket is such a crapshoot," she said. In the four years since I'd seen her last—she'd defended before I had—she had somehow polished her book, published it, and secured a tenure-track job, all while looking like a cryogenically frozen specimen of L.A. She was a woman who always lived up to her brand. Online, she posted pictures of herself and her minimalistic, modern workspace—a giant white shag carpet, a rainbow of book spines, all the necessary brands: Apple, Moleskine, Blackwing. All the necessary causes: Vote, Time's Up, Self-Care.

"What are you up to?" she said. "Writing fiction at all?"

"Oh, you know."

She frowned. Creative writers have a habit of thinking every other literary professional is just a failed novelist, though in my case, it was at least partially true.

"I always thought you were one of the most . . . creative in our program," she said. It sounded less like a compliment and more like I was a whimsical yet incomprehensible amateur. "You were writing those unromantic love stories for a while," she added. The least generous way to define the project.

"Couldn't ignore the siren song of an academic dissertation," I said noncommittally.

Aliana forced a laugh. Her body stiffened. She tapped the steering wheel as we waited at the light, looking around as if it were a city she missed dearly, but we were just on a random stretch of road that looked even more generic than usual in the misty rain. The light turned green and she accelerated. "I'm kind of surprised you took a job at Rosedale," she said. "I mean, did you want to work with Tom? Seems a little strange, no?"

It was a weird accusation. What could Aliana possibly know about Tom and me? And why would she care?

"I didn't even know he was back in the country," I said, shifting in my seat.

"You must have known he left SHU."

"I had no idea until, like, two weeks ago," I said, feeling so uneasy by Aliana's shift in tone, by some hidden implication, that my voice slipped and it sounded like a lie.

How would I have known, anyway? I'd slowly fallen out of touch with everyone from our cohort, all those people who, for over a decade, had been my only people. They had all moved—for fellowships, for postdocs (in Seattle, in Helsinki, in Sydney, in Detroit), for partners, for marketing jobs, for start-ups. Most had graduated while I was still holed up in my carrel in the stacks, trying to write an academic dissertation I was almost sure I was incapable of writing. In the past year, the text messages had waned significantly. I couldn't tell if it was their fault or mine. Many of them were in precarious situations, too, but each of their successes made my failures feel more acute. I'd spent the past few years bracing for the future that had just come to pass, in which an old classmate had beaten me out for a tenure-track job.

Aliana breathed heavily through her nostrils, as if calming herself down. "Listen," she said. "Just let it go now, okay?"

"What are you talking about?" I felt like I'd walked into the middle of a play ostensibly about my life, except I couldn't decipher the premise.

Aliana made big, disbelieving eyes, then composed herself. "I'm not gonna do this," she said, shaking her head. The defensive architecture of a rich woman who had done years of therapy. Hyperaware of her emotional output, spending it all on speaking her truth or plumbing for the answers she felt she deserved, then popping up "boundaries" real quick, so you never had a chance to respond. Self-awareness, terminating at the self.

We pulled into Lot A at Lewis. I peeled myself off her seat, where plastic flakes of rain jacket had stuck onto the leather. I tried to wipe them off, embarrassed by the metaphor of my disintegrating coat.

I extracted my duffel from the backseat, putting the strap around my shoulder like a regular person. The repeating spines of *Rolex* made me dizzy, and when I looked away, they clouded my vision as fluorescent afterimages, the spines slatted like blinds.

"I'll have to get one," I said.

"Oh, of course not." She reached around the seat and pulled out a copy. Then, in one fell swoop, she extracted a baby-blue Lamy fountain pen from her leather purse, popped off the top, and signed the cover page in elegant cursive. She handed the book to me and smiled, one side of her mouth too upturned to be friendly. "Maybe Tom will sign his new book for you, too."

My airways felt tight as I raced toward the adjunct office at Lewis while the Google search loaded on my phone with a predictable lack of urgency. I clicked the first link that appeared, waiting in an echoey stairwell as the cover revealed itself in tiny increments.

CASUALTY

it said, large and in all caps, and though I couldn't tell from the image, I imagined the letters were beveled, the mark of a book predestined for success. You could argue that Tom himself had been beveled at birth. Below the letters, a black-and-white photo of a disheveled man in a blazer, sitting at a messy desk stacked with papers and books, flying high on the myth of the mad-genius professor.

The figure's face was scribbled over with neon pink pen that made me think: bitchy schoolgirl, childish revenge. All I could really make out from beneath the angry tumult of magenta was one beady eye, staring at me, condemning me for staring back.

The last strip of cover loaded, as if to emphasize a point:

BY THOMAS STERNBERG

I scrolled down to the description:

Twenty years after the heralded debut that thrust him to literary superstardom, Thomas Sternberg returns with a powerful, genre-bending portrait of a professor reckoning with his checkered past.

In the fast and loose days of 1980s academia, a prominent professor finds himself entangled with a younger female student, a promising yet unsure scholar. What begins as innocent intellectual conversations and heartfelt correspondence grows into something more charged after she writes a letter to him detailing her discovery of his sex toys while house-sitting. A disappointing sexual encounter leads to the dissolution of his marriage, and the two lose touch.

Years later, as a feminist movement sweeps the nation, the former student publishes a think piece telling her version of the story. The professor is bewildered to learn that she considers him responsible for her subsequent personal and professional failures—and the institutions are swift to respond. Forced into retirement, the professor begins to grapple with his past through profound and surprising encounters with literature, culture, and memory. This is a wholly different story of accountability, asking us what we gain from the momentum of a movement and what we lose to a lack of nuance.

A fiercely honest and vitally important novel for this historical moment, *Casualty* is an unforgettable examination of privilege, power, and passion from a writer who has waited—who has made us wait—twenty years to dazzle and challenge us all over again.

ADVANCE PRAISE FOR *CASUALTY*

"Masterful."

"Unlike anything I have ever"—

I skipped the blurbs, reread the synopsis—once, twice, three times—came back to the blurbs, read them twice, found the publication date (October 29), scrolled up and down past the cover, scrolled all the way to the bottom of the page and up again, kept scrolling until the forearm muscle connected to my thumb began to ache and the 11:15 classes let out and the students started stomping and clacking up and down the stairs, their voices echoing in the stairwell. I backed up against the wall, clicked off the phone, dropped it in my pocket. I wanted to read the book immediately and I also wanted never to read it and I also wanted to throw up.

I had a student meeting at 12:30; I had Survey of American Lit I at 1:25; I had office hours for Lewis at 2:30; I had to come up with a lesson plan for American Lit II's 8 a.m. class tomorrow; I had to plan all the classes after that; plus, there was an onslaught of job apps due soon, Samford and St. Mary's and St. John's. But I could only think about Tom's book.

Aliana's words echoed in my head in her stiff, annoyed, incredulous tone: "Did you want to work with Tom? Seems a little strange, no?"

The details didn't match up—not even, I'd argue, the "intellectual conversations." The book could be inspired by anyone or no one. Maybe he was combining stories, making a composite, that fiction-writer specialty. Maybe the book had to do with another student—who? someone in my cohort? I felt a pang like jealousy, then a pang of embarrassment for feeling it. I could picture the sex toys, important enough to make the cover copy: the silicone rabbit, the glass dildo, the blindfold and the lube and the feather on a stick.

Trying to settle myself, I walked from the adjunct office to the faculty lounge, looking for coffee, but there wasn't any in the pot. I walked to the bathroom and washed my hands with the almond-scented soap. I was only freaking out because of Aliana's accusatory tone. The book couldn't have anything to do with me. In the past, I'd let myself imagine I was special, and I didn't want to make that mistake twice.

—

The tow lot closed before I could get to it, so I had to take the bus home from Lewis. An extravagantly bony guy with a blue bandana wrapped around his head ambled onto the bus, the skin under his eyes sagging, revealing a pink, wet strip of eye socket. He sat down next to me, even though there were plenty of seats, eyed me for a few blocks, then said, "Got a boyfriend?"

"Mmm-hmm," I said without looking up from *The War Between the Tates,* which I was barely reading, distracted by the thought of Tom's book and the smell of the bus—astringent, like piss mixed with nail polish remover, which someone at the back of the bus was, in fact, using. I envied her disregard for others.

The War Between the Tates was the only novel on either Rosedale syllabi written by a woman, and despite the very 1970s feminist take, the plotline was familiar. Tom's book was apparently joining a rich tradition of campus novels about a male professor having an affair with a student.

"He treat you right? You take shit from him?" the guy asked of my invented boyfriend.

"Never," I said.

"Those motherfuckers!" a homeless man shouted, apropos of nothing.

"Relationships don't have to be a *drag,*" the guy said, then he began monologuing with a combination life history/lecture about failed relationships, best practices, lessons learned, etc.

Because I couldn't read while he was talking, I looked out the window as we passed bright murals, check-cashing shops, pawnshops, unisex barbershops, people on street corners, nobody on the street at all, someone sleeping on a "Greatest City in America" bench. Attempting to rebrand, the city had emblazoned this slogan on all the benches, a move so absurd that the irony itself became its own achievement.

Like other cities with attrition problems, Baltimore held tight to its unique and specific claims to fame: Edgar Allan Poe and Mr. Trash Wheel, Frederick Douglass and Utz potato chips, the Baltimore Orioles and Natty Boh, the champion of cheap beer in Baltimore with an iconic one-eyed mascot. King of camp John Waters was a regular at local haunts. A plaque in a 7-Eleven on Charles Street claimed the Oujia board had been invented in that very spot, by Elijah Bond, who was now lying six feet under a Oujia-board grave in Green Mount Cemetery, where John Wilkes Booth was also buried, pennies covering his grave.

I once was charmed by Charm City, but it's a difficult place, sprawling and strange, an abandoned dream of the industrial era, a city that could have been and wasn't, that defies the logic of a city, the purpose of a city, because it isn't really walkable, the public transit sucks, and there's an almost impressive lack of grocery stores.

But what did I know? I wasn't from Baltimore. I was white. It wasn't really my city.

Baltimore has a majority Black population and is strictly divided along racial lines thanks to 1900s redlining and the structural racism that followed. To the city government, *revitalization* meant luring rich transplants to the "White L," which stretched down Charles and across the Inner Harbor, while the "Black Butterfly," which spread east and west, remained in poverty and was ignored. A bougie market popped up in the White L's Mount Vernon neighborhood, serving five-dollar dumplings. An eighteen-million-dollar independent theater, funded by my alma mater SHU, was built on North Avenue, right across the street from an indie theater that had long been a city staple. The new independent theater was apparently, predictably, hemorrhaging money. People constantly implored you to go to the theater and support the arts, as if it were *your* fault the theater was failing when nobody had asked if you wanted it there in the first place. And they certainly hadn't asked the people streaming out of the methadone clinic down the street.

Recently, the president had called Baltimore a "dangerous and filthy," "rodent-infested mess" to score points against his political enemies. Democrats had come to Baltimore's defense, proclaiming their love for the city that they had run for years, a city packed with neighborhoods they had underfunded, overpoliced, incarcerated, and scapegoated for the very real problems it faced. The criticism and the defense of the city both felt like posturing. The lives of the people in the Black Butterfly didn't seem to matter to anyone at all.

I didn't spend time in the Black Butterfly. In grad school, I ran in a tight, relatively wealthy circle of transplants who made the city feel small-town. A friend once claimed that Baltimore—that is, the sliver of it we thought of as ours—"celebrated its own mediocrity and sold it as quirk." Which is ungenerous but does explain the Natty Boh.

"BUS IS TURNING," announced the bus. A detour sent

us right, past Long Nails and Mattress Firm, and suddenly, the road stretched out and relaxed, gained a grassy medium, gained sidewalks studded in trees and streetlamps. We bumped past the Painted Ladies, a strip of homes in bright colors mimicking the more famous ones in San Francisco. The transition from forgotten to well-funded was so quick it gave you whiplash.

During the spring of 2015, the Baltimore police killed a twenty-five-year-old Black man named Freddie Gray, and the people rose up, revolted, the already obvious injustices of the city now a gaping wound. Protestors teemed in the streets, chanting and shouting, the city electric with anger and hope. Tanks rolled in along with the National Guard, as if the citizens were the threat, as if they were the people prone to violence. *Riots,* said the news on one segment. *Unrest,* they said on the next. It was either the chaotic, flailing whims of a crowd or it was nothing, a toddler who hadn't slept well.

Less than two years later, I watched the 2016 election unfold from a bar in Station North, my stomach a pit. The feeling that change might really happen had slipped away long before, but the results were an even bigger *fuck you* than I had imagined.

All that energy, and for what? What was a movement when the foundations wouldn't budge? And what could I do about it? So I had stood on the street with a sign? So I was angry? So I was a gentrifier anyway? So I could hardly pay the rent? I had no idea how to support the cause; I was barely managing to support myself.

"BUS IS TURNING," the bus announced again, and there it was: my grad school alma mater, Samuel Hudson University, a compact college town plopped down in the middle of a city, protected by a fortress of campus police who stood at all the main access points. A strange mix of regret and nostalgia rose in me, part stomachache, part heartache.

We drove past the iconic statue of Samuel Hudson himself, his bust on a pedestal that rose above two other statues sitting on the base: a man who represented knowledge and a woman who represented healing. She was bare-chested and her breasts were smooth, a brilliant golden color from years of wear, because it was good luck to feel her up. Men in particular did it with gusto, a full, meaty grope. I'd tried it myself, a shy swipe when no one was looking.

My bus acquaintance stopped trying to convince me to break up with my invented boyfriend and looked out the window with me as we chugged down Charles. "Now, if only we'd gone to school there!" he shouted.

Chapter 3

THE MASCULINE VOICE

"We're still human, after all" was what Sophie said that Friday when she proposed drinks at Chuck's. In the onslaught of the semester, our face time had already dwindled.

Behind the bar, small plastic skeletons gripped the necks of bottled spirits. It was only mid-September, early for Halloween decor, but the skeletons may have always been there. Not one memory from frequenting this bar during my grad school years was anything other than a smudgy vignette.

As I waited for my Natty Boh, I mentally scrolled through the to-do list I had shirked in order to be here. I had to write lecture notes and discussion questions for *The War Between the Tates, The Great Gatsby,* Anne Bradstreet, and Faulkner. I had to read the supplemental critical papers for *The Doctor of Desire,* and I had to start reading *Lolita* and *The Scarlet Letter.* I had to finish writing my duffel-bag review, correct the homework on claims for English Comp, and prepare a class on acknowledgment and response. Plus, I still had to write job applications for Samford, St. Mary's, and Western Connecticut State. And maybe wash my sheets and buy groceries.

The to-dos were a low, constant hum that grew deafening

when I wasn't working on them, which mostly allowed me to ignore a more abstract, underlying unease I didn't want to admit was about Tom.

I sat in a red pleather seat as Velvet Underground's "Heroin" began playing. As I took my first sips, it started slow, with the guitar and deep drumbeats. By the time the lyrics dropped in, I was already feeling better, the knot in my chest loosening with hope of being untied, and by the time the song sped up into cacophony, Sophie appeared in the doorway wearing red lipstick and an oversize navy blazer. Her face was always shining and bright, as if her life were a constant rush of excitement, exaggerated now by the wash of the bar window's red neon light. I gripped my wet pint glass, watched as she looked around the bar and the song released back into slowness. She was searching for me, but it didn't seem urgent, as if, were I not there, she'd simply sit at the bar and talk to strangers all night.

"I'm exhausted," she said once she'd found me and settled in with a gin and tonic. "What are you drinking?"

"A Boh," I said.

"Interesting."

"What?"

"It's kind of the PBR of Baltimore," she said. "A bad beer everyone loves. I thought it was a kind of hipster posturing, which didn't really seem like your thing."

"It's not my thing," I said. "It's the cheapest drink on the menu. My philosophy: The worse the drink, the slower the drinking, the less the spending."

"Good strategy," Sophie admitted.

As the bar filled up, we surveyed the crowd. "I always think

I'm going to get laid," she said, "and then I just don't have the energy."

"Have you used Tinder or anything?"

"Have you? I mean, what's a picture have to do with anything?"

"I think it's less about looks than vibes," I said. Between the music and the crowd, the bar was getting so loud that we had to shout across the table, and eventually she just moved over, sitting beside me as the seats across from us were taken instantly.

"Poli Sci is a cesspool," she said, her breath warm in my ear. "Half the people are completely insufferable. Georgetown was horrible, a big ol' boys' club full of pretentious dicks looking for government jobs and hardly any vaginas at all. And Lewis? I mean, the adjuncts, no offense, don't exactly exude sensuality."

I was apparently included in the category and tried not to feel bad. Someone once told me that I was a black box of sexual energy, that he felt unstable interacting with me—there was a jarring lack of information to work with, just his input and my unpredictable output.

I let my hair down, combing through it with my fingers as Sophie retrieved a second round on which she insisted and I barely protested. It was the first time I'd been able to relax in weeks, and now that I'd had a taste of sweet relief, I didn't want it to end.

She returned to the table with a Boh for each of us and two shots of whiskey. I fished out a ten and she took it.

"How's the job search going? Find anything good for next year?" I asked.

"The truth is, I'm not sure I want to participate in the predation of students whose families can't pay for college or the perpetuation of privilege for students who can," she said, a predictable answer. Her brown bangs had lost their slight pouf and now lay flat against her forehead, as if this conversation were as exhausting as a workout.

"It's really fucked up," I agreed, nodding, though it seemed like we were both participating regardless, even as exploited cogs in the big machine.

"Higher education is basically a pyramid scheme," she shouted over the noise. "Everyone but like ten people are getting fucked, and not in the good way. The students are paying hundreds of thousands of dollars for an education that's going to maybe land them a decent job when they get out, maybe not. And professors are living in poverty while paying back student loans?" She looked me in the eye. "Do we really want to be part of that?"

"No," I said. I sipped my Boh, feeling almost frightened for her. This was prime hunting season. Applications for most of the big jobs were due between September and October. There would still be postings in November, but not nearly as many.

I'd been on high alert for openings since midsummer, doing a weekly circuit on MLA Job List, The Chronicle of Higher Ed, HigherEdJobs, Higher Education Recruitment Consortium, and, absurdly, Twitter. There was no single place you could find every posting. Occasionally I visited the crowd-sourced Academic Jobs Wiki, where people anonymously provided updates about the status of an active job, which was usually how you learned a position had moved on to the interview stage and you weren't invited.

"But you must be concerned about job season regardless?" I said.

"I guess," she said with a roll of the eyes. "But I'm going to focus on public universities, which at least aren't *as* exploitative. I don't know if I can stomach working at a private college."

"With a market this tight, don't you pretty much have to apply to everything that vaguely fits your profile? I mean, adjuncting is obviously not sustainable."

"And yet the entire system relies on our labor." She shook her pint glass, the final inches sloshing around. "Maybe I could be a bartender. Tending, that sounds nice." She combed her fingers through her exhausted bangs. "Can we go outside?"

Sophie bummed a cigarette from a group of film students in extra-large sweaters. I was surprised she smoked, because in every other way, she appeared to have higher standards than I did. She took a drag, offered the cigarette to me without interrupting her conversational flow, seemed to know I would decline, and seamlessly brought it back to her lips. She asked the students what they were studying, talking not as if she were one of them—we were professors, after all, or ostensibly—but as if it didn't matter, as if she were beyond public judgment. She mentioned some contemporary art-house films and up-and-coming directors I had never heard of. She blew smoke off to the side, away from me. I surreptitiously inspected the cigarette: no lipstick marks.

Sophie turned back to me and stomped on the cigarette. "I'm starving," she said. We looked across the street at the tapas restaurant, which emitted a warm glow. "That place is bougie as fuck," she said with a grimace, and suggested we walk past to see what people were eating.

"Mussels," she said. "Manchego." She was walking too close, as if window-shopping at a jewelry store. "Oysters." Our reflections hovered ghostlike in the window. I squinted beyond myself and saw that behind my own chest sat, of all people, Tom. He was looking not at us but at the woman across from him, who was merely inches from me, her back to the window, shiny hair, and shoulders that were all blade. He picked the eyeball out of a smoked fish.

I grabbed at Sophie's arm, pulled her back.

"He knows what he's doing," she said. "The eyeball is the best part."

I turned slightly away from the window and slumped to make my silhouette less familiar. "Come on," I said, and started walking.

"Who was that?"

"Nobody."

"You know that guy?"

"Kind of," I said.

"Asshole?"

"Well . . ."

"Affair?"

"No," I said quickly.

She narrowed her eyes.

With the excuse and reality that Sophie was too drunk to drive home, we walked back to my place. In my bedroom, I felt the slight spin of drunkenness as I slithered out of my skinny jeans and into sweatpants. I switched shirts quickly, taking off my bra the stealthy way. Sophie didn't bother, removing her T-shirt entirely to unclasp her bra, revealing breasts round and pale as two moons. Then she pulled her T-shirt back on and crawled beneath the covers in her underwear as if it were her room and her bed.

"How do you know so much about contemporary film?" I asked.

She waved her hand around, as if such knowledge came from the ether.

I stared at her face. How did people know all these things? Art-house films and directors and that you were supposed to eat the eyeball of the fish? Where did women learn how to make lipstick stay on their lips, to make their hair shiny, to paint their nails without painting their skin? Did you have to be Michelangelo to contour your face? If Kim Kardashian could do it, couldn't I?

"How do you do that?" I asked.

"Do what?"

"Like, what's your lipstick trick?"

"Expensive lipstick," she said.

"So, not CVS."

"Like Sephora."

"How much is that stuff?" I asked.

"Just pocket the testers."

"Does it ever come off?"

"With soap, yeah," she said. "It's not a tattoo."

"But, like, if you made out with someone, would it come off?"

She raised her eyebrows, laughed. Her eyes were agate, hazel, green ringing a starburst of brown. "Well," she said, and though I hadn't meant it as a line, I moved closer, let my tongue slither in. She flicked it with hers, then moved away from me and laughed.

"Pretty resistant," I said.

"You want to mess around or what?" she said. "I don't have a ton of energy for a whole big thing, but I'm pretty horny right now, to be honest."

"Oh," I said. "I mean, yeah, sure, okay."

"You're the one who got this rolling," she said, and crawled on top of me, grinding against my leg, eyes closed. She put her hand on my chest to steady herself or to get more momentum, all her weight leaning into that hand, so my breastbone began to ache. I was extremely turned on, in part by the suddenness of it, the novelty, and also because of her breasts, which I had seen briefly and which I was imagining now.

She lifted one of my hands, put my finger in her mouth, sucking on it, then pulled my hand around her, directing me to the less conventional location. "Do it," she commanded. I awkwardly complied with half a digit. Her breath turned heavy as she rubbed against me. She took her hand off my chest, heat spreading across the spot like a bruise, and sort of crouched over me as she humped, her hair flung over my face, into my mouth and eyes.

"Oh fuck oh fuck oh fuck," she said, having brought her own hand into the mix. It was amazing, how easily she did this, so unembarrassed.

I was worried she'd wake Brianna. "I have a roommate," I said, but Sophie didn't seem to hear.

After finishing, she stared at me, then laughed, and I realized I needed to remove my finger so she could crawl off me.

"Oh my God," she said, "you have a roommate?"

"You think I can afford this place alone?" It was startling, to be back in a normal conversation. I was holding out the hand that had been inside of her, the pointer finger pointed away from the rest.

"I can't with roommates anymore," she said. "Anyway, what about you? You want to jerk off or what?"

"I'm good."

"I can eat you out or something?" she said, as if offering me a snack she could scrape together from what she had lying around.

"It's okay, I don't usually come anyway."

She sat up on her elbow, looking at me like an interesting specimen. "Really? But you *can* come?"

"Yes."

"Makes sense if you're used to fucking guys. You're basically straight, right? Straight women come way less." She lay back down on her pillow. "What about with that guy from the tapas place?"

"No," I said.

"Not even with him," she said, musing.

"Let me just go to the bathroom," I said, wiggling my finger. "One sec."

I washed my hands in the dark. We had a little night-light shaped like a lava lamp next to the sink, but I didn't flip it on. I was half grossed out, half turned on, something that felt like it was happening beyond context, though there was obvious context. I jammed my fingernail into the bar of soap, wiping it back and forth.

I considered getting myself off, but the luster of drunkenness was fading directly into a headache, as if for every action there was an equal and opposite payback, and I began to wonder if I'd ruined my whole weekend, which would be a crisis.

Sophie was asleep when I crawled back into bed. My mind wandered as the headache gained ground. I was still holding my hand away from me, finger pointed, as if I hadn't washed it. My face grew hot. Why had Sophie kept laughing? What was so funny about it, anyway?

I awoke with a pounding pain that radiated either to or from my jaw. My toothache was getting worse. I was desperate for water. Sophie felt like a figment of my imagination, an unfulfilling erotic dream.

She was sound asleep. A section of bangs on her right side stuck vertically into the air, and her cheek was imprinted with pillow wrinkles.

My bedroom faced a tiny courtyard—a square of grass, really—and so I saw other windows from mine, and other windows saw me. One of my blinds was three quarters of the way down, the window cracked to let in air, and I realized that we had been on full display, if anyone had been awake to see us, if we had woken anyone up.

The apartment directly across from mine had been under renovation for weeks but appeared to be finished now, someone moved in. The walls were royal blue with white molding; paintings hung on the wall in fat gilded frames. It was like a unit from another building, another city, another timeline or plotline. People had started moving down from D.C. in droves because Baltimore was cool and cheap. It raised rent prices for us, just as we—the grad students and the artists—had raised rent prices for the Baltimore-born-and-bred. I wondered if these fancy people had seen us and regretted their move.

On the floor, Sophie's and my pants were in perfect squashed piles, the two leg holes revealing the blue rug beneath, as if they had just dropped from us cartoonishly and we'd stepped out of them.

I was reinserting myself into my pair when Sophie groaned, "I am so hungover." She stretched a hand out to me. "Help. Coffee?"

She gulped it down black, standing in the kitchen, in a rush to get to a catering gig she had only just remembered.

⁓

After Sophie left, I spread my papers out across the kitchen table and tried to detach from my headache so I could focus on The Masculine Voice and The Campus Novel, which had some crossover.

Masculinity studies had become a genuine field of academic

inquiry in the nineties. The purported purpose was not to reinforce masculinity but to challenge its norms, to ask questions like: How are we raising boys? What's the root of toxic masculinity? And, more recently, what's the deal with incels?

Theoretically, masculinity studies was in conversation with feminist, gender, and sexuality studies, but some institutions situated it separately. It seemed odd to me—or exactly on point—that masculinity would be considered exceptional enough to burst out of the bounds of gender studies and into its own separate field.

I had wondered initially if the class intended to examine the masculine voice critically and in relation to feminist theory. It did not. As per the course description:

> Our present-day fixation with gender has led us to forget what we mean when we say "masculine." In this course, we return to American literary classics to consider cultural narratives of masculinity. What is masculinity? How is it performed in a text? What is the relationship between authorial voice and narrative voice? Readings may include Cheever, Carver, Roth, Bowles, Baldwin, Booth, Nabokov, Steinbeck, Salinger, Johnson, Joyce, Updike, Hemingway, and others, along with related critical texts. Ultimately, this return to the classics will allow us to think through not only the problems with the masculine voice but also its promise and potential.
>
> Professor Carpenter

The issue with *promise and potential* was that they were available only to those with the privilege of proving themselves later. The rest of us just had *problems.*

One of mine was that I was now teaching a class designed by a reactionary whose sexism—and certainly racism—was barely disguised as a protection of American classics. The class had an odd mix of students taking it earnestly, randomly, and ironically—Risky Business, the undergrad I'd met at orientation, appeared to be in the latter category. Since the students had already bought the books and downloaded the essays, which had already been hunted down and scanned by the library, I had to balance the high-profile academic's bullshit with my own scholarly sensibilities, not to mention my moral compass. Hard to do generally, harder with a hangover.

I'd recognized the name Carpenter immediately. He was an Ivy Leaguer of the old guard who'd written a piece called "Bad Men: The Female Gaze in Contemporary Literature," a rebuttal to an article by a young feminist scholar that had caused a stir in certain academic circles. The gist of his argument was that our obsession with the male gaze had obliterated any talk of the female gaze, a gaze that often reduced men to "bad men." This lack of dimensionality, he said, was a kind of objectification.

His argument missed the point, but the argument itself wasn't the issue. Rather, it was the way a senior scholar had so viciously gone after a junior one—an easy target, an unfair fight. The uncomfortable reality was that the feminist scholar's work was not particularly good, and the entire debate devolved into an academic battle of the sexes in which the main characters fell easily into stereotypes: The woman lacked intellectual rigor, the man was brilliant enough to be excused for being an asshole.

The journal that had published the feminist scholar's article—one entirely dedicated to William Booth—had been criticized previously for publishing mostly men, and some argued that the feminist scholar's paper had been accepted only because she was a woman. It's possible this was true and betrayed the journal's misogyny most of all. They wanted to fulfill a requirement and couldn't be bothered to believe in good scholarship by women. Or maybe the problem was this: Most women were kind of over talking about William Booth. Even I—who had come of age reading him, who still held his short stories in high regard—was kind of burned out on the endless discourse.

Carpenter, and I by proxy, had assigned an article called "Misreading Misogyny in Booth" to accompany Booth's novel *The Doctor of Desire*, which we would read in both The Campus Novel and The Masculine Voice. In the article, the author argues against the criticism that Booth was a navel-gazer and misogynist, claiming that such critiques are leveled by unimaginative readers who haven't considered "narrative distance" or "irony." The conclusion, some twenty pages later, is that while the main character in the book is misogynistic, this in no way confirms anything about Booth himself. There was some logic–bro scoffing to this argument, wrapped up in pretty academic bows, and a vague undertone of annoyance with the "project" of feminist scholars.

The problem, I wanted to tell the author of the article, was that anything an author writes betrays his worldview even when it's not aligned with the main character's. Besides, the rest of Booth's canon, never mind his actual biography of constant womanizing, really did confirm that Booth was a misogynist, so what was the fucking point?

My roommate, Brianna, appeared in a high school swim T-shirt, booty shorts, and sparkling silver mules. She yawned extravagantly. "You're up early," she said. Our conversations usually felt like half-hearted duels, and I braced myself for a low simmer of passive aggression.

"I have a lot of work."

"You're *always* working," she said, walking into the kitchen. She enjoyed getting my attention and then disappearing. "*Almost* always working," she called. "Coffee?"

"There isn't any left."

"No, do you want some? Like, more?"

"Sure," I said cautiously.

I had found Brianna via her Craigslist ad. What sold me on the place was her laissez-faire attitude about the whole thing—no up-front security deposit, no signing on a dotted line, no harsh punishment for late rent. What sold her on me was that I was quiet and had no furniture or social life. Later I realized that her parents, both dentists who did Botox, were paying for the apartment, and my presence was a secret, scoring her an extra $750 per month, which she appeared to use for clothes, subscription boxes, and takeout. This explained why she was surprisingly chill about the late-rent repayment plan: Just get her the money as soon as I could.

Brianna was twenty-six—seven years younger than I was—and had a job in merchandising at the headquarters of a national athletic apparel brand. She was a tall Black woman with perfect teeth. Born and raised in New York City, she had a degree in marketing from NYU and had moved to Baltimore for the job, but she wanted to leave as soon as possible without messing up her résumé—i.e., after two or three years with the company. First, she said, Baltimore was barely a city compared to New York. Second, all the transplants at the company assumed she was from Baltimore while all the people in Baltimore knew she wasn't, that being

Black was complicated everywhere but especially complicated here, in a majority-Black city where segregation had created such extreme inequality that, just one mile apart, the life expectancy varied by twenty years.

I learned her feelings about Baltimore during our most intimate conversation one night when she woke me up by using the air popper at one a.m. She'd come home from a night out, and she looked so depressed that I just pretended I couldn't sleep.

Mostly, though, we tried to stay out of each other's way.

Brianna started the coffee, then shuffled back into her room while looking at her phone. It occurred to me that, for the first time ever, she was acting deferential. I thought of Sophie's "Oh fuck oh fuck oh fuck" and wondered whether I'd earned cache or Brianna just felt awkward.

On my way to the bathroom, I heard her on the phone. "I figured out what's wrong with my roommate. She's just a lez who finally got her rocks off." A pause. "I mean, yeah, sure, I guess she could be bi or pan or whatever, but then what's the big deal? I mean, come on, it's the twenty-first century."

Back in the kitchen, trying to make oatmeal, I became irate over the lack of available supplies. Brianna hoarded spices and condiments and silverware and plates in her room. Where was the cinnamon? Had she used up the last of the milk? Was the saltshaker still missing? I found a jar of pink Himalayan sea salt wrapped in a white bow. She'd gotten it as a party favor at one of a string of recent friend-weddings, and afterward spent days moping around the apartment, talking about her future as a "cat lady."

As soon as I took a bite of oatmeal, a pebble of salt hit my sensitive tooth, and pain radiated out along my gums. I grabbed the jar of sea salt in my fist, crushing the wire bow, and shoved it to the back of the spice drawer.

Was I mad Brianna had called me a lesbian? Hadn't Sophie, just last night, called me straight? I had never been straight enough for people not to wonder, never queer enough to actually be queer. Easy for Brianna to say "it's the twenty-first century," having barely lived in another one. She was from the era of *Broad City*. I was born during the AIDS crisis, had grown up in the age of Ellen DeGeneres getting blackballed for coming out on her sitcom.

When I was younger, I variously worried I was a lesbian because I wasn't that interested in men and worried I wasn't anything because I wasn't that interested in women, either. I couldn't help but be repulsed by the reality of people up close, their smells and their pores and their moles, their pus and their sweat and their ingrown hairs. Alcohol helped because it made people abstract, unspecific.

Sex had been an acquired taste, something I'd had to come around to, the same way I'd had to cultivate a taste for coffee and beer. Apparently some people genuinely liked these things—how else could you explain decaf coffee and alcohol-free beer? It was as if my taste had never matured, and now my liking existed as part of a not liking, the repulsion part of the thrall.

"Questioning" your sexuality had always been framed as a process of coming to terms with what you had repressed, easing yourself into what you had always secretly known. I kept waiting for that kind of clarity, even asked myself which sex organ I'd rather have in my mouth. Neither? Both? Thinking sexual attraction might work by accumulation, I'd gone on a bender of hookups in grad school, but it just felt like the optometrist clicking back and forth between the blur of A or B, A or B, A or B. And Tom, how did he fit in?

I'd had a thing for Tom, clearly, but I'd always had a thing for teachers. How could I begin to categorize such a relationship? Mentor seemed so bland. It didn't convey the power or the reality of a person who stretched into so many roles: teacher, parent, friend, counselor, confidant. If I liked a teacher, I basked in their attention. I'd go out of my way to walk down her halls or near his buildings, imagining our potential interaction. The possibility was enough—as with window-shopping, the daydream was the thrill. I had a friend once who felt the same way about her therapist, was always looking for him when she was out.

If my feelings toward certain teachers could be categorized as crushes, they were like the crushes of middle schoolers—the longing was not to be touched but to be understood, to be paid attention to. Why was this feeling more powerful when the object was a man? Because society itself imbued men with more importance? Because I'd been trained to think a relationship with a man was more prone to elicit a sexual charge? Because it felt good to be an object of male attention? Because I wanted some father-figure fill-in, since my father had died when I was thirteen? Who could untangle it all?

Mostly my sexual desire was abstract and nebulous, like hunger without a specific craving, which is not to say gender didn't matter, just that my sexuality felt like a moving target and I was shooting arrows into the dark. I had the impression that bisexual people just liked whoever they liked, regardless of gender, in a way that made gender seem beside the point. But for me, gender seemed exactly the point.

Women were more physically attractive than men, obviously, which made me feel like a lesbian. I liked the way the light hit the soft hair on their forearms. I liked their dimples and—like a repressed Victorian—the nape of the neck. I liked the stray hairs that sprang forth around their temples because what I liked most about women were the moments they didn't notice themselves, when they were just being—the bite of the lower lip as they worked, the furrowed brow, the tousled hair, how it fell from a bun. And boobs, obviously.

What I liked about men were the dark, glistening hairs on their knuckles, the tufts sprouting from their armpits—primal, apelike. I saw sex with men as an invasion, but an exciting one I could provoke. I liked their deep laughs, the crinkles next to their eyes when they smiled. I liked the mystery of them, that centimeter of unknowableness that existed between my sex and theirs. I liked when their attention zeroed in on one person, and I liked when that person was me.

When I rolled over in bed and looked at a man snoring by my side, he seemed impenetrable and vaguely grotesque, like a crab you had to kill with a rock so you could eat what was tender inside. When I looked at Sophie, I felt like I'd gotten handsy at a sleepover, like I'd pocketed something at the drugstore and was high on my own lawlessness. The idea of dating her seemed like a farce, like playing house, fun but ridiculous, which made me feel like a straight girl who kissed other girls for sport, the kind lesbians hate.

Maybe I was a half-hearted bisexual, or an asexual who had come around on sex. On TV, bisexuals were classically indecisive, double-crossing, sex-obsessed, and diabolical. Now bisexuality was a character trait denoting casual coolness, reserved mainly for hot, thin, feminine women. Now you could act queer for clout, like Katy Perry when she'd kissed a girl and liked it, but how much did you have to like kissing a girl for it to be not a performance of queerness but actual queerness?

I took a bundle of Brianna's clothes, which had been piled on the couch for a week, knocked on her door, dumped the clothes on her bed, and delivered armful after armful as she talked on the phone and gave me dirtier and dirtier looks. I never felt I could get very far with equity in the apartment, especially now that I was late on rent.

I lay down on the couch and tried simultaneously to relax my jaw muscles and plan my day, like pushing and pulling at the same time.

Brianna appeared, annoyed, telling me she was *going to* clean up the pile, but she had been *on the phone*.

"Well," I said, "and where's the table salt?"

"What's *table* salt?"

"Like the regular salt." Did no one say *table* salt anymore? "Like the saltshaker. All your clothes are out here, and all of the seasonings are in there."

"You're being passive-aggressive because I use the condiments?"

"The salt should always be available," I said. "It's called *table* salt because you leave it on the table for everyone to use."

"I've never heard of *table* salt, but okay," she said, and stomped off, I hoped to excavate the salt from her room.

A text from Sophie flashed on my screen: so hungover 🫠

My phone was at 5 percent. Before it died, I managed to reply: same, not sure how I'm going to get anything done today 😭😭😭

Brianna had recently told me that emojis weren't "a thing" anymore. I was never cool, per se, but what I didn't realize until it was no longer the case was that I'd once had an osmotic understanding of the trends. Brianna was constantly informing me that things were uncool or out of date or different than before. I'd once, in passing, mentioned my tomboy phase, and she'd looked at me like I was crazy. "Tomboy?" she'd said. "What were you, born in the fifties?"

"I *was* a tomboy," I'd told her.

"Do you understand how problematic that word is?" she'd said.

The changing times didn't change what I had been, what I had called myself—declared myself—for two years after I had cut my hair short, renamed myself Sam, refused to wear skirts, put all my Barbies in the attic, and started collecting G.I. Joes. Perhaps, were I a child today, I would have envisioned myself as something different—nonbinary hadn't been an available category at the time. Or perhaps the constraints of girlhood had widened enough that no one would have blinked an eye if I'd stalked the courtyard with a toy rifle, or they would have blinked for new and different reasons. Perhaps if TV shows and books had been rich with women who were scientists and skateboarders and not just secretaries and nagging moms, if feminists hadn't been vilified as hairy lesbians angrily burning bras, then I wouldn't have found it so fucking embarrassing to be a girl in the first place.

Who was Brianna to imagine I could retroactively understand myself outside of the context in which I'd been raised? She acted as if people in the past had always had the advantage of future options but were too lazy to consider them, like we weren't all just trudging through our daily lives assimilating received opinion, as if we could ever draw breath without breathing the air. We all came blinking out of our own humiliating pasts eventually.

My mom was once brushing correction fluid over a typewritten page, just as my dad was once lying on a shag carpet trying to listen to a record backward, just as I was once swiveling the antenna on my boom box trying to tune into Z100 so I could record a Fastball song on a cassette. And now my mom didn't know how to open a second tab on her browser, and I was conveying meaning with laughing-crying emojis, and one day Brianna would awaken to find that everyone on Snapchat was wrinkled and complaining about a new cut of jeans, and maybe you—if you are reading this in some future, if these words become more than a diary of rants from under a desk, maybe you will think, That's out of date, nobody uses Snapchat anymore, but that's the point: One day you will be ridiculous, too.

The Masculine Voice, we scoff, and I scoffed most of all, two times a week on my way to class. But there was a time when I might have signed up for it earnestly. I felt a little bad for Carpenter. One day, if we're lucky, we'll all be dying breeds.

Chapter 4

THE CAMPUS NOVEL

The sun rose, the sun set, I missed it, and we did it all again. I made the coffee, I forgot the coffee, I burned the coffee. It grew cold, I reheated it, I found it on a desk the next day, the inside of the mug looped in geological brown rings. I made copies for my Rosedale classes at Lewis, I wrote a duffel-bag review in the computer lab at the library, I sent cover-letter drafts to my own email, so my inbox looked like a conversation with myself. My phone died, was reborn, died again. I ran out of deodorant, took on the scent of the adjunct office, where I also fell asleep, occasionally or often, between classes, late at night, my tooth aching as I woke to a text from Sophie revealing the drop point of abandoned food. We occasionally passed each other in a hall with knowing, exhausted looks, as I lugged my duffel of printer paper and bagels behind me like contraband. And it was still September; I hadn't yet been paid.

The adjunct office at Lewis was filled with a rotating array of humanities teachers and an entire floor's worth of HP printers along with a large photocopy machine, an old Dell with a tower running Windows X, two tables that were too high, several mismatched chairs that were too low, including a broken office chair that could not be raised, so if you sat on it you were a mere foot from the linoleum floor, which was dotted in a confetti of crushed brown leaves from the dead ficus in the corner. The air pulsed with the heat of the printers, and a ripe nervous-sweat stench hung in the humid air.

Personal items were jammed in every corner: a travel toothbrush and a half-empty bottle of mouthwash on the bookshelf, a dress hanging off a lamp, a plastic grocery bag of stinky gym clothes under the computer table. All around us, students jogged down halls, yelled across lawns, squealed in and out of vast parking lots, coming and going from their actual lives: part-time jobs, full-time jobs, families. Lewis's campus was fluid, like a train station. Twenty thousand students, mostly in-state, always on their way somewhere.

Taped above two of the HP printers in the adjunct office—and on an additional piece of paper that had fallen on the floor, now watermarked by a shoe print—was a note that said: DO NOT PRINT COPIES ON PRINTERS. USE THE COPY MACHINE. Ironically, these appeared to have been printed on one of the HPs. Taped above another printer was a sign that said: DO NOT TURN OFF PRINTERS! THIS CAUSES CHAOS FOR PROFESSORS TRYING TO PRINT.

All over the adjunct office and into the faculty kitchen were pleas for decorum delivered in all caps:

CLEAN OUT MICROWAVE AFTER EACH USE.

DO NOT LEAVE DIRTY MUGS IN SINK.

DO NOT LEAVE MUGS
OF COFFEE IN OFFICES.

CLEAN OUT COFFEEPOT.

BE RESPECTFUL!!!!!

<u>DO NOT</u> BRUSH TEETH IN SINK.

An entire English department reduced to the typographical sin of all caps, underline, and exclamation points.

The only useful note was a yellow Post-it Scotch-taped to the monitor of the shared computer. READ_ME, it said in all caps, like a tag on a bottle in *Alice in Wonderland*. Under it, in small writing, a cryptic parenthetical: *(in THINGS)*.

THINGS was the sole folder on the desktop PC. It was a folder of folders, a Matryoshka doll of folders, the Aleph of folders. In it were folders designated by class name, class code, code word, by nondescript generalities like MORE THINGS, ME, and ACTUALLY ME. The folders contained handouts, student papers, eleven-by-seventeen Excel spreadsheets tracking job postings and application requirements for full-time positions. Among all of the things in *THINGS* was the most important thing: a .txt file that said READ_ME. READ_ME was a collection of adjunct tips, like how to submit grades (through the self-service banner in the LCPortal), how to change your classroom from a windowless dungeon to something with a view (you had to ask a student with a departmental work-study job to do it), how to get around your printing limit (use printer code 6969 instead of your personal code). Because the adjunct office was so chaotic and the room-request portal had access limitations, I had met students for office hours in the library, a sandwich shop, a vestibule with a couch.

One morning I was, as it were, double-69ing, printing Langston Hughes poems for American Lit II. (*What happens to a dream deferred?*) I'd moved the Harlem Renaissance up two weeks, lopping *The Grapes of Wrath* off the syllabus completely, because I knew the students wouldn't read a book that long. One of them had told me straight up, "You can honestly just give me a zero on that." Realistically, I didn't have time to read it, either.

I watched an adjunct conked out at a table with his mouth wide open, a dark spot of drool on the forearm of his sweater. How could he sleep through another teacher playing the sexual-harassment video at top volume? Sleeping peers made me nervous. I'd read an article—we'd all read the article—about an adjunct who died in her office and nobody realized for almost a week. Other professors kept walking past the office, complaining about the smell as her body decomposed. I pressed my hand into each warm sheet of paper before the next one shot out. DO NOT LEAVE DEAD ADJUNCTS IN OFFICE could be another useful sign. I strained to hear the sleeper's shallow breath.

"Look, Leandra," said the boss in the sexual-harassment training video. "Why don't you relax?"

"I'm fine," she replied, stiff and sour.

The video had an after-school-special vibe. I'd tried to watch it on my phone, but a zoomed-in segment of the upper-left corner took up the whole screen. The module, it was noted, was better viewed on a desktop in Chrome.

Lewis's video was more dated than Rosedale's, which at least took place in the social media era. The Rosedale video had several parts, each one bookended by lessons from a Mrs. Rogers-y narrator. In one, a group of male professors ogles a female colleague's Facebook photos. Mrs. Rogers talks about "the gray area" and what I'd broadly call "using common sense." At the end, she explains the process of making a sexual-harassment complaint, but no contract laborer would dare do so if they expected to be hired the following semester. These videos sucked. Even the gray area was a sham.

"Can you make fifty copies?" said a voice, and I turned to find the woman who'd side-eyed Sophie and me in the faculty lounge. She tried to hand me a stack of paper.

"I'm not— I'm a lecturer," I said.

"And I'm a professor and I have class in ten minutes."

"I'm in the middle of a print job for my own class."

"You"—it was a general *you*—"act like you own this stuff just because you're in here," she said. "These are department printers."

I glanced at the other adjuncts, but they were too busy or asleep or dead for solidarity. The state of the office embarrassed me. At MBMU and other places I'd worked, the adjuncts had strained to keep the offices neat, to prove they were professionals, but it was impossible here, with so many of us and so many printers and so little space.

I watched Leandra's pained face on the screen as her boss massaged her shoulders and suggested she "put on something nice" for a happy hour with clients. The video was working against itself. The boss was a slimeball, sure, but why did they have to make Leandra seem like such a buzzkill, a spineless party pooper, and a prude? It didn't help that after toting my duffel around for weeks,

I would've killed for a shoulder massage—from a sketchy boss or a Neanderthal, I didn't care.

"Please," said the professor in a way that suggested I was being completely unreasonable.

I stopped the job, stepped aside.

"Thank you," she said thanklessly.

I had a soft spot for a kid in my American Lit II class at Lewis. On the first day, I'd arrived early to prepare and was sitting at a desk in the classroom going through my notes when he came in, sat down next to me, and started devouring a Subway sandwich.

"Wait, did we have homework? Like, already?" he asked with his mouth full.

"No," I said.

"Oh, damn, good," he said. "You're just, like, studious?"

"I'm teaching the class." I'd never nailed the professional look or the self-confidence that gave so many of my peers automatic authority.

"But where's the *prof*?"

"Right here," I said. "Me."

"Like you're a sub?" He licked dressing off his fingers.

"I'm your instructor for the semester?" It came out in the unconfident, lilting uptalk for which the women of my generation have been so often maligned.

"Are you sure?" he asked.

"Yes," I said, nailing the punctuation.

He crumpled up the wrapper and successfully free-threw it into the trash, then pulled out a five-subject spiral-bound notebook and wrote *AMERICAN LIT II: THE RECKONING* at the top of a page. After that, every time I ran into him at Lewis, he would shout, "Yo! Prof Sam!" and wave.

One day he came to office hours at an on-campus café, where we each ordered a drip coffee—the cheapest thing on the menu—and I learned he didn't really believe in punctuation. He found commas particularly useless. "Aren't the other ones way more important?" he said. I told him the "eats, shoots, and leaves" joke. "Wow, I'll really have to think about that," he replied. It was his earnestness, his openness, and the fact that he called me Prof that endeared me to him. I promised myself that if I managed to do one thing that semester, it would be to make Subway Sandwich understand the thrill—or at the very least the purpose—of a well-placed comma. Maybe hyphens, I dreamed. Maybe colons.

Two stone walls flanked the mouth of Rosedale's long driveway. It would be easy to think you were entering an estate as you wound through the bright green woods, passed the stone benches set under vine-covered pergolas, admired a neat green field complete with a horse and its rider, the rider wearing actual riding boots and an equestrian helmet. But then the black paved parking lot would rise into view, and a crop of modern buildings would reveal themselves, including a three-story glass library that jutted off the back of an old stone building like the hull of a beautiful but useless ship.

Rosedale students ventured beyond campus only if they were leaving for good or coming right back, like mental patients on a field trip. Five thousand mostly out-of-state students, ever in orbit.

In the library, each sat in a little silo of noise-canceling headphones, while those of us without would hear the gentle thump of nearly silent MacBook Pro keys, broken only by the tectonic vibration of a phone and the accompanying Pavlovian jolt of everyone in the vicinity.

Because Rosedale's adjunct office had no printers, no copy machines, no clunky old computers with mysterious beeps and overheating fans, the noises I heard most were the squeak and click of shoes, students making their way toward Tom's office—where, I noted, he always kept the door ajar. The building's AC was set to arctic, so I had to dress in two ensembles every day, peeling off leggings and sweaters at Lewis, putting them back on at Rosedale, like Superman but with no one to save but myself.

Of the two adjuncts I apparently shared the office with, I only ever saw one, a lawyer in her mid-forties named Renata who taught Writing the Law on Wednesday nights. She'd had some local success writing crime novels that hinged on obscure legal precedents, and she taught the class "for fun," often saying, "God knows we don't do this for the money." Occasionally she whirled into the office with a student, talked their ear off, talked mine off, and then departed.

Several of her novels were featured in a glass display of BOOKS FROM THE ROSEDALE FAMILY. Renata, referred to as a lecturer, was the only author I could identify as an adjunct. Either adjuncts were too embarrassing to claim, or they'd never had time to write a book.

Ten Four, of course, was front and center, soon to be replaced by a handsome hardback of *Casualty.* That cover had begun flashing on the campus-wide digital signage, beside Tom's face, to promote a reading at Rosedale's largest lecture hall a few weeks before the book's release.

—

During the first week of October, it rained for seven days straight—Lewis a blur of black umbrellas twisting in the wind, Rosedale all sleek raincoats and Wellingtons, *the apparition of these faces in the crowd,* me with my shoes drying under my desk/table as I wrote on the giant flip-over pad I had found in a storage closet at Lewis, the air thick with the gasoline scent of Sharpie, which was what Dr. Brighton noticed when she appeared in the doorway of the adjunct office.

"What's that?" she asked, sniffing. These were the first words she'd spoken to me since orientation back in August. I searched with my feet for my wet shoes. My arms were covered in goose bumps. I had misplaced my leggings—perhaps and probably they were sitting on top of the toilet paper dispenser in a bathroom stall at Lewis, where I often changed before heading to Rosedale.

"Preparing for class," I said. I tried to cover the flip-board with my arm because I'd written, *Should we even read Lolita????* in pink Sharpie. A day prior, Risky Business had come up to me after class and said, "Should we really be platforming a book about pedophilia? I just sort of thought we'd gotten past this kind of thing."

"How so?"

"Like, MeToo happened," she said.

"That definitely adds context."

"Don't you think we should be platforming the voice of the victim, if anything?"

"Well, it's fiction."

"No, like, victims generally," she said.

I mean, sure, if it were my syllabus, if I had the time, I might have assigned *Lolita* alongside *The Lover* by Marguerite Dumas, but here we were.

"Is that what you would do if you were teaching the class?" I asked.

"This isn't exactly the class I would choose to teach."

"But it is the class you chose to take."

"Honestly, I just don't think I'm comfortable reading this book," she said.

I bristled at the quick retreat to personal comfort but tried to be empathetic. I didn't know anything about her life, what she might have been through. "Listen," I said, "if this book is genuinely going to mess with your equilibrium, if you're going to lose sleep over it, if your stomach will churn and you won't be able to eat, don't read it."

"What do you mean?"

"Skip class, use your absences, don't raise your hand, whatever."

"But won't that affect my grade?"

"If you do well on everything else, you'll be fine. But I will also say this: If it's just going to make you run-of-the-mill uncomfortable, then read it. The book is controversial, and ultimately, it *asks* you to be uncomfortable, so these aren't unusual feelings to have about it."

I mean, the point of the book was the mindfuckery. It was about manipulation—not just of the girl, Lolita, but of the reader by the unreliable narrator and, on top of it, by Nabokov himself.

This conversation had given me an idea: We would have a class debate about whether or not we should read the book at all.

"Is that a giant pad of paper?" Dr. Brighton asked. "Where's your laptop?"

I looked at the flip pad with surprise, as if I had no idea how it had gotten there or why it wasn't a computer.

Dr. Brighton's face tightened. "Parents are paying fifty thousand dollars a year for a top-tier education," she said.

I considered the ironies but only nodded. "Of course," I said. "I just thought, you know, different media sparks different brain centers."

"Ah." She lingered. She slipped her spoon into a parfait, extracted a multilayered bite with yogurt, jam, and granola. My stomach audibly groaned. I had forgotten to pack a lunch. The cool yogurt would feel so nice on my increasingly problematic tooth. "Have anything on the docket for the next week?" she asked.

"Well, teaching, of course," I said, unsure what she was getting at. "Really digging into Carpenter's syllabi and enjoying the students. And I'm working on a paper for *Critical Inquiry*." This was true insofar as "working" involved perpetually toting around a book that one of the reviewers had recommended and I hadn't yet opened.

"It's so essential to find time for writing and research," she said, nodding.

"It really is."

"I do have a project you might be interested in."

I perked up. Maybe she needed some help with footnotes, indexing. I wasn't sure if it was humanely—that was a typo, but apt—possible to squeeze one more thing into my schedule, but I was acutely aware of my résumé's optics. It would be nice to have something fresh, especially since I didn't have the funds to participate in conferences, and work on the *Critical Inquiry* revision had stalled.

"I have this conference in Las Vegas next week," Dr. Brighton said.

"Oh, you're going to CAWW?" The Conference of American Women Writers, which everyone pronounced *Caw.* "I presented there once, on psychological trauma and the otherworldly."

I'd given the presentation while still exploring the otherworldly within the trauma narrative. My research was about how the intensity of traumatic experience can overwhelm conventional logic so thoroughly that it requires expression through fantastical elements (read: Trauma feels so unreal that only the unreal can describe it). I'd analyzed Toni Morrison's *Beloved,* which uses a ghost story to show the psychological impact of slavery, and Kurt Vonnegut's *Slaughterhouse-Five,* which uses time travel to explore the trauma of war. But there was a lot of preexisting scholarship in this area, and *trauma* generally was starting to oversaturate the market. I felt like I was researching things I already knew rather than following new thoughts to the mysterious places they led. It had been a panel at CAWW that had led me to the theme of embodiment and the altered state, which had become central to my dissertation.

"Hm," Dr. Brighton said. "Well, it's a bit of a ridiculous place for a conference, if you ask me. I think next year it will be in Denver. Maybe you can go to that one."

"Hopefully," I said. "By the way," I added, a clunky transition but I had to work it in, "I was wondering if I could cover Carpenter's spring classes."

"Well, he only had one in the spring, but I think so," she said, poking at her parfait. A cartoonish –$4,400 cha-chinged in my mind.

"Maybe there's something else I could teach, too."

"Maybe," she said. "Anyway, why I'm here: I'm taking a week for the conference, and I have a picky cat and a few plants that will want to be watered while I'm away."

Disappointment set in.

"Not *too* needy," she clarified, perhaps detecting something in my expression. "Once a day is fine for the cat. And this is just the indoor plants. The gardener takes care of the exterior. I can offer a hundred dollars for the week, and I live just over in Homeland." She licked off her spoon. "Yes?"

Homeland was an upscale suburb within the city limits that had been designed by Olmsted. It probably did seem like the Homeland to the people who lived there—the news anchors, the museum curators, the professional lacrosse players, the tenured professors, Tom among them.

Could I justify saying no to a hundred dollars or to a woman who had the power to rehire me next semester?

Because I was getting paid only four times over the course of the semester, my September paycheck had been significant—between all five classes and the product-review job, I'd made around $4,000 after taxes. But it had gone quickly. My rent, utilities, and car insurance totaled about $1,000 a month; I also had my $500 monthly student loan payment, $900 in credit-card debt to chip away at, and four months of back rent. After paying back two months of rent, settling the previous month's expenses I'd floated on credit—which included groceries, gas, and towing fees—and paying off $250 in credit-card debt, here I sat with $426 in my bank account.

"Sure," I said. "That would be great. Thanks."

"Happy to help." She dropped her $5.99 parfait, barely eaten, into the trash, then left with a tap of the doorframe.

I stared at the parfait, buoyed in the bin by a pile of take-out containers. I was, in fact, reaching for it when Dr. Brighton's head popped back into the office. She registered my gesture, I was sure of that, but then decided to ignore it.

"This," she said, waving her hand at the flip-over pad, unable to assign a noun, "isn't a good look. Maybe at a public college, but not here." She tapped the doorframe. "*Really,*" she added, ducking out again.

The sky was insanely blue as I drove north on Charles toward Homeland. Dr. Brighton's block was dotted with speed bumps and massive houses—boxy brick or Tudor, stone facades, bay windows, gabled roofs. Tree branches crowded over the road, their leaves vibrant green against the bright blue sky, nothing like the lethargic green-brown of the spindly city trees outside my apartment. Maybe it was a trick of foregrounding, the neighborhood and the sky.

I'd been up here a million times, not just for classes on Tom's terrace but to house-sit, keeping his Lab, Cheever, company for fifteen dollars a day.

I slammed the rusty door of my car shut in Dr. Brighton's driveway as two women speed-walking with hand weights gave me the evil eye. This neighborhood was straight from *The Purge,* security cameras everywhere to keep out the riffraff.

Dr. Brighton's house was three stories, set on a neat lawn with a flagstone path and bulbous trimmed bushes wrapping around the porch. The mudroom looked like an overgrown greenhouse, which surprised me because Dr. Brighton had such a neat office. It took me turning the doorknob to the house to realize that she had stuffed all the plants in the mudroom and locked the door, which had a flap for the cat. Through the glass, I saw the kitchen and part of the living room, a gradient of white to beige. On the white couch, the throw pillows looked fluffed by karate chop.

Instructions were in a three-ring binder. The first page was all about the cat, Daisy, and the litter, water, and wet-food situation: ahi tuna, mackerel, sea bass. Each page after Daisy's included a photo of a plant along with care instructions, which I was sure some student or adjunct had put together.

I put my thumb in the soil of each of Dr. Brighton's pots, testing for some nebulous metric of moistness, then began the process of filling and refilling the needlessly small, long-spouted enamel watering can from the spigot outside, my shoes getting soaked. The silver faucet of the kitchen sink, a mere ten feet away, flashed in the sun.

Why did people always think I'd be good at taking care of their plants and their pets and occasionally even their children? I had always liked that professors doled out jobs to grad students, little things to earn extra money or learn the ropes. My friend Isaac had read for an anthology. Pretentious Hardik had apparently edited Tom's personal work. Aliana used her social and cultural capital to run the graduate reading series at a local bar, which was a big success.

Tom never asked me to do anything remotely literary or artistic outside of class, unless you counted the time he asked if I could sew because he needed some pants hemmed. I *could* sew, actually. I did hem his pants. ("Don't get handsy," he'd joked, but I didn't do the measuring-tape thing, just sat cross-legged on the floor and eyeballed it, pins between my teeth.) When SHU hosted a big-name writer I happened to love, Tom asked if I would sit next to the guest of honor at the departmental dinner hosted on the writer's behalf. Tom confided in me that the school was trying to woo said writer, and that it was well known he had "a taste for renaissance women." What I hoped Tom meant was a woman of many talents, but what I knew he meant was confirmed the night of the dinner when I saw the flanking parties were Felicia and me—our curvy figures more or less matched.

I ran through my cohort and couldn't think of an exception: Men did the reading, editing, and compiling, women the hosting, house-sitting, and admin. We were all thankful for it regardless, the chosen ones.

I had been thrilled the first time Tom asked me to house-sit. He trusted me with his things, and also, I would get to see his things, which so far I'd glimpsed only through the window when our workshop had met on his terrace. The job was also appealing because it meant spending less time in my own house, a government-subsidized row home with poor plumbing and loud roommates, and because I would make some money, all things that Tom mentioned when he'd offered the job. This excited me, too, that he knew details about my life, that he'd been listening.

He was usually out of town for a conference or a guest lecture or a "boys' weekend." I gathered his wife commuted to and from New York City, where she worked at an advertising agency, coming into Baltimore mostly on the weekends. I assumed Tom occasionally went to New York with her, but he never mentioned it. Even on their salaries, it was difficult to imagine owning a house in Homeland and an apartment in Manhattan, but his wife was the granddaughter of some power-tool mogul. Tom's family had money, too—there was a black-and-white picture in his living room of his father (presumably) with Jimmy Carter.

Tom's instructions were always written on a page pulled from the grocery pad posted to the fridge: when to feed Cheever, the ideal number of walks to take him on, perishable food I should feel free to use up. He didn't mention the plants, but usually the soil was bone-dry, so I watered them anyway.

Unlike Dr. Brighton's house, Tom's looked lived in—more homey than messy. Inset bookshelves bursting with fiction, beds laid with handmade quilts, warm natural wood accents: an old oak desk in the study, a butcher block island in the kitchen. "Touch anything," he had told me more than once, almost a dare. "Use it all. Open all the drawers, look under the beds, I don't care." So I used the lavender bath salts and salon shampoos in his oversize tub. I cooked his apples from the basket on his counter with his brown sugar in his cast-iron pan, which I helpfully washed because I didn't know anything about cast-iron pans. I filled his laundry machine with his detergent and my clothes—a relief not to have to go to the laundromat. I ate his popcorn from his air popper as I watched his cable TV, cuddled on his couch with his dog, a pile of his books by my side, many of them personally inscribed by the author. I found postcards and letters in a drawer—one from an ex-girlfriend, another from an editor at *The New Yorker* vacationing in Key West, obligatory mention of Hemingway's six-toed cats. I paged through his daybook, saw his running regime, his tennis lessons, his couples therapy every other week. I discovered the sex toys in a photo box peeking out from under the bed: rechargeable silicone Rabbit, clear glass dildo, black leather blindfold, feather tickler, plenty of lube. Which of these things did he want me to find?

I thought again of the descriptive copy for *Casualty*. Was some fictionalized version of me suspended in those pages, crouching next to a bed, pulling out a box, thinking whatever thoughts Tom gave me?

I was afraid to read the book, afraid I'd find a version of myself there, doing things I had definitely done and things I definitely hadn't. I was afraid I would be misunderstood, and I was afraid I would be understood exactly, exposed in all my awkwardness. But what embarrassed me most was a fear that underlay the others, one I barely admitted to myself: What if I didn't find myself in the book at all? Tom had taken up so much of my mental space. What if I hadn't taken up any of his?

After the hookup, Sophie and I fell easily back into our routine without any discernible unease. To her, the hookup had been less romantic fulfillment than itch-scratching, and to me it felt abstract, like a hazy dream. Partly because of the drinking, yes, but also because the night existed so wildly beyond the cadence of daily life that I felt disconnected from it. Now that I was back on the hamster wheel, everything else was a blur.

I told Sophie about teaching The Campus Novel at Rosedale, how the room where I taught the class was so epically and classically academic that I thought Carpenter might have specifically requested it. It had two large arched windows overlooking the green quad, five rows of fixed wooden seats with narrow fold-down tables where students precariously balanced MacBooks, and an old chalkboard with a wooden frame. After the flip-pad incident, I'd bought Crayola chalk for $1.89 in the toy section of CVS.

Four campus novels in—I taught a new one every two weeks—and I'd gotten the gist. The struggles of professors were variously: affairs, aging, ennui, envy, exclusion, hypocrisy, narcissism, sexual attraction to students, and writer's block. ("Where do you have to be on Maslow's hierarchy of needs to be plagued by ennui?" Sophie asked.) Some of it was satire, setting the high-minded ideals of academia against the pettiness and stupidity of actual people.

Carpenter's anxiety about "being canceled" threaded its way through the syllabus. The novel we were reading now was about a professor who believes he should be more famous than he is and hates teaching. He has an affair with a student that, based on the description, could arguably be categorized as rape. You're not supposed to like the guy. He refuses to apologize, claims he loves the student, and is forced to leave the university.

The article Carpenter chose to accompany the novel was his own freshly published essay about students' reactions to the book. In it, he complains that in the MeToo afterglow, the professor is summarily, almost frantically dismissed by his Rosedale students. Carpenter looks down on such a response as surface-level. He believes the professor's mulling and moping is character depth and spends most of the paper explaining in detail how he plays devil's advocate with the students, thus proving that the professor, much like himself, is complex and the students are simple and stupid. In so many words.

Sometimes I felt academic essays were merely an excuse to give unreasonable and extensive credence to emotional reactions or opinions you couldn't otherwise justify saying aloud, like that your students were idiots. Carpenter was right, the students did frantically dismiss the professor, but was that so dissimilar from Carpenter frantically dismissing the students? The main difference between them wasn't instinct or intelligence but finesse.

In a strange twist, I felt Carpenter himself was immune to cancellation. He was a conservative voice on a liberal campus desperate to prove its dedication to a free exchange of ideas—regardless of whether those ideas were bad or good, apparently. Carpenter had become a kind of token representing "diversity of thought."

"You should write a campus novel," said Sophie. "Except instead of it being about professors with status anxiety living coddled existences in old Victorian houses, it's about adjuncts with survival anxiety stealing bagels from department meetings and buying office supplies in the toy section of CVS."

"The problem is it'll sound like satire," I said.

"That's exactly the point. We're *living* the genre of satire. All of us are, probably since Ronald Reagan. Our president is an orange billionaire, and academia isn't any less absurd. Take SHU—it's basically a gentrifying urban developer fronting as a university, snatching up all the property it can in East Baltimore to sell or use when it's convenient for them." She seemed so powerful when impassioned, so much energy emanating from such a tiny body, you could see every muscle appearing and disappearing as she moved. "Most universities are debt-collecting hedge funds. They've got departments that study the best way to implement counter-insurgencies. They design nuclear weapons systems to cow their adversaries while holding the rest of us hostage in the global balance of terror. They tout anthropology departments founded on a history of sorting the world by race. And fuck, some are *literally* built on plantations! The whole thing is absurd."

There was another problem, I told her. Perhaps the main unifying criterion for a campus novel was its setting. Usually a campus novel was contained, like a novel of manners that plays out in a mansion or a workplace sitcom with only one set. The novels typically conjured a romantic image of university life: picturesque campuses in the Midwest or New England, plaid skirts and mad-genius professors (mostly men) with messy offices, messy hair, and bursts of insight delineated in frantic chalkboard scrawl.

In fact, two of the novels on Carpenter's syllabus took place at a disguised version of my own undergraduate alma mater, Cornell. It was an ideal setting. During my first semester there, the campus had ignited in an academic wet dream of fall, the craggy trees ablaze in red and orange, the stone arches echoing with a cappella, the whiteboards packed with equations and conjugations, and—I kid you not—local apples available in special vending machines campus-wide.

Cornell had been out of my league, so to speak. When I'd decided to apply, it was with low expectations and on a whim, two weeks before the application was due and without having taken the required SAT IIs. I submitted the application with the same brief, giddy hopeless hope you feel as the Powerball numbers pop into place. The shock of getting into that school never quite left me. For four years, I wandered across quads with the awed desperation of someone who was "just happy to be there" but who had also done the math, who knew exactly how much it cost to be there.

"So a campus novel would take place at Rosedale, not Lewis," Sophie said.

"And certainly never both at once."

I taught "Hills Like White Elephants" twice, once at Lewis for American Lit II and once at Rosedale for The Masculine Voice.

At Lewis, Subway Sandwich got the class discussion rolling by saying, "I don't get it."

"It's a lesson in subtext," suggested a woman who, at least once a week, wore a heather-gray sweatshirt that said COLLEGE in capitalized serif across the chest.

"But what *is* the subtext?" Subway Sandwich asked.

"He wants her to have an abortion," said a guy at the back.

Subway Sandwich opened his mouth in shock. "How do you even know that?"

The guy pointed to his Lenovo. "Wikipedia."

"Don't use your computer during class," I said.

"But that's how I'm taking notes," he said.

"Don't use Wikipedia during class," I said, though I had surely read this Wikipedia entry in the course of my own education.

"You could also just, like, read the dialogue and think about it?" suggested COLLEGE.

"Tell me where it says the abortion thing," Subway Sandwich insisted.

A student raised her hand. She was smart but rarely on time, and her papers seemed rushed, ever on the cusp of their full potential. "I think it might be all that stuff about the operation," she offered.

"Does anyone know what *white elephant* could be referring to?" I asked, writing their ideas down on the chalkboard: *An elephant in the room. A gift exchange. An unwanted gift.*

"Oh, dude," said Subway Sandwich. "*Unwanted gift.* Like a *baby.*" He wanted to know if the woman was going to get the abortion.

"It's up for debate," said Wikipedia. "The story is purposefully ambiguous."

"Let's not focus on what the internet says," I said.

"Would you consider this a feminist story?" asked Smart but Rushed. "I mean, bringing up abortion in a story this old is kind of radical, no?"

"Does anyone have thoughts?" I asked the class, hoping one of the other twenty-three students might speak up.

"It's anti-feminist," said COLLEGE. "The guy in the story is pretending to be all cool with abortion, but he's just saying it. It's lip service."

"It can be read as feminist or anti-feminist," said Wikipedia. "I read that before I stopped reading Wikipedia," he added quickly.

"Whoa whoa whoa," said Subway Sandwich. "This is about *feminism*?"

"I don't know if this is how you're supposed to read it," said Smart but Rushed, "but I think I agree about it being lip service. I have this sense—I don't know—that he's trying to pressure her into having an abortion while also minimizing the trauma of abortion?"

So we dove into the text to find out if and where we saw that on the page.

The dialogue, the subtext, the ambiguity—these were the

qualities that had sold academics on this story for a century. But I didn't like it. Maybe it was because I'd read it too many times, but I thought the supposed depth was cheaply won. I was annoyed by the main character, who was an asshole, and the author, who was Hemingway, who wrote in short sentences that sometimes seemed to me—sacrilege!—less profound than telegraphic, less ambiguous than noncommittal. Hemingway made the pregnant girl seem irritating and unlikable—like Leandra from the sexual-harassment video.

At Rosedale, the class on "Hills Like White Elephants" went down differently. I'd begun by explaining the context—that the story had been written a century ago, which mattered in terms of both subject (abortion) and style (totally new for the time!). I kicked off with a question about the dialogue, and after the requisite thirty seconds of silence, Risky Business dared speak. "Much of the story takes place beyond the dialogue, in what's not said," she explained. "This is what gives the story layers and ambiguity, which is one of the reasons why it's stood the test of time." Textbook answer. Not very risky business. Maybe she'd also read the Wikipedia page or had already been taught the story in high school, in a creative writing class, in a survey of American lit, all three.

"Anyone else?" I asked.

The students looked at their desks. I could see the painful, tentative way the next hour would proceed if I didn't change course. Two women in the class had come to see me the first week of the semester with scanned copies of their prescriptions for anxiety meds, as an explanation for why they couldn't speak in class. ("What do you think the therapist-to-student ratio is like at Rosedale?" Sophie had asked when I'd told her this.) They wanted alternative assignments to make up for the class participation grade.

What would Carpenter do? He would say the kids had become soft and ridiculous. He would have conjured "back in the day," when people just set their jaws and did the work whether it killed them or not. Easy to say *back in the day* when *back in the day* had been very kind to Carpenter's kind. Did I really want to take his side?

But it was a moot point—there was no time to invent alternative assignments. If I had to speak in class—my voice sometimes shaking as I threw a query into the void they made no effort to fill—so would they.

"Here's a question," I said. "Do you like it?"

So simple, and yet no one raised a hand. I was trying to free them from their preconceptions about the story and the idea that there was a right or wrong answer. I wanted to snap them back into their own thoughts.

A bird outside cawed, and several students looked toward the window as if it might have an answer. Risky Business stared at me, blinking.

"Do you?" I asked her.

"Do I what?" she asked. "Like the story?"

"Yeah, do you like it?"

"Whether I like it or not is not that interesting."

This is what we had been taught, all of us, that in English class, whether or not you liked something was beside the point. "Do you have to *like* the quadratic equation?" my own high school English teacher had asked, and for a long time I had accepted it as fact, that liking something and learning something should be amicably divorced, that academic rigor was devoid of—what? taste? But literature is not math, there are no right answers, you are always just feeling your way through. Was feeling really beside the point, then? Or was it the point exactly?

EMBODIMENT

I had not intended to go to Tom's prepub reading, but Dr. Brighton's flight from Vegas had been delayed, and she'd sent an email full of typos asking me to drop off her mudroom keys at the event, which she would be heading to directly from the airport and assumed I'd be attending. My plan was to get in and out before it even began.

I wanted to know what was in the book, of course, desperately, but I didn't want anyone to know I wanted to know—that is, I didn't want Tom to see me there. Even if the book was completely unrelated to me, I didn't want Tom to think I cared what he was up to. But then that seemed self-important; Tom probably didn't care what I cared about. So nothing good could come of going to the reading, interpersonally or psychologically, and the book would be on the shelves in less than a month. I could wait.

The auditorium was packed with students, most of Rosedale's Literature Department, and—what I hadn't expected—many of the English and Comparative Literature faculty from SHU.

Tom stood at the front in a T-shirt and navy blazer, chatting chummily with Mateo, the department head from SHU, a short, affable guy nearing seventy. I'd wondered if Tom's departure had created a rift, but apparently not.

I'd always liked Mateo. He'd more or less convinced me I was capable of completing an academic dissertation. One year, he and his wife, Hannah, had even invited me to Christmas dinner when they'd found out I wasn't going home for the holidays. He was friendly but firm, like a generous boss, a sort of anti–Dr. Brighton. Any pretension was cut by the kind of jolliness required to deal with dozens of different personality types a day. From the undergrads to the dean, he appeared to like everyone equally. But I knew he had been especially tight with Tom, in part because Hannah and Tom's ex-wife, Lydia, had been friends.

I turned away, hoping they wouldn't spot me, and looked around the room for Dr. Brighton. My toothache had emerged with renewed vigor in the late afternoon—I blamed the sandwich I'd torn through between The Campus Novel and American Lit II. I wanted to go home and take some painkillers, lie in bed listening through my walls to Brianna and her friends throwing clothes around the room, doing something inexplicable with their eyebrows, preparing for a night out.

I glanced back at Tom. His head turned to the doorway, and mine followed: There was Aliana in a tight-fitting, high-necked knit dress, hair pulled into a silky ponytail, smile big and bright. A magazine version of womanhood. She hugged Tom, then Mateo, then marched around the circle shaking hands, patting shoulders, and offering smiles. I hadn't expected her to be here.

Aliana scanned the room and registered me instantly. My face flushed. I threw a terse smile as I turned my head, pretending I had just happened to catch her eye. Then I got into the line for hors d'oeuvres.

When I turned back around with my plate of Brie and jam, Aliana was right in front of me.

"What are you doing here?" Her tone was accusatory, but she smiled like a ventriloquist talking through her teeth. She glanced at my plate as if it were a funny choice to consume food when you could just live off air.

"I work here," I said. A gaggle of girls who looked like teens in a nineties movie squeezed past us, forcing us to move, so now my back was literally against the wall.

"I know, but don't you think it's a little weird," said Aliana, "considering the book."

Adrenaline shot through me and my throat tightened, the same elixir of excitement and dread that activates during an emergency or the climax of a novel. The jacket copy flashed in my head: *disappointing sexual encounter, personal and professional failures.* I pressed my fingers into a strip of Brie. "The department head asked me to be here," I said. "But I'm about to leave."

Pursed lips, cocked head, gently furrowed brow, all on Aliana's perfect face: the textbook picture of pity. She sighed in the tone of someone who had promised herself that she would no longer do the emotional labor of explaining things to other people but found herself ever resigned to the task. "I know this MeToo stuff is making everyone rethink things—and rightly so. But wanting to reframe, I don't know, embarrassment or regret or personal failure as something else, after the fact, is not feminism."

The air felt oppressive, hot and thick, like I couldn't take enough in. My mind raced. This was who I was in the book? A vengeful failure? "I never framed anything," I said. When had I ever spoken a public word about Tom? The closest I'd come was during the PhD exit interview, when asked why I'd switched tracks. But I'd deflected follow-up questions, so it hardly counted.

I was alarmed, too, at my visceral aversion to being looped into the flood of MeToo accusations. The movement had been exciting at first, epic, the way it unveiled how lives had been ground up in a horrible machine. But I was uneasy about the frenzied confessions that followed, by the lack of nuance, by the people who saw the Aziz Ansari story as one of sexual misconduct somehow on par with Harvey Weinstein's. I was annoyed, too, by those quick to dismiss the Ansari story simply as an awkward encounter with no other lessons to glean.

If we take the woman "Grace" at her word (and assume her story was accurately recounted by the reporting news outlet), Aziz was being a relentlessly pushy creep, behaving inappropriately but not illegally. But it didn't have to be assault for the encounter to reveal something seriously wrong with dating culture. Alarmingly, I believed that Grace could legitimately categorize it as one of the worst nights of her life at the same time Aziz could've felt, as he later said, that everything seemed okay.

I could see how a not-so-reputable news outlet could convince Grace to share her very clickable version of the story and what they would gain from framing it dramatically as abuse. I understood, too, how the date could leave her feeling violated and confused. Grace did not know how to claim what she wanted. Aziz knew exactly how to claim what he wanted. These were archetypal characters. Why? How had we gotten here?

The group who saw sexual misconduct in the Aziz story used it as an example of why sex absolutely required verbal, enthusiastic consent. The people who wrote it off as a cringey encounter every woman was bound to experience blamed Grace for her helplessness, saying she should've just walked out. The upshot was the same: Women should simply assert themselves.

I was uncomfortable with the wash of empowerment rhetoric that the movement had become. It was as if all women had to do was learn to stand our ground, delineate our boundaries, and use our voices, and the patriarchy would fall, as if the patriarchy hadn't created the very conditions that primed women to behave passively in the first place.

"I just find it suspicious that, after everything, you took a job at Rosedale," Aliana said.

"What's 'everything'? Do you understand that Rosedale called me? That I needed a job? That I had no idea Tom was working here?" Confrontation made me feel lightheaded, drugged. "I don't know what to say to you, Aliana. Why do you even care? If Tom wants to talk to me about something, he can talk to me. Otherwise, leave me alone." I did a heel turn, trashed my plate of Brie, and looked for the closest exit, heart racing.

A hand on my arm as I made my way through the crowd: "There you are," said Dr. Brighton. She was wearing a loose olive green dress you might call a shift and sweeping a hand across the shoulder of an older man in a chair. "This is the esteemed Professor Carpenter."

A low-rent Paul Newman in his salad-dressing years—bright blue eyes, bushy brows, a blur of white hair. He was sitting, I assumed, because of the fall, or his age, or some combination. I didn't want to talk to him or anyone. I needed to go somewhere and think. Or go somewhere and not think. I needed to go for a run, to channel this anxious energy somewhere productive. Or maybe somewhere not productive. I needed to find a computer. Maybe they had finally put up an Amazon preview of the book's first chapter.

"She's covering your classes," Dr. Brighton said.

"Very good," he said. He smiled perfunctorily, then turned back to Dr. Brighton, already done with me.

"I have to handle a little audio issue," she said. "I'm sure you two have plenty to discuss."

"Wait," I said desperately, but she was already off.

Carpenter raised his eyebrows, as if challenging me to find something worthy of conversation.

I turned slightly, so I was facing away from the front of the auditorium. "I just read one of your articles," I offered. A slight unfriendliness, perhaps, seeped into my tone.

"I should hope so, if you're teaching my class." He pursed his lips and pushed his head back, staring at me as if sizing up an enemy. "Just out of grad school?"

Two years—did that sound too fresh or too stale? "Recently," I said.

"And now you've ended up teaching both of my courses?"

"Yes. Interesting classes."

"I never felt *interesting* conveyed much information."

It conveyed a lot of information. It was a passive-aggressive way to say you didn't find it interesting at all. "I was considering some changes to the Campus Novel syllabus, actually," I said.

"The class has functioned quite well for the past twenty years."

"Have you read *The Idiot*?"

"Of course."

"The new one," I clarified.

A breathy scoff. "Oh, there's a new one?"

"It's a campus novel that I think would resonate with the students."

"It's a slippery slope, pandering to student taste."

"There's something to be said for connecting with the material."

"You'd like to trash the classics based on the whims of the youth?"

"Have you read 'Voltaire Night'?" I asked.

"Going for obscure?"

"It's about an adjunct professor," I said. "It doesn't really take place at the university."

"Then it's not a campus novel," he said. It was, in fact, a short story. "Funny that someone would be teaching my class who doesn't understand the genre." He smiled, made a show of patience that we both knew was a lie—he was basking in what he felt was my incompetence.

"No, I get it," I said. "I understand the class."

"I'm sure you think you do." He craned his neck to find someone to rescue him, then turned back to me, disappointed. "The campus novel is about academia as an *institution* and a *place*," he said. "The closed environment is what makes—"

"I'm just not sure the premise is relevant anymore," I interrupted.

"No?" he challenged.

"At this point, the university employs so much low-paid contract labor—" and so Sophie's favorite rant began to tumble out of my mouth.

"The campus novel is about hierarchy, my dear," he said. "Why is it a surprise to people nowadays that one has to do time in the ranks?" His face had the beige shine of Silly Putty. I wondered, if you pressed the page of a book to his face, would all the words stick on backward?

"It's not a surprise," I said, but I was unable to conjure Sophie's confident sense of injustice. The charge from the conversation with Aliana was wearing off, mutating into pure anxiety. I could not get in a fight with this man. It would change nothing except, possibly, the chance to be hired next semester. And since most of the full-time positions I'd applied for wouldn't start until next fall, I desperately needed the income.

I swallowed my pride, glanced around the room. "Big turnout."

"Indeed," said Dr. Carpenter, and we went on this way, me holding up the entire useless conversation as if I were the only one floundering.

When Dr. Brighton returned, I handed her the key immediately.

"House-sitting," she said to Dr. Carpenter.

"Odd jobs never hurt anyone," he replied.

From deep in her dress pockets, Dr. Brighton pulled a white envelope that said *house-sitting $$$* in blue ballpoint. Not even my name, first or last, and certainly nary a *Dr.* Also, one *$* would have sufficed.

Quickly, I squeezed my way toward the door, trying to escape through the back, when I spotted the guy I'd locked eyes with at Rosedale the very first day. He was sweaty and frazzled and not particularly well shaved, like someone who'd been rescued from a desert island and airlifted to a work event. He saw me, his face brightened, and he began excusing his way from his row of seats to get to me.

"Gabe," he said, holding out his hand. "Are you in literature as well?"

"Yes, hi, I'm Sam," I said, shaking his hand. "Part-time lecturer."

He told me he was a visiting assistant professor—temporary but much better paid—in his second year of a two-year contract. He was teaching a four/four—four classes in the fall and four in the spring, a heavy workload. "I'll admit I haven't read any of Sternberg's work," he told me. "I'm just here because I was brainwashed by three weeks of daily emails."

"Luckily, I'm apparently too temp for anyone to remember to put me on a listserv," I said. "Anyway, we should meet up sometime, but I have to—"

"Um, sorry," Gabe interrupted. "Are they looking at us?"

I turned to see Mateo and Aliana at the front of the room, staring through the crowd right at me. Mateo averted his eyes, but Aliana's gaze lingered for a moment to let me know she was in total control.

"Me," I said. "They're looking at me."

"Did you commit some kind of crime?"

"I know them from grad school."

"Where you committed a crime?" he joked.

"Framed," I said.

They were nervous. What did they think I would do? Stage an independent protest? For a book I hadn't even read? Fuck them. Why should I let them chase me out? Besides, if I left now, what kind of statement would that make? Would it say I was a coward? That I felt threatened, which in turn would suggest I was culpable? No, I couldn't leave now.

Gabe and I found seats just before Aliana tapped at the microphone, and the noisy lecture hall faded into a hush as she began the inventory of Tom's accomplishments. The adrenaline came pumping back, as if I had strapped in for a horror movie. It made sense that Tom would tap her to do an intro—her presence gave him credibility, approval from a younger, popular, vaguely feminist writer.

Soon Tom took the stand to thunderous applause and a dash of whooping from a group of girls near the front. I began to feel I'd made a mistake. What if he started with a description of a woman who looked exactly like me, pulling a box of sex toys out from under his bed? My face was hot. I pinched my sweaty hands between my thighs.

He smiled, did the obligatory thanking, related a charming anecdote about a faux pas he'd made at his very first reading many, many years ago, which was also a joke about how long it had taken him to write this book. Then he began.

"'I'm writing from an old oak desk.'" He glanced up at the crowd. "'I'm writing at two a.m. in a remote cabin in the woods. I don't have an office, not anymore, or not really.'"

I leaned forward in my seat.

Tom's narrator, it turned out, did have an office. It was no longer at a university but, rather, in a cozy house in the woods of Vermont where everything seemed to be hand-carved straight from tree trunks. The character spent the chapter shuffling around, poking at the fire, perusing his books. The tension is that you, the reader, don't know exactly why he was kicked out of the university, but you feel it might have been more justified than the narrator implies.

Relief and disappointment washed over me when the crowd finally broke into applause. There was no girl, not yet, but I couldn't bear to sit through the Q&A. People were still clapping, standing up, standing O. "Can we go?" I whispered in Gabe's ear.

"Let's do it," he whispered back.

⁓

We had dinner at the Thai place on Charles, where I slurped down my curry like a last meal, chewing delicately on the solids because of my tooth, then post-dinner drinks at the Brew, Gabe paying for everything, any pretense of feminism gone in light of my financial situation.

He told me about his family. His mother was from Taiwan and, in her early twenties, had moved to Seattle, where she met his father, New England–born and –bred with European roots. Gabe was raised in a Connecticut suburb, where his parents still lived. I told him my truncated backstory—grew up in New Jersey, dead dad, remarried mom.

"Let me ask you this," I said. I wanted to talk about Tom, but I couldn't figure out how to make my question casual. "What did you think of the reading?" My fingers curled tight around my pint glass.

"It was interesting," he said.

"You didn't like it."

"I wouldn't quite say that."

"Wasn't there something off about it?" I said. "Something, I don't know, scammy?"

Gabe pursed his lips. "Okay, I'm kind of relieved you say that, actually—not because . . . well, because I felt that the tone of the book was *ostensibly* progressive but perhaps not actually so. Obviously it's leading to some sort of revelation about a sexual-harassment scandal, and the narrator is going to think the complaint is bogus. There seemed to be some authorial winks suggesting the author disagrees with the narrator. What I mean is, the author seems to be trying very hard to make you think he's fair, even if the narrator isn't. But I couldn't shake the feeling that there was another author beneath this presumed author, leading us to some regressive core."

"Yes!" I said. So Gabe was one of those people who could put words to something that for me was only a vague, inarticulate thought. It was a rarer quality than you might expect in academia, where sounding smart sometimes took precedence over being smart.

I looked into that little alcove where Tom and I had sat together so many years ago.

"Are you okay?" asked Gabe.

"Yeah," I said. "It's just weird to still live in the place you went to grad school."

"I can imagine."

"There's so many Baltimores in Baltimore, and I've been so many versions of me in Baltimore, and some are more embarrassing than others." I finished the last of my beer, waved the glass. "This is honestly just what I needed." It was the first drink I'd had since the night out with Sophie, and the buzz released all the stress that had built up since.

We ordered more beer and discussed other books as I wheeled the coaster around on the table, back and forth with my index finger, back and forth with names: Felisberto Hernández, yes, Bolaño,

Borges, of course, Jun'ichirō Tanizaki, Tommaso Landolfi, yes, Annie Ernaux, yes, Bruno Schulz, yes yes yes, we must have been on *in translation*. He was fluent in Spanish, Italian, and French. Theoretically I could read French and Spanish, but I was mostly too lazy to plod through the original.

I missed having conversations about literature. When you were reading and teaching at high speed, it was hard to remember the thrill, especially when certain books were already so entrenched in a particular set of analyses.

Gabe looked at the beer menu, pointed to Mr. Trash Wheel's Lost Python Ale. "Sometimes I feel like culture is getting so esoteric I have no idea what's going on anymore."

"You moved to Baltimore when?"

"Last July," he said.

"You haven't seen Mr. Trash Wheel?"

"I have no idea what you're talking about."

Mr. Trash Wheel sorted trash out of the Inner Harbor, using a simple design that could be replicated easily and cheaply—basically a canopy over a dumpster with a giant wheel that ran on solar power. The canopy made it look snail-like, and someone ingeniously added giant googly eyes and gave it an Instagram account, in which Mr. Trash Wheel shows off the weird garbage he's "eating," like naked baby dolls and beer kegs and, once, a live python, as immortalized on the aforementioned beer's can.

"But you've been to the Inner Harbor?" I asked.

"I forced myself to wander around and go to the Aquarium. But it was just . . . sad?"

"The Aquarium or the harbor or you?"

"All three, I guess. It was a hundred and two degrees."

"There are only so many bears you can a-build in the harbor," I said. "If you had walked a bit farther past the Aquarium along the water, you would've run into Mr. Trash Wheel."

"And a python?"

"Maybe you should invest in a guidebook."

"I know," he said. "But I've lived in three cities in the last four years, and I'm tired of being a tourist. And try being a tourist in Lincoln, Nebraska."

And so we arrived back deep in the heart of the Rome all roads lead to: the state of academia. We said the word so much that it began to lose meaning, to feel round in my mouth, an unswallowable, uncrackable nut. An *academia nut.*

We talked about the classes we were teaching and the research we weren't doing. We traded dissertation spiels. I told him about mine, "Embodying the Altered State: Breakdowns, Drug Fugues, and Childhood Wonder in the Literary Imagination." The gist was that mental breakdowns and drug fugues warp sensory perception, motor control, and emotion, creating states that burst beyond the bounds of what we like to call reality. The twist was that I also framed childhood wonder as an altered state. Like those who are high or manic, children don't have access to ordinary cognition, are driven by intuition rather than thought, and attribute meaning to the mundane (which manifests in children as enchantment but can manifest in adults as paranoia).

The theme of embodiment was central to the project—the word describes how authors make readers feel by evoking sensations and experiences in their bodies. It's a direct contrast to representation, where authors use symbolic language to engage a reader's conscious mind. The altered state is a paradigm of embodiment because the altered state exists, well, *in the body*—beyond cognition, beyond articulation, beyond narrative, beyond time, even. How—constrained by language, by the logistical reality of putting one word after the next—does an author articulate non-articulation, chronicle a-chronology?

Gabe, I gleaned, though he strained not to brag, had had some fairly successful academic papers and a book contract that would be an updated version of his dissertation on postapocalyptic and ecological fictions, though he had extended the submission date twice.

He also told me about his plight over the last six years to find a tenure-track job—or any academic position with a contract longer than two years. He suffered from severe migraines, and the constant moves meant starting from scratch with a new doctor every year or two. When a migraine came, it could debilitate him for days. Because his visiting faculty and postdoc positions were mostly teaching-based, he had little time for research, and when a migraine hit, his own work was always the first to suffer—well, after him, of course. So he wrote less and less, published less and less, attended fewer and fewer conferences, even as he became an ever more experienced teacher.

"I don't think I'm ever going to get a tenure-track job," he said.

"I'm starting to feel like, if you're not anointed out of the gate, it's a losing battle." I was referring to the grad students hired for positions straight out of, say, Princeton, emanating the emerald shine of possibility that we had already lost. "Like Tom—he got hired before he even published a book."

"That's the world we thought we were walking into," said Gabe. "Before the financial crash. You were supposed to get a job so you could write your book, not write your book somehow as an independent scholar so you could get a job—or, as it were, not get a job."

"But someone *does* have to get the jobs. I mean, look at you, a visiting professor."

"So? Only twenty percent of faculty are tenure now. An escape from the adjunct trap is an escape from sub-minimum wage work, but it's not an escape from exploitation. Even my 'lucky' friends tolerate a lot of shit until they get tenure review—heavy teaching loads, no research budget, tons of service. This is what I'm hoping for? This is the lottery I want to win?"

The coaster I'd been rolling around wobbled like a spun quarter, then lay flat.

"I'm sorry," said Gabe. "I'm just frustrated. I don't mean to be depressing." He took a sip of his drink. "Can I ask: Why did you want to get a PhD . . . originally?"

"The economy was bleak and . . . I liked books? I liked . . . words."

I liked them as if they were objects, trinkets or iridescent pearls that shone different colors in different lights. I liked how, when strung together, the whole hit you before the parts. I liked when a sentence stuck in me like a barbed thorn. The right's fear of trigger warnings was out of hand, but I also felt there needn't be such warnings on literature. Literature was all trigger. Kafka and his axe were trying to tear us apart. It was exactly what I wanted.

I'd liked the thinking, too: the teasing of threads, following them to the strange places they lead, trying to tie them back together in the sober light of language, which had created them in the first place. But I never felt I could get into the groove of academic writing. My work was always too "voicey"; there was too much "me" in it. I couldn't get rid of her.

"I liked books, too," said Gabe, smiling. "Still do."

I took another sip of beer, lowered my voice: "I also had some vague idea I was going to write one," I said. "Like, not academic. A novel. I started on SHU's creative track. That's really why I went to grad school."

"What made you switch?"

"I wasn't good enough," I said. For who, though? For the program? For Tom? For myself? For myself because of Tom? Tom and Mateo had both encouraged me to switch, so I'd switched.

I once loved writing. I wrote my first story in fifth grade: "JCPenney and the Secret Cavern," about a girl who gets locked in a JCPenney at night. She tries all those fluffy display beds, then somehow drops into a cavernous abyss hidden beneath the store. (Excuse the under-desk commentary, but younger me was prophetic, almost: a story about the promise of capitalism as manifested in a nineties department store, packed with things I could only admire for a moment before I fell into the dark underworld below.) The first part was inspired by *The Mixed-Up Files of Mrs. Basil E. Frankweiler.* My story was the semi-suburban counterpart, based on my youth, where culture was driving thirty minutes to the mall.

In high school, I wrote emo poetry that I thought was clever: a sonnet about sonnets, a sestina about eating disorders, endless free verse, like "The Divine Grocery Store," in which Adam and Eve lust over apples in the fruit aisle at ShopRite. The last line: *And the credit card runneth over.*

In college, I wrote about doomed relationships. Poets liked to describe moons, whereas I liked to describe burning summer suns: like cotton balls, like jawbreakers, like severed rabbits' tails, bald as full moons. I wrote a story about a woman whose breakup made her feel so untethered that she floated up into the sky. I wrote a story called "Going South" about a couple heading for a breakup on a road trip to South Carolina. In real life, I had never had a relationship, never mind one passionate enough for the gravitas of "doomed." It all rang false.

I started to write in the third person, which, I gathered, was more literary. I pasted myself in a chair and wrote the biography of a synesthetic male painter living in the mid–nineteen hundreds, told it in color rather than chronological order, from black, through the spectrum, and into white, into "the very canvas of the universe." I set a timer for two hours every day and wrote a Western in which, at the end, instead of the main character waking up from a dream, the twist is that it's all a film set, the whole thing is a movie, which is why weird flashes of the future keep appearing and disappearing, Coke cans and cell phones. Clever enough to get me into grad school, but in retrospect, it was all tricks, no heart.

At SHU, I started writing what Aliana would come to call "unromantic love stories," whose anti-drama was more real to me than anything I had invented before. They took place in the context of misconnection and misunderstanding, of permeating loneliness and alienation. In one story, a librarian who has never understood the allure of romance novels befriends her stalker, not realizing that he is stalking her. As their friendship grows, the stalker's obsession lessens, which he frames as "falling out of love." The problem is that, up close, she exudes an aloof, almost anti-sexuality. At the end of the story, the librarian picks up a romance novel while restocking the shelves and begins reading, with some implication that she may have a burgeoning sexual interest in the stalker-turned-friend.

Sometimes, writing these, I felt as if I'd tapped some primal well, less like I was creating something than giving birth to it. Then I went to workshop and had to act like a regular human who had not basically bled out onto a piece of paper.

Tom liked the stories at first, or claimed to, but then there were problems because I began using the first person more and more, and he couldn't get behind the confessional tone—the mark of an amateur.

After that, I had a dry spell. The next jolt of inspiration wasn't until years later, when I discovered the work of Bruno Schulz, quite late in my dissertation. He wrote about childhood, that magical space where the commonplace—discarded objects, cheap art supplies, advertisements in magazines—shimmers with an otherworldly significance. Schulz didn't sentimentalize or use a childlike voice. Instead, he wrote as an adult, treating childhood enchantment as serious and sacred, as an "age of genius" he seems almost desperate to recapture, the way drug addicts chase the first high, or some bipolar patients go off their meds, bored by life without mania.

In this passage, for example, Schulz describes a child sitting on the floor in a square of sunlight drawing on scrap paper as a transcendent experience of art-making:

> And I sat among the piles of paper, blinded by the glare, my eyes full of explosions, rockets, and colors, and I drew wildly, feverishly, across the paper, over the printed or figure-covered

> pages. My colored pencils rushed in inspiration across columns of illegible text in masterly squiggles, in breakneck zigzags that knotted themselves suddenly into anagrams of vision, into enigmas of bright revelation, and then dissolved into empty, shiny flashes of lightning, following imaginary tracks.

While reading that passage, I remembered, in a flash of feeling, the experience of writing "JCPenney and the Secret Cavern": the soft braided rug where I lay on the floor, the cool winter light from the sliding glass door falling across my page so that the silver spiral of my notebook gleamed, and the big graphite cursive loops—my writing—sparkled.

I wished to have just a dash of this sort of transcendent experience while writing my dissertation, but I was thinking too much, I was too scared of failing to let myself feel, and academia wasn't about feeling, anyway. We were always pretending there was no *us* in our work. Even on the creative side, we either peddled our lives as fiction, disguised the details so we could smuggle in real feelings or, when less successful, forgot the feelings, focused on flourishes, style at the expense of art. On the academic side, "research as me-search" was an anti-intellectual embarrassment. But dig into any dissertation, and you'll find the author there, her anxieties and obsessions and secret desires.

The bar was a haze, Gabe the only clear pinpoint. I couldn't tell if I was buzzed or drunk, which should have been a clue. Our glasses were empty. "I don't live that far from here," I said.

"Should I walk you home?" he asked, understanding, as they say, the assignment.

We flicked off our shoes in the dark hallway, my ears pulsing in the anti-bar silence of my apartment. Brianna's door was closed, no light from the bottom strip. She must've been asleep. I felt like I'd won.

"We can't go in the kitchen," I whispered.

"Why not?"

"Things are rotting."

"*Things are rotting,*" he repeated, laughing.

"Something's rotten in the state of my apartment," I whispered.

"So it goes."

"Poo-tee-weet."

"Why not lights?"

"What's that from?"

"No, I'm asking," he said.

"Oh. My roommate," I said. "Room?" I gestured toward my door in the grainy dark. Two PhDs in literature. Dr. Tarzan and Dr. Jane.

No lights in the bedroom, either. I preferred the anonymous feel. I didn't want the night to devolve into a make-out session, didn't want to think about his mouth or face in any specific, physical way. The Brillo-y little hairs sprouting on his cheeks and upper lip, the spittle at the corners of his mouth, which gave me the impression that his lips would be sticky. I put my hand on his crotch.

In so many books, they skip right over the sex, as if it were a clean and easy negotiation, a set of communication standards so universal that you could just jump-cut your way through and get the gist, but to me—was I doing it wrong?—there was so much subtext in the brokering.

"Hey," he said. I paused for the reveal, the hidden wife or the STD. It seemed absurd to have my hand on his groin as I waited for information. "I mean, should we talk about expectations?" he asked.

"Now?"

"My position is over at the end of the year." He tried to say something else and failed. My hand was still on his crotch. I felt a downward tick.

Lines of poetry flitted through my head. Sometimes, when I was drunk, I felt like a Dadaist collage.

What lips my lips have kissed, and where, and why,
with dreams, with drugs, with waking nightmares, alcohol
    and cock and endless balls
so many things seem filled with the intent
to be lost that their loss is no disaster.

Nothing I could say aloud.

"You're not looking for a relationship," I said.

"I don't even mean that," he said. "I *am* looking for a relationship, but of course, my situation is never particularly conducive . . . There's this looming end point, and I don't know—I just thought it was possible you'd want to talk about it first?" I felt it tick down again. How did men rule the world when they were the ones who had this ridiculous, humiliating organ with its big tell?

"We don't have to talk about it now," I said. "Just pretend I'm not anyone specific."

I knelt. I liked the visceral scratchy sting of the indoor-outdoor rug on my knees. It had a grounding effect, something concrete and easier to hold on to than the abstract dread of daily life. I unzipped his fly. You'd think this would be worse than a mouth, but mouths, at first glance, seemed so innocuous, only to reveal a raw wetness inside, whereas this complied completely with my expectations. I took his hand and put it on the back of my head, pushed against it a little, to indicate that a certain roughness was fine, and up it went, taut as a diving board.

Did I like it? Not an uncomplicated question. I wanted to do it because it seemed both more and less personal than other options, because by focusing on his pleasure, we didn't have to focus on mine, because I wanted to be the kind of girl who would do this, and by doing it I was.

Embodiment. It's what I wanted most: to feel my body, to understand it effortlessly. I wanted to know how people intuit themselves, so I'd sat down each day at my carrel in the stacks and tried to articulate the articulation of the inarticulable. How many layers of articulation did you need to understand pure experience? Was I perhaps missing the point, trying to intellectualize what I just needed to feel?

Well, here I am, jump-cutting anyway to four a.m., hungover, tooth aching, knees rug-burned, Gabe snoring. I couldn't see a way to pull out a blanket without disturbing him, so I tiptoed to the bathroom naked, peed, then wrapped a beach towel around myself and went into the kitchen, where, indeed, something was rotting.

I gulped down a glass of water, which streamed from the corners of my mouth as I chastised myself for waiting so long to hydrate, for not peeing before I'd gone to sleep. There was a fifty-fifty chance I would get a UTI. My body was bent on defending against foreign entry. In grad school, a tenacious UTI had traveled to my kidneys, and I'd almost passed out while teaching. After class, I'd walked in tiny steps to the health center, the sky cobalt, winter biting my burning-hot face.

At least I'd had decent health insurance back then, through SHU. Now, with a seven-thousand-dollar deductible, I was fucked. There would be the cost of the doctor's appointment, the urine culture, the antibiotics, plus the half day I would lose to the whole thing. Hetero sex was a time suck, a money pit. Maybe society had steered me toward straightness, but my body was steering me away.

I lay on the couch with my towel wrapped around me, the throw thrown on top, thinking about Tom's stupid smile when he read the word *co-eds,* as if to laugh at the narrator for his outdated ways. I thought about how much work I had to do and how much harder it would be with a hangover, my second of the semester. The couch was basically an upholstered board with button tufting and a few random springs that dug into your back. My body felt unbalanced with a sense of uncompleted action—I hadn't come, what's new. My nervous sweat from the reading intermingled with the BO scent of old onion wafting from the kitchen. Dawn approached as the birds began their chaotic chirping.

I gave up on trying to sleep. I plugged my phone into the outlet next to the table and sat on the floor, towel-wrapped, knees-to-chest, and googled Tom. I found *Casualty* on a most-anticipated list in *The Guardian: Daring, elegant and brutally honest, Tom Sternberg's much anticipated second novel is a deep and nuanced examination of power, responsibility, and punishment—in particular, how much punishment is enough?*

I skimmed the rest of the listicle, then closed the browser, then reopened it, then started googling things like "what if someone writes a book about you" and "DIY root canal?" and "lazy or burned out?" and "free dental clinics" and "at-home UTI remedies" and "the low, humiliating premise of union gluck poem" and "sexuality quiz" and "successful adjunct professors" and "adjunct nightmares," as if there would be some pop listicle or BuzzFeed article, but there were only desperate blog entries and that famed *Atlantic* article about the adjunct who died from being overworked and underinsured.

As my hangover improved, my toothache worsened. I wrapped an ice pack around my jaw. It was a gel pack with beads in it, velvety on one side, designed for your lower back. I strapped the elastic band around my head, the Velcro scratching at the skin below my eye.

I checked Facebook, saw the new army of fat babies who had burst from the loins of high school classmates I hadn't seen or spoken to in more than a decade. I checked the trash heap that was Twitter, an academic hangout spot for humble brags, all virtue and outrage. Aliana had retweeted a tweet from Tom, which itself was a retweet from *The Guardian*.

I closed the browser with a flick of the thumb. To lighten the mood, I rewatched an episode of *The Handmaid's Tale*. I was attracted to the bad guy—the fascist who hated women and wouldn't let them read. Maybe I was the agent of my own oppression. Maybe my job was perfect for me, maybe it was what I was destined for, maybe it turned me on.

I awoke to Brianna's shiny golden mules shuffling past the kitchen table. I pulled the lukewarm ice pack off my face and rubbed the sleep out of my eyes, listening to her sigh as she emptied out yesterday's coffee grounds, listening to the coffee machine gurgle, listening to the microwave whir, listening to Brianna yelp "Ouch!" as she did every morning when she took the bowl out of the microwave with her bare hands, listening to the coffee hiss, hiss, hiss onto the hot plate as she poured herself a cup before it was finished brewing, which she also did every morning.

I watched the mules again, passing under the table, saw the spoon drop. She set her bowl and mug on the table, and I held my breath as she leaned down to pick it up. From five feet away, I could see the whites of her eyes, the whites of her AirPods. She picked up her spoon, didn't notice me at all.

Five minutes later, as I passed her open door to go to the bathroom, she looked up at me, startled, from her bed, where she was sitting with the bowl of oatmeal propped between her legs. "Where'd you come from?"

"Here," I said vaguely as the door to my room, catty-corner to Brianna's, opened and Gabe appeared.

"Hi," he said. He was fully dressed.

Brianna looked stunned.

"Brianna, Gabe. Gabe, Brianna," I said, throwing my hand between them.

"Hey," Brianna said.

"Hi," said Gabe. "Nice to meet you."

All the sexual energy of the night before had vanished or, perhaps more accurately, reconfigured itself into a kind of elephant in the room. It amazed me, what you could do to each other, what parts of each other you could have in your mouth or elsewhere, how many boundaries could be eliminated, how instantly they could be redrawn.

"How did you sleep?" he asked.

"Good," I said. "I mean, bad. Fine. You?"

"Okay," he said. "I can't believe I slept this late." It was only eight-thirty, but I understood.

"It's not a problem if you have to go," I said. "I mean, obviously you can have coffee if you want—food, whatever—but it's not a requirement."

"I mean, what do you want? I'm flexible. Do you need the time to work, or—?"

"We both probably have a lot of work," I said.

Brianna watched on, bewildered but all in.

"Yeah, okay, cool," he said. "So I'll just head out?"

"Yeah, no problem."

"I had a really good time, Sam."

It was lame, maybe, but hearing my name made my heart swell. "Yeah, same," I said.

As soon as the front door shut, Brianna yelled, "What the fuck was that?"

"Nothing," I said, returning to her doorway.

"That was weird as hell," she said. "Plus, I thought you were a lesbian." She slid a bite of oatmeal into her mouth. "Not that it matters. I mean, people don't even come out anymore. It's whatever."

"I'm not a lesbian," I said.

"You're bi," she said. "My second guess."

"Sure," I said, shrugging.

"No?" she said. "Pan?"

I shrugged again.

"What? Asexual?" She screwed up her face, rejecting that one out of hand. "Aromantic? Demisexual?"

"I don't even know what those are," I said.

"Demisexual is—"

"It doesn't matter."

"*Experimenting?*" she asked, exasperated.

"I thought the whole thing with your age group was that you could be whatever you want."

"I mean, obviously whatever is fine," she said. "It just seems lazy to not even have a word for it when, like, every word is available to you. Plus, aren't you a writer or something?"

"Or something."

She raised an eyebrow. "You *teach* writing."

"Kind of."

"Kind of? Is there anything you *definitely* are?"

Was there? Was I employed? Sort of. In a relationship? Not really. In two relationships? Kind of, but also no. A daughter? More or less, though less and less. A writer? Or something.

What I felt like most acutely, overwhelmingly, was a toothache.

"An adjunct," I said. "I'm an adjunct."

Brianna pushed air from her lips, the auditory equivalent of an eye roll. "No, I mean like: I'm a cis, heterosexual, hetero-romantic, neurotypical, Gen Z, Black woman from New York City with occasional anxiety who works in merchandising."

"You're Gen Z?"

"Well, I just identify more with Gen Z."

I used to think new words only increased possibilities, but they were starting to feel like restraints. There were too many of them, and there would never be enough. I understood the need for identities and diagnoses, but sometimes I felt as if we were, societally, acquiring an unhealthy attachment to them, drilling our identities down to strange minutiae, to strings of words, trying to make ourselves static and definable when really we moved, changed, slid along some multiaxial diagram of being that defied categorization.

Why were we so desperate to contain the uncontainable, tame the untamable, name the unnamable, to corral the in-between and force it to fit in? Maybe we felt that by nailing our identities down to a word, we'd at least have something to hold on to while our lives fractured into the chaos of the gig economy, the climate apocalypse. But it made me feel worse when every word was available to me and none of them made sense.

I said some truncated version of this to Brianna. "You only have to make sense to yourself," she replied.

"Do you make sense to yourself?"

"Pretty much," she said. "Not to other people. Most of them can't comprehend that I could be Black—and, what!—have parents who are *dentists*? a summer house on the Cape? a *white* grandmother? But fuck them, you know? I am what I am."

"I need an infusion of that Gen Z confidence," I said. "Being a white millennial woman adjunct from suburban New Jersey is pretty embarrassing."

"You're lucky to be such a neutral person," she said. "But it will help your street cred if you're gay somehow." She took another bite of oatmeal. "So, as an adjunct, you just teach, like, regular college classes or what?"

"Yeah," I said.

"Doesn't *adjunct* basically mean, like, temporary? Like you're a temp?"

"Everything's temporary," I offered. I used to be afraid of change, but now it was the only comforting thought.

"In the scheme of things, maybe," she said. "What's your sign? You've got to be a cusp."

"Scorpio," I said.

"See!" she said, pointing. "You *are* something!" She shook her head. "Wow. *Scorpio*. That makes so much sense."

I went back to my room and took one of my five precious Vicodins, left over from another dramatic medical situation a few years before. The big sell is that dental issues are your own fault, and yet I brush and floss every day, it's as close as I get to prayer, and still my teeth rebel as if my gums are a prison from which they're desperate to escape.

I texted Sophie my Bitmoji avatar flipping over a desk of school supplies.

Sometimes it took her hours or even days to respond, but she wrote back immediately: Lol

I wondered if she'd been out drinking last night, too, had just ushered someone out the door. A woman, thin and attractive, like she was?

Is that supposed to be you? she asked, since I had taken liberties to give my avatar wrinkles and belly fat.

I put my phone on my night table, and another text dinged in, a picture of a sweet potato so old that its eyes had grown into stalks.

Found this small, lonely creature, read the accompanying message. Things are rotting here, too.

It was Gabe, not Sophie.

You look geriatric 😂, Sophie texted.

In real life? I wrote back.

I got up and scoured the fridge, searching for something terrible, and was rewarded with a Tupperware container that had grown a mold culture like the terrain of an alien planet. I suffered through the putrid act of opening the lid to take a picture that best conveyed the planetary look without losing the context. I wrote: found its home planet.

fucked up, came the reply.

I'd sent the message to Sophie. sorry, did not mean to send that! newest mars rover shot, I added, as if that explained things.

She didn't reply. I thumbed over to Gabe, sent the picture to him, then switched my phone to silent. I needed to work. No, I needed to lie down, just for a few minutes.

Head on my pillow, I closed my eyes, and in slunk a man and in slunk a woman—generic, featureless—and they took care of things, each in their own way, and for the first time in months, I came, quite hard, my poor pained teeth clacking together.

Chapter 6

TEXTS

I told my grumbling stomach to shut up. The antibiotics for the UTI had just kicked in, and I felt like after three days straight of needing to pee, my body shouldn't be allowed to make further requests. Rosedale was dead quiet. A warm glow emitted from the library onto the dark quad, so its columns were dramatically silhouetted. I had four job applications left to write for the big October 15 deadline, two for tenure-track positions at Altoona Midwest and Naylor, and two for non-tenure-track, open-rank lectureships at KIT and St. Francis, all of which had starting dates of next fall. I'd been able to borrow a Chromebook from the Baltimore public library to finish them up.

The KIT job required a cover letter, CV, three letters of recommendation, three sample syllabi for courses I'd taught in the past, three sample syllabi for courses I might develop at KIT, a writing sample, teaching evaluations from at least two classes, a teaching statement, and a diversity statement. The job was a theoretically renewable one-year contract that required teaching a four/four, advising undergraduate capstone projects, and contributing to the "excellence of the department" (read: being on committees). It didn't support research, and it paid forty-five thousand dollars a year.

I opened the last cover letter I'd written, from the BYC job, then saved a new copy as COVER LETTER KIT. My stomach grumbled again. I'd made the mistake of looking up pizza delivery options online, in a private browser tab, as if it were porn. I couldn't stop thinking about the picture on the website, a stock photo of a slice being pulled from a pie, glistening cheese stretching away in long melted strings. A large pie cost fourteen bucks, plus a five-dollar service fee for the delivery app, plus the five-dollar tip I would add on for the delivery person, out of guilt and solidarity. I couldn't justify spending twenty-four dollars on a pizza, not when I was trying to keep groceries under two hundred a month.

If I really wanted to order, I would have to order two pizzas to justify the extra fees, and then I'd have leftover pizza all week and not have to eat another cannellini-bean-and-tuna-fish salad, my quick dinner, which I called the Toucan (two-can, ha ha) Special.

Forget the pizza, I told myself as I started editing the cover letter to match the job description. I needed to sound less like the composition and rhetoric professor they'd wanted at BYC and more like a generalist who could cover survey courses and writing workshops and also teach classes "in queer studies, Afro-diasporic literatures, or the environmental humanities."

In grad school, my friend Isaac helped me revise my cover letter and CV. My issue, he said, was an "almost self-sabotaging lack of pretension." It was as if, he told me, I expected people to be swayed by simplicity, straightforwardness, and common sense. Academia wasn't a meeting of minds so much as a battle for limited resources, and to get resources, you had to puff yourself up like a rooster and convince everyone you were a genius. Private school kids had a leg up, he told me (he was a private school kid), because they were taught to be entrepreneurs, but the product was you, and you were taught it so thoroughly—it underpinned your entire education—that you weren't even putting on a show. A rooster puffs because that's what he does. "That is all to say, Sam," he told me as he handed back my application materials covered in red pen, "you're really going to have to douche it up."

Douche it up, I said like a mantra as I rewrote the third and last paragraphs. Absently, in a pause between paragraphs, I reopened the private browser window where the pizza sat. I felt the drooly drag of saliva under my tongue and a pang of nostalgia. I'd grown up in Jersey with New York–style pizza, the kind that looked straight out of a *Teenage Mutant Ninja Turtles* cartoon. My mother, a perpetual dieter, refused to eat it, so every few months I went with my dad to a strip-mall parlor with red gingham cloths on the tables and wedges of cardboard under the uneven feet. We always got the Monday special after my dad had worked the weekend, and we never ordered drinks. "One pie, two waters, no ice," he'd say. What did we talk about during these outings? I couldn't remember.

"You gotta douche it up," I repeated to myself.

It was well after eight now. I hadn't eaten since eleven-thirty. I could just order the pizza. I could just do it. What was the point of living? How could I focus for the next five or seven hours this hungry? If I went home to eat, I'd lose momentum.

I ordered the pizza, my heart beating fast as if I'd impulse-bought a Ferrari, then read over my cover letter one more time.

I checked my phone. A little dot tracked the person in possession of my pizza, a mile away.

I saved the cover letter, found my most recent diversity statement, and made a new copy for KIT. The whole thing was a showpiece, a stopgap, a sham. As if academia, by its very nature, didn't root out diversity long before the job application. As if poor people just streamed into graduate school—never mind college—as a matter of course. As if people of color might never feel out of place or get tired of being told that their stories weren't universal.

My phone was dying, so I crawled under the table to plug it in, watched the dot as it entered the building and got trapped in the maze of Bowen. I wanted to help it, go to it, but I knew a dot's location wasn't all that accurate inside a building. It shifted around, back and forth, like a fly caught between windowpanes. I was still staring at the dot when a voice said, "Hello?"

"Hello?" I said from under the table. "Sorry, my phone—"

Subway Sandwich stood tall in the doorway with my pizzas, like a character from one book suddenly popping up in another.

"Prof?" he said.

I shot up, dusting my knees. "Sorry, my phone cord is about two feet long." The smell of pizza was overwhelming. I felt attuned to every scent, like I was high: the richness of the cheese, the yeastiness of the dough, the acidic delight of the tomato sauce.

"What are you doing here?" he asked.

"Oh, I teach here, too," I said.

"You can do that?"

"Contract labor."

"Like the gig economy?" he said. "For professors?"

"Yeah," I said.

"Cool."

"Yeah, except there's this market issue in which the supply is greater than the demand," I said. "How many hours a week do you work?"

"Basically, like, whenever I'm not asleep or at school or doing homework," he said. "That's why I signed up for your class, eight a.m. Nobody orders delivery that early. But I'm getting the degree so I don't have to do this shit—I mean, sorry, Prof, *stuff*—for the rest of my life." He put the pizza boxes on the desk. I swallowed my saliva. "What about you?" he asked. "How many hours a week do you work?"

"Oh," I said. "Always. Whenever I'm awake."

The Grapes of Wrath? Nobody, and I mean nobody, had time for *The Grapes of Wrath*. And yet who could deny: *and in the eyes of the people there is the failure; and in the eyes of the hungry there is a growing wrath.* Not to be dramatic.

Subway Sandwich looked out the window. "Damn, this campus is insane, like from a movie. I didn't even know this place was here. I thought it was like a horse farm or something. Lawn looks like a golf course. You'd think if they had this much money, they'd label the buildings, you know?" Lewis was plastered with maps. "Anyways. Any hints about that, like, army of mushrooms?"

I had assigned a Plath poem for American Lit II about a multitude of mushrooms silently pushing their way up from the earth. "Don't worry," I said. "We'll figure it out in class."

As soon as he left, I tore open the box. The pizza, still moderately warm, shone golden. I felt ill with joy. I pulled out a slice, flipped it onto the lid to absorb some of the oil, then devoured it and started on another. This time I took a more measured approach, forcing myself to be gentle on my tooth and to savor bite by bite as I worked.

With greasy fingers on the keys, I considered how to approach the diversity statement at a school that skewed center-left. Your best bet generally was to throw yourself under the bus, shimmy your way out of the closet, flay yourself in exactly the appropriate way. *As a woman,* you were supposed to say. *As a member of the LGBTQ+ community. As a survivor of sexual assault.* Be proud of your identity. Italicize a word in your mother's native tongue. Mention mental health abstractly, not as illness but as work-life balance, balanced more toward work. Mention a disability that's not too debilitating. Be different, but prove you'll fit right in.

They wanted palatable diversity, which is to say they didn't want to deal with the setbacks diversity might entail. They wanted hardship that had already been overcome. Diversity sans structural conditions. Diversity as merit badge, no baggage allowed. They wanted diversity romanticized, straightforward and quantifiable—there was no space for gradients. By economic diversity, they meant abject poverty; they couldn't fathom the existence of the suburban lower-middle class. My own queerness was not even nameable to me, never mind claimable on an application.

At many institutions, it was too radical to say you wanted to queer the classroom or decolonize the syllabus—forget about the actual world—you never knew the political attitudes of the hiring committee. They preferred a lukewarm repertoire of "diverse" teaching experiences, preferably at top-tier institutions and private colleges. Teaching at a community college was basically career suicide, and adjuncting was just an unemployed academic's maintenance phase. Two thirds of academics were on short-term contracts, and the richer you were, the longer you could afford to hold out hope for something better.

For an adjunct, it was better to teach two classes at one university than four at two, so you didn't seem disjointed and directionless. Better to use that free time for conferences and committees, research and publications. It was as if money were not a factor, as if time weren't money, as if teaching classes weren't money, as if conference fees weren't money, as if your entire undergraduate education weren't money, as if you didn't need money to live.

My curser blinked. *As a woman . . .* I began.

"I just can't care anymore," Sophie said when I asked her if she had to teach soon. We were sitting in her car in Lot A, eating a veggie pizza straight from the box, which Sophie had scavenged from a student government meeting—salad course to the leftover pizza in my freezer at home.

"I doubt that's true," I said.

She contorted herself extravagantly to retrieve a water bottle from the footwell behind her. "You're coming to the meeting about unionizing, right?"

"Text me the info. I need to put it in my calendar," I said. "Do you have napkins?"

She popped open the glove compartment with one hand. "We need to do something," she said. "I mean, some of us are on fucking food stamps, on Medicaid."

"Wait," I said, patting oil off my slice. "How did you get on Medicaid?" I didn't think I qualified because of the way we were getting paid, four lump sums that put us over the monthly limit.

"Why are we telling kids to go to college?" she asked, not

hearing my question. "Wouldn't we be better off telling them to go into the trades?"

"The trades?"

"Plumbers, electricians. Economy tanks, people still need their pipes fixed. You fix a pipe, then you forget about it; you don't have to stay up all night thinking about some kid who's a horrible student but is going to be deported if he gets less than a C."

"Do you think you'd really be happy as a plumber?"

"We sit around pretending we're doing the Lord's work—which, by the way, is how we get completely fucked over pay-wise. I believed in all this academic bullshit when I started. Like it was smart and honorable. Whatever." She took another slice of pizza, chewed as she talked. "Plumbers do work that actually affects people's daily lives. We should bow down at the feet of the plumber."

I felt uneasy. The faultless plumber doing God's work. Her monologue smacked of the hidden condescension that I had once overlooked in *Ten Four.*

Hadn't she said more than once that she was on food stamps, Medicaid? No, she had said "some of us."

"So be a plumber," I told her. "You can do manual labor if you want."

"I mean, I fucking am," she said. "I have like ten jobs. It's not less-than to work a trade."

How was she turning this on me like I was the elitist? "You know, my dad pumped gas for years," I said. "Delivered packages."

"I don't know about gas, but deliverymen? That's a good union job, right? Don't they have set hours? Overtime? You're your own boss?"

"You aren't your own boss," I said. "All he ever did was work."

"All *we* ever do is work."

I pulled a strip of green pepper off my slice. "What do your parents do?"

"It's funny, actually," she said. She took another bite, chewed it with her fingers over her lips, buying time, as if she hadn't just been talking with food in her mouth.

"What?"

"They're screenwriters," she said, shaking her head with a laugh.

Everything I knew about Sophie coalesced, congealed: the directors and the lipstick, the gin and tonic and the eyeball of a fish.

"Seriously," she added, "screenwriting's not as glamorous as it sounds. It's constant hustle, constant schmoozing. It's writing spec scripts for straight-to-TV movies that never get made."

"But did they get made?"

"I mean, yeah," she said. "Sometimes. I mean, they were lucky."

"You grew up in L.A.?" I asked. How had I not clocked this earlier? Pedigree usually revealed itself not just in the pretentious or the preppy but in people who tried to hide it, because the scent of class lingered, like cigarette smoke in carpet.

"Fucking hellhole. Honestly, I've felt more welcome shooting whiskey at a dive bar in Knoxville than sipping some pink shit in a West Hollywood cocktail lounge."

My mother's parents had lived in the South, and I was often annoyed about the general attitude that Northeast liberals had about the region—that it was so full of backward and stupid people that they deserved the Republicans they voted for. But this opposite sentiment annoyed me, too. Maybe the South was charming when you could hop in, ignore the Confederate flags, marvel at the cowboy boots and the lack of pretension, then head back to another reality.

"At least they like gay people in California," I said.

She rolled her eyes. "Yes, the performance of liberalness is a distinctive part of California culture. But commercialized Pride isn't exactly the utopia we all dreamed about." Her blasé attitude reminded me of Brianna's "it's whatever," like we were post-Pride, like everything was good now, like I should just be chill.

"You know that book *Rolex*?" I asked.

"Oh my God," Sophie said, shaking her head. "That girl. What's her name? She went to prep school at Heritage. Dated my brother's friend for, like, one minute."

"Oh, wow," I said stupidly. "Aliana. We were in grad school together." I had mentioned the book only because its take on L.A.'s depraved high society seemed relevant, not because I'd imagined that Sophie and Aliana ran in the same social circles.

"Small world," Sophie said.

But it wasn't a small world. It was a big, big world brimming with horror, and we were cordoned off in a tiny part of it, riding around in our academic bumper cars.

Cornell had been packed with kids like Sophie and Aliana, outclassing me everywhere I went. I thought of my first college party, all red Solo cups and name-dropping, philosophy lessons from sadboys, eighteen-year-olds vying to be most highbrow. I didn't know what anyone was talking about. When someone mentioned Freud, I was relieved. I had somewhat randomly read his lectures on psychoanalysis in high school because I'd found a copy for a dollar at the library book sale. But it quickly became clear that having read the book wasn't an advantage. I had come to the book blind, with little context, and seemed to know only random minutiae. Everyone else had a common language of keywords, an understanding of what history had extracted. It didn't matter that they hadn't read the book.

My peers' knowledge went deeper than education or intelligence; it was born of a lifetime of gleaning. It came from the air they breathed, it was the conversation at the dinner table, it was the family friends, the radio station in the background, the newspapers and magazines around the house. As with learning a foreign language, one had to be immersed. Even fluency, when it came late, didn't override your accent. The muscle memory of your mother tongue always licked its way through, revealing you.

Even now, more than a decade later, with a BA, an MA, a PhD, I was missing something essentially "academic," something tied to class that I couldn't quite explain. I felt like an interloper, a step behind, watching what everyone else did, some more subtle version of Leonardo DiCaprio not knowing which utensil to use in *Titanic*. Sure, you could mimic Kathy Bates, but it didn't really matter: The ship was going down and you were in steerage.

Sophie checked the clock. "Okay, now I'm truly late to class. Lock the doors on your way out, okay?"

Sophie left me there, with the last slice of pizza pooled in grease I didn't tap off, napkins fluttering in the open glove box as I searched online for her parents. Sophie's dad had been a Hollywood psychiatrist, at some point consulted on a movie, then had begun a career as a screenwriter, cowriting several psychological thrillers with Sophie's mom. He'd also been nominated for an Oscar in the category of Documentary Short.

Information about my own parents, of course, is not online. They married young, though not each other. I was the product of their second marriages. My dad met my mom and his first wife the same way, as a gas station attendant in New Jersey, one of the few states where you aren't allowed to pump your own gas.

My mom had recently divorced the man she'd married at twenty-one and was trying to get back on her feet, living in an apartment over a pharmacy and making minimum wage as a secretary for a large plant nursery where we'd later get our yearly Christmas tree for free. Her car had been behaving badly, and my dad offered to look under the hood. Her oil had turned to sludge. Not only had she never changed it, but she'd never thought to change it, because she didn't know a car's oil needed to be changed.

My mother told this story often, until my dad died (cancer, lung) when I was thirteen. Then she stopped telling it and, little by little, stopped mentioning him at all.

We didn't have many books in my house growing up, mostly just my mom's grocery-store mass-market romance novels. But on the top shelf in what had been my parents' bedroom were several cheap paperback classics that I knew to be my dad's. My mother had gotten rid of his clothes and other things quickly, but she had left his books.

I'd never seen him open them—had he read them before I was born? Did he have some secret interest in literature? My father, unlike my mother, hadn't gone to college, but occasionally he bought the Sunday *Times* at the deli.

Months after his death, I sat on the edge of my bed and opened the first yellowed page of *One Hundred Years of Solitude,* the fattest of the top-shelf books. *Many years later, as he faced the firing squad,* the novel began, *Colonel Aureliano Buendía was to remember that distant afternoon when his father took him to discover ice.*

As I read the sentence, my throat clenched with longing so acute it seemed to lodge there. I closed the book and put it under my bed, but the sentence embedded in me like a trapped splinter.

Many years later was an insane way to begin a book. In a single sentence, time twisted back on itself, the *now, then,* and *later* all collapsing into one another. But what hit me hardest was the specter of impending death and the phrase *took him to discover ice,* which captured nostalgia for the childhood era of all-knowing parents and constant wonder.

A few months later, I read the whole book in cycles of boredom (how many pages left?) and awe over what the back-cover copy called *magical realism.* I kept thinking: Can you *do* that in a book? It created a sense of possibility I had never felt in real life.

But there was another layer to my reading. Word by word, I felt like I was stepping on a stone path, following my father. I read as two people: me and him.

When I finished the book, I suggested my mother read it, knowing full well she wouldn't. But it made me feel good, to be in a club with my dad and not with her, because I missed him and felt she did not.

"Oh, I tried about two paragraphs once," she said. "It didn't make any sense."

"Because the first clause is *many years later*?" I asked.

"What? The first clause?"

"The first sentence is really striking."

"Honestly, Samantha, how would I remember the first sentence?"

"Maybe it's why Dad liked the book."

"Honey, your father never read that book." Her words sat in my gut, indigestible. She was lying; she was saying it to be mean. "When would he have had time?"

"Why would he *have* the book, then?"

"I think he picked it up from a free box at the gas station. Maybe he wanted to imagine he would read it." So many conditionals! The sentence said nothing. That was my father now: all conjecture.

"Why would you keep it if it didn't mean anything?"

"I honestly forgot those books were even there," she said.

Many years later, though, when I got into Cornell as an English major, my mom told me, "Your dad would be so proud." This struck me as profound, the tears in her eyes genuine, because by then she'd stopped talking about him at all.

I often wondered about that book over the years, about the possibility that he had read part of it, or that it revealed a secret aspiration he'd never realized, which he'd passed on to me.

When my dad got sick, my mom couldn't stop talking about the burden of his coming death, about her impending singledom. She needn't have worried; she was already seeing someone six months after my dad died. No, not just seeing him, he was already walking around our house half naked, already commenting on my boobs, already asking my mom for a blow job over breakfast, occasionally joking that I could be a suitable replacement if she wasn't in the mood.

I used it to my benefit. I'd put on a push-up bra and a V-neck and ask for a ride. "Well, who could say no when you're wearing a shirt like that?" he'd say. Mostly I ignored him, but he was everywhere, his little dark hairs in the sink and shower, a ridiculous replacement for my loving father, with more ridiculous replacements yet to come.

For this, and a bunch of other shit, I haven't forgiven her.

Later that week I found, preserved on my old phone from grad school, which itself was preserved in its original glitter case, all the texts between Tom and me. They were jarring to read: cringey, juvenile, mundane. But now I could see something clearly. He appeared when he was bored and lonely, pushed the envelope, then dropped away the instant he was otherwise entertained. I stayed at the ready, thrilled to respond, thrilled just to be there, to even be considered.

Back then I had no sense of digital permanence. A text felt as fleeting as a note passed in class, destined for the trash, though when those texts came from Tom, they might as well have been wartime correspondence, secret instructions I would have to memorize and then swallow.

I just realized the book is in the house! he said in his first text to me. I was dog-sitting Cheever and was sure he meant the text for someone else.

I think in the office—the shelf by the wall near the trash can—probably near the top he wrote a few minutes later.

You can just stand on a chair to get it, he added.

A few minutes later: Not the cane chair, the other one.

This is sam, I wrote back.

Him: I know. The Wood book I was telling you about is in the house, you can borrow it.

I hope I didn't wake you.

Me: You didn't! I'm in bed but not asleep. Thanks for letting me know about the book!

Him: I hope not in bed with the classicist.

Me: Who? Jonas? I was just being friendly in the hall.

Him: Okay, good. Jonas is not worthy.

Me: It's just me and Cheever.

Him: In bed with Cheever? Impressive! What other literary greats have you scored?

Warning: they're all a bunch of dogs. ;)

Me: Ha!

Him: Avoid literary types at all costs.

How could I have been charmed after such a low-effort pun and an unearned winky face? Plus, the quantity of my exclamation points was mortifying—like the indiscriminate, doofy tail wagging of an ever loyal Labrador.

I could hardly stand to reread the messages. It was like looking at a picture of myself in middle school, waterfall ponytail and boxy Disney tee. But no, that was different—I could forgive my eleven-year-old self her fashion sense, but I flushed with embarrassment for the me of my early twenties, for my naïveté intertwined with a desperation to be liked.

Him: Anyway, probably I should not be texting at this hour. Just wanted to inform you about the book.

Me: Should I get the book now?

Him: Whenever you'd like.

What are you doing awake so late? Night owl or insomniac?

Me: Second leading to first.

You?

Him: The latter, brought on by existential dread.

Me: Everything ok?

Him: All but existentially, so that's something.

I'm grading papers, actually. Do you think this one is a joke?

Here he sent a picture of a poorly written sentence in a student paper, but the photo was no longer accessible in my text history.

Me: LOL. WOW.

If you have existential dread shouldn't you at least be doing something else. IE not grading papers.

Him: Like what?

Me: Watching TV? Or aren't there parties at conferences?

Him: The academic party scene at the Hilton leaves much to be desired. I am drinking, if that helps. Probably shouldn't drink and grade. Don't tell.

Me: You're secret is safe with me

*your, duh

Him: What are the kids watching on TV these days?

Me: I've been told I have terrible taste

Him: You have great taste! Except in the case of Jonas.

Me: I wouldn't exactly say Jonas is my taste

Him: You are much, much too good for Jonas.

Me: oh come on

Him: I'm serious. You have a curiosity and hopefulness about you. An innocence? Jonas is . . . it's just that Jonas would not appreciate it or would ruin it.

This had pleased me. It suggested Tom was both protective and envious; it was evidence he cared.

Me: Innocence?!

Him: I just mean it's an orientation to the world people lose as they age. It's a good thing.

The observation seemed genuine and heartfelt. It was proof that Tom thought about me beyond our immediate interactions. I imagined him sitting in his office, considering my orientation to the world. Throughout my life, when an authority figure made me feel important, I glowed.

Him: Anyway, I know you're not innocent—rumor has it you are in bed with Cheever right now.

Me: LOL

you make it sound like you're 80

Him: Marriage, mortgage, 401K.

Me: life partner, pet dog, award-winning novel

401K!!!

doesn't sound that bad

Him: Correction: nominated. Life-partner thing not going quite as planned. No much-anticipated second novel in sight.

Me: are you panning adulthood or what?

Him: 2 out of 5 stars

But no reason to bother you with the drama of the elderly. Where are you, anyway? Guest bed or did you secretly take the master bedroom?

Me: Guest room. Very cozy!

Him: Okay, good, wouldn't want you snooping around the bedroom . . .

Me: You *did* tell me to snoop around.

Him: Did I? Did you?

Me: maybe a little

as instructed

Him: what did you find?

Me: you know . . . various

sundry

Him: what? the box under the bed?

Me: I did see that

Him: scandalized? :)

Me: no, not scandalized :)

Him: What was in there?

Me: Don't you know?

Him: Of course I know.

Just trying to assess the level of your snooping :)

Me: High-level snooping.

Him: Did you partake?

Me: no!!!

Him: You must have some yourself

Me: What do you think?

Him: I think you do. I think I probably can't even begin to imagine what you have under your bed. Still waters and all.

I remembered this moment, too, how my heart raced as I lay in his guest bedroom, a stack of books he had recommended towering next to the nightstand. No, there weren't sex toys under my bed. There were just poster tubes and craft projects and dirty socks, but I liked the idea that he thought there were. The small thrill of texting with my professor late at night had escalated to something more shocking, more exciting. My discomfort didn't dampen the feeling but fed it. I was special, chosen. *Still waters and all* echoed in my head.

Reading the texts now, a decade later, I thought of the letter referenced in the copy for Tom's book, a detail designed to show that the student had wanted it, too. These tentative, awkward texts were far less grand, but wasn't I implicated nonetheless? He was testing the waters, dipping a toe, and I was waving him in, or at least not stopping him from going just a bit deeper.

I thought, too, of my mother's former boyfriend, of the rush I got from making him tick. If I was being truthful, hadn't I dressed each morning—low-cut V-neck, short skirt—a little for him? Because I wanted to—what? Compete with or annoy my mother? See that shine of lust in his eyes, as if it could replace the twinkle of pride I remembered in my father's? I felt shame with every possibility.

I had learned something, perhaps: how to keep a man's attention without committing to action. But with Tom, I had not been navigating uncomfortable vibes in my childhood home. I'd felt happy when I was with him. He and my mom's former boyfriend were worlds apart. Set on a scale of creepiness, Tom couldn't compete.

Me: Maybe I'm not as complicated as you think. ;)

Him: I've read the weird shit you write, Sam.

Me: Is it really weird?

My question hung painfully in the air as I waited for a response. Was it too self-indulgent? Could I course-correct by complimenting his writing style without sounding like a sycophant? Or maybe ask more about his existential dread, about what stress he had going on in his life? I knew his mother was having health issues. Maybe better not to bring that up. But he had just mentioned marriage troubles, so that door was open. But it seemed rude to press for details. Before I could come up with something worthy, he texted again.

Him: Hey, sorry, I have to go. Sweat dreams to you and Cheever.

Me: Are you going to sleep?

I dozed off waiting for a response, my feet pinned to the bed by the weight of the dog, the phone fallen on my chest.

The next day, I lay on Tom's couch with the Wood book but couldn't concentrate. Instead, I spent my mental energy constructing follow-up texts that I didn't send. I felt like I should apologize for something but wasn't sure what. Two hours before he was expected home, he called.

"Could you stay one more night?" he asked.

"Is everything okay?"

"Everything's fine."

"Did you sleep?"

"Yes." It was as if we hadn't texted the night before.

"Did the conference run long?" I asked, though I wasn't sure that was a thing a conference could do.

"I just ran into an old friend," he said. The tone was a smile; the friend, I understood, was a woman.

"Oh," I said. "Who?"

"Can you stay?"

"When will you be back?"

"I don't know, tomorrow afternoon," he said, irritated. "Do you have other plans?" He asked it as if I couldn't possibly. He covered the phone with his hand, but I heard him say, in a more pleasant tone, "Claire? Are you back? Hold on a second." Then he returned to me. "All I need is for you to let Cheever out in the morning and feed him; you could even leave before I'm back tomorrow." But I loved that transition time when he paid me—not just in money but in attention, too.

"I'll give you an extra twenty, and all you have to do is just stay where you are, in a nice big old house with lots of food." He paused. "And no roommates! No mice! No newts!" With that, he won me back, he remembered my life, that it existed beyond his schedule, that a newt recently had been snapped in half by a mousetrap in my kitchen, a story that had amused him when I'd relayed it, though it was pretty gross when it happened.

I agreed. My original plan had been to pack up my stuff strewn across the guest room upstairs, then make breaded chicken and salad for dinner, enough so he could eat the leftovers when he got home. Instead, I found Annie's mac and cheese in the cabinet and ate it while watching *Law & Order: SVU* reruns, first an episode about an exchange student whose host father sells her sexual services to colleagues, then another about a series of rapes in which the rapist wears a clown mask.

When I heard a clattering of keys and felt a breeze from the front door, I thought: Robber, rapist. But the woman who walked in did not look criminal—if anything, white-collar crime. Cheever abandoned my feet, ran to her, jumping all around. She was attractive: thin with jet-black hair. Her pants were pressed; her cream-colored double-breasted coat was pristine.

"Good boy," she said. "Good, good boy." Tom's wife, Lydia. I had seen her a few times at department events, not to mention in photos around the house.

"Put your hands behind your back," said a cop on TV, arresting someone who was probably innocent, since the episode had only just begun.

Lydia still hadn't looked at me when she said coolly, "Who are you?"

"Sam," I said. "A grad student."

She thumbed through the mail I had set in the wire basket on the credenza. She wasn't looking at me—I was less important than what she had come here to do.

"Why are you here?" I asked.

"It's my house."

"Tom didn't say—"

"Tom doesn't have to *say*."

I felt stupid, sitting on her couch, under her throw, with her bowl on the coffee table, her mac and cheese in my stomach, her remote control shining with my grease. It hadn't occurred to me that what I thought of as Tom's Things, or occasionally as Tom's Wife's Things, were at least as much Lydia's Things, and maybe even *more* hers if she made most of the money. Was Tom's permission her permission? Would she have said, Yes, please, look through my daybook, my sex toys, wash my cast-iron pan?

"I— Are you staying?" I asked.

"I have a train to the city at nine," she said. I had no understanding of their logistics, where she had been or where she was going. "I stopped by to deal with some paperwork." She walked over to the dining room table and started slicing open mail with a miniature dagger. "Is there some reason you still need to be here?"

"To feed Cheever," I said.

"I'm sure you've already fed him. Or no? It's what, seven-thirty?"

She well knew it was impossible not to have fed him by six. By five-thirty he was already giddy with expectation, running around the house with a tennis ball in his mouth. "I fed him," I said.

"Cheever can stand to be alone for an hour or two until Tom gets home. Unless there was some other reason you wanted to stay?"

"No," I said, realizing she didn't know Tom wasn't coming home and that she thought I was fucking him. My face flushed with shame, as if it were true. "I think he's— Are you sure he's coming back tonight?" I said, my voice froggy.

"Oh, please," she said. "Just go, please."

I didn't dare go upstairs to collect my things—I would come back for them after she left. I just stepped outside into the loamy darkness, the fall air cool against my hot face. How embarrassing that I had flirted with Tom by text; that I had looked through his things; that his wife was much more beautiful than I was; that even so he was with some other woman; that his wife thought the other woman was me. The humiliation was enough; the repercussions I could not have imagined.

Risky Business, sans sunglasses, pulled her MacBook from her maroon leather tote, opening up the Word doc for the paper I had returned to her twenty minutes before in The Masculine Voice. She gave me a frank look, her jaunty brown ponytail swinging behind her.

"I'm not really sure why I got a B on this," she said. The paper was on *Lolita,* which the class and Risky Business had decided to read after all. Her thesis statement was about how the image of "Lolita" as a seductress was a pop-culture invention that perverted the original intention of the novel. But what she had set out to do in an eloquently written first paragraph, she had failed to achieve in the rest of the paper, which descended into a meandering account of different cultural representations of Lolita instead of an argument that hinged on a close reading of the text.

Risky Business was right: The popular image of Lolita—ponytailed teenager in a crop top, sucking a red lollipop—was not the Lolita of the book, not the kidnapped and abused prepubescent kid crying in hotel rooms every night.

She aimlessly flicked at the trackpad, so her paper scrolled up and down, up and down, making me dizzy. "Maybe you don't know this because you're new, but you're a much harsher grader than the other lit teachers at this level."

Well, that wouldn't be great for student evaluations.

"A B is an opportunity to grow," I said. "Learning, the very nature of it, should push you outside of your comfort zone."

"Tell that to a prospective employer."

"I'll let you in on a secret: Once you graduate, no one really cares about your grades."

"I doubt that. Besides, I might go to grad school instead, and they definitely care."

"Oh," I said. "Grad school for what?"

"I don't know, English."

I felt the urge to wave my hands, warn her from imminent danger.

"And if I go, I would want to go to a really good school, obviously," she said. "Like, I mean, my parents basically forced me to go here because I got a partial merit scholarship and my dad was having a midlife crisis and wanted a convertible." It was a plight for which I could not, at the moment, feel pity. "I mean, at least this isn't a state school, but it doesn't have name recognition." She shrugged. "I mean, more pertinently, it's in the middle of nowhere."

"Baltimore is a minor major city," I said.

"Oh my God, I would *not* go into the city."

"You haven't been downtown?"

"I mean, the Harbor, yeah, but everywhere else is pretty dangerous," she said. "Didn't you go to SHU or something?" I was surprised that she had looked me up. "Dr. Sternberg used to work there."

"You have a class with him?"

"Yeah," she said. "He's pretty good. He said I should go to grad school. That I was writing excellent papers or something." She half rolled her eyes, unable to commit to the full brag. "But, like, you seem to disagree?"

"You show real brilliance in some parts of your work," I said.

"I'm just trying to get you to meet that level the whole way through your papers."

"But, like, you wouldn't go to grad school if you were me."

"You would be an excellent candidate for grad school," I said carefully. "But I do wonder if it's really a viable career path right now. I mean, for anyone."

"You did it. Dr. Sternberg did it. Whoever made up this class did it. Aren't there, like, a million colleges?"

I'm not doing it, I wanted to say. This isn't doing it. "I'm not trying to discourage you," I said. "I just know that when I started out, no one talked to me about the reality of the job market. I was promised a lot of things. I would just say to look into it. And who knows, it might work out for you. Besides, if you love it"—did I really believe this?—"then that's what matters most."

We went through her paper line by line, cutting out extraneous words and repetitive ideas while identifying places where she could add textual references. Soon the seven-page paper had dwindled to five, and we weren't even halfway through.

She flicked through the pages on her screen, incredulous. "But the paper had to be seven pages," she said.

"Now you have all this space to say more. To deepen the argument with a close reading."

"So you think I should write an entire paper, delete half of it, and then write more?" She slumped back in her chair. I tongued my problem tooth. My duffel bag buzzed. Our heads snapped to it.

"Did you get a message?" she asked, as hopeful as if it had come from her own phone. The bag kept vibrating: a phone call. "You want to look at it?"

I did want to look at it. "I can wait," I said.

She frowned just as her phone buzzed. I could feel the vibrations of text after text radiate from her back pocket. We looked at each other.

"Okay," I said. "Let's both check."

Before I even found my phone, Risky Business was typing at furious Olympic speed. "Sorry," she said. "Just a sec. It's a whole thing."

On my phone, a call from an unknown number, no message. Probably spam. I clicked off the screen, watched blue bubbles blip-blip-blip on Risky Business's phone.

I looked out the window. Thirty students were strewn across the quad, lying on their backs in the grass, flowing shirts billowing in the breeze. What the fuck was happening? Apocalypse? Poison? If so, they might have to cancel classes.

Suddenly, synchronously, they all stood up and started mock–sword fighting with invisible weapons.

Disappointment coursed through me. They were probably just filming a TikTok.

"Good?" I said after a few minutes.

She shrugged, typed something else, put her phone facedown on the table, restrained herself from picking it up when it immediately buzzed. "So much drama," she said. "You married?"

"No, I'm not."

"Because guys are horrible?" she said, moany half joke.

"They really can be," I agreed.

"My friends and I have this epic problem." She sighed. Her phone buzzed again, and the energy it took her not to check it channeled itself into her monologue: "Some masters' students from St. Mary's who, like, drove up here for a weekend? They drove us around and took us out for crabs and bought us drinks. They were super into whatever we were reading for classes and what we were learning and stuff, and they were making all these plans with us for this big trip to Assateague, you know, like, with the ponies on the beach? Then we were trying to get back in touch after they left, and we literally thought something horrible had happened to them, and then there are these pictures of some other girls from some other school with, fucking—oh my God, sorry—but with ponies on the beach! So, Assateague, obviously. And we were, like, trying to figure out what's going on, and then suddenly they just got back in touch with us yesterday and were like, Sorry we were so busy, and, like, now they wanna hang out again?"

"They sound pretty bad," I said.

"They're super nice guys, though."

"But didn't they ghost you?"

"Well, not really, because they reappeared."

"On brand for a ghost," I said. I didn't know that the guys were doing anything explicitly wrong, but it seemed like they were being self-centered assholes, picking up and dropping the girls like toys, partly because the girls didn't have enough experience to know better.

I wondered if I should tell her as much, but also wondered if that would ruin the whole thing. Risky Business went to class, worked at the library ten hours a week for spending money, ate meals in the dining hall, gossiped in dorm rooms with her friends, then basked in the attention of older guys who took her to eat crabs and drink beer. There was a great excitement when you were young and felt on the edge of something illicit, which was how so many things felt at that age. But once you had drunk enough alcohol and done enough drugs and fucked enough people, the transgressive thrill lost its luster. Why should I be the one to break the spell? And why did I think she'd listen to personal advice when she wouldn't even listen to me in class?

I couldn't get a handle on the students, how much they knew or understood about life. Sometimes they seemed mature and knowledgeable: They had thoughtful questions, genuinely profound insights. But other times, as I waded my way through the word soup of a one-page run-on sentence or listened to a rant that so obviously contradicted reality, I realized they were, essentially, children.

I once babysat a six-year-old who spent a half hour telling me about dinosaurs whose names I couldn't pronounce. "Not all the dinosaurs were around at the same time, you know," he explained. "A lot of people think that. The Massospondylus is from the Jurassic Period. They were thirteen feet long!" He must have seen me trying to figure out how long that was. "Like here to maybe the wall," he explained. "Herbivores. You know, like, vegetarians." I am an idiot, I thought. But ten minutes later he proceeded to have a temper tantrum about soup, tears streaming down his bright red face.

Had I been like Risky Business once? Some strange combination of earnest and cynical, the cynicism presented like a badge of honor? I had constantly questioned the minutiae but believed the premise on a grand scale: If you got good grades, you would be successful. She was smart but green, taking everything at face value, even the subtext, as if subtext weren't an invitation to dig deeper but a final answer, a dead end.

Risky Business was about the same age I'd been at the start

of grad school. The idea that I would ask her to house-sit or to hem my pants—or, my God, lead her on a treasure hunt to my sex toys—was ludicrous.

My phone rang again, the same unknown number. I flipped it over, then pointed at Risky Business's paper, which had dimmed on her screen. "I think if you do this very exercise with your next paper, then you'll be in good shape. Get it down to essentials, then add depth. Reference the text. Do it over and over again. You have some great ideas in here."

"I guess," she said. Her head was somewhere else, and really, so was mine.

The unfamiliar number called again that night. I was sitting up in bed, pillows wedged under my knees, reading American Lit I essays on the Puritans and *The Scarlet Letter,* trying to hurry but constitutionally unable to half-ass it because I had a sick dedication to student improvement.

Curiosity overcame me. I answered the phone.

The woman introduced herself as Leslie Chen, a freelance journalist writing a profile about Tom for, I gathered, a major national media outlet. "Do you have a minute to talk?" she asked.

"Um, I don't know," I said. "What's the piece about exactly?"

"An author profile," she said. "A little about this book, his history, his teaching. It won't take long. I'm calling a bunch of Dr. Sternberg's former students. You took some of his classes in graduate school, is that correct?"

I had an impulse to hang up, and another, greater impulse to find out what her angle was. "Yeah, he was my adviser," I answered.

"And how did you like Dr. Sternberg?"

"Very smart and well read, obviously," I said vaguely.

"You switched to the academic track in your second year?"

"Yes." The question made me nervous.

"What led you to do that?"

"I'm sorry—can you explain a little more about the piece you're writing?"

"As I said, it's a profile. I'm just curious if there was a particular reason you switched."

"I just changed my mind," I said.

"It wasn't because of the nature of your and Tom's relationship?"

My stomach lurched. I felt like I'd dropped through the floorboards of a house I'd walked into knowing it wasn't structurally sound. How did the woman have this information?

"So it's not just general questions," I said. "You wanted to ask me specific questions."

"I want to know if you made a complaint against Tom."

"What? No."

But it hit me: Maybe someone *had* made a complaint against Tom in real life, and he'd used that as inspiration for his book. Maybe that was why he'd left SHU. It wasn't uncommon, this "pass the harasser" magic trick that wiped records clean. Like those pedophilic priests switching parishes to avoid the paper trail.

Maybe the article was a takedown. Maybe the journalist was trying to show a pattern of untoward behavior. I wanted to support the mystery complainant, but I felt I didn't have a right to complain. I was implicated. I had waited for his texts. I had responded to them over and over and over. Regardless, I didn't want my personal life made public, and certainly not in any way that might connect me with Tom's book.

"No?" she said. "Can you tell me about your exit interview with the university?"

My mind raced back to the interview. A representative of the Graduate Studies Committee conducted them with every graduating doctoral student. She had asked about the strengths and weaknesses of the program, my relationships with peers and professors, my most positive and negative experiences.

"It was an exit interview," I said. "It went how they go. I talked about my time at the university."

"The good and the bad," she said.

"Of course."

"What was the bad?"

The bad was that I'd had to switch tracks, which was what I'd told the representative interviewing me. She had worn a slate-gray pencil skirt and had a friendly but professional tone. The more follow-ups she asked, the more confused she became. Had my adviser or someone in the department requested that I switch because I wasn't doing well? There was no evidence that I wasn't doing well, was there? If I'd wanted to switch, why had it been a negative experience? If I hadn't wanted to switch, why had I?

"Just tell me what you're getting at," I said to the journalist. "Or else I have to go." I was clicking the button on top of my retractable pen rapidly, I realized, and forced myself to stop. It was a red pen, because I'd thought it would be mildly funny to give the students red A's on papers about *The Scarlet Letter.*

"I want to confirm—if it's true—that, during your exit interview, you discussed switching tracks because of your relationship with Tom," she said, "and that you were read a question from Title IX about Tom's sexual conduct."

What did she mean "relationship with Tom"? Certainly I hadn't used that phrase. But then what had prompted the representative to read the question straight out of Title IX: Did Tom engage in any sexual conduct that was "sufficiently severe, persistent, or pervasive" to limit my "ability to participate in or benefit from the education program, or to create a hostile or abusive education environment"?

So much from that interview was vague in my memory, but my answer to that question stood out crisp and clear, and it had come without pretense, straight from the gut: *Yes, no, I don't know.*

"Sam?" said the journalist.

"That's true," I said. "I was read a question."

"About Tom's sexual conduct?"

"Yes."

"You taught at the university yourself, so you know about mandatory reporting?"

A hatch in my throat seemed to open and close, like a precursor to vomiting.

Had that *yes* counted? Hadn't the follow-ups negated it? When had that interview happened? Late 2017, at the height of MeToo? I felt rage at the trigger-happy woman who had conducted the exit interview. Had Tom really left SHU because of me?

"I didn't . . ." I stammered. "I didn't intend to complain about anything."

"Could we go back to the question about why you switched tracks?"

"Because you can't *be* a writer." I was clicking the pen again;

surely she could hear it through the phone. "It's not a job for regular people." You couldn't be a professor, either, it turned out, but I hadn't known that then. "Look, I have to go," I said. "No comment," I added, like an idiot.

I hung up the phone, unsure if I was trying to protect myself or if I was inadvertently protecting Tom or if I was betraying the feminist cause.

Chapter 7

EMERGENCY

We read "The Legend of Sleepy Hollow" in American Lit I just as the leaves began to turn, not Northeast-brilliant but a muted red-brown. Then it was the fever pitch of midsemester: of grading midterms, of students crying during office hours, of waking up to the dull trill of my alarm with the pages of a campus novel pasted to my face, less a sound than a sneaking suspicion that something terrible was about to happen.

One morning I walked to my car on Preston in the crisp dark to find the side window shattered. Glass was everywhere, strewn across both seats, the footwells, the sidewalk. The only missing item—the only thing to take—was my *Simon and Garfunkel's Greatest Hits* cassette, which I found disemboweled and smashed on the sidewalk. It had been my dad's. I remembered sitting in the passenger seat next to him on summer afternoons with this tape playing full blast, the windows open, the breeze on my face. I'd felt like royalty sitting up there. Where were we going, just me and him? To pick up corn and tomatoes from the farmstand? I seemed to remember holding a paper bag in my lap. Every memory of my father was like this, a piece of film cut haphazardly from the roll. I salvaged the J-card from the broken case, which was nothing really, just a picture of the duo, sunlit in blazers, and a giant UPC code.

Money seemed to liquefy, pour from my bank account: $300 to replace the side window, $40 for an Uber while the car was being fixed, $200 for the urgent-care appointment I'd needed to get the antibiotics for the UTI. I caught up on rent only to have to pay it again, money down the drain, my credit card holding me over until my paycheck at the end of the month, an article on the internet saying millennials aren't "wired to save."

Dawn broke as I drove up 83 on a Monday—no fresh yolk of sun, no fluorescent fanfare, just the grainy gray lightening of the dark. Even this early, I usually had to circle up the dizzying Guggenheim spiral of Lot D, searching the darkness for the even more darkness of a free space. But today I found a spot right away, lower level.

What could account for the deranged optimism with which I thought, Sometimes you're lucky for once, even as my block heels echoed in the gray emptiness? Was I riding high on my newly fixed side window? Was it a delusion built by sheer exhaustion? I'd been up until two a.m., first commenting on topic proposals for English Comp, so the students would get them back before they had to write their essays, then grading papers for The Campus Novel, which I felt obligated to finish so they could have feedback before their next paper was due. I'd woken up with a start at six a.m. on top of my covers, at the epicenter of the papers strewn across my bed, a used piece of floss next to my head, my almost dead phone lying on my chest. The browser was open to The Chronicle of Higher Ed—I vaguely recalled scrolling for late-release academic job postings.

I didn't dare wait for the whims of the shuttle bus but jogged toward campus, wearing my duffel like a backpack, knot in my chest tightening as I passed one nearly empty lot after another.

What was going on? Bomb threat? Gas leak? Active shooter? Apocalypse? I hadn't passed a single human. Had there been cars on the road? I couldn't remember the drive. What if everyone on the planet had disappeared overnight?

I slowed to a stupid jog-walk and checked my phone. There was still life on earth, I discovered. People were still interneting, still posting, still committing random acts of violence but also of kindness, even if they were filming it. I checked the date (yes, Monday), my email, the university's Twitter account, each page loading at a snail's pace. Lewis hadn't posted anything in two weeks. The school probably had some emergency messaging system that I wasn't on.

I felt nostalgia for the quaint and personal era of the phone tree, parents calling parents calling parents to let them know about a two-hour delay, or else we'd all just tune into the radio with a hope and a prayer. I also felt nostalgia for those innocent pre-Columbine years. Once a month, we lined up for fire drills and marched outside, high on the fresh air, the timed multiplication-table tests abandoned at our desks, the adrenaline rush of potential but unlikely disaster coursing through our veins.

Then came the horrifying buzzkill of active-shooter drills, where we barricaded ourselves behind desks and hid in closets as the administration wandered the halls throwing tennis balls at those unfortunate enough to be locked out of classrooms. It put you on edge every time you had to take a piss. As if the smack of a dodgeball in gym class weren't enough, now you had to endure fake death by Wilson, compliments of your guidance counselor, which was better than the alternative, real death by real bullet, compliments of your unhinged classmate. Maybe that's why all the students today had anxiety disorders.

I jogged up the steps into the empty building, my heart pounding. I tried to tiptoe—the heels of my boots had worn through the sole, which meant a loud, clacking thump with every hit of the heel. I had to pee, but in the bathroom, the sound of my pee seemed like all sound, the only sound. What the fuck was going on? Should I hide? Should I leave? Should I keep slinking toward the adjunct office? Should I open the door, which was almost never shut?

The office looked as if it had been abandoned chaotically. A half-full coffee cup on a desk. A jar of peanut butter with a spoon sticking straight out of it. A stack of ungraded student papers on top of a printer. Running tights, which, upon closer inspection, had a pair of underwear inside. A copy of an Elizabeth Bishop poem—was that mine? for American Lit II?—waiting in the scanning bed of the Xerox machine.

My throat tightened. The giant desk calendar hanging on the wall was not up to date. Every morning someone put a big X through the previous day, and, on Monday, the previous three days, but there was no X on Friday, Saturday, or Sunday. I walked slowly to the calendar, put X's through the three days. Why did we do this? We were afraid of death, yet we counted down. The X-less days, those weeks and months to come, doubled my dread. *Tomorrow, and tomorrow, and tomorrow, / Creeps in this petty pace from day to day.*

Outside the window: a square of blocky buildings, a patch of sidewalk, a triangle of grass. No movement.

The smell of burnt coffee. Someone was here or recently had been. I took off my loud boots, slid silently in my socks toward the kitchen, my heart beating wildly.

At the round table in the center of the room, a person—Sophie?—slumped, head on the table, brown hair fanned out. I was tiptoeing toward her, looking for the rise and fall of breath, when my phone rang. Her head jerked up, eyes wide open. "What the fuck," she said. *Ding,* my phone alerted. *Ding, ding, ding.* Texts from Gabe.

Sophie blinked several times as if resetting the picture. Her trademark glistening skin was not glistening, her rosy cheeks were not rosy. She had dark bags under her eyes.

"Sorry," I said, flipping my phone to silent.

"Why are you here?" she said at the same time as I said, "Why isn't anyone here?"

"It's fall break." She sounded annoyed, and nasal. She sneezed in her elbow.

"Shit," I said, backing away. "Right now?" Had anyone told me this? Fall break was next week at Rosedale.

"It's just two days," she said. "Long weekend."

"Why are you here?" I asked.

"They've been doing construction on my street, and the power's been fucked up." I began to worry that she was mad at me, even though I felt I had a right to be mad at her after our last conversation.

"Are you okay?" I asked.

"Well, October Surprise, I'm obviously sick." She walked to the coffee machine. "And I have a ton of shit to do," she said, pouring coffee. "Two hundred pages of student papers to grade and a catering gig at noon."

"Yeah," I said. "I should get to work, too." I hesitated. I started to speak, stopped, started again. "Is something wrong?"

"With what?"

"I thought maybe you were annoyed with me?"

"What do you think?" she asked as she put the milk back in the fridge and closed the door with a jerk.

"I mean, based on you saying that, I would say yes."

"So you don't even realize?"

The whole morning felt like waiting for a shoe to drop, and here it came, plummeting to the bottom of my stomach.

Whereas I would have kept messing with the coffee, cleaning the pot, anything not to make eye contact, Sophie turned and looked at me. "You weren't at the meeting," she said.

I racked my brain. What meeting?

"Unionizing," Sophie said, incredulous.

"Fuck," I said, looking down at my socks. When even was that meeting?

"Everyone pretends they're on board, but when it comes down to it, they don't want to do a fucking thing."

"I completely forgot. I guess I thought you were going to text me the info."

"I mentioned the meeting, like, what, probably ten times? We agreed you were going."

Why was she always *we*-ing me, as if we were in the same boat, as if we had the same psyche, which she apparently controlled. "*We* agreed you'd text me the info," I said. "You have to remind people if you have something going on."

"I *did* remind people," she said. "I spent the last two weeks reminding people, but I thought I didn't have to worry about you. I thought you were a given. You act like this is *my* project, like you forgot to come to my school play."

"Well, it *is* your project." I swished my toe in a semicircle along the linoleum floor, cold in my sock feet.

"No, it fucking isn't."

"I'm not saying it doesn't involve me. Or, like, relate to me, but it's your wheelhouse."

She snapped each knuckle with the thumb of the same hand. "Do you think you're special somehow? Do you think you aren't going to be a permanent fixture on the adjunct circuit?"

"I would've come," I almost pleaded. "You didn't send me the info. At this point I'm just trying to get through each day, you know?"

"What about next week?" she said. "Next month? Next year? How are you going to get through those? Guess what, I have news, there are no real jobs anymore. It's too late, we haven't been chosen, we're fucked."

"We don't know that. We're right in the middle of job season."

"We *do* know that. We all know. Every casual employee, every contract laborer, every postdoc and part-time lecturer knows," said Sophie. "And if you don't, you're delusional."

"It took me ten years to finish my PhD, it would be pretty ridiculous for me to just give up hope now. I have research I want to do. I have classes I want to teach. I have to believe there's something better. I put all my eggs in this basket."

Sophie pursed her lips in a near grimace. "Find another basket, Sam. I mean, sorry, but it's true." She turned back to the coffee machine, dumped the rest of the pot in the sink, then shoved it back on the hot plate, where it sizzled.

I slid my way back to the adjunct office as I read the messages from Gabe:

> this is going to sound crazy
>
> feel free to say no.
>
> I have two nights at a campground next week—Fri & Sat
>
> Probably weird to ask, since we basically just met, but I don't have other friends here 😂
>
> I have all the camping gear & food worked out
>
> and it's all paid for
>
> No pressure in terms of . . . you know.
>
> Just looking for someone to hang with!
>
> Sorry if this is weird.

I typed back: not weird

> But don't you teach Fridays?

Him: Not next Friday

> Fall break!

Me: I would love to get away but I have to teach next Friday 😭

> fall break is apparently this week at Lewis ☹️

But I wanted to go. Getting away during the week of Tom's book release seemed like a good idea; it might save me from obsessively scouring the internet for coverage.

Him: it is totally absolutely fine if you don't want to go

so no pressure

but hear me out . . .

sick day?

—

The campsite was tucked in a cool and loamy patch of woods with a lake not very far down a dirt path lined in pine trees. Gabe jostled sticks to start a fire, a determined look on his face, as I sat in a camp chair reading an essay on the aesthetics of enchantment for the *Critical Inquiry* rewrite.

The car ride had been awkward. I couldn't think of anything interesting to say. It seemed ridiculous that his penis had been inside me. He was like a meteor in orbit, catastrophically close and then floating far away again, off in space.

I had been nervous about taking a sick day, but no one seemed to care or even notice. It felt like a victory, that I'd cracked a spine in the name of academic research, but who was I kidding? How much reading was I going to get done in the woods? Why did I think I had the luxury of a weekend away?

I had already squandered too much time this week. I had followed the release of *Casualty* frantically for two days. Good reviews in the trades, a positive mention in *WaPo,* a review in *Harper's* I couldn't access, Amazon preview pages that matched those Tom had read aloud. I was unable to glean anything significant beyond what I already knew from the back cover and blurbs. The Baltimore public library had a waitlist that I didn't want to put my name on, and I refused to pay twenty-eight dollars for the book. Every time I opened my phone, even to look at the time, the thumb jerk to a private browser tab was reflex, and I found myself googling Leslie Chen. But I couldn't find an article, and instead of lessening my panic it transmuted into the diffuse anxiety of postponement. By Thursday morning, I'd sworn off my private browser searches.

I was exhausted to the point of delusion, partly because my toothache was now keeping me awake at night. The novels I read for classes felt like fever dreams, and it didn't help that, in The Campus Novel, we were reading a Pynchon-y counterculture cult classic that felt like a fever dream itself. I was surprised a guy like Carpenter had assigned it—maybe he tore it apart in his lectures. The first time I'd read the book, many years ago in grad school, I had been into the experimental writing, but now all I could think about was the scene in which the main character, a male student, has sex with a woman, admits to her he didn't wear a condom, is a blasé asshole when she freaks out, and then gets sulky and depressed about his inability to find love.

I also had to write a product review for an Infinity pillow, which was less pillow than stuffed infinity scarf. It was designed for people who expected to be exhausted in all kinds of configurations. Yet when you lay down with it, it unwound, slithered away, refused to comply with the definition of *pillow*. As with every other travel pillow I had ever tried, it always came down to this: Humans were not designed to sleep standing up or sitting down. I, myself, seemed no longer designed to sleep at all.

Gabe finished with the fire, then tossed me a can of beer, which I immediately placed on my hot jaw.

"You okay?" he asked.

"Just a little tooth thing," I said.

"It does look kind of swollen. I didn't mean to drag you along if you weren't feeling up to it."

"Sorry."

"Not at all," he said. "I mean, it sucks you're feeling bad. But to be honest, I'm just glad to be having a conversation with someone over twenty-two."

"Some people prefer conversations with twenty-year-olds."

"Other twenty-year-olds?" he joked.

I wiggled the tab on the can of beer, then popped it open and took a sip. "Would you ever hook up with a student?"

"Oh my God, no."

"Is that the knee-jerk party line?" I asked. "You've never even thought about it?"

"Genuinely, no."

"Why not?"

"Would *you*?" he asked.

"No."

"Never mind the ethics," he said. "I just can't . . . I mean, the writing?"

We both laughed. "Oh, do you need me to supply a writing sample?"

"But you know what I mean?" he said.

"Okay, but what about a grad student?"

"I don't think it's *inherently* or *necessarily* wrong, but it is tricky ground with the potential power imbalances," he said. "In terms of professors dating students, I think there's a pretty good litmus test."

"What's that?"

"Is the guy a serial creep?"

"That's legitimately good," I said, laughing. "This girl I

know—" But why was I saying it like that? "I have a friend, Sophie. She's really smart, very . . . She's confident, self-possessed . . ."

Gabe raised his eyebrows.

"What I mean is, she's somehow able to look critically at some aspects of the MeToo movement and not seem like an anti-feminist psychopath. She says the hashtag was supposed to be democratization, for and of the people, but instead it became for and of profit, a chance for news outlets and content mills parading as feminist websites to extract women's confessions for clicks, fuck nuance, never mind compensation."

"I also think it's worth separating the critiques of living in a capitalist society from the ideals of a movement which has raised genuinely important questions about power, gender, and consent," said Gabe. "But I do get the point. Women's stories 'must be told,' so the labor of telling them is often unpaid. Which makes it even more ironic that someone like Sternberg is freely able to capitalize on the movement. I'm just surprised people aren't warier of his narrative."

"Wait, did you read the book?"

"No," he said, "I just read a few reviews."

"Which reviews?" I asked, forcing myself to sound calm. "Any profiles? What did they say?"

"Oh, just like *The New York Times Book Review*, the *Post*, *The Guardian*," he said. Now my personal ban seemed stupid. Why hadn't I set a Google News alert? "They generally see the narrator as flawed but sympathetic. The gist is that the student was obsessed, and he just sort of regretfully succumbed. But I'm still kinda uncomfortable with the framing."

"Yeah," I said. "Me, too."

We grew quiet. The air was electric with the rustle of leaves, the crackle of fire. A Rorschach of clouds blotted the pale moon.

Perhaps because it was dark and we were drinking and we were looking not at each other but into the fire, perhaps because we didn't know each other all that well or because we were in this strange pocket of time that seemed to exist outside of our actual lives, we began to talk about our families, about how we'd grown up.

Gabe told me that he and his sister were two of only six Asian kids in his school system, and he'd always felt self-conscious about being smart, as if perpetuating a stereotype. He leaned into the humanities instead of math, and into his American side instead of his Taiwanese side, which he now regretted. His dissertation had been completely Eurocentric, something he was trying to remedy in his book manuscript. When he was growing up, his foreign-sounding middle name had felt like a liability, and he'd simply used an initial. Now hiring committees wanted diversity, and he felt guilty about strategically using his whole middle name after having denied that part of himself for so long.

He felt that not fitting in had made him less pretentious than many of his classmates, who had sailed through smart and uninhibited to their familial destiny. Many of those classmates were now making bank at their father's company. Meanwhile, his parents couldn't understand why finding a steady job was so difficult for him when there were so many universities.

I told him about my mother. About how she'd married a widower called Don, taken his last name, and moved to Pennsylvania during my first year of college. It had happened so suddenly that I'd had to cancel a carpool home for Christmas. It also had cemented my future financial problems, legally binding me to a man I didn't even know, so that when I filled out my FAFSA, his income was included, completely fucking up my financial aid. But when my mom decided to marry, she was, of course, not thinking about my FAFSA. She had always wanted a big family. I had never even met her only sister, my dad's family had disappeared after his death, and I suspected there was some fertility issue that left me solo. Suddenly she had acquired three teenage sons who she instantly loved.

I'd managed to scramble together a last-minute multi-part bus ride to a strip mall near the subdivision where she lived in East Bumblefuck, PA. The neighborhood was a serious escalation of the eighties/nineties suburbia I knew from growing up in small-town New Jersey. This was true suburbia, the stuff of horror movies: big houses on postage-stamp lawns, clean white sidewalks nobody walked on, freezers packed with Lean Cuisines. I was constantly getting stuffed in the back of a van with one or all three teenage boys, ostensibly my stepbrothers but actually strangers, condemned to stand for hours on the sideline of a wrestling match or to sit on a metal bench at a humid indoor pool, waiting for the endless heats to wrap up.

Worst of all, because Don was Evangelical, I was inexplicably sitting in a pew on Sundays, watching not the gesticulating preacher but the bewildering devotion of my mother, wide-eyed and expectant, as if at any moment she might be called to rise up or fall to her knees. In New Jersey, we'd been half-hearted Methodists. I remembered church mostly as bake sales and brightly colored Sunday-school pamphlets, my dad pretending to fall asleep during sermons to amuse me, until the preacher burst into song or my mother elbowed him in the ribs.

Something odd happened that Christmas at Don's. My mom had a desperate interest in my dating life: Had I met anyone nice at college? Did I have a boyfriend? Don, with his bristly gray goatee, was always glancing over, keeping track. At first I thought she was trying to prove to him that even if I wasn't exactly a good Christian, at least I was chaste. Funny, considering the years she'd spent so loudly fucking her boyfriend on the other side of the wall. This last part I didn't say to Gabe.

"Did you ever bring an SO back from college?" Gabe asked.

"Not to an air mattress in an office covered with Eagles memorabilia, no," I said. A joke to avoid revealing two truths. The first was that I hadn't had a significant other in college; I hadn't put any effort into the endeavor. I was reading, studying, writing stories—none of it out of a sense of duty or even purpose but because I wanted to suck that school dry. I had felt singular and haughty: I had so much more time than everyone else, and I was getting so much more out of college. But I also felt strange, delayed: What essential piece of my humanity was I missing that I gave a shit about dating only in so far as I felt left out? The second thing I didn't mention was that the following year was the last I would be home for Christmas, the last I would visit Don's at all.

Gabe jostled logs in the fire. I tried to understand why I was so sure I would fuck him tonight, why I even wanted to. Was I horny? Did I desire Gabe romantically—if so, what did that mean? Did I want Gabe to want me? Was I trying to prove a point? To whom? Myself? My mother? Who had the time or money or insurance for therapy to figure it out? I guzzled my beer, grabbed another, resting it on my cheek before opening it.

Sex was one of the few acts I engaged in that wasn't instrumental to my existence. I used to sleep in, not just sleep. I used to cook, not just suck on stale bagels and broccoli steamed to mash. I used to read for fun, not just to teach books I didn't even like. I used to keep my own plants alive, not just other people's. Fucking was such an extraneous, useless waste of energy. How wonderful to realize I had a little energy left to waste.

I woke up sweating, in intense pain, the lower half of my face burning. I sat up, and immediately: some relief, like the blood draining out, the vise grip loosening around my jaw. But then a second tier of pain rushed in. I put my duffel bag behind my head, trying to get more vertical. I closed my eyes and tried to think of other things, to meditate the pain away.

Candle flickering in the dark.

Curtains blowing in a breeze.

Rushing waterfall.

Tooth, pain.

No, candle flickering in the dark.

Fire. Face on fire.

No: Candle flickering in the dark.

But: Face on fire.

I crawled out of the tent, zipping it behind me as quietly as I could, my eyes adjusting to the darkness as goose bumps rose on my skin.

I slipped on my sneakers and made my way down the dirt path to the car using my phone's flashlight. I wanted something from the cooler—ice or a beer or anything—to soothe my face. I felt raw, all of me. Rubbed raw, my own fault, raw from the cool breeze, raw nerve in my jaw, raw from overwork. The sex already felt a million miles away, had the patina of a dream.

The car was locked. I sank next to the driver's side door and laid my cheek against the cool surface.

With my face plastered to the car, I checked my phone: two-thirty a.m., 11 percent battery. The parking lot was surrounded by the shadows of trees. It occurred to me to be afraid. I texted Sophie, all the anger I'd felt from our last interaction gone in the light of dramatic circumstances.

Me: my fazce is hon fire

Me: *ON

Me: *face

I thought she'd see it in the morning, but the dots—they blinked! I could cry. I was crying.

Her: in a good way or a bad way

figuratively or literally

Me: in a literxal figuraztive way

vhat IS thue good way?

y r u awake?

Her: Why are YOU awake baybay?

Baybay was mysterious and new. I didn't know why she was calling me that, if it was some diminutive of *baby*, or if it was a reference to a meme or something. It seemed weird that she would give me a new name that had nothing to do with my actual one, but it also felt like a gift she had picked out just for me, even if it wasn't the gift I would've picked for myself. My face, I typed very carefully.

The leaves rustled. I clicked the phone screen off, squinted into the darkness. Probably nothing. Probably a bear that would eat me alive. I glanced around the car for a stick as a blinding light hit my eyes.

It was Gabe, of course.

"What's going on?" he said.

I rubbed at my wet eyes, the afterimage of his phone flashlight hovering in my vision like a black moon.

"My tooth," I said. "I had to ice it."

"Ice it?"

"Well, the car was locked. But then the surface was pretty cold."

"Can I see?"

I peeled my face from the car, turned my head toward his light.

"Sam, it's completely swollen," he said. "You have to go to the hospital or something."

I shook my head, then plastered my face back on the car door. "I can't afford it."

"You can't afford to be dead, either."

"I mean, technically cheaper for me."

"I'm not going to let you die in the woods in the middle of the night."

"Would it ruin your vacation?"

"Yeah," he said. "It would ruin my vacation."

"Good story for a dinner party."

"A better story for a dinner party would be the one where I'm a hero, rushing you to the hospital in the dead of night."

"I mean, if it's good for your social life, I guess."

Outside the emergency department, a woman paced with an IV pole in her fist, the IV taped to her arm, the wheels getting caught again and again in the crack between two cement slabs, the automatic doors opening and closing each time she walked past. "I have been here for eight fucking hours!" she shouted. "I'm leaving . . . If I die, I'll sue them!"

Gabe and I looked at the ground so as not to catch the woman's eye, trying to walk at the right pace to cross through the doors when she wasn't in front of them, like video game characters avoiding an enemy guarding a gate.

The waiting room had that defeated purgatory feel. The chairs were all stuck together, unmovable. A woman with a drawn, pale face emitted occasional groans. A man with a stomach so distended he looked pregnant listened to a podcast on low volume, holding the phone to his ear. A sweaty child was huddled in her mother's arms. An old man was parked in a wheelchair, a fleece blanket with a candy-cane motif wrapped around his shoulders. A new woman sat down, her face swollen and pink—not just with infection but with the adrenaline rush of emergency, the naive hope that she would be attended to soon.

That last one was me.

On the TV, *Felicity* reruns played soundlessly. Felicity was sitting in the giant bay window of the world's most spacious dorm room. Gabe came bearing gifts—an ice pack, two bottles of Coke from the vending machine—smiling through his exhaustion. The strangeness of my own body, its insurrection, made everything feel strange. I usually didn't even notice my body. Gabe was such a random person. I hardly knew him at all. His red cheeks made him look boyish and eager, like a love interest in a teen movie, the one she rejects for the rebel. Were there teen movies anymore? Had the plots changed? Did he have rosacea or was it just windy outside? It was a thing I had always liked about women, the prickly red spots on their upper arms which made them seem at once fragile and determined.

There's no use making you suffer through the next seven hours along with me. No reason to describe Gabe falling asleep in his chair, snoring gently, or Felicity cutting off her hair (a scene I remembered though I had never watched the show), or the jaundiced sun rising in the window. No reason to describe the live-wire pain emanating from my tooth, how it crackled through my jaw so I felt like a constantly breaking dish, how I detached from it like a figure from a bathroom sign, just a ball of head floating above a body, how, by the time I saw the doctor, I could no longer understand how my pain related to anything, least of all the pain scale. "Seven?" I said, pointing to the red frowny face. "Six? Eight?" But when it became clear that the endodontist's first appointment for a root canal wasn't until Tuesday, I started to cry, full-blown, like the teary-eyed, beet-red number ten.

CONFESSIONS

I sandwiched my twelve-hundred-dollar root canal between my two Tuesday classes, which, for various reasons, I didn't think I should cancel. My jaw was so numb that I felt unreal, like I was made of blocks, like I had the wooden chin of a marionette. In English Comp, I talked from one side of my mouth, the way a stage actor might dramatically pretend to whisper, as I dabbed the other side for drool.

The cost of the root canal was even more painful than the procedure which had been complicated by how the infection had spread. And that total didn't include a permanent crown—I would have to make do with a temporary. I'd put the charge on my credit card because my bank account was down to $498 even though I'd just gotten paid. Most of the money had gone to settling up with Brianna on rent, but the ER bill was on the horizon.

Gabe appeared in the adjunct office holding a brown paper bag next to his head. "Chocolate pudding, applesauce," he said. "Plus, I have a certain essential device. Though I wouldn't expect too much out of it; it really cranks." At some point during the camping trip, he'd offered me his old laptop.

I pressed the cuff of my shirt to my mouth, assuming drool,

then scratched at my arm. I had all these little bumps, maybe some kind of skin irritation? Because I hadn't washed my sheets since—when? August?

Gabe sat next to me in the faculty lounge, reading student papers as I booted up the laptop. I peeled open a single-serve applesauce, and just as I set the first cool spoonful on my tongue, Tom appeared. When he saw me, he pursed his lips, then turned them quickly into a smile, nodding. "Oh, hi, Sam, Gabe." His tone was weird, artificial lightness.

He started toward the coffeemaker, changed his mind, walked to the fridge, pulled out an orange LaCroix.

"We enjoyed your reading," said Gabe.

We had?

"Ah, thank you," Tom said, and relaxed a little. He looked at the can, looked at us. "You know, I do want the coffee." He put the LaCroix back in the fridge and started making a big pot while talking to Gabe about a set of four students they both had in their classes—two men and two women who were perpetually shifting partners. Gabe wasn't abreast of the details. "No?" said Tom. "You don't pick up on that tension? They make class feel like a key party."

I pretended to be busy by logging into my email on the laptop. On Friday, Margret who ran the Writing Seminars program at Lewis had emailed asking if I wanted to teach two sections of English Comp in the spring, but between camping and searing pain, I hadn't had a chance to reply. I wrote back that I was interested and could she send me the class times.

Tom recounted the drama of the undergrads as the coffee gurgled behind him. He wiped his graying bangs from his forehead with three fingers that looked like a claw, so I saw his receding hairline, a hidden spray of age spots, and, in a flash, the face of the senior citizen he would become.

Sonia and Calvin were dating, he said, but really Tyler wanted Sonia, which is why he and Ottessa had broken up, and now Ottessa longed to be involved, something Tom surmised because she had emailed him a "very ardent" manifesto about polyamory, "as if I would be opposed."

Tom had always fed off the interpersonal drama of his students. I would never engage with them the way he did, would never receive an ardent manifesto on polyamory, I was sure of it. Being too close to the undergrads would undermine my authority and possibly even feel icky, but Tom had the gravitas to do what he wanted.

In some ways, I understood his impulse. There was something undeniable about the fresh, eager energy of eighteen- or twenty-year-olds, which they sometimes threw into their work but more often into their relationships. They were more alive than the rest of us. Literally, yes, their bones and their brains, but also their passion was more acute, less blunted by failures. Despite the teenage years, they had yet to become entirely disenchanted with the world.

But now that he was fifty and they were still eighteen, his overinvestment took on the tone of desperation, like a decrepit hand reaching toward the elixir of youth. He meddled in their affairs, half pretending he was one of them, but he always had, at the ready, the upper hand of extensive past experience.

Tom had deluded himself into thinking that the students' energy would rub off on him. It wasn't contagious, it was secondhand smoke. You could catch the whiff but never the high. It was like watching a toddler run toward a Christmas tree—you could delight in their delight, but you would never again embody that sense of wonder yourself.

A new email appeared from Margret. I'm sorry, but because you didn't respond to my email, I assumed you didn't want these classes and have assigned them to someone else. Best, Marg

My heart clenched; an ache began to emerge from the numbness of my mouth. What the fuck? Had I lost nine thousand dollars just like that? Because it had taken me two business days to respond to an email in the middle of a health crisis? Now all I had lined up for next semester was a single class at Rosedale, which meant I would have to start contacting department heads across Baltimore, once again begging for classes to teach in the spring. The thought exhausted me, made me feel as ancient as Tom now seemed.

I emailed Margret back anyway, asking her to please keep me posted on any other openings, as Tom and Gabe moved on from student gossip to the state of the academic job market. By the time I'd finished the email, Tom was standing by the sink with a cup of coffee, and they were volleying names back and forth to see who they had in common. They were both connected to a certain Midwest contingent of Comp Lit scholars.

"You know Miles Garwood?" Tom asked, and we did, of course, we all knew of him, though he wasn't asking me, he was asking Gabe, they were buddies now. "I went to school with him. Totally brilliant guy. He drove all the way out to Iowa City in a snowstorm once to see me read. Anyway, he's at Michigan. Happy to connect you."

"That would be great," said Gabe. "I'd really appreciate it." What disturbed me more than the chumminess was Gabe's shift in tone, not just of voice but an almost bodily shift I couldn't put my finger on. He seemed more masculine, with a dash of pretension mixed in, a change in registers to match Tom's.

"Any jobs for me?" I said with a laugh.

Gabe and Tom looked at me with the same face, uncomfortable by my artless interruption of their conversational flow.

"Jobs for everyone, I hope," said Tom. He slapped the counter behind him. "Anyway, I should probably get going. Leaving for a reading in New York in a few hours."

I looked back at my computer screen. Another email appeared, this time from Isaac. I hadn't heard from him in months. All it said was: Did you read the article????? Is that you? More soon! X

My eyes blurred. I read the URL as if through water. My mouth, I realized, had fallen agape. In the face of overwhelming physical pain, obsessing over Tom's book had taken a backseat.

"You okay?" said Gabe.

"Just looking at the news," I managed.

"Did something happen?" said Gabe.

I glanced at Tom. He looked back at me with an expression of—what was it? Apology? Embarrassment? Dread? No: pity, perhaps, like that of a fortune-teller who didn't want to break the news.

"No," I said, closing the laptop. "Same shit as always. I need to get another Vicodin."

A STARTLING CONFESSION AND A LITERARY COMEBACK TWENTY YEARS IN THE MAKING

Decades after Dr. Tom Sternberg's acclaimed debut, a controversial confession and a follow-up he didn't think would see the light of day.

By Leslie Chen

Dr. Thomas Sternberg and Dr. Aliana Williams sit together on an emerald-green velvet sofa in the library-like living room of Dr. Sternberg's Victorian home on the outskirts of Baltimore City, not far from Samuel Hudson University. The shelves are packed with campus novels and books about injustice and exile.

Dr. Williams, 39, bestselling author of the novel *Rolex,* smooths the lap of her black slacks. "Let's get this out of the way," she says. "Tom was my professor many years ago at Samuel Hudson, but we never had a relationship when I was a student. We reconnected years later at a conference."

"We were on the same panel. We had become equals," says Dr. Sternberg, 50. "Well, actually," he adds with a laugh, "she's probably sold more books than me."

The point, Dr. Williams says, is that Dr. Sternberg's new book is not about her.

"That should go without saying," says Dr. Sternberg. "It's fiction."

The book in question is *Casualty,* Dr. Sternberg's first novel in twenty years, following his breakout debut *Ten Four,* which was nominated for the National Book Award. *Casualty* follows a professor who is forced into retirement because of a short-lived affair with a student. The novel has been praised for landing some magnificent genre-bending tricks as the professor reckons with his past by combing through classic and contemporary literature, then looking beyond it, to books that were never part of his canon, from Afro-futurist to feminist writings.

Dr. Sternberg would rather talk about craft than how his novel relates to his personal biography. "For me, it's always much more interesting to discuss what's on the page," he says. "But in this case, people are asking, and so I think it's my responsibility to be perfectly clear about my past."

He explains that many years ago, as a professor at Samuel Hudson, he had a brief sexual relationship with a graduate student in his department, a former advisee who was no longer taking his classes. "It was consensual," he says, "but we didn't end on good terms. She was very angry, and at the time I didn't really understand it."

During #MeToo, Dr. Sternberg began reflecting on the relationship and trying to empathize with the student's perspective. He cites this as the seed of inspiration for the novel but says the book strays far from that initial seed.

"What interests me is the bifurcation between how people see themselves and how others see them, and how that changes through different movements, milieus, cultures. How does one navigate a world in which there is this vast gray area that shifts not just through time but from person to person, from place to place, and how do you respect that shift without losing your sense of self?" says Dr. Sternberg. "One reason I chose a main character in his 80s was to offer this more expansive sense of the timeline."

Writing a campus novel wasn't about fictionalizing his own experience but about plumbing a rich genre. The campus is a protected space that fosters intense closeness. "Graduate school in particular creates these lovely, vulnerable spaces, you might say the gray area made manifest," says Dr. Sternberg. Professors often open their homes to students for writing workshops, invite them to informal dinners, and hold reading groups at bars. "It's not just intellectual discussion—I mean, it is a lot of that—but it's also shared joy and pain and all those human things. So how does one navigate that? How does one allow all parts of the human experience into the classroom without bumping up against, well, the human—human foibles, human sexuality."

Dr. Sternberg wrote *Ten Four,* his literary debut, in his late 20s, fresh out of a PhD program at Princeton and already an assistant professor at Samuel Hudson University. For those who fell in love with the novel, Dr. Sternberg admits there's been quite the wait for a follow-up.

He brings out a manila folder of old photos and articles snapped, snipped, and saved by his late mother, Dr. Gail Sternberg, an economist at Yale who was a regular on the morning-show circuit in the '90s.

Dr. Sternberg examines a photograph taken a few weeks before *Ten Four*'s release, when he was 29. "I was a kid," he says. The photo has all the grainy charm of 35mm film. In it, he stands on a porch at twilight, bangs falling over his eyes, so baby-faced that the cigar in his hand seems out of place. "It was a long time ago," he says. "I had no idea how to handle the attention, the pressure. I was extremely lucky, of course. But it made me too self-conscious to write."

Dr. Sternberg came to terms with being a one-hit wonder, turning his attention to teaching and building a new Creative Writing Department at Samuel Hudson, which eventually became an integral part of the university's PhD program in English and Comparative Literature.

By all indications, he's an excellent teacher. His energy—eye-glinting, exuberant—is undeniable, says Maya Johanna, who earned her PhD at Samuel Hudson in 2012 and is now a consultant. "He's just magnetic and insanely smart," she says. "Even now, a youthful charm shines through." She admits that kind of attitude can be misconstrued.

Clee Ferris, who also earned her PhD at Samuel Hudson in 2014 and now teaches literature at Hunterton College in North Carolina, says that Dr. Sternberg "was one of us. He never treated us like kids. And his door was always open." She is not surprised he won the university-wide teaching award three times in less than ten years.

But Dr. Sternberg no longer teaches at Samuel Hudson. His decision to leave, he says, was entirely his own. "I did want to try something new, I think. But I also wanted to protect Samuel Hudson from any potential fallout." He is now a professor at Rosedale, a small liberal arts college in Baltimore.

Dr. Sternberg wrote the first draft of *Casualty* in five weeks. "It came so quickly in part because there was no pressure—I wasn't planning to publish it. It seemed like career suicide," he says. "And no, this is not me conjuring the woke mob or fearmongering about cancellation—people have a right to boo the asshole on the stage. I support MeToo wholeheartedly, and part of not wanting to publish this was the fear that it might come off as critical of the very heart of MeToo. That's not what this is. It's really the opposite."

Dr. Williams, who has been a vocal supporter of the #MeToo movement on social media, did not share Dr. Sternberg's fears that the book would be considered anti-#MeToo, at least not by the thoughtful reader.

The publishing industry seemed to agree. *Casualty* was reportedly sold in a mid-six-figure deal, and the publisher rushed the book to print nine months after acquisition, citing its importance to the national conversation.

"It's exactly because of the MeToo movement that Tom's

book is so vital right now," says Alex Riel, Dr. Sternberg's editor. "There are no easy answers in this novel, and that's the point. It exists beyond this dichotomy of 'good' and 'canceled' and moves us to a place of open dialogue and reconciliation. It shows a path forward."

The novel has earned rave reviews in *The New York Times Book Review, The New Yorker, The Guardian, The Washington Post,* and *Harper's.* In a mixed review from the *Los Angeles Review of Books,* however, Becca Adamski, a PhD candidate at UC Davis, questions Dr. Sternberg's choice to have the student in the book aggressively pursue the professor. "The female seductress is a trope as old as time, and in *Casualty* we are apparently supposed to take it at face value. The professor grapples with his past, but he never grapples with that framing because it is the author's framing."

But several former students of Dr. Sternberg noted that the relationship bears resemblance to the worshipful behavior of some students toward gregarious academic authority figures like Dr. Sternberg—and perhaps to one student in particular.

They described a peer who dropped out of the creative writing track that Dr. Sternberg directed and shifted to the academic track. Samuel Hudson's bylaws permit student-teacher relationships as long as a student isn't directly under a teacher's charge. The student's dropping out of Dr. Sternberg's program would have allowed a consensual sexual relationship to take place without institutional pushback. When asked about this, Dr. Sternberg declined to comment further in the interest of preserving the student's anonymity, but he said, "I did encourage her to stay in the program."

Years later, a Title IX complaint was filed against Dr.

> Sternberg but then withdrawn. When called for comment, the student allegedly involved confirmed that she had switched tracks to widen her career prospects but provided no comment on the nature of her relationship with Dr. Sternberg before or after. She claims she did not intend to make a complaint.

Blame it on my bad mood or the Vicodin or the shock, but I couldn't seem to finish the article. I felt something at my edges that could only be described as detached, like a door that had lost its frame, like I was losing touch with the context, as if Tom had carefully, screw by screw, removed me from my hinges and installed me somewhere else.

I opened a new browser window on Gabe's old computer and googled my name—nothing unexpected. I opened Twitter, where I scrolled through a flurry of hot-take tweets and think-piece threads from the academic/literary set. Even those who did not condone Tom's actions—or felt they couldn't publicly—were cautiously impressed by how he'd taken accountability. After all, these tweeters mentioned, it appeared he was confessing to sleeping with a student who wasn't even technically his student at the time, yet he didn't harp on that, he didn't let himself off the hook, and what was more, he wanted to protect this student's identity. They agreed with Tom's editor—this could be a rudimentary template for men who had made mistakes in their past. Many of the tweets were tinged with condescending sympathy for the anonymous woman ("I feel for her").

Cowards, I thought. What bullshit posturing. How could you blame Tom for anything if you believed the article, chock-full as it was with humble self-reflection and lie upon lie and a sweeping indictment of "the anonymous student" compliments of my former classmates? And why was no one talking about the article's tone-deaf Golden Age–inspired photos, like a portrait of Aliana lounging with a highball glass of lemonade on Tom's velvet couch?

I cringed at the detractors in the comments. He was in a👏position 👏of👏power, said one. Sleeping with TWO former students? 🤔 wrote another.

I was surprised by Tom and Aliana's relationship, but I didn't have any kind of moral issue with it. They hadn't dated in grad school, and even if they had, it would have been different. Aliana was six years older than I was, for starters. But more than that, Tom wouldn't have dared to start some scammy late-night text conversation with someone as put-together and self-assured and socially mobile as Aliana, because she wouldn't have been into it.

I searched for a tweet from the *LARB* reviewer, Becca Adamski. She had a thread that began *The problem with the article is the problem with the book* and ended with *If we have learned anything from #MeToo, it's that when a story is delivered by the person in power, that is when we should most ardently interrogate it.* But it was just one voice, lost in the noise of many.

I replied to Isaac: I just read it. WTF. Can we talk? Then I closed the computer and went to teach "The Brigadier and the Golf Widow" to The Masculine Voice.

During my second semester of grad school, Tom and I started meeting up more and more. At first in his office, then at a coffee shop every other week, then after work—a happy hour here or there—and then one of his meetings would run late and we would end up getting together in the evening for drinks, where his usual charm morphed into a darkness I mistook for depth.

We vaguely held on to the premise that we were meeting to discuss my work, but mostly we discussed him. He was having several midlife crises related to his elusive second novel, his deteriorating relationship with his wife (they hadn't had sex in six months), his mother's Parkinson's, and his fortieth birthday. As someone in my early twenties, I found assimilating his age almost impossible. I could remember pieces of my own mother's fortieth birthday—the OVER THE HILL banner, the bundle of black balloons. My father was dead by forty-one.

The Brew was full that night, but Tom and I were tucked in our own little corner. I had torn my cardboard coaster to bits, shredded one final piece in half, and set it on top of the pile. Tom watched me with one of those delighted half smiles that made my heart race. His face glowed by the light of a tea candle in a small glass jar.

"Sorry," I said.

"You can't be still, can you?"

"I guess not." I plowed the pile to the edge of the table and into my cupped hand, then dropped the pieces back on the table.

"It's cute, to be honest. It's charming." He glanced at my cleavage in the V of the shirt I had worn purposefully. "You look very nice today."

My face felt warm. "Thank you."

Tom took a sip of his drink and looked out the doorway of our alcove into the greater bar area. "Is it just me, or do the students get more attractive every year?" He was looking at them as if they emitted a magical, youthful glow, all the delight in that half-smile now beaming out at them.

"I think you're just getting older," I said.

I'd meant it as a joke, or I'd meant to mean it as a joke, but he slumped back in his chair and frowned. "That I am."

I couldn't seem to keep up with the nuances of his mood, kept trying to recalibrate. "But it's true," I said. "They are. Everyone's so attractive now."

"I probably shouldn't have gotten married at twenty-five," he said gloomily. "I don't recommend it." I felt a simultaneous pang of jealousy that his wife existed and pride that he was willing to confide in me about their relationship. The idea that I would get married in a couple of years seemed almost as ridiculous as hanging out with someone who'd already been married for fifteen. To think there was a day when I was eight—pre-pageboy haircut, cute curly hair—and Tom was out there reciting his vows.

"Why not?" I asked.

"I wasn't ready. I wasn't totally . . . honest."

"You mean with yourself?" What useful thing could I say about marriage? I was always trying to strike some balance with him, to seem unfazed and older than I was while also being young and charming, a manic pixie dream student.

"Not quite like that," he said. This was the dance. I pretended that I understood something, he let me know that I did not and imparted some wisdom. "It's more like . . . you'll get married and your husband won't be able to do all of the things you need him to do, and you won't be able to do all the things he needs you to do, and you'll have to find ways around it without hurting each other too much. You know what I mean by *needs*?"

"I think so."

"Emotional, sexual," he said. "To put it broadly."

"Right."

"Everyone has those needs: me, you. We can't ignore them. It's the human condition."

I felt that low pang of ambivalence, my differentness, pushed it away. "You can't," I agreed.

"Is this conversation making you uncomfortable?"

"No."

He took a slow sip of his drink. His mood downshifted again. "You know that time last semester? When I asked you to house-sit for one more night?"

"Yeah, of course."

"I made a very bad mistake that night."

"The friend," I said. "An ex?"

"Oh, God, if only it were that simple." He picked up his glass, moved it in tiny circles so the ice clinked around the edges, then set it back down. "You know, I've slipped up before, a long time ago, at a wedding. Lydia and I worked through it. We got over it. I think we have some tentative agreement that this can happen once in a while, and we'll be okay. But this wasn't some stranger, Sam. This wasn't some random woman."

I waited for him to say who it was, but he didn't. So I offered, somewhat randomly, "Diego Rivera cheated on Frida Kahlo with Frida's sister." I had always loved Frida—the way she'd taken a bad hand and turned it into a career, working outside the male-dominated artistic establishment. I would not be deterred by her sudden mass appeal.

"And how did that turn out?" he asked.

"Frida cut off all her hair to spite him, and then they got a divorce. But later they got remarried."

"Yeah, well, artists," he said.

"You're an artist."

"Lydia isn't, that's for sure. When I so much as uttered the words *open marriage,* she flipped out. A marriage can feel claustrophobic, like you're trapped in a fucking elevator together. But that's no excuse. Even in an open marriage, you can't have sex with whoever, somebody's friend."

"Ah," I said.

"Somebody's *best* friend, for example," he added miserably. It seemed flippant to tell him this was fine, and judgmental to say it wasn't, so I just nodded with the empathetic vacancy of a therapist and waited for him to continue. "Lydia suspects something is going on," he said. "The important thing is that she doesn't find out *who.*"

Had I been the one to make her suspicious, that night at the house? Or had I somehow confirmed suspicions she already had? "How does she know?" I asked.

"Sixth sense, I don't know. Everything has been off for months. I will admit I transgressed; I'm not going to let her think she's crazy. But if she knew *who*, it might actually kill her. It would, in fact, be uniquely devastating to everyone involved."

I wondered if I should mention Lydia's reaction to me that night, but I didn't. He clasped his hand over his lips, staring into space, thinking, then looked back at me. "It's cliché, I know, it's a way people let themselves off the hook, but in this case I really believe not telling her who is what will protect her most. I'll have to carry the guilt of that alone. I'm just trying to do something right after I did something very wrong. Do you think that's horrible?"

"No, not if you've really thought through your options and

their consequences," I said. He looked relieved. I was surprised by this—was I so important that my permission might wash away his guilt? "Can I ask a question?" I said.

"Shoot."

"Did you do it because you wanted what you couldn't have?"

He smiled slightly, laughed. "I wanted what I *could* have, that's the thing," he said. "The sexual tension had been building for years. Years. I've known her since Princeton." He leaned toward me. "I mean, do you want to know why I did it, really?" I nodded. "Lydia, for all her exceptional qualities, is a tentative woman in the bedroom. Lydia denies herself so much. Sex with her is like eating a decent meal, meat and potatoes, fills your caloric goals but not your dreams. Not Michelin-star. But this woman: She wants it. Does things Lydia will not do. For example, and excuse the crassness, she wants it in the ass. Practically begs for it." I felt vaguely grossed out—why was he telling me this?—and turned on—transgressive sexual details!—and embarrassed—was I being prudish or perverted?—and proud—I was his confidante. He leaned back. "Where can I write a review to the maker?" he said. "Because it seems like a design flaw, that humans are capable of catastrophic guilt and overwhelming passion at the same time."

"Major design flaw," I said.

"Do you ever just give in completely to something you want, Sam?" he asked. It made me feel warm, to hear my name come out of his mouth. "Some people deny themselves everything, you know. But we aren't those kinds of people, are we?"

I shook my head: No, we aren't.

He finished his drink, wiped his mouth with a damp cocktail napkin, then checked the time. "I need to let His Majesty out," he said, referring to Cheever. He reached around the candle and cupped my hands, beseeching. "Should we meet tomorrow to discuss your latest?" he asked, reverting to the premise. "Come by the office in the afternoon." I had scheduled lunch with a friend, but there was no question I would cancel it, no question I would hover by my email in the nebulous vicinity of afternoon and wait to be summoned.

He paid for the drinks as I waited by the door, then we stepped outside into the warm Baltimore night. He lingered, looking up and down the sidewalk as if to gather information about the night or the people out in it.

"Cheever loves you," he said.

"We're buddies," I said.

"Buddies? That's quite the slight. Cheever has professed his *love*."

"Well, okay, of course I love Cheever."

"Maybe you should come over," Tom said. "Tell him yourself."

My system flushed with excitement, then dread, as if I had been waiting in line for a roller coaster and was surprised to find myself next to go. "Now?"

I watched his lips tighten. It was the wrong answer. "Up to you," he said with a shrug. "I can drive you home after."

If this were a choose-your-own adventure, would changing my answer change the ending? Would some other web of possibilities open, or would I always end up here, shivering under this desk, trying to write my way to some kind of clarity?

I knew Tom's house. I knew the cast-iron pan, the bookshelves, the TV remote, the light switches, the guest room and its feather pillows, the quilt that had probably been handmade by some grandmother or great-aunt. I knew it all, but I didn't really know Tom in it.

He was cheerful once we were there, though perhaps, in retrospect, not quite sober enough to have driven. First thing he did was take off his button-down and hang it over a kitchen chair, so he was in a white undershirt, chest hairs crawling out of the V. He knelt, petted the drooling dog. "Cheever, look!" he said. "It's your buddy! It's your buddy Sam!"

Cheever and I followed him into the kitchen. "Roll over," Tom said. "Shake hands!" Cheever offered his paw, Tom took it and clapped his thighs, revealed the treat, then got up and started opening cabinets as I knelt to rub Cheever's tummy.

"Whiskey? Or do you prefer gin? I can make you a gimlet," he said, pulling down different-shaped glasses. His arms were so thin; you forgot it when he was in a button-down.

"What even is a gimlet?"

He laughed. "Have you read *The Long Goodbye*?"

"Cheever?"

The dog whipped his head toward me, tail wagging.

"Chandler," he said. "You're thinking of 'Goodbye, My Brother.' "

"I thought that was Roth?"

"That's 'Goodbye, Columbus,'" he said with a laugh. "I know someone who knew the girl in that story. One of my old professors. Stripped down to her underwear and did a flip off his diving board in the backyard."

"Which girl? The main woman?"

"The one who refused to get a diaphragm," he said.

"I thought she *did* get the diaphragm."

"Anyway, Chandler swore by Rose's lime juice." He took two limes out of a fridge packed to the gills with fruits, vegetables, milk, beer, and glass containers of leftovers. "But he was wrong."

He served the gimlet—gin, simple syrup, and lime juice—in a wide-mouthed glass with a lime wedge hooked on. For himself, he poured whiskey in a squat glass. When I had cooked at his house, I'd cleaned each item as I'd gone along, making sure the kitchen remained spotless. I was in awe of the extravagant way he left everything out, soft bubbles of pulp strewn across the cutting board, a stream of simple syrup running from the lip of its bottle, the spout of the juicer dripping onto the counter.

"Let's sit down," he said, nodding me toward the living room where I had, many times, fallen asleep watching cop shows about sexual predators and serial killers.

He turned on some music, flipped on a lamp—low, buttery light—and sat on the couch, supporting his back with the turquoise throw pillow that I always laid my head on. Cheever sat at his feet. My teeth chattered. I chose the chair on the other side, which I immediately understood as ridiculous.

"You okay?" he asked. He pushed his bangs up a bit, revealing a swath of forehead. What was playing? Was it "Crash Into Me"? Was this a wet-dream song? I had never really listened to the lyrics.

"I'm fine," I said.

"Just making sure." He held up a finger. "Hold on, Cheever has something to say." He leaned down toward the dog. "Yes?" he said, nodding and responding the way you do when pretending to be on the phone with a child. "Yes, right. Right." He sat back up. "Cheever thought you came here mainly to pet him? And he's a little disappointed in the small number of pets he has thusly received."

"Thusly received?" I repeated.

"Thusly received." He leaned back in his seat, one leg crossed over the other, whiskey in hand, in a way that felt like: Your move.

I stood up. I walked over to the opposite side of the couch to pet Cheever.

"You're going to sit over there?" he said.

"Well, Cheever's over here."

"So you want *me* to move?" He laughed and inched over to me, taking his pillow with him. "Hey," he said, as if to calm me. He put his hand on my back, rubbing it gently.

My jaw tightened. I finally had his undivided attention, and now that I had it, I didn't know what to do. I felt like a dog who had, much to his own surprise and horror, caught the rabbit who'd been taunting him all summer.

"Let's just talk," he said. "We're not so bad at that, are we?"

"Okay," I said. "What should we talk about?" My voice was high from nerves.

"Hm, I don't know," he said. Then, in a joking tone: "Maybe we should go look at my sex-toy collection. Or, wait—you already explored that when you were snooping around the house."

"You told me to snoop," I said, trying to match his easy tone.

"I did," he said. "What's your favorite?"

"Sex toy?"

"Sure."

"I'm versatile."

"Are you?"

I couldn't stop thinking about the pillow behind his back.

That was his back pillow. Night after night, he put it behind his back while watching TV or reading a book. It must have absorbed so much sweat. And then I would come to house-sit, and it was where I laid my head.

Everything seemed wrong. *He* seemed wrong. His body was so thin, yet his face was so round—smooth and mushy, like a thumb with bangs. The bangs suddenly struck me as a lame and unsuccessful reach toward youthfulness.

He let the sex toys go, perhaps sensing my unease. "What's the gossip in the department?" he asked. "Who's everyone sleeping with these days?"

"I don't know. Aliana and that French guy."

"The actor, of course, yes," he said. "What about you?" Then he held up his hand flat so I wouldn't answer: "No, don't tell me. Isaac? Jonas?"

"Isaac and I are just friends."

"So, Jonas?" he said.

"What's wrong with Jonas?" This was a ploy; I wasn't sleeping with anyone.

Tom raised his eyebrows. It was obvious what was wrong with Jonas: He was an alcoholic, basically, who would sleep with a worm if given the opportunity. A self-centered asshole, albeit with redeeming qualities. Jonas always showed up when someone needed help moving, for example. If you got down on yourself for being an asshole, he stood by your side because he understood it deeply.

"We shouldn't talk about Jonas," he said. One finger made spirals on my back. "I don't want to think about where Jonas has been." He was hard, I saw. I felt a ripple of nausea.

I chastised myself for the disgust. I had answered every single one of Tom's texts quickly and with glee. I had constantly cleared my schedule for him. Why? What had I wanted if not this?

"You deserve an actual adult," he said. "Someone who isn't intimidated by your talent." Subtly but definitely, Tom opened his legs, jutted his pelvis forward with a tiny sigh.

I felt desperate to hold his interest without touching him. "So you think I have talent?" I said, trying to sound flirty.

"Come on, Sam," he said sweetly. "Obviously. Yes."

"Tell me more," I said, as if joking, but I wanted to know.

"You have a way of capturing . . . you have this postmodern sensibility."

"Oh?"

"I mean you do *modernity* very well," he said impatiently. "The way people talk, for instance."

"Dialogue?" I asked. I was losing the sexy—if I'd had any in the first place—to brass tacks.

"Yes, but elsewhere as well," he said. A thread of annoyance now.

"Elsewhere where?"

"Are we here to talk shop?"

"Well, you're my professor, my adviser."

He sat up, his hand springing from my back. "What's that supposed to mean?"

"Nothing," I said quickly. "I didn't mean anything. I just, you know. Well, it's nice to hear about my work sometimes."

He scratched his forehead crazily, like I was making him lose his mind. "Do you have some issue with being here right now?"

"No."

"Tell me: Why did you come here?" His face was all disgust, like I had wronged him, like he had unmasked a traitor.

"Like here?" I said, pointing around me, because for a second I thought he'd meant graduate school.

"Yes, to my house, Sam."

"Because you asked."

"I know I asked," he said. "But why did you say yes?"

"I just did."

"That's not an answer."

"I don't know," I stammered.

Cheever crawled under the chair I'd been sitting in earlier and began to whimper. I was holding the gimlet with one hand. I took a sip of it for something to do, but it didn't taste good, all astringent, no sweet. The more I thought of the word *gimlet,* the more I thought of *giblets,* turkey organs, slimy things. You could cup a wet heart in your palm.

"You can't answer the question?" he asked.

"I don't know why you're mad at me," I said, looking at the floor.

"I'm not *mad* at you," he said, sounding mad. "I just want you to take some responsibility for what's going on here."

"Why does anyone need to take responsibility for anything? I'm just here, and you're just here, and I guess it feels weirder than I thought it would."

"I didn't lure you here."

"I know."

I was once curled up on this very couch where he now sat with a pillow behind his back. I once texted him about sex toys from this very house. *This* guy who had a pillow behind his back and those bangs? One day, surely, I would also slide a pillow behind my back, but not today.

Cheever whined plaintively, long and low.

Maybe I wasn't the dog at all but the rabbit. All this time, I'd believed we'd been only playing, that the boundaries of his marriage or his job were as good as a fence. Now, in the jaws of reality, I was horrified by where I'd ended up. Crossing the line ruined the premise, ended the game. Now he just seemed like a guy who was older than I remembered, and meaner. He was *forty*. He almost had an entire *me* on me.

"You're going to pull this crap about how I'm your adviser *now*?" he said.

"I wasn't trying to . . . I just really wanted to talk about my writing."

"And you thought this would be the perfect time?" His face was pink.

"I wasn't trying—I didn't mean to. I don't know what's happening."

"You *don't know what's happening*? Bullshit, Sam."

I reached toward his belt buckle. He grabbed my wrist, set my hand back on my lap with a jerk. "Are you kidding?" He stood up. "Not anymore."

Without looking at me, he walked over to the credenza where Lydia once flicked through the mail. He picked up the phone and called me a cab.

A week or two later, some grad students gathered at the Village Pub after Victorian Lit. Hardik was there. Isaac was there with his new boyfriend. Jonas was there, talking too much, his eyes bloodshot and glassy. Aliana wasn't there. She rarely came out, lived a life beyond the program with her French actor boyfriend.

It came up in passing that Felicia, another grad student who was also at the bar, would be taking care of Cheever the following week. My throat was so tight that I could hardly get down my Natty Boh. Cardboard beer advertisements hung from the ceiling on fishing line, turning slowly. The Natty Boh guy, with his fat handlebar mustache and single giant eye, winked at me as he turned, like he knew what I was thinking and wouldn't let me get away with it.

Felicia's beer was hazy, a bitter IPA. She was pretty, polite and cheerful, the kind of person who would only project *you* back to you, saying things like "Oh my God, yes, the rain has been crazy!" or "Yeah, the rain is beautiful!" depending on your own reaction to the rain.

I'd forced down most of my beer when Tom walked in. Our heads turned toward him like magnets. "Look who we have here!" he called.

"Well, hello!" shouted Clee. She had a cool, easy confidence, an Afro, and everyone's phone number. She was always sending texts inviting people out, never omitting anyone based on some level of coolness or uncoolness that the rest of the group had silently determined. Clee had a confidence that didn't require anything from anyone, was friends with a lot of guys in a non-flirty way. She would leave a party whenever she felt like, showed no fear of missing out. Everywhere Clee went, *she* was the thing that was happening, but when Tom came, *he* was the thing that was happening, and she was fine giving him the floor, which he always took.

Tom squeezed in next to Clee with a whiskey and started a long story about a recent conference. The climax involved him being accidentally drunk at the hotel bar with a famous older woman author. Let's call her Largret Latwood. I watched Felicia, who was taking in Tom's performance with an awe I recognized.

Tom surveyed us, his audience, as he spoke, passing over me with a vacant neutrality—not overcompensating, not completely freezing me out. It was exactly how he dealt with me in class. This is what you wanted? he seemed to say. You got it. Tom noticed Felicia's empty pint glass and called an intermission. I forced myself to go to the bar and order another Boh, not wanting to make some statement by leaving. Clee was waiting for her drink beside me. "Heard you came to the dark side," she said.

"What?"

"That you're switching to the academic track."

"Wait, what? Where did you hear that?"

"Sternberg," she said.

I hadn't switched. It hadn't even crossed my mind. Why would Tom say something like that? Had Clee misunderstood? I had a brief sensation of moving backward even though I was perfectly still, the physical feeling of my body revolting against reality. I put my hand on the bar.

"Oh, I don't know," I said. "I haven't decided anything."

"Why not?" she said with a shrug. "Maybe it's better to get some distance."

"From what?"

"Writing fiction. Honestly, better the judger than the judged."

The group reconvened. Tom finished his story. At the end, he and Largret had traded shoes, so that he was in black pumps and she was in loafers, which were large on her feet and made her look clownish. He couldn't even squeeze his heels in the back of her pumps, so he was just tottering around and praising women for their ability to balance and trying to do a sort of runway walk across the red carpet of the hotel bar.

That was when the president of SHU walked in, looked both of them up and down, turned on his heel, and walked out again.

Clee spat some of her drink back into her glass, then the whole table was in hysterics. Felicia laughed, too, in a more reserved and self-conscious way. Tom offered her a special smile, the kind of smile that made space for her shyness and insecurity, the kind of smile that had once made space for mine.

I lingered at the bar with Jonas after everyone else had gone home. We escalated to shots, escalated to being at his house, in his room, which had only an IKEA dresser and, on the floor, a rectangle of mattress and stacks of books that jutted up like stalagmites. No curtains, no pictures. He took off all his clothes instantly. I stared at his sweaty face. Long nose, long eyelashes, almost cartoonish, his features interchangeable like on a Mr. Potato Head, as if you could pluck out his mouth and put it where his ear had been. I thought of Tom's bangs, of his back pillow, moist with sweat. I unfocused my eyes, let myself descend into dizziness, tucked away my disgust behind the drunkenness.

What can I even remember? He was in my hand, my mouth. "No, no, like this," he kept saying. The entire house shook, a blinding white light shining in my eyes, as if we'd been caught in the beam of a police helicopter or an alien spaceship. I blinked into the light, surrendering to it, then it flashed away. It was a train—the tracks ran through Jonas's backyard, eye level with his bedroom windows. I felt as if I'd been shaken apart, split open, then zipped back together, reconfigured to look the same on the outside. I was embarrassed to have surrendered so easily, to have surrendered to nothing.

A few days later, I went to see Tom during office hours. He kept the door wide open, sat behind his desk, didn't roll his chair out, didn't lean forward. A dark broodiness emanated from him.

"Guess what happened," I said, trying to settle back into the old groove of banter, but it was too late, we were already on a different course.

"What's that?" he asked without interest.

"My house filled up with literal shit." The sewage system in my shared decrepit rental had backed up, and everything had come spewing out of the kitchen sink.

"Were you able to get it fixed?"

"Yeah, but we had to bleach all of our dishes and utensils in the bathtub upstairs, and so now, whenever you're eating, you just kind of wonder: Am I eating shit?"

"Remind me not to go to a dinner party at your house," he said. He threw me a smile, but it was not an invitation. It was punctuation, a period.

He fanned through the pages of the manuscript I had submitted the previous week, which he had barely touched, just a few stray copyediting marks in red. "Should we get to the task at hand?" he asked, as if we had ever gotten to the task at hand. "I want to hear what you think about this. Do you think it's working?"

"You don't?" I asked.

"What do *you* think? You need to have some kind of intuition about this kind of thing. Knowing is part of the art."

"Then what's your job?" I said in a joking tone.

"My role here is more like park ranger than tour guide," he said seriously. "I can't walk you everywhere, can only point the way. You have to go on your own journey."

"Okay, well, point the way."

He sighed, adjusted in his chair. "If you're writing what you need to write, then you shouldn't give a shit what I think," he said. "The important thing is *your* opinion. You have no opinion about your own work?" He set the papers on his desk. "They say early work is always autobiography. If *you're* stuck, then your characters are stuck. If you don't know what you want, your characters don't know what they want."

"The characters are finding out what they want."

"And how are they doing that?"

"I don't know."

"You don't know?" he said in mock surprise. "These characters are floundering, Sam. They're flailing. They have no direction. They're acting like twenty-year-olds."

"They *are* twenty-year-olds," I said.

"At some point, they're going to have to grow up."

I wanted to say, Yes, that's how age works, you grow up. Hadn't he done it himself?

But no, my characters were too young, much too young, he could not believe how young they were. Anyway, first-person narration was amateurish, anything verging on "confessional" was self-obsession (though not when he did it), and endlessly self-destructive female characters were an unsophisticated trend he refused to call literary. He always imagined himself as the ideal reader.

"By now we're all pretty familiar with your exploration of the aromantic," he continued. "Verging, possibly, on the asexual, a sort of neutered defense mechanism that I don't totally buy. Anti-charisma has its own kind of charm, but of course charm can be a gimmick, and a gimmick can be, what, a cop-out? Can it sustain a body of work? Or at some point does it disguise a total lack of substance? One thing a story shouldn't be about is its own aboutness; it's a sort of tautological failure."

"So it's not good," I said stupidly.

"Again, that's not a question you should have to ask me," he said, never having needed to ask the question himself. He was like Aliana, who always nodded as we gave her comments, taking notes as if attending an important lecture. She submitted work as if on her way to fulfilling a destiny, and each response seemed only to reveal our commitment to her potential. In my case, each piece of criticism only further proved my inadequacies.

"Don't pretend like I'm shooting puppies here," he said. "I'm not being harsh for the sake of harshness. You asked for my opinion. This isn't undergrad. This isn't even an MFA program. It's a PhD. Narrative laziness isn't going to get you anywhere, nor is it helpful for me to pretend it will. You have to ask serious questions about what you are doing here, and why, and how to proceed if, indeed, you should proceed at all."

My heart fell into my stomach; the *if* echoed in the empty chamber of my chest.

Tom pushed air through his lips, looked off to the side, tapped his fingers over his mouth. Then he turned to me, fist under his chin. "Do you like writing?"

"Sometimes," I said.

"Sometimes," he repeated. "Sometimes isn't enough. Sometimes doesn't sustain you. You have to want it. The thirst to write must burn beyond hope for success. If you can see yourself doing anything else, you should do that. You shouldn't do this."

The horrible refrain of writing teachers everywhere, a practical axiom of the profession. What it meant was this: If you're capable of being happy doing something else, do it, because you'll be unhappy as a writer. What a luxury. How condescending. I wondered what asshole had said it first. Perhaps it had been co-opted from God or Zeus. *If you can be anything other than Zeus,* said Zeus, falling back into his throne of clouds, exhausted from fucking Leda, *be it.*

Of course I could be something else. Most people *had* to be something else. I could be a caterer or a copywriter or an adjunct. I could be a reviewer of duffel bags and Infinity pillows. I could be a homeless person under a desk.

"Maybe your strengths are more in criticism," Tom said with a shrug, as if it were nothing, as if saying I might be better at cooking carrots than peas. "It's a very, very tough literary market out there. Only a few people rise to the top, and I want to be honest about where you're at here."

"You said . . ." I began. That wet pressure was building up behind my eyes. "I mean . . ." I wanted to say, You told me I was talented, but it felt juvenile and desperate.

"You're skilled, obviously," he said, and I felt worse because he knew exactly what I wanted to hear. "Your sentences? Pristine." This wasn't true. I wound my way into sentences and couldn't find my way out. Had he just picked something random that a graduate student should be good at? Or had he actively chosen something I was bad at, to prove a point? "But you're unsure. You *have to* have an intuition about this stuff."

I felt a pang. He was right. Intuition was what I was missing, not just in art but in life. I had been told over and over the kind of things I was just supposed to know about myself. If I searched deep inside, I would know if I was straight or had been gay all along. I would know if I wanted to fuck someone or if I just wanted them to like me or if I wanted to be like them or if I was just surrendering to the narrative. I would know, deep down, if I was a writer because I would thirst for it beyond hope of success or a home or a meal.

I reached down into my heart and hoped that a fire for words was burning there, but the fire was not for language, it was a fear that I would never be good enough. And it was a burning anger at Tom.

"Intuition," he said again. "That's the art. That—and I'm sorry—but that you can't fake."

Chapter 9

BARELY VISIBLE THINGS

A week after the *Times* profile and Tom's whirlwind book tour, the department hosted a reception to celebrate the release. Rather than spend the afternoon avoiding the faculty lounge and boycotting the sheet cake I desperately wanted to eat, I went home after my last class at Rosedale.

I squeezed through the door of my apartment to find the entry hall littered with empty boxes. It was unusual for Brianna to be home this early. She usually existed as a presence of absences, the missing dishware and condiments, the broken appliances. But I could hear her showering and listening to a podcast at top volume as I tripped down the hall. "Trigger warning," one of the hosts said, then commenced to read a truly gruesome autopsy report.

I dropped my duffel, briefly tried to massage my own shoulders. A mountain of clothes had been piled on the couch for weeks, a combination of thrifted and new items still in plastic wrap.

Brianna had explained that she changed her wardrobe every year, supplementing with "original thrifts" and "seasonal flourishes." Most astounding was that "rotating the wardrobe" appeared to involve donating certain clothes made with delicate materials—silk, wool, beaded details—so she wouldn't have to deal with washing them.

I heard a noise in the kitchen—a rat? There had been a rat—not a mouse, *a rat*—the week before. The building manager had put out a trap, and the next morning I'd found a tail and a trail of blood. I felt bad for the rat, who was only trying to eat like the rest of us. I wanted him to survive, but I wanted him to survive somewhere else.

I sat down at the kitchen table, plugged in Gabe's laptop, and checked for a new message from Isaac, who had reached out via Facebook. Because he was living in Finland for his postdoc, our conversation had been a halting multiday string of messages that only a seven-hour time difference can produce.

[WED 8:11 AM]
ISAAC: OMG, what is going on?

I honestly cannot believe Tom said all of that in a national newspaper.

Plus the STYLE section? Hilarious.

Plus Tom and Aliana are fucking? Did not see that coming.

How are you feeling?

[THURS 3:59 PM]
ME: Did not see the Tom and Aliana thing coming either . . . wow

Feeling eh

I guess that student is supposed to be me . . . ? But the article is full of lies? It doesn't add up.

I'm just confused.

(Also sorry for the delay, I was teaching three classes yesterday.)

How is Helsinki, by the way?

[FRI 2:52 AM]
ISAAC: Sorry, I just slept eleven hours straight.

It's kind of a nightmare.

The sun sets at 4PM.

What are the lies?

[FRI 4:03 PM]
ME: For starters, I didn't sleep with Tom.

[SUN 4:21 AM]
ISAAC: wait whattttt 🤯

really?

But then did you still make a complaint?

Because why did he leave SHU?

[SUN 6:12 AM]
ME: No, I wasn't trying to make a complaint.

Do people really think I, like, mean-heartedly threw Tom out of SHU?

[SUN 4:12 PM]
????

If there are rumors please just tell me

[MON 3:47 AM]
ISAAC: Yes, sorry. I was asleep.

What I heard is that Tom left SHU because you guys had slept together like ten years ago or whatever and you just made a complaint about it in the last year or two.

[TUES 5:39 AM]
ME: And you thought that was true?

[TUES 6:02 AM]
ISAAC: I don't know??

You were always kind of weirdly private about your dating life?

And you did seem really close with Tom at the beg of grad school but then it seemed like there was a falling out at some point?

so in that way it kind of tracked

[TUES 6:33 AM]
ME: So everyone basically thinks I ratted out Tom?

[TUES 2:39 PM]
ISAAC: Well I think the bad vibes are also because

And this is just what I heard

people feel like you orchestrated sleeping with him. Like not even just angling for it on the night you guys were drunk and banged—allegedly!—but because you dropped out of the creative track SO you could sleep together and then you were really pissed when he was like, "No, I want to make things work with my wife."

So that made your complaint seem less justified and more like you were leveraging/manipulating the moment for elaborate revenge.

I felt vaguely ill reading the last messages, which were new. When had the rumors started and with whom? Tom or Aliana, I assumed. Must've made it easy for Leslie Chen to get her quotes. I scratched at my shoulder, my forearm. More red marks had appeared on my skin, everywhere, a constellation of tiny welts. Could you break out in hives from sheer stress?

Why would Tom want people to believe we'd slept together? What was the point? Couldn't it only hurt him? How could all these smart people not question the framing, Tom as a hero for ad mitting a flaw? Why did he get to be a "kid" during the publication of his book at twenty-nine, and I, sitting in the Brew at twenty-two, did not? Why would Aliana participate in the interview—did she believe Tom? Why was Tom's twenty-year-long writer's block so fucking important? Why the Style section? A dry spell was a luxury, and the Style section was luxury, so I guessed it all made sense.

I'd thought contact with my grad school peers had petered out over the last many months because of me, because I was envious and also busy, but maybe it was they who had created the distance, the way you might back away slowly from a deranged person. To support that point: No one except Isaac had contacted me about the article.

To Isaac I typed, TOM TOLD ME to switch tracks.

He wrote back right away, though it was the middle of the night in Helsinki: Okay, that's fucked up if that's how it happened.

But then I don't really understand why he would lie about all this?!

I was suspicious of the tone—the *if,* the *then,* followed by a question mark and an exclamation point, which read as an attempt to soften his skepticism.

I wrote back, I don't know. It doesn't make any sense. Publicity???

For the third time that week, I checked to see if the price of *Casualty* had decreased on Amazon. It hadn't.

I considered texting Aliana. I considered confronting Tom. I considered bursting into his office and shouting, "We didn't have sex!" or making an appointment to sit down in front of him and ask, "Why would you tell everyone that?"

The more I thought about it, the more genius the article

seemed. Tom's "admission" created controversy, press, and sales. He was trying to get ahead of the story in case I decided to speak up. In a way, it precluded people from believing what had really happened—or hadn't—between us. Not only had the article called my character into question, but the truth would've read like backtracking, a de-escalation of his more dramatic admission. Even if, for some reason, I'd told Leslie Chen we hadn't slept together, his version would've still taken precedence because he was more respected and he had more to lose. Because why would he risk his career for a lie? I would have come off as defensive, embarrassed. What was more, what was worse, was that he'd made such a show of taking responsibility, of introspection, of concern, of reasonableness, that he'd essentially exonerated himself.

"So much skin under her fingernails," said the podcast host from the bathroom, "that one of her nails had broken off."

There were always worse problems.

No reply came from the cold, dark tundra of Finland, so I closed my computer, then cleared Brianna's take-out containers to find the strata of mail.

I discovered a letter from my insurance company telling me the ER visit would cost $1,300. It had come so quickly, it was as if they were making a point: "We will not let you get away with this." THIS IS NOT A BILL, it said, taunting me further, but I knew it would become a bill soon because I hadn't reached my $7,000 deductible.

Since I'd finally paid back my late rent, I resolved to use most of my November paycheck to settle my October expenses, which included the root canal. Then I'd pay as much of the ER bill as possible and float the rest on credit.

If there was one thing I'd learned from my student-loan debacle, it was to not get behind if you could help it, to never pretend you had money you didn't, and the best way to do that was to give it to whoever you owed as quickly as possible. But it was like trying to slay a hydra. For every bit of debt you managed to repay, interest and new expenses sprouted to replace it.

In a padded envelope, I found three different kinds of earplugs (foam, wax, silicone) for my next product-review assignment.

"Her eyeballs had been replaced . . ." the host reported from the bathroom.

I rolled the orange foam earplugs between my fingers, inserting them in my ears, where they expanded into a muted silence.

That was the trick, to tuck reality behind whatever makeshift barricade you had at hand. To proceed, I would have to block out the noise, all of it, the murder podcast, the ever depressing news, Tom's book, the article, Isaac's response, the itchiness of my skin. If I severed the mind-body connection, then these little welts wouldn't be a problem at all, they would simply go away someday or kill me.

I found steam-in-the-bag broccoli in the depths of the freezer, heated it in the microwave until I heard a dull beeping from beyond the foam, dropped a pad of butter into the bag, didn't waste my time pretending I would find suitable salt, and ate it directly from the package while standing in the kitchen.

A figure appeared in front of me, and I jumped, primed to claw my attacker, to get a little skin under my fingernails, but it was only Brianna. I twirled the earplugs out of my ears.

"Oh," she said in a way that sounded like *ew*. She was dewy from the shower, energetically scratching her shoulder.

"Did they find the killer?" I asked.

"What killer?"

"The podcast."

"That's not the point of the podcast."

"They don't tell you who did it?"

"Obviously they do, but that's not *the point*," she said, scratching at her arm. "It's about the victim and it's about justice. Are you just eating broccoli from the bag?"

"Are you scratching your arm?"

"I have these fucking, like, mini mosquito bites or a rash or something," she said. "I took a shower, but they still itch."

I showed her my arm. "Maybe we have bedbugs."

"Probably not," said Brianna, looking scared.

"We also have that rat," I said.

"If we have bedbugs, it's from you. You work at, like, a thousand different places. Plus, you take random people home."

"I've only brought *two* people home," I said. I considered accusing her of being classist or homophobic, because I knew she would turn herself inside out to prove she wasn't, and I'd gain the upper hand, but decided it was counterproductive on a grand scale. "You leave your food and take-out containers everywhere, and you just brought piles of clothes home from the thrift store."

"It doesn't even matter where the bugs are from," she said, realizing where they were from. "What are we supposed to do?"

"Email Tyronne," I said, referring to the building manager.

"No way."

"Why not? He probably knows what to do."

"No," she said like a militant child. "What if he makes us move out? My parents will *never* forgive me if I mess this up."

"We have to get rid of them somehow."

"How can something so tiny cause so much chaos?" she whined. "What are we supposed to do?"

"Google it?" I asked.

"Why don't *you* google it?"

"Should *I* email Tyronne?"

She whipped out her phone. What used to be her leverage—her name on the lease—was finally, briefly mine.

The peeling paint on Sophie's row house glowed in the late-afternoon light that slatted through a line of trees across the street. The trees were meant to obfuscate the sudden land-drop plummeting to the highway below.

With a garbage bag full of clothes slung over my shoulder, I pushed open the waterlogged wooden gate covered in lichen. The backyard was a narrow strip of balding lawn, half covered in dead leaves fallen from tree branches that hung over the tall fence marking off the neighbor's yard. A small platform attached to the back of the house seemed more like a dock than a deck. Two dirty blue plastic chairs cupped crunchy brown leaves. Back here, the sun was already gone, the light a dusty gray.

Brianna had agreed to try a bug bomb, and Sophie had agreed to let me stay with her for a few days as long as I followed instructions, which she had sent via text, addressing the message to Baybay.

I shivered, waiting for Sophie at the edge of the deck, my bag in the grass, as I'd been instructed. The meeting felt illicit, like I was here for anonymous Craigslist sex.

Sophie appeared in her black-and-white catering ensemble and yellow kitchen gloves, holding a box of tissues. "Move back," she said. I jerked the bag up with one hand and moved back, soldier-like, leaves crunching beneath my feet. "Not with the bag," she said. I moved forward, dropped the bag, moved back.

Sophie dumped its entire contents on the deck. I had tumble-dried everything on high, as she had instructed. She squatted down to inspect the pile for bugs. She had gone through a bedbug situation in college.

"Take off your clothes," she said.

"What?" Despite the fence, I was in view of the neighbors' second-story windows.

"Don't worry about them," said Sophie. "Do you know how loud those people have sex with the windows open?"

"It's also kind of cold?"

"It's a risk, taking you in. If you want to be here, we have to be sure you are bug-free. It's not embarrassing, it's just the situation." Both, I thought. So many things seemed like they should be one or the other but were actually both.

I took off my shoes, dropped my pants, peeled off my sweat-shirt and my T-shirt, and stood there in my bra and underwear, goose bumps rising on my skin, which was covered in red welts and streaks from scratching. I felt like I was trapped inside the unlikely premise of an amateur porn video. The next thing she would do was touch me, check places that were stupid to check, places you wouldn't check, invading my privacy until we were somehow fucking in the leaves with the neighbors watching.

She leaped toward the new pile of clothes, picking through them on her haunches, then looked up at me, held out her hand, and said, "Underwear."

I hesitated.

She rolled her eyes.

I slunk out of my underwear, handed them over, unhooked my bra, hands over my chest, feeling prudish.

She did not touch me, just directed me to a pink-tiled bathroom where the water pressure was so good and the water was so hot that it felt like little pins sticking me all over, scratching my welts. I felt with my finger—indeed, I was turned on. Sophie had been all business, but that didn't stop me from jerking off as the water scratched my back.

When I opened the curtain, I saw that Sophie had left out a towel and a pile of her clothes for me, black cotton leggings and an oversize T-shirt. Heat prickled across my chest. When had she even come in?

Sophie was reading a book in the living room, my backpack leaning against the squat yellow couch.

"You got a text," she said without looking up.

It was on the lock screen: coffee break tomorrow? whenever you are free? Gabe.

"That the guy you're dating?"

"We're not dating."

"No?" she said.

As I crept past Tom's office on the way to The Masculine Voice, I saw the wedge-heeled foot of a student bouncing up and down, one leg crossed over the other. "A reformed rake makes the best husband?" she asked. I stopped in the hall several feet from the door as the question hung in the air, awaited his approval. This was a line

Tom often said in relation to eighteenth-century literature. I knew they were reading *Wuthering Heights* because I had seen it flash on the iPads and Kindles of the women lined up outside of his office.

Wuthering Heights was inexplicable to me as a romance novel. Heathcliff falls in love with his nonbiological sister, Catherine, leaves home, returns a rich dick, finds Catherine married. Even though Heathcliff is a true and vengeful asshole with almost no redeeming qualities, Catherine is desperately in love with him. When she dies, Heathcliff challenges her to haunt him forever. On his own deathbed many years later, he admits that seeking revenge has brought him no joy, but he also insists he didn't do anything wrong.

What I liked best about *Wuthering Heights* was the eponymous, ethereal Kate Bush song told from the perspective of Catherine's ghost haunting Heathcliff. When I first heard the song, without really listening to the lyrics, I thought it was about the newspaper comics—Heathcliff the garbage-flipping, female-feline-loving orange cat, and Cathy the *Ack! I ate too much chocolate!* thirty-something serial dater.

"Right," said Tom to the student. "The trope here, and who knows, maybe the truth"—I pictured the cocked head, the furrowed brow—"is that 'bad boys' are attractive." I pictured her smile. "What do you think? Are you attracted to 'bad boys'? Is Calvin, for example, a bad boy?" Calvin was not in the book. He was one of the students Tom had talked about in his conversation with Gabe.

I pictured her flirty forehead tilt, the big eyes, expected a little laugh of surprise and delight. Instead she said, "Oh." Like she was caught off guard. "I don't know. I wasn't really thinking about that." A thread of disgust in her voice.

"You and Calvin are still dating?" he asked, misattributing her tone.

"Yes."

"But you're also interested in Tyler. Who has not been to class recently, has he?"

"Tyler and I are just friends."

"I've heard that one before," said Tom with a laugh. "Listen, Sonia, you are doing some good work in this class, but you care too much about what I think. You've got to let loose a little. Only when you bring your own world into the world of the novel do you ever really learn anything, do you ever really *feel* anything. Yes, of course, when you're writing an academic paper, they *must* be separated, but first you have to feel here." He was surely tapping his chest with a flat hand.

"But how?" she asked. Was she humoring him? Playing dumb because she understood what could be gained by appeasing him? My younger self had stupidly believed every word out of this guy's mouth.

Maybe he was losing his edge. Maybe because of his age, his charm no longer held. Students, as Tom himself had said, were getting younger and more attractive by the year. Tom, meanwhile, was only getting older, droopier. Or maybe the movement had done something tangible; perhaps the younger generation had an eye for creepiness now, could spot a man who was high on his own supply, who had the power to get away with something.

"I mean, you can start by asking yourself real questions and connecting them with the work. For instance, what is it about the 'bad boy' that turns a woman on?"

"Honestly, I'm thinking of becoming a lesbian," she said in a joking tone. She was as aware of his fragile ego as she was of her impending grade. Like so many women, she was an expert in redirecting without offending.

Tom would surely read this as flirting. The axiom of his life was promise and potential, his own inherent worthiness. His anguish over failing to write his second book directly reflected his certitude of his own importance.

"Maybe it's not even a *reformed* rake that makes the best husband," she said, feeding him. "Maybe it's just a rake."

"Which begs the question," said Tom, "did Heathcliff reform? What do you think?"

We think, I think, not.

I woke up at my desk/table at Rosedale with the Infinity pillow-scarf wrapped around my neck like a noose and orange foam earplugs in my ears and *Wonder Boys* stuck to my forehead. It was my thirty-fourth birthday. I was supposed to teach the book tomorrow, and I still had a hundred pages to read. The novel was about a professor who couldn't finish writing his 2,000-page book and whose wife left him because he was having an affair—not, for once, with a student.

Scholars often said the campus in an academic novel was a "microcosm," but I was beginning to see it more as a biodome, less a reflection of the real world than a curated exemption from it. The professors in the books were free not just from the struggle for time and money but from being faithful to their wives, from the mess of raising their own children, from having boundaries with students. And when they fucked it up so much that they were forced to leave, it was like being cast out of Eden.

As an undergrad, I'd felt my exempt status acutely, like a soldier gone AWOL—the brief glee of freedom tinged in the anxiety of eventual return. I couldn't believe I'd managed to ditch nearly every responsibility to basically read books. But I'd felt the breath of reality on my neck, and as graduation had approached, I'd panicked. I applied to PhD programs.

Recently Sophie had been on a jag about political states of exception, apropos of the ongoing pro-democracy protests in Hong Kong, which I had failed to follow, and I wondered if exemption was essentially the other side of the coin.

States of exception were when a ruler suspended a law, often in the name of a national emergency. Guantánamo, created after 9/11, was a prime example. The current president, of course, had suspended environmental regulations to build the wall, had suspended human rights as he packed detention centers. Surely certain norms were being suspended in Hong Kong to deal with the protests, as they had been suspended in Baltimore during the uprising after Freddie Gray's murder.

States of exception created casualties, and the people who suffered were those who "didn't matter." The philosopher Agamben talked of "bare life"—that is, dehumanized biological beings who were considered expendable: the prisoners of Guantánamo, the migrants in the detention centers.

Campuses, I thought, were places where the rules were suspended. They were places of exemption for some, like the tenured professors in the academic novels, and states of exception for others, like the adjuncts, bare life caught under the sovereign wheels of capital.

I couldn't help but wonder what, if anything, this had to do with embodiment. You might think bare life—just a body!—experienced pure embodiment, but no, that made the experience seem simple and good. When you were expendable, you felt expendable. Your only recourse was making a state of exception for yourself by reaching an altered state—embodiment divorced from reality—or by disassociation, reality divorced from yourself.

I was over campus novels. I was having a harder and harder time empathizing with books about professors cast out of academia because of their own bad behavior. At least they had some time in the system, enough to publish books, pay down mortgages on nice houses.

The campus was not a contained world, tenured professors whining about exclusion were just in the privileged position of thinking it was. They never walked out of the story, into another story, and then back into the original story. They did not spew out, like adjuncts, onto other campuses, into other employment schemes. They were not moonlighting as caterers or writing product reviews on the side. We were half the teaching force; we defied a genre that couldn't exist without us.

I opened a fresh page in my notebook and wrote not about exemption or embodiment or even the campus novel but about my Infinity pillow: *Combine an infinity scarf with a cloud, and you might get a sense of how this sleek Möbius strip of down feels upon first inspection. Yet the Infinity Pillow Sleeper—Regular Fluff isn't adjustable, so it always felt either too loose or too tight wrapped around my neck, and I got the unsettling sense, during a fitful nap at my desk, that I was being asphyxiated by something that looked nice and seemed clever but was ultimately not designed for me.*

On the computer Gabe had lent me, a million tabs were open,

all from Craigslist, just purple peace sign after purple peace sign, mocking the chaotic reasons why people are on Craigslist in the first place. My chaotic reason was this series of texts from Brianna:

> I am really really sorry.
>
> I truly do not want to have to do this.
>
> But you have to move out.
>
> I can be really flexible about when you have to come get your stuff.

I called her immediately. She answered with a sheepish "Hello?" In the ensuing conversation, I gleaned she had admitted the roommate scheme to her parents, framing it as "entrepreneurship" while also implying that I was the source of the bedbug problem. She couldn't do anything about me having to move out. She was so, so sorry. Her parents were paying for the apartment; I had to go.

I had less than $400 in the bank, and the Craigslist options were dire. Even the miniature one-bedrooms were over $1,000 a month, plus utilities, plus first and last months' rent, plus a credit and income check. It became clear that I had to start looking in the Rooms & Shares section, but most of them required some kind of security deposit of at least $400. You couldn't get within an inch of Rosedale for less than $1,000, because the college students' parents had inflated the prices, some of them even buying houses to rent out to other college students. There was a nice room in a Victorian row house in Charles Village, but it was $950 a month. For $550, there was a carpeted basement room near Lewis with seventies wood paneling and no closet, in a house full of college students. Anything under $500 had a catch. NO DRAMA & NO DRUG ADDICTS!!!!!! said one. Another asked for headshots. Another highlighted the lack of background checks as a major draw. A "rent-free" situation featured a shared bedroom, no photos, and a request for "help around the house," the ideal opening for a true-crime podcast.

Renata, the lawyer-adjunct, squealed into the room, said something to me that I couldn't hear because my earplugs were in. "Good morning!" I replied, too loudly, I sensed, and also it was four p.m.

I closed the laptop. Something fell from my cardigan and plinked onto the floor. I picked up an object that was small and hard and white: a tooth. My tooth? I tongued the empty space in my mouth. My temporary had fallen out again. I put the fake tooth in my pocket, then made my way toward the coffee machine in the lounge on my two-inch heels, which I'd inexplicably grabbed instead of the shorter ones when I'd gone to Sophie's. Thanks to the bedbug-killing high-heat regime, many of my clothes had been destroyed or shrunk. The dress I was wearing was too tight. I'd had to safety-pin the V-neck higher up and kept pulling down the hem.

I returned to the adjunct office with coffee, checked my email, clicked on an ecard from my mom featuring an angel hovering like a drone over green pastures. Her typed message said: *Happy Birthday Samantha! Love, Mom.* The full name made me feel almost viscerally like a child, as if the elastic of a puff-sleeved dress were cutting off the circulation in my arms.

The card stayed in my mind, reminded me of the second and final Christmas I'd spent at Don's. The glowing white angel sitting atop the ten-foot artificial tree had hovered in the reflection of the seventy-inch flat-screen TV as if suspended in air.

I stared at that angel as my mom talked to me over the granite countertops of Don's kitchen island in the gut of suburbia where we were drinking low-calorie hot chocolate. She asked me point-blank, clasping my hands: "Are you a lesbian, Samantha?" She looked so serious and sad that, for the moment before I felt like I might throw up, I almost laughed. "We can get through this together," she said.

I wanted to say yes out of spite, and I wanted to say no because I didn't want to be a lesbian, actually. That look on her face, the pity and terror, conjured all I had understood about lesbians growing up, how ugly they were with their stocky, mannish walks and bad haircuts. I didn't believe it with my mind, but I believed it with my horrible heart.

I wanted to hurt my mother, literally, to slap her hard across the face.

How stupid of me to think she was worried about premarital sex. She seemed to know the truth and was suspicious of it: I had yet to sleep with anyone at all, and what else could that mean? She would've forgiven an abortion as long as it meant I had fucked a guy.

The angel behind her, porcelain and pretty, floated uncannily. Perhaps she'd glide on over and grant me the reprieve she'd granted Mary: immaculate conception, straightness sans sex. *Immaculate,* what a word. No mess.

Not that I cared if I lied to my mother, but it struck me that there was no answer I could give that wouldn't feel like a lie. "Come on, Ma," I said, throwing her hands off me. "No. Why would you ask me that?" She looked at me sadly. We were both disappointed that I didn't have better proof.

I x-ed off the Craigslist ads one by one, washed my coffee cup in the kitchen. Outside, darkness had fallen over the quad. A couple in long black coats wound their way through the parking lot in the misty night. More cars than usual, probably some faculty event. A gray cloud drifted, exposed the moon. I thought of Sylvia Plath, the O-*gape of complete despair.*

When I turned to leave the lounge, I noticed, at the center of the round table, a thick book, splayed open, as if it had fallen from the sky. It was an old course catalog, like a missive from a lost time now that the catalogs lived online.

I picked it up, thumbing through the thin pages, my fingers graying from the newsprint, as it all came rushing back to me, the thrill of walking down to the registrar each August to pick up the course catalog with its three-inch spine of possibility, the tingle I felt while flipping through it back in my dorm. I had chosen my major freshman year by putting a check mark next to all the classes I wanted to take, then tallying which major had the most checks. Go to college, everyone said. Choose a major you love, they said. Work hard. You will be rewarded. You can be anything, they said. You can be whatever you want.

In the arms of a giant course catalog, in the cradle of the humanities, in the air-conditioned dorm, in the endlessly stocked dining hall, in the all-access pass to the student health center, I believed it. I put my head down, didn't make many friends. It was lost on me that the crux of the whole thing was connections. How naive: What I liked about school was school.

I left the catalog on the table, packed up my duffel, took a back exit, and cut through the wet grass, trying to avoid people, balancing my weight on my toes so my heels wouldn't sink into the soil, pulling at the hem of my skirt, my bare, unshaved legs freezing.

On a bench in the grass, a man flicked at his lighter. A flash of Tom's face before it returned to the blurry darkness.

Had I imagined him? He smoked sometimes when he drank. The figure put his head in his hands, then lifted his head again, then brushed his hair back in an annoyed motion. I hadn't put my temporary in, and that gap in my teeth felt enormous, a doorway left wide open.

He hadn't noticed me. It was so cold that I began to feel as if my body weren't even mine, like I was a ghost, somehow subtracted from myself. In some stories, the ghost jangles things and everyone freaks the fuck out. In others, a misty hand touches an object and the hand mists right through.

"Hey," I called, tiptoeing in my heels, trying not to descend into the dirt.

He startled, looked around, trying to attach the disembodied voice to a body. "Hello?" he called back. Yes, it was definitely Tom. "Hello?" he said again, as if I were haunting him.

I was three feet in front of him before he finally saw me. "Are you cold?" he asked. His brown scarf was wrapped around his neck. "You must be freezing."

Fucked up, but I felt the old visceral craving to impress him, maybe with some profound observation about the moon, but all I could think of were other people's lines: *that lozenge of love . . . Wandering companionless . . . staring from her hood of bone.*

"I'm fine," I said.

"I'm sure you don't want to talk to me," he said, and took a drag. He was inebriated in that gloomy, self-hating way that, in my twenties, I had somehow failed to identify as sulking.

"Was there some event?" I asked.

"Yeah."

"Aliana here?"

"She's in D.C., mostly here weekends," he said, tapping his cigarette. His head lolled back. He was drunker than I'd thought. He squinted up at me. "You look ethereal in the moonlight."

I felt a question inside me, in my chest, like my heart was the question and it was coming up my throat. Fuck it, I thought. "Is that supposed to be me in the book?"

"It's not *not* supposed to be you."

"It's a composite," I said.

"It's fiction. Everything is true; nothing is true," he said. "Contrary to what you may believe, I'm not wandering around seducing students left and right. Yes, I am a sensual guy, but the thing with you—I wasn't in a good place, Sam. My marriage was falling apart; my mother was sick; my writing was not going well. I couldn't even place a fucking essay in a magazine. I wasn't getting one single thing I wanted."

Except your wife's best friend, I thought of saying. Instead I said, "Why did you lie in the article?"

"Why did you make a complaint about me?"

"I didn't. That whole thing was misconstrued."

"Yeah? So I left SHU for no reason?" he said. "You know, women have somehow managed to survive fucking their professors for generations."

"Funny, because the only thing I didn't survive was *not* fucking you," I said. "I don't understand why you would make that up."

"What, do you have a tape recorder?"

"What?"

"I seem to remember that you liked me."

"But you didn't really like me, did you? You wanted your ego stroked. You wanted to be flattered."

"Isn't that what everyone wants?" he said, annoyed. "Isn't that what you wanted?"

"Well, I didn't get it," I said. "You told me I wasn't good enough."

"For what?"

"To be a writer."

"I didn't say that."

"You *did* say that. You basically kicked me off the creative track."

"Come on," he said. "You don't need me to be a writer."

"I did though, since you were my adviser."

"If you want to be a writer, you should be a writer." These old lines. "You were talented. Talented ruin." Summoning Baldwin. "Everyone's talented in their own way." He took another drag. "Like Aliana. People love it. It's easy to swallow. Unfussy. It's *for the people,* you know?" Tom once told us that you should never reveal character through drunkenness, that it was a lazy narrative device. But in real life, it seemed the surefire way to discover the truth.

An inky cloud drifted over the moon. He tapped ash from his cigarette, stared moodily into the dark.

"They say that only suburban soccer moms read books anymore," he said.

"Your book seems to be doing just fine. You hit the moment right."

"I do get it, you know. Times are changing. Power structures. The patriarchy. But sensuality, passion, it's magnetic, it's inescapable, it's not an insult. To turn sexuality into an ever looming danger, it's cutting us off from this true enjoyment."

"Well, it's not a danger for you."

"Oh, come on," he said. "I never put you in any danger. That's ridiculous."

"I don't mean physical danger, I mean—I don't know." I gave up with a sigh. "Why would you tell everyone we slept together?"

"I never said your name." He brushed his hair out of his face again. I had him, right here, drunk and in some confessional mood, and yet I knew he was never going to give me any of the answers I wanted. He couldn't even seem to comprehend my questions.

My calves were cramping. I relented, let the heels sink into the ground. A relief to give in.

"I should go," I said.

"What did you think of my book?"

"I didn't read it," I said.

Chapter 10

ORAL REPORT

On Friday night, when Sophie got home from whatever job, I abandoned class prep to regale her with the funniest of the Craigslist ads as she rummaged for food. "Just stay with me," she said. "You can find another place over winter break when you have time to look."

"Really?" A fierce wind rushed outside in the dark, seeped in through the cracks. My skin was covered in goose bumps—Sophie had turned the heat way down to save money.

"Yeah," she said. "I mean, why not? I have the space."

"That would be amazing." A weight lifted off me. A shadowy branch shifted outside the window, and for a moment I thought it was an arm or a creature trying to get in, and I felt extra cozy and safe by mere contrast.

Toast leaped from the toaster, burned. "Shit," said Sophie. She tossed the piece between her fingers, dropped it on a plate, then picked it up again several seconds later to scrape the burned layer into the sink with a knife.

"Why don't I try to conjure up some dinner?" It was something my mother used to say.

The fridge revealed an arsenal of condiments lining the doors and a few moldy items on the shelves: a greenish block of cheddar cheese, squishy clementines, almond milk, a rotting pineapple, a half-drunk bottle of champagne, an untouched six-pack of Boh.

"We should figure out rent," she said.

For some reason, I had imagined that it would be a Snow White situation, like I'd take on a bunch of the chores and cooking to earn my keep, chip in generously on groceries. But of course I should contribute to rent. I felt stupid for not offering. "What do you think is fair?" I asked.

"Well, the place is two thousand a month total."

I tried not to look shocked, but still I said, "Oh, wow." That's why she worked so many jobs. Or was she not paying for it all herself? How had she even gotten approved for a lease? Her parents must have signed the promissory note, at the very least.

"I mean, that's pretty average for around here," she said. "Why don't we just do, like, seventy/thirty?"

Six hundred a month? For a couch in someone's living room? "Sure," I said as I opened the cabinets: a half jar of natural peanut butter that had begun to separate, opened bags of petrified snacks—wasabi almonds, high-protein power bites, dried mango. Expensive stuff, Whole Foods.

"Does that include utilities and everything?" I asked, concentrating on pulling out several almost expired staples: canned tuna, canned corn, canned cranberry sauce.

"I mean, I feel like we should split those at the end of the month."

"Cool." I shouldn't be mad, I thought. Splitting utilities was fair. I just didn't have any money, that's why I was annoyed. I should make the dinner nice, and I should be nice because Sophie was doing me a favor, because anything from Craigslist would be much, much worse.

While Sophie was in the bathroom, I put some tuna in a bowl, heated the corn, slid the gelatinous cylinder of cranberry sauce out of the can, then cut it into thick slices and fanned them on the plate, as my mother had done every Thanksgiving.

I opened drawers looking for a candle but came up empty, finding dish towels instead. I chose one in red and white plaid, spreading it out as a table runner, then set everything out, wiping the edges of the bowls with a paper towel so they looked nice. After my dad died, my mom gave up on cooking. We ate packaged foods—Hamburger Helper, Stouffer's, Stove Top—but, now that I thought about it, she always made the table nice: place mats, candles, triangle of napkin under each fork.

We sat down, and Sophie pulled the cranberry rounds toward her, shook the plate to watch them jiggle. "So weird," she said. "Does anyone actually eat the canned stuff?"

"I found it in *your* cabinet," I said. "It was almost expired."

"I don't think I bought this. Can it expire? Isn't this basically some kind of a kitschy joke food, like Spam?"

"I think it's pretty standard among the masses."

"It's not a class thing," she said. "Maybe it's regional." She pulled a round off with a fork, then spread the sauce on her toast like jelly.

"I have never witnessed anyone make whole cranberry sauce," I said. This wasn't even true. In graduate school, someone was always at the stove making cranberry sauce, smashing cloves with a pestle, zesting an orange, pouring in Grade A maple syrup from a glass jug.

"You basically pour frozen cranberries in a pot," she said. "It's not like you have to be Ottolenghi."

"What?"

"Oh my God, you should try some of his recipes," she said self-consciously, not sure if I knew who he was but understanding what it sounded like to have this guy as her go-to celebrity chef. "He's this *amazing* cook," she said, her enthusiasm a kind of backtracking. "So yummy. Like, Mediterranean, Middle Eastern stuff. Veg-centric." She took another bite of toast, tried to class-correct. "Hey, you want a Natty?"

Gabe and I rummaged through a sad mishmash of holiday decor in the blue plastic bins that said *Various, two for $1*: spiderweb table runners, battery-operated pinecone candles, embroidered Santa ornaments once painstakingly stitched. Gabe kept picking things up and making jokes, like putting a plastic tarantula in his hair and asking if it was a good look.

We'd barely seen each other recently, even at work, so the thrift shop run was double duty: a hangout and a way to replace some of my clothes destroyed in the bedbug purge.

I picked up a plastic Abominable Snowman Happy Meal toy whose arms twisted 360 degrees, clutching him so that his biceps rested over my fist. "Look," I said. "I'm the shitty feminist remake of King Kong. The twist is: *Now the woman is the monster.*"

" '*The Atlantic* praises *Queen Kong*'s radical feminism,' " said Gabe in the tone of a theatrical trailer, " 'while the right predicts that, in just a few years, the monster won't be just a woman but a lesbian, too, leading to the downfall of humanity.' "

We picked through more *various,* but when we couldn't think of anything else funny to say, we moved on to the books. "What did you think about that profile of Sternberg?" Gabe asked.

"Suspect," I said lightly. We hadn't talked about Tom since the day they'd seemed buddy-buddy in the lounge, and I was afraid of what I might reveal if we discussed the article. I pulled out *THINK BIG: Unleashing Your Potential for Excellence* by Ben Carson and showed it to Gabe, rolling my eyes.

Gabe glanced at the book. "Funny," he said. "I don't buy the way he was conveying the complainant."

"Me, either," I said, flipping through the book. "This is even better than I thought. Did you know 'THINK BIG' is an acronym?"

"No," said Gabe. "Do a lot of people switch tracks at SHU?"

My jaw tightened. "I think it's more common than at other universities because of how the Creative Writing Department is housed within the larger Lit Department," I said, not looking up from the book. "Okay, so H is for *hope*. Guess what the N is for?"

"Negation," he said. He knew, didn't he? He knew I was the student in the profile? No, he *suspected,* that was different.

"Nope, it's for *nice*."

"That's not even the same part of speech."

"The B is for *books*."

"Personally speaking, *hope, nice, books* haven't gotten me very far," said Gabe. He dropped the line of questioning but sounded disappointed.

I started reading aloud from the book theatrically, the Abominable Snowman still clutched in my hand as Gabe kept browsing. I was midsentence when I caught sight of a woman catching sight of me: Smart but Rushed, my student from Lewis who was always late. Her back straightened and her eyes darted toward a boy, four-ish, who was frantically pressing a button on a barnyard toy to no effect. Now I understood why everything she handed in sounded like a first draft.

"Hi," I said brightly, walking toward her. I flicked my tongue to my temp, checking that it was in place.

"Hi," she answered just as brightly. She was holding a stack of kids' clothes. To the boy, she said firmly, "Come here, please." He looked at the toy, his mother, the toy again, then decided he should listen.

"This is my friend Gabe," I said, nodding.

"This is one of Mommy's professors," she told her son. "Say hi."

"Hi," he said to the floor.

"Hi," I said.

He peeked up. "Mom's going to college," he offered. He pointed at the Abominable Snowman in my fist. "I didn't even see that toy."

"It was with the holiday stuff."

"I want that," he said.

"That isn't polite," said my student. "He has tons of toys at home," she said to me. "You have kids?"

"I don't."

She smiled down at hers, who eyed the toy that I did not want to give him.

I had no idea what to say to her outside the paradigm of the classroom. What I came up with was "Got to wash the clothes in here on hot. I know someone who got bedbugs from a thrift store."

"Oh, seriously?" she said.

"Had to move out of their apartment."

"Oh, wow. Yeah, we'll definitely wash these. That's horrible."

For a moment I wondered what we were waiting for, and then I realized it was me. She was being deferential, waiting to be excused. What power I had, to say random, boring things while she pretended I was interesting.

"I should let you go," I said.

I abandoned the theatrical reading of Ben Carson, and Gabe and I moved on to the clothes at the back, trying to seem more professorial until the student left.

"Kids are amazing," said Gabe as I struggled to pull shirts from the overstuffed racks. "They really go for it, you know?"

"I should've given him the Abominable Snowman."

"Hey, you found it first."

"Remember when we used to get toys in cereal boxes? Plastic dinosaurs, color-changing spoons?"

"Weird to think those were the quaint days of capitalism."

"I loved that stuff," I said. "Sometimes my dad would take me to McDonald's and get the cashiers to give me free toys. We didn't even buy a meal."

The memory appeared as I said it, my father convincing the cashier to give us free toys even though we were just buying a soda, how the cashier would plunge a hand into the great sea of plastic and toss the toys on the counter with the magnanimity of a king throwing coins to a crowd. I remembered the almost violent joy I felt picking through, like my heart was a bird flapping its wings so hard that it could burst from my chest, break through to some even higher, uncontainable level of happiness. I got all of the *Lion King* toys in one go: the wild-eyed hyena, the crouching yellow Simba that, if you pulled it back, would shoot across the floor. Many years later, as she wandered through the thrift store, I thought, Sam was to remember that distant afternoon when her father took her to discover McDonald's toys.

"When I have kids," said Gabe, "that's exactly the kind of thing I'm going to do."

The certainty of his *when*, the offhandedness of the comment, surprised me. Sophie was always talking about the unpaid labor of motherhood, from the pregnancy to the breastfeeding to the endless household chores, about all the couples she knew who couldn't live up to their own feminist ideals, the wife staying home because childcare was too expensive and nothing else made financial sense. Creating a nuclear family, Sophie said, was as good as giving up, was absolute resignation to neoliberalism.

I agreed; I agree. Even the word *motherhood* made me recoil. But I didn't tell her the disgusting truth: I loved babies. I loved their chunky arms and their unbridled laughter and their ridiculous massive eyes. My primal pull toward those cute little time sucks, those adorable money pits, those anti-feminist nightmares, felt like a betrayal, to myself most of all. And the nuclear family? Even that was alluring, since mine had basically disintegrated. Sophie's parents were still together, writing movies and going to matinees.

Why waste my time thinking about babies? I was in my mid-thirties and sleeping on a couch. Sometimes I woke up shivering, sunk between the cushions, my hip bone jammed against the wooden frame.

I collected basics, plus an oversize pink blazer that reminded me of Sophie, and tried everything on. Gabe slipped a sequined dress over the fitting-room door as a joke. "What do you think?" he said. It had an over-the-top eighties vibe, with colorful sequined stripes extending into an extravagantly zigzagging hem.

I loved it, actually. It fit me really well. We even found a pair of three-inch pink heels to match, and I clicked back and forth across the linoleum floor with a hippy swagger, laughing, though on the lookout for students.

With gentle insistence, Gabe bought me the dress and heels. Then we went to Five Guys, which made me think of Obama's lauded lunch excursion to get a cheeseburger, back when we were all so filled with H for *hope*.

When it was time to pay, the cashier asked, "Together?" and my own hesitation, however brief, bothered me.

"Together, yes," Gabe said, handing his card over.

Soon I was sipping the last inch of my milkshake as we idled outside of Sophie's.

"This was really fun," said Gabe.

"Yeah, it was."

"The campout was fun. After the reading was fun." He had big expectant eyes. He wanted to be invited up. I eyed Sophie's car, parked along the curb.

"Yeah," I said. "Thanks for coming with me today."

"My pleasure." He leaned over and kissed me on the mouth. I felt robotic. Typically I would respond to such a gesture by touching the other person's body or head in some way, but I was sitting on one hand, warming it between the heated seat and my butt, while the other was holding my milkshake. How much feeling was it possible to convey with the fishlike parting and reparting of lips?

He drew away. "I just like spending time with you," he said, as if to defend himself.

"Agreed. I mean, I also like it with you."

He sank back in his seat. "How'd you manage to get into this place so quickly?"

"It's actually a friend's place," I said, extracting my hand to smooth my skirt. "Another lecturer at Lewis. Just temporary."

"Oh, I didn't realize that. Cool. Your friend Sophie?"

"Right, yes. Good memory. She's just letting me stay while I straighten things out."

I told him I should go, waved from the mailbox as he drove away, then headed inside, already regretting that I hadn't made a move. I could've gone down on him in the front seat. Nobody was ever on that street. Sophie never hung around the windows, as if she would even care. The neighbors had probably already seen me naked in the backyard. Why was it that the farther I got away from someone, the more the idea of fucking them turned me on?

When the TV used to buzz with static, we called it snow, we called it noise, like the cover of a composition book, like a Magic Eye in black and white, the pattern crawled. The snow fell outside Sophie's front window, and I was mesmerized.

The potholes and the brown grass and the junk in people's yards were covered in fresh, smooth white curves. Even the broken mailboxes seemed charming with their Seussical lilting, their hats of snow.

It was impossible not to think of Joyce's "The Dead": *His soul swooned slowly as he heard the snow falling faintly through the universe and faintly falling, like the descent of their last end, upon all the living and dead.*

I felt as close to at peace as I had all semester. The blizzard was perfectly timed—right before Thanksgiving break but not during it, so we'd score almost an entire week off.

I was wrapped in a fleece blanket, trying to catch up on grading. I had a stack of over 150 pages to mark, which should've been returned weeks ago. I had been stuck for an hour on a deep edit of Subway Sandwich's four-page paper. He had overcorrected on punctuation, so now he was using it everywhere, and I felt as disoriented as I sometimes did while reading Emily Dickinson, with all her wild dashes and capitalizations (*As Freezing persons, recollect the Snow— / First—Chill—then Stupor—then the letting go—*). We had just covered Dickinson in American Lit I, as we moved toward the pinnacle of Whitman.

I hoped Sophie would be home soon. I couldn't keep track of her. She had recently started working for this app where she did tasks for people, helping them put together IKEA furniture or walking their dogs (or, in one case, a potbellied pig named Cheerio). She'd even been hired as a "guest" on a "podcast" recorded in a walk-in closet stuffed full of pillows, and for the entire hour-and-a-half recording, she thought it might be a setup for her murder.

Some days we merely caught glimpses of each other as she breezed in and out, changing between work ensembles: her black-and-white catering gear; the matching blazer-and-pants set in which she taught. I heard her footfalls from my couch/bed, saw the light from the kitchen brightening behind my eyelids as she made herself a late dinner. One night—just one—she didn't come home at all.

I imagined Thanksgiving together, just the two of us. A turkey in the oven, sweet potato casserole, some compromise of cranberry sauces which we could laugh about. On the TV, the soothing buzz of the Macy's Thanksgiving Day Parade, band after band, brand after brand.

I awoke at midnight from a dream in which I was trying to read *Song of Myself* aloud to my class, but we were outside, and I was blinded by the sun reflecting off the bright white snow. In the dream, I panicked, kept saying the same three lines over and over: *Do I contradict myself? / Very well then I contradict myself, / (I am large, I contain multitudes.)*

Sophie was stomping her boots as quietly as she could on the doormat. "You don't have to be quiet," I called to her.

"What?"

"I'm awake," I said, trying to sound awake.

"Driving out there is a nightmare."

She peeked in the doorway, backlit. Still, I saw her shining face, her hair wet with melted snow. She left to eat and didn't reappear.

I found her in bed watching *The Kardashians* on her laptop. Take-out containers were strewn on the floor. Her hair was up in a bun, and she wore an oversize T-shirt that would've looked awful and shapeless on me but on Sophie looked great. The devil-may-care casualness that only thin girls could pull off.

"I'm freezing," I said.

"Come in here," she said. "I'm under like fifteen covers."

I crawled into bed next to her, feeling strange, still dazed from sleep, in a trance of snow.

I had never watched an episode of *The Kardashians,* and yet I knew the name of every single woman on the screen. They looked like cartoons of themselves, eating massive bowls of salad in a pristine white kitchen. They were trying to get the brother to start some sort of sock business, but he couldn't get up the gumption to do it, even though other people would do all the work and his last name would sell the socks. I hated the brother, who seemed lazy and kind of high, who was not even trying to be hot or interesting.

"Do you like this show?" I asked.

"It's trash," she said, but she didn't turn it off.

"You know that guy we saw in the window of that tapas place?"

"The professor guy?"

"He wrote a book about a professor who sleeps with his student."

"Wait, is it about you?" she said, looking up from the show.

"I don't know. Maybe, ostensibly."

"You slept with him?"

"No."

"Huh," she said, disappointed. "So not about you."

"He tried to sleep with me."

"You said no?"

"Yeah."

"Good for you." Her attention was back on the show. "You give a guy like that an inch, he tries to take a mile."

I was disappointed. Sophie, so full of outrage, couldn't muster a little on my behalf? But was it really fair to expect empathy when I hadn't given her any information? If I told Sophie the whole story, I feared she would either minimize it or politicize it, and either way I would wind up feeling like I'd handled the whole thing wrong.

I got bored of the show. I pictured myself in the backyard, naked among the leaves, following Sophie's commands. I pictured her in my bedroom, crawling off me after she had come, laughing. Shame coursed through me. But why? Because she'd laughed? Was it all a joke to her? Wasn't I the one who thought that being with women was a farce, a playhouse? But if we were going to play house, shouldn't we do it, shouldn't we play?

I pushed the tops of my cold, stockinged toes on her leg.

"Holy shit, your feet are freezing," she said, but she didn't move away.

Now I pressed the undersides of my cold toes against her leg.

She squealed and threw me a cute smile. "Are you trying to torture me?"

"A little."

The light from the laptop glowed on her face. I flexed my toes so the tops were against her skin again.

"Fuck," she said with a squeal. "At least take your stockings off; they're scratchy."

I dipped under the covers, trying to pull the stockings off my feet without my toenails ripping them.

"Do you always take your stockings off like that?"

"I don't know," I said from under the covers.

"Are you drunk?"

"No," I said, surfacing. "Do I seem drunk?"

"Somewhat."

"Hm."

I was kissing her. Her lips were dry. I was wet. Her mouth tasted like garlic and cumin. She moved the laptop to her nightstand but didn't turn off the show.

I wanted to touch her breasts, to take each one in a hand and feel the soft weight, the gentle curve, but it seemed too intimate.

Her face would be right there, her hazel eyes, and what if she laughed at me?

Instead I went under. I was overwhelmed by first the smell, then the taste. What was I supposed to do down here? I hardened my muscle of tongue. The alphabet? I couldn't remember how to go down on a woman.

Maybe I *was* straight? Wasn't oral sex supposed to be some kind of litmus test? But wasn't there a big joke about how straight men were afraid to eat pussy? Like eating pussy made them seem gay somehow? And hadn't I felt exactly the same about men's junk until I acclimated?

Instinct failed to take over. I was too self-conscious, too sober, too sick, suddenly, over what felt like a betrayal of Gabe, though we had never defined or even talked about the relationship. I started worrying that my temporary tooth would fall out.

A memory flashed in my mind as I worked on the project at hand. Jonas had returned to Baltimore after a summer in Barcelona spent working out and going to the beach. By then we were sleeping together—often, occasionally, almost randomly, always drunk. He was excited to show me something. "Look," he said. "There." He'd pulled down his pants a little and was pointing to a spot between his groin and thigh.

"What?"

"That cut," he said. It was a divot, a trough between muscles. The sight alarmed me. It made him look manufactured, like a doll where you could just pop out the leg.

"Ah," I said. "Nice. A new feature."

"Come on," he said, taking my hand so I could feel it.

"It's like a crevice."

"A crevice? It's a V-cut. From working out."

"Cool," I said.

"Every last girl I have ever been with loves that *crevice*," he said, irritated. *Every last girl.* Except for me.

That night, as usual, I'd gone down on Jonas, an almost compulsory prelude to sex, or at the very least what you did when you didn't know what else to do, when you were mimicking the imagined actions of *every last girl.* I can't say I ever really learned to like the dick of it. Instead I learned to like being wanted, found a kind of perverse pleasure in the sense of my own subjugation.

Here with Sophie, without the fucked-up gender dynamics, I didn't know what to like.

From under the covers, I heard my phone *ding,* then *ding* again. *Ding-ding-ding.*

Sophie opened a crack in the covers, looked down at me. "If you're not into it, just don't do it."

"I'm not *not* into it."

"So you're not a lesbian. It's fine."

My face got hot. "But I'm not *not*—"

"If you don't like pussy, it's a pretty good sign."

I surfaced. She put her laptop back on her lap and started watching the show again. She seemed less hurt than vaguely—but not catastrophically—annoyed, like why had I disrupted her show for this failed attempt at getting her off?

I was annoyed, too. What right did she have to tell me what I was or wasn't? Maybe she thought I was using her to test my sexuality? (Was I?) But hadn't she instigated it the first time around? There was nothing romantic about the relationship between Sophie and me. We were friends, that was all; even when I had my face between her legs, it just seemed like I was engaging in a hobby that I wasn't good at. Maybe I was incapable of being romantic and therefore incapable of bringing out anyone's romantic side. Maybe fucking me was like playing catch with a wall—you could do it if you were bored, but there wasn't a lot to work with.

The romantic love portrayed in classic novels had always disappointed me. It seemed unearned, unexplained, leading me to believe it was so universally understandable that no one felt you had to describe anything other than its effects.

I understood hunger, thirst, even sexual desire—they were essentially cravings born of over- or understimulation. I understood attraction, even, in a broad sense, that you were pulled to some people over others. I understood platonic and familial love, how a bond could form over time. But romantic love? If I didn't know any better, I would think it was an authorial invention to get out of explaining why a relationship between two people—one of whom was often an asshole—was strong enough to be their downfall.

I pretended not to be embarrassed, to be chill. I checked my phone.

Gabe: My flight home was canceled. Any Thanksgiving plans?

> Sounds like some profs from Rosedale are doing a kind of impromptu tday
>
> (because so many people's plans are messed up)
>
> Interested in coming with?

"Gabe is asking me about my Thanksgiving plans," I said to Sophie.

"Who? The academic?"

"Aren't we all?" I said. "I guess his flight home was canceled."

"So, what, he wants to do Thanksgiving with you?"

"Apparently some of the profs at Rosedale are doing a potluck."

"You gonna go?"

"I'm not sure it's my milieu."

"You do work at Rosedale."

"I'm not exactly in the *in* crowd," I said. "I wasn't directly invited. Like, I don't know what your plans are, but I was thinking you and I could stay home and do Thanksgiving here."

"Just do your thing," she said. "I'm not really a big Thanksgiving person. American nostalgia, football, traumatic brain injuries, the nuclear family, the genocide."

"Right," I said. "But in terms of a nice dinner, a break from work?"

"I think it's going to be a really good day with tasks on the app, to be honest."

"In the snow? On Thanksgiving?"

"Shoveling driveways? Putting chains on tires? Running out for last-minute dinner items? Plus, people are more generous tippers on holidays," she said. "Out of guilt."

"That makes sense."

"Do your thing with the bourgeoise. It'll be interesting, at least. Plus, there'll probably be like a hundred different pies."

Chapter 11

SOMEONE SPECIFIC

The vents blew concentrated blasts of warm air in my face as my thighs began to unfreeze on Gabe's heated seat. Outside, dirty snow, plow-compacted to ice, lined the slushy roads like the walls of a maze. Cars crept along the streets so slowly that the traffic lights seemed moot, artifacts from another time or merely an aesthetic, a wash of yellow, red, green against the blue-gray snow.

On my lap sat a cold pumpkin pie, an orange-brown circle with a crack down the middle, like the surface of some sludgy moon. Peeking from beneath the finger-crimped pie crust, the metallic pleats of a single-use aluminum pan.

Gabe's contributions sat in the backseat: a six-pack of amber ale and a bottle of red with a silky orange ribbon tied around the neck. I smiled at the thought of him tying it on himself, but it was probably something they'd done at the store.

Between caffeine-fueled grading sessions, I'd slid my way on foot to the closest grocery store, an overpriced organic market where the ingredients for the pie cost more than twenty dollars, mostly because of the exorbitant prices of ground ginger and cloves. One of the problems with moving so much is that you keep losing your investment in spices.

"Hmmmm," Sophie had said, surveying the pie that morning on her way to fill a travel mug with coffee. She already had a task, which was to pick up a flat-screen TV in Glen Burnie, then install it at a house in Timonium, preferably before some big football game. "Are you bringing that?"

"Yes . . . ?"

"Oh, okay," she answered.

Now I stared at the pie, and it stared back, unblinking. I felt mad at it, like it was a third wheel who'd invited itself.

"Hey, you okay?" asked Gabe, glancing over at me as we crept along.

"Yeah," I said.

"All your teeth in good shape?"

I laughed, trying not to sound half-hearted.

"You seem quiet," he ventured.

"Just thawing out."

I was nervous about the event, where I didn't belong, where Tom and Aliana might be. In grad school, Tom often stopped by our communal Friendsgivings, a postscript to his own family meal with—whom? Was it his family or Lydia's who lived in the DMV?

Grad school Thanksgivings were legendary, sprawling potlucks that started in the afternoon and extended late into the night, food fading into games into food again into dancing into lying on the floor drunk, just feeling the music. Clee always hosted at her house in Charles Village, dragging card tables up from her basement, covering them in the annual array of mismatched tablecloths, including a seventies *Star Wars* sheet someone had bought at the Salvation Army. Another tradition: Each year, a different person was tasked with creating a centerpiece, the sillier the better—a turkey made of gourds, state-fair stuffed animals spilling out of a cornucopia, a basket of crunchy brown fall leaves, a cake stand piled with pom-poms. Had these traditions lived on? Was there a group of grad students in a row house, at this very moment and not far away, spreading a *Star Wars* sheet over a card table?

Was it only one Thanksgiving or every Thanksgiving that I was lying on Clee's front porch trying to cool off, stuffed and drunk, surrounded by the diffuse light of a Baltimore night, curled in the nook of Isaac's arm, listening to Arcade Fire songs about snail mail and suburban sprawl? Was it only one Thanksgiving or every Thanksgiving that Jonas and I fucked for five minutes on a dusty mattress in the cold basement, then came upstairs five minutes apart, trying to be discreet? Was it only one Thanksgiving or every Thanksgiving that someone recited "Animals" by Frank O'Hara before dinner, pre-nostalgia in lieu of a prayer? *Have you forgotten what we were like then / when we were still first rate . . .*

We cheered when our professors made cameos, plying them with whiskey and pie, trying to convince them to stay longer, performing our youthfulness while also trying to prove we were really adults, drunkenly hoping to say something smart about life or literature or whatever.

Tom always dropped by late and alone. That first Thanksgiving, he arrived in the middle of a game of Ham Chunk, which other people call Celebrity. Classically you wrote the names of celebrities on slips of paper, but we wrote all kinds of things—movies, books, phrases, the names of people we knew. Each round, you pulled slips from the same pool of words, and your team had to guess them as quickly as possible. The first round, the words or phrases were guessed based on verbal clues; the second round the words were acted out; and the third round you had only a single word.

Clee gave the clue: "A professor who flirts with all the students," and several people shouted, correctly, "Tom!" and we all laughed, including Tom, who threw his arms up, like *Who, me?* In the shuffle of moving on to the next player, I smiled at Tom from across the table. We locked gazes, then let them drift apart, the way spies trade suitcases at a busy airport, then walk off casually in opposite directions.

When I turned, Isaac was looking at me, eyebrows raised. He shook his head, ever so slightly, not a judgment but a warning.

Dr. Brighton's driveway had been plowed and salted, the snow shaken from the hedges, the flagstone path shoveled, the mailbox freed from the wrath of the plow so the mail truck could pull in, and even the top of the mailbox had been wiped of its little pyramid of snow. The yard was untromped. It looked like the set of a romcom in which my boyfriend would meet my sweetly married or comically divorced parents for the first time.

In Dr. Brighton's mudroom, the throng of plants had been replaced with a throng of outerwear: Patagonia puffers, North Face parkas, navy peacoats, cashmere scarfs. My own dingy puffer was the color of a lightly roasted marshmallow that had fallen in the dirt. I tried to stuff it behind the other coats, the three-dollar hot-pink CVS mittens pushed deep in the pockets. There was no legion of shoes at the door, as with Friendsgivings of yore. Through the glass I saw shiny black and brown leather loafers and booties treading over hardwood floors and white carpet. I used to think removing shoes at the door was a sign of class: We keep this house clean, like respectable people! But, of course, you could reach a level of wealth at which someone else dealt with it later.

Dr. Brighton appeared, radiating a buzzed hostess's high-energy hum. "Gabe!" she said, as if they were great friends. She held out her hand to me. "Do I know you from something?"

"She teaches in the Literature Department," said Gabe.

"Where?"

"Rosedale," I said.

"Which department?"

"Literature," Gabe said.

"Part-time lecturer," I said. "I plant-sat."

"Oh, Sam, yes."

"She's my plus-one," said Gabe.

"Ah, okay," said Dr. Brighton.

"Wine and beer," said Gabe, holding up each hand in turn.

"Oh, how sweet." She took the bottle and the beer. "So thoughtful. Thank you."

"And a homemade pie," I said.

I sensed her smile was also a cringe, but she said, "Wonderful, we can put that straight in the fridge. Come in, come in."

Sides from Whole Foods were stacked in the fridge, along with four boxes of pie from a local shop, where I knew single slices sold for seven dollars. I balanced my pumpkin offering on top, fiddling with the budget-brand cling wrap, which kept clinging to my hands.

In the living room, people stood in small circles, chatting while Norah Jones sang in the background. It was all blazers and button-downs, structured dresses and tortoiseshell glasses. I knew hardly anyone because I wasn't invited to department meetings. A few kids flit around, gel-haired boys, a girl in a velvet dress. The deep green plants, the soil perfectly moist, brightened the white room, which had appeared so stark through the window when I was trapped outside. Appetizers were distributed throughout: crostini, crudités, canapés. During my freshman year of college, I had publicly called them *ca-NAPS*.

Tom and Aliana stood in a group at the edge of the room, Tom in a sky-blue button-down and black slacks, his shaggy bangs trimmed. Aliana wore heels, pearl earrings, and a structured, sleeveless sheath dress in rusty orange. Her long hair was loose and parted in the middle. Very Girl Boss, very professional chic. The two seemed to be telling a story in tandem, handing it off to each other or talking over each other, laughing theatrically, some public performance of coupleness. This was Tom's usual, but Aliana typically commanded a room more subtly, without so much gesticulation.

She spotted me but merely acknowledged my presence with an empty glance before looking away, no nudge to Tom, no squawk of warning that an intruder had arrived, like maybe the intruder was no longer a threat now that the book and the article and the relationship had gone public, had been received well.

They exuded a power-couple aesthetic reminiscent of Tom and Lydia's. Like Lydia, Aliana was attractive, poised, smart, and successful. I sensed that Tom liked to have someone he could show off while also feeling like he was the virtuous one who hadn't sold out. Tom's literary success contrasted nicely with Aliana's pop-lit success and Lydia's corporate success. He wanted a strong, confident woman for his public-facing partner. The fawning he could get elsewhere.

I roamed the party with Gabe, appetizers, and an IPA until Dr. Brighton tapped her fork on a wineglass, apologized for the fact of a buffet, toasted to the semester being almost over, toasted to the success of Tom's book, toasted to us being able to gather impromptu. Diana Krall started singing a cover of "A Case of You." If anyone wanted me, I wouldn't be at the bar, I'd be in an adjunct office somewhere, I couldn't even tell you which one. I was definitely buzzed. My attempt to pile my plate modestly was a wash.

I eyed Aliana's plate: a gathering of green beans, a few shreds of turkey, a taste of chunky cranberry sauce, a plop of mashed sweet potato, which she was dipping into and then sliding the fork into her mouth, less of a bite than a suck. I was close enough to see a green vein pulsing in her forehead. It occurred to me that her unusual gregariousness might just be anxiety. Her facial aesthetic tended to porcelain doll, unyielding yet delicate, and the vein made it look like she was starting to crack. Once, in grad school, two weeks before her dissertation was due while she was also working on a deadline for a *Rolling Stone* piece (she knew someone at the magazine), this very same vein had begun to pop.

A couple I didn't know appeared in the room, late arrivals. The man smiled at Gabe, whose hand was already drawn. They took each other in with a kind of horizontal high five that ended in a handshake. The guy held out a hand to me, chummy. "Rick," he said.

"Sam."

He turned back to Gabe. "What the hell are you doing here?"

I could already tell he was one of those overconfident, bro-y types who would explain first-aid techniques to the nurses from his deathbed. The woman he'd come with had been absorbed by another group. Gabe and Rick knew each other from grad school. Rick had a postdoc in Dallas, following postdocs in Oslo and Hamburg. He'd arrived in Baltimore right before the storm.

Gabe pointed at me. "We're both at Rosedale."

"Dude, cool," Rick said. "Permanent thing?"

"Visiting," said Gabe.

"Lecturing," I said.

"What do you teach?" he asked me.

"Literature."

"Right, but like what?"

"Various," I said. "Modern American, mostly."

"Do you know Ravi?" Rick asked. "He used to teach at Rosedale."

"Didn't he get a permanent position at VCU a while back?" asked Gabe.

"No, you're thinking of Rami. Ravi's at CVS now," said Rick with a grimace.

"Wait, what's that?" I asked.

"The drugstore," said Rick. We all looked at each other, aware of our possible futures, then dropped it.

"Is Marissa still at VCU?" said Gabe.

"She moved to Hollins," said Rick.

"You know there's a job open there," said Gabe.

"They already scheduled on-campus interviews," said Rick.

"Shit, when did that happen?" asked Gabe. I'd applied to that job, too.

"I don't know, it's on the Wiki," said Rick with a shrug. I'd stopped checking the Wiki. The updates ranged from desperate to depressing: *Is this a real job?????? . . . Please, has anyone heard anything from this one? . . . Heard they canceled this search.* All I ever seemed to learn was that more and more jobs I'd applied to either weren't jobs or had already scheduled first-round interviews, which meant I wasn't even in the running.

They volleyed names back and forth, and I felt Gabe's tonal shift, the same shift I had witnessed in the lounge with Tom, his usual warmth yielding to a dash of masculine pretension. It created a space between us, like I was an outsider.

I took a bite of turkey and felt the hard, jagged fact of my temporary crown on my tongue. Pretending to wipe my face, I spat the tooth into my napkin as nonchalantly as possible.

One of the roaming kids appeared and began marching two toy dinosaurs up Rick's leg, to Rick's total lack of amusement.

"Are you good with kids?" he asked me.

"Are you?" I said.

Rick gave me a half eye roll. "Chill. I didn't mean because you're a woman." He looked down at the kid. "I don't think those dinos are even from the same epoch," he said, trying to logic-bro his way out of this.

"If *Jurassic Park* mixed epochs," said Gabe to the kid, but as repartee with Rick, "you can, too."

The kid shrugged but seemed offended, and the dinos proceeded to fight viciously on Rick's shoe before the kid growled and sulked off.

Rick glanced around the room, lowered his voice. "Can you believe Tom Sternberg moved to Rosedale? Big loss for SHU, right before his big book came out."

I tongued the empty hole where my crown had been.

"Certainly the book was a liability," said Gabe.

"I feel bad for the guy," said Rick, whispering now. "Honestly, what an idiot. Doesn't matter how obsessed a student is with you, you should keep your dick in your pants, or at least don't fucking *announce it*."

"In a national newspaper, no less."

"Why do you feel bad for him?" I said. "His book's doing well. He's got a permanent position."

"Probably an unpopular opinion, but don't you think SHU should grow a backbone?" said Rick. "I mean, do we really think he left voluntarily? What about academic freedom? I mean, okay, *freedom* is a loaded word co-opted by the right, but I think it's ultimately a leftist impulse. I'm all for taking down sexual predators, but the pendulum swings too far and you get, well, casualties. Are you really going to stifle literature? Especially from a guy who is basically apologizing?" Rick turned to me. "What year did you say you went to SHU? You must have known the girl."

"Could be anyone," I said.

"It had to have been around the same time you were there," said Rick. "Do you know anyone who switched tracks?"

"I don't think it's any of our business who it's supposed to be," I said too harshly. Gabe looked at me, I looked at the sweet potatoes on my plate. One second ago, so appetizing, now radioactive sludge.

"Oh, come on, don't moral-high-ground me," said Rick. "I mean, if she's a stalker like they say, shouldn't we all be wary? Maybe she needs help."

Gabe picked up his beer from the edge of the planter, took a self-conscious sip.

"Have you considered that rumors aren't always the best source of information?" I said.

"Gossip is a legitimate method of information dispersal, traditionally used by the oppressed—by women, in fact," said Rick, "to warn each other."

"Don't moral-high-ground me, either," I said.

Gabe ineptly changed the topic. "Oh, you know, I was wondering, did you guys apply to the Montevallo position?"

"They already scheduled first-round interviews," said Rick. "Oh, and Portland's a spousal hire, and Naylor is an internal hire, but they're making a big show of going through all the motions." Universities had to publicly post jobs and interview external candidates, even if they already knew whom they were hiring.

"They make us do all this fucking work, then it's not even really an open position?" said Gabe. I had never seen him annoyed like this. "Are there ever any actual jobs?"

"What about Carpenter's position?" said Rick. "I mean, it's not gonna be tenure-track, but it's still a job."

"Carpenter's retiring?" I said.

"You didn't know?" said Gabe. "They sent it to the department listserv."

"I'm not on the listserv," I said. "You applied?"

Sheepishly Gabe said, "I'm applying for everything that comes up."

"You can't go in there," said the girl in a wine-colored velvet dress, sixish, as I approached the downstairs bathroom. Food was crusted on her upper lip. She rubbed her hand across her chest to feel the soft velvet, leaving a pale track going in the wrong direction.

"My mom's in there." She stared at me without smiling. "I *hate* potatoes."

Yeah, fuck potatoes, and fuck everything else, I wanted to say. Instead I said, "They're okay." I was holding my phone in one hand and my crumpled napkin in the other, trying not to crush the temporary crown with my fist.

"I *hate* them," she said again.

That was what I liked best about kids, their complete lack of social bullshit. If her not-boyfriend had not told her about applying to her not-job, she would have thrown a temper tantrum instead of lamely excusing herself to go to the bathroom.

How had I missed the listing? What a stupid question. There were a million websites to check, high season was over, I had let down my guard. But how had Gabe not told me?

Nearby, two boys played with plastic dinosaurs.

"Do you like dinosaurs?" I asked the girl.

"They're okay."

"You don't want to play with them?"

"I know I can play with boy stuff." She shrugged. "But sometimes I just don't want to."

One boy's dino had the other boy's dino by the neck, and the kid with the attacked dino was now convulsing on the floor, as if he were that dino and he was about to die, which was something I felt deeply, this craving to overdramatize pain.

"You should probably go upstairs," said the girl. "My mom has IBS."

My throat expanded with relief as I ascended to the second floor. I felt like a middle schooler with a hall pass, didn't care that permission had been given by a child.

The bathroom was clean and spacious, double sinks and a rainfall shower with two showerheads and a shampoo brand I'd never seen—i.e., salon stuff, not CVS. I put my phone on the counter along with my balled-up napkin, the crown inside, a dumpling from hell.

I peed, then washed my hands with a smooth lavender bar soap. This soap spent its days cradled in a pristine white dish. At Sophie's, we used Dial, set it in the wet mucus of itself on the back edge of the sink. Would a clean soap dish and a beautiful bar of lightly scented soap make my life better? The chicken or the egg. I was reminded of the essentially conservative assertion that making your bed could change your life. It presupposed some things, like that you weren't sleeping on a couch.

While perched on the toilet lid, I called my mom, the obligatory holiday contact. "Samantha," she said. "So good to hear from you! Happy Thanksgiving!" Then, away from the phone, "It's Samantha, everybody, say *Happy Thanksgiving.*" "Happy Thanksgiving," said some voices, not in unison. "We wish you could be here!" said my mom, as if saying it along with other people. Then, not to me, "No, no, set the timer for ten more minutes, it's not done."

"I can let you go if you're busy," I said.

"No, no. Are you having a good Thanksgiving?" I could hear her hurrying off somewhere, the click of a door.

"I am. We weren't sure if we could even do it." This was a passive-aggressive attempt to remind her we'd had a blizzard. I knew she wouldn't ask me to define *we.*

"Of course we'd rather you were here," she said.

"Because of the big snowstorm."

"Oh, right," she said. "The roads are still a mess?"

"They're kind of okay now. I mean, we're creeping along."

"What address should I use for your Christmas card? Or I can just send you a picture."

"Sure."

We talked aimlessly for a few more minutes, then said our goodbyes until our Christmas call. It softened me to her, that she'd retreated to the bathroom or wherever to have this conversation. She may have become a homophobic right-winger, but she was still my mother.

My phone dinged. A picture of the Christmas card held between my mom's fingers, the nails polished a brilliant red. Above a big family photo, it said *Faith, Love, Joy* in variegated gold cursive. Faith in what? I wondered. Loving whom? Joy, generally? Were words accessories now, abstract vibes, absent of any real meaning?

The photo was of Don, my mom, the three sons, and the three girlfriends/fiancées, two of whom wore giant white turtleneck sweaters and knee-high brown boots over light-wash skinny jeans. There was a soft-focus, almost sepia tint to the photo. The women's eyelashes were thick and their hair was basically the same, even my mom's, the wiglike look of a straighten and then a curl. Maybe they'd all gotten ready together. On my mom's décolletage, the shine of her gold cross pendant. Gems lined the pockets of her jeans. I was embarrassed by this stupid picture that I wasn't in, by its suburban banality. It looked like a sample from a greeting-card website. Who even had a family like this?

My mom finally had money, but she couldn't buy class, couldn't understand the cultural signifiers. She was not capable of looking cool as she slid cranberry sauce out of a tin can or drank a cheap beer, which most of my peers could pull off with an ironic pride, earning cachet by performing what they imagined were the quaint customs of the masses. I had gone to college and grad school thinking I could come out the other side better than I was, but I was left feeling just superior enough to my family to feel inferior to everyone else. Was it precisely because my mother was my mother that I had spent my whole life judging her? What did I expect from her? Some anachronistic, feminist story? Who's to say what I would have done in her time, in her shoes?

I was such an asshole. It was a nice card.

A knock on the door. "Sam? Are you in here?" It was Gabe.

"Yes."

"Can we talk?"

"Not right now, please," I said.

"I would really like to talk to you."

"And I would really like to be left alone."

He left. The modern man, not pushing it. I reinserted my tooth and tried to recite Allen Ginsberg's "America" poem, which I had memorized in high school, as if I knew it would one day apply. *America I've given you all and now I'm nothing.* I couldn't remember the third line of the second stanza, required it to get to the line after, could only picture its place on the page in my slim black-and-white City Lights edition of *Howl.* I gave up, opened the medicine cabinet, whispered the brand names of the medication: aspirin, extra-strength Excedrin, ibuprofen. I sat on the toilet lid again and texted Sophie.

Me: You were right about the party.

Her: Bougie? Lots of pies?

Me: Yes. Boxes and boxes of fancy pies.

Her: Well I'm eating peruvian chicken in bed and watching SVU reruns

Me: Sounds amazing

I tried typing a few other things, typing and deleting, typing and deleting, then gave up—I didn't want her to watch those dots blinking, not blinking, blinking again.

⁓

When I finally exited the bathroom, Aliana was standing in the hall.

"Oh, sorry," I said. "I didn't know anyone was waiting."

"I haven't been here that long," Aliana said, leaning lethargically against the wall, the bulging forehead vein now a faint blue crack.

"Is that woman still in the bathroom downstairs?" I asked.

"Oh, I don't know. Just needed a little break from the constant—" She waved her hand abstractly.

Wasn't I supposed to confront this woman? Here was my chance: Fuck you, Aliana! Or I could be the bigger person. I was tired enough for this to be an alluring thought: I could let it go. We could all just move on.

"Same," I said. "Though also someone was in the bathroom downstairs before." I waited for her to go into the bathroom, but she stood there, looking at the floor. Then she put a knuckle under an eye, the mascara-save gesture of a woman about to cry.

"Wait, are you okay?"

"Yes, yes, sorry, I'm fine," she said.

"Did something happen?"

"No, it's just—I haven't slept." I nodded and let the silence hang, to see if she'd continue, and she did. "It's just too much, you know? All the committees and conferences and advising student projects, plus coming to Baltimore every weekend from D.C.? It's just too fucking much. I don't know how I'll write a single word of my own work until I get tenure, which— Should I even write another book? With all this hate mail about what a cunt I am because I wrote a book where I'm, like, a sexual being?"

She seemed like a soft pink balloon deflated into concave rubber, her shoulders forward, her chest cupped. "Sounds like the people sending you hate mail are the real cunts," I said, feeling generous. A peace offering in the spirit of Thanksgiving, though who wanted to take that metaphor too far.

"Thanks," she said. "I know I shouldn't complain. I know I'm lucky to have a job. I'm sure your situation is much worse."

She was lucky, of course: an office, colleagues, a title and an accompanying institution that allowed her to apply for grants or sabbaticals, a real salary, enough time for a vaguely functioning relationship, never mind the rest of it: her book, her beauty, her birth into a world where she knew everyone who mattered. And still.

"Academia sucks," I said. "Why can't Tom come to see you?" Generosity again, mentioning Tom so casually.

"He doesn't get it," she said. "I mean, he's a great partner," she added quickly. "He gets *so* many things, but it just wasn't the same for him."

"An oblivious academic baby of the prefinancial crash," I said, nodding.

"Yeah, and just . . . a dude?" She laughed a little. "I mean, he literally made reference to my biological clock."

"Oh my God," I said. "Why?"

"He . . . wants kids?"

"Wait, what? Since when?"

"Since this morning?" she said. "It's like it just came to him. I'm sure he's thinking posterity, not playdates. He just cannot comprehend what is blatantly obvious to me: It will ruin my career."

I was shocked. Aliana didn't want kids? I had pegged her—pigeonholed her?—as a lean-in, have-it-all woman, with the means to make it happen. If Aliana couldn't do it, who could?

"I'll be fine," she said. "I'm just having a moment. Just need to get more sleep."

She was about to go into the bathroom when I said, "Hey. One thing."

"Yeah?"

"I don't understand why you participated in that Style piece."

Her shoulders straightened into a wall. "I thought we were being friendly here?"

"That's why I thought—"

"Don't," she said. "You should be grateful. That article let you off the hook. It's entirely your fault Tom left SHU, a place he loved. Now he's teaching at fucking Rosedale."

"Wow, must be hard," I said sarcastically. "It's not my fault Tom left SHU."

"Oh, come on," said Aliana. "You made a misconduct complaint in the middle of a nationwide sexual-harassment shitstorm, Sam."

"That's not what happened."

"Okay, sure."

"I thought your whole thing was *believe women*?"

"One thing that you really, really shouldn't do," said Aliana, "is twist this into some story about how I'm anti-MeToo. I've been through my own shit—actual shit, Sam. At its core, the movement is about accountability. And I wonder if you've ever taken any accountability? You were a graduate student and an adult, and you had a giant crush on Tom. Frankly, it was embarrassing to watch. Yeah, I get power imbalances, but I also get nuance. You think it's somehow feminist to say, hey, grown women aren't capable of making their own choices? What is he supposed to do? Deny women their agency?"

I had a hard time with agency. I framed all my sexual experiences in the passive voice, as if those people had just appeared there, on top of me, inside of me. As if I had just arrived at Tom's house, as if my feet hadn't carried me, as if I had magically floated.

But I hadn't floated. Why did I go that night when part of me knew exactly what he wanted? And what had I wanted? I'd wanted to bask in his attention a little longer. I'd wanted approval. I'd wanted to feel smart and good and worthy. I had wanted it to be about my work, but those weren't his terms, so I'd wanted what I could get. My agency, as defined by his. And why couldn't he take responsibility for that?

Aliana had pinpointed the essence of my discomfort with where MeToo had led us. The movement wasn't just about holding wrongdoers responsible for their actions but about one's own responsibility to be assertive. "Enthusiastic consent" was now the gold standard of sexual experience. "Yes! Yes! Yes!" shouted MeToo's ideal woman, a woman I couldn't identify with at all. My entire sexuality was built on ambivalence—if enthusiasm were a requirement, I'd still be a virgin. Not knowing what I wanted made me a traitor to the cause.

Tom's book now existed in the frame of MeToo, and because of it, I had entered the frame of MeToo, and I felt as if it had subsumed my story without my . . . consent? Was it really solidarity when you felt left out and forced in at the same time?

"You pursued him relentlessly," Aliana was saying.

"Which is what Tom told you," I said. Here we stood, two female doctors spectacularly failing the Bechdel Test.

"It was obvious you had a crush on him."

"Yeah, and so what?" I said. "That's his whole thing, students are charmed by him. What the fuck is *relentless* supposed to mean?"

"Um, I don't know, the texting at all hours. The sitting outside of his office waiting for him. The night you went to their house and Lydia found out about the whole thing. Oh—here's one—switching to the academic track just so you could be with him? When he begged you not to?"

Anger flared inside me. "He practically forced me out of the program," I said. "He told me to switch, but not before he told everyone else it had been my decision. I lost so much time because of it. I had to change my entire plan, I had to start over. It wrecked my confidence in myself." It hit me that this was all true, irrevocably true, that I had a right to be angry with him—very fucking angry.

"You were turned on by his power, by his authority, and you threw yourself at him," said Aliana. "He made one mistake, one night, a drunken mistake that you were *desperate* for him to make, and he lost his marriage because of it, he lost his job. Fucking a teacher is a *trope,* Sam."

"Well, be more original, then," I said.

"I meant you."

"But we didn't actually . . . Tom and I never fucked," I said.

"Don't bullshit me."

"We never even kissed."

"Come on," she said. "That's ridiculous."

"Maybe I had a crush on him, maybe I flirted with him, maybe I went to his house one night, but when he made a move, I left. Tom really told you we slept together?"

"Of course."

"Why do you believe him?"

"Because why wouldn't I? Because if you and Tom didn't have sex," said Aliana, "then what the hell are we all doing here? It would be a pretty fucking huge and pointless lie, wouldn't it?"

"I don't know what to say, Aliana."

"Everyone knows," she said. "Tom, Mateo, Mateo's wife, me, Tom's ex-wife, obviously; it's why they got divorced."

"Tom said that?"

"Obviously there were problems," said Aliana. "They tried to make it work, but it just deteriorated after that revelation."

"Tom had an affair," I said, "but not with me."

Aliana blinked at me. I could hear the chatter of people downstairs, the click and squeak of their shoes on hardwood. "Come here," she said. She waved me into the bathroom, closed the door behind us, locked it, then acted like I wasn't there. She inspected herself in the mirror, tucked her smooth hair behind her ears, rubbed the blue vein in the middle of her forehead as if to smudge it out, washed her hands with the lavender soap.

"I'm not messing with you, Aliana," I said. "I didn't sleep with him."

"I get that you're saying that," said Aliana harshly, glancing at me in the mirror. She regained her composure as she dried her hands on the towel, then turned around to face me. "But Tom says that you did." She was calm now. "He says you were both drunk, that it was a difficult time for him—his failing marriage, his mother's illness. He knows it was a big mistake. And maybe you feel the same way. Maybe you had a bunch of shit going on in your personal life, too, and you wanted some comfort and you regretted it later and now you wish it never happened. And you know what? I get that, I really do. But I don't know what you're hoping to accomplish here by denying it."

"I get it, too," I said. "I get that it's my word against his, that you're dating him, that you want to believe him, that I can't prove what didn't happen. All I can say is: I'm confused, and I'm tired of being a part of this."

She searched my face, looking for a lie, hoping for a lie. "If you didn't sleep together, then explain to me why he would admit it to Lydia, to me, to Mateo, to the public? Why would he want everyone to believe a lie that could only hurt him?"

It was a good question. Why did people lie? To protect themselves, to get away with something, because the truth was harder to bear.

It hit me then, the whole story. I leaned against the door, feeling dizziness on top of my anger. It was entirely predictable, how unimportant I was to the narrative. In the scheme of Tom's life, I was a nonplayer. As in a classic campus novel, I was a plot device, an inciting incident, a casualty of someone else's story.

The night Lydia found me at Tom's had led her to believe he was sleeping with me. And Tom had let her believe it. He'd said it himself: He would tell Lydia about his affair, but he would lie about who. At the time, the lie must have seemed less destructive than the truth. Did he tell Lydia he'd slept with me before I went to his house that night, figuring he should at least be able to do it if he'd already admitted to it? Or did he tell her after?

Getting me to drop out of the program had proved to his wife that he was keeping his distance from me while they tried to work things out. It also gave him immunity for his own lie, because he couldn't get in trouble for sleeping with one of his students if I wasn't one of his students.

Perhaps it was also a way for him to punish me for what he saw as a rebuff. Maybe that's what underpinned the whole thing: He was trying to protect his ego. He was embarrassed that, despite all his power and authority and supposed charm, he could be turned down by someone he considered beneath him. What's worse than sleeping with a student? Trying to sleep with a student who rejects you. For Tom, the truth was the most damning version of the story.

"Aliana, I was a scapegoat," I said. "Tom told me that Lydia thought he was cheating. She assumed it was me because I was over there house-sitting. It was easier for him to explain than the truth, which was that he was fucking her best friend."

"What? Who?"

"Claire Somebody from Princeton."

"Fuck," said Aliana. The name seemed to click. She pressed at the vein in her forehead with her thumb, bowed her head to stretch her neck. She took her time, rolled her shoulders, then looked back up at me. "In this scenario, probably Lydia told Hannah"—Mateo's wife—"and Hannah would have told Mateo." And so the lie became the story. "What did you say in the exit interview?"

"They kept asking me about my relationship with Tom," I

said. "I hardly told them anything, but it was the height of MeToo, and they just kind of ran with it."

Why did I feel the need to defend myself over a complaint I would have been justified in making? Tom felt entitled to use me as he pleased in his book, yet I felt I had no right to simply say what had happened? I was supposed to shut my mouth because a movement I had no part in might "overreact"? I never wanted to ruin Tom's life. But the truth was, Tom behaved badly. He saw me as an object of desire first, a student second, and a writer least of all. He kept thrusting me into the former category, and by doing so, he had fucked me over. Because the greatest offense—that he'd essentially kicked me out of the program—hardly seemed to register. Maybe he didn't even believe he'd done it.

"All I know is that the exit interview really concerned Mateo," Aliana said. "He knew about the affair—supposed affair, whatever. And even though it was all technically aboveboard because you weren't on the creative track anymore, Mateo felt that *the zeitgeist had its own agenda,* and if there was a chance you'd speak up publicly, he didn't want there to be any fallout at SHU."

Aliana looked blankly into the air. She combed her fingers through her hair, unparting it, flipping it to one side with a jerk. She seemed to be deciding something, and then she seemed to have decided it. "I probably shouldn't tell you this, but before MeToo, there had been a few other—really general—complaints against Tom over the years. Just stuff like *a flirtatious atmosphere.* Mateo and Tom didn't think the complaints were anything to worry about, so they never really went anywhere." I didn't know what to feel about this. Mad that no one had considered the obvious solution: that Tom change his behavior? Glad that maybe Tom hadn't tried to sleep with other students—in which case, I'd been special after all? Was my self-worth really still wrapped up in this? "But I don't know," Aliana continued, "your situation seemed more serious, especially in the middle of MeToo, and with this record of complaints, it just didn't look good. So that's why Mateo helped Tom get the job at Rosedale."

Et tu, Mateo? Mateo, who had invited me over to Christmas dinner? Mateo, who was so theoretically *nice*? Mateo had saved Tom not once but twice. The first was when he encouraged me to switch to the academic track; the second was when he orchestrated Tom's escape to Rosedale.

"That's extremely fucked up," I said.

"But it just seemed . . ." Aliana looked miserable now. "The way Tom told the story . . . you know Tom. He can tell a story. The way Tom explained your behavior at SHU, your relentlessness. It was super-alarming when you showed up at Rosedale. We didn't know if you were stalking him or bent on revenge; it felt like there was no telling what you might do or say."

It was laughable that they were worried I would make a stink. What did they think I would do? Email who at what media outlet? Publish my own article on some clickbait website that, at best, no one would read and, at worst, would become a viral touchstone in a debate about consent or student-teacher relationships? Some would accuse Tom of abusing his power, others would highlight my age and reprimand me for continuously engaging, but any way you sliced it, an article like that would be job-search suicide.

"He didn't have to do the Style article," I said. "Honestly, he didn't even have to publish the fucking book."

"After twenty years, that would have been a hard pill to swallow," said Aliana. "And with the Style thing, it just seemed better to get out ahead of the story with a sympathetic ear, to preempt the conduct questions that would surely come in light of the book, which was why he got in touch with Leslie. At the time it seemed, you know, bold and courageous to come forward and exactly in line with the lessons of his novel."

"Tom knew the journalist?"

Aliana looked at her feet.

"So, not the biggest gamble," I said, "because he could tell the story that fit the existing narrative, the story everyone else believed anyway. Easy. With one small casualty: me."

I left Aliana shell-shocked in the bathroom and walked back downstairs. I could hear a woman monologuing loudly, drunkenly—not wasted but not quite hitting the consonants, either. "Yeah, I mean, *obviously* there are valid critiques of the security state," she was saying. "But people *do* want security, people *do* want safety, and we're still going to need to work with the police to get that safety. At *best*—if we want to give people the benefit of the doubt, although I'm not sure we should, considering the populist impulse to do God knows what—at *best* this burgeoning police abolition movement is born of naïveté, and it's certainly bad marketing."

"Yet you can't blame people for being distrustful after what's happened," said Tom, who didn't notice as I passed. "Even if police reform may well be the more realistic and convincing approach in the end." Ever equanimous Tom, ever supposedly empathetic Tom, ever blandly liberal Tom. He was so sure that, at its core, the system worked—and it did, always, for him.

Gabe didn't notice me, either. He was talking to Rick and

the girlfriend, his back to me. They couldn't seem to stop saying "Anthropocene," as if it were a competition, who could say it more, who could say it five times fast.

I walked past Dr. Brighton, who was taking out the pies. Rustic apple cinnamon. Bourbon pecan with its neat wheel of nuts. Sweet potato chai with piped whipped-cream trim. Pumpkin spice cheesecake with a sleek herringbone cream-cheese design, perfect as a parquet floor. And right beside it, the apocalyptic hellscape of my pumpkin pie with its great slimy ravine slashed through the middle.

I doubled back to the fridge, grabbed two beers. In the mudroom, I pulled on my ugly coat and then stuffed a beer in each pocket, so I was weighted down, a modern Virginia Woolf, sans a room of her own. A tasteless joke, a poor comparison, not least because I'd never written anything interesting.

Outside, the plowed snow was an impressive gradient of gray, like a cross section of earth, like Dr. Brighton's parfait, like a textbook illustration of geological time. What was the difference between an epoch and an era? I could only think Jurassic. I could only think Anthropocene. What about Meta . . . something? Metamorphosis. Metazoic.

The breeze bit at my cheeks as I walked and whispered to myself: "Metazoic. Metazoic. Metazoic." The more I said it, the more it sounded like a type of rock, a ring from a Jared commercial, a literary term. Meta-zoic. Meta-stoic.

The road was all gravel and sand. My tooth was not-tooth, just the darkness of my mouth. The sky was Earl Grey gone cold. The walk was, what, two miles? Piece of cake. Piece of pie. I could pick up another can of pumpkin puree on the way home, if anything was open. Well, it was America, of course things would be open.

I had the other ingredients already, so it would be easy to make a second pie, a pie for me and Sophie. I could skip the crust. The crust was too difficult. It could be a pudding.

Me*ta*zoic? Wasn't that cells, not dinosaurs? Many cells? Like animals? Did it just mean animals?

Me*so*zoic, that was dinosaurs. Maybe, millions of years ago, right here, some dinosaur was clomping around. I tried to picture it. I was getting screeching pterodactyl. Braying brontosaurus. I was getting volcanoes and conifers and ferns. I was getting *Fern-Gully*, actually. This after decades of education.

I wasn't going to make another pie.

My skin broke out in goose bumps, and to make matters worse, I was drinking one of the beers. I felt like a character in a television show. Self-destructive self-pity seemed so generationally on brand that I couldn't figure out if I was doing it naturally or theatrically. Regardless, I was walking down a major thoroughfare in the freezing dark, a mere metazoa in the Anthropocene in America in Maryland in Baltimore on Roland Avenue, where the snow was encroaching on the road, and the darkness was encroaching on me, and my own life, set on any geological or historical scale, was nothing.

⁓

By the time Gabe pulled up alongside me, I'd already walked a mile and finished a beer and was so freezing cold that it didn't take much convincing to get me in the car.

"You just *leave*?" he said before I'd even buckled up. "Without saying a word?" The hermetic seal of his niceness had broken. Once the dirty air rushed in, you couldn't go back.

"You just apply for the job that replaces me?" I said, flipping on the seat warmer. "Without saying a word?"

We lurched into the darkness. "I assumed you knew about it," he said.

"You'd think someone would've mentioned it. Like you, for example."

"I thought you'd see the listing and bring it up if you wanted to talk about it."

"Or you thought that if I didn't know about it, I wouldn't apply."

"Is that what you think of me?"

"What should I think?"

"I don't know, that I've been a nice person this whole time and I wouldn't do that?"

"You should've told me."

"Yeah, and maybe there are a few things you should've told me."

"What's that supposed to mean?"

"Tom, for example," said Gabe.

"What about Tom?"

"Come on," he said. "We talked about him a hundred times, and you acted like it was all hypothetical. Then this article comes out, and— I mean, do you think I'm stupid?"

"I thought you were *skeptical of the narrative*? Or are you two friends now?"

"What are you talking about? The lounge? How am I supposed to navigate that, Sam? I have to work with the guy," he said. "And I *am* skeptical of the narrative. I'm not *blaming* you for anything. I'm saying you might've told me you were involved. The specifics are honestly beside the point. It's indicative of a larger problem, this distance you keep."

"What distance?"

"You don't tell me anything."

"Yes, I do."

"What about Sophie?"

"What about her?"

"See," he said. "You're doing it again, you're doing it now. If I were important to you, there are some things you might have mentioned."

"You're the one who told me you didn't want a relationship."

"I didn't say that, I said my life has never been particularly *conducive*—"

"You never brought up a relationship."

"You never made it feel like a possibility!"

"I thought you wanted something casual."

"What's *casual*?" said Gabe, venom in his voice. "What does that mean? Indifferent? Accidental? Thoughtless?" He squinted into the night.

"How are you turning this on me?" I said. "You're the one who applied for my job and didn't tell me."

"I didn't know you didn't know," Gabe nearly shouted. "That's the thing. You *do* know what I don't know, and you refuse to tell me. The point is just give me some fucking information so I don't feel extraneous."

"You're not extraneous."

"No?" he said. "Are you sure? We go out to bars, to restaurants, to the thrift shop, to Thanksgiving. I take you these places, and I wanted to take you to these places." He didn't say *money,* but I felt it simmering beneath, because that was where it always sat; you were never supposed to talk about it, but I'd let him pay for everything. "It would be fine if I felt like you wanted to reciprocate somehow, if I felt like I wasn't generically convenient to have around, if I felt like you cared about me in some specific way."

"Come on," I said. "I do care about you in some specific way. You're smart, charming, thoughtful. The list goes on."

"But that sounds like you're trying to complete a homework assignment," he said. "I don't *feel* it. I don't feel like you're interested in me."

"Then why do I keep hanging out with you?"

"Because I'm here," he said. "That's what it feels like." He paused, considered his words. "I don't know how to say this, but it's also . . . I mean, the physical stuff. It's so disconnected. Do you even want *me*? There's no *us* to it. I feel like I could be anyone."

We crept through the icy gray streets, snow globe of dirt. Was that how I treated him? Like he was replaceable? I knew the feeling. It was how my mom's family treated me, how Sophie treated me sometimes, how Tom had treated me, how Lewis treated me, how Rosedale treated me.

Just pretend I'm not anyone specific, I'd said to Gabe the first time we'd slept together, house rules. Maybe I felt that if you didn't have anything in the first place, you couldn't lose it. But I was finding that you could lose what you didn't have, you could lose the secret dream of it—the career or the partner or the mother you always wanted. Maybe I was trying to keep my distance with Gabe while also trying to hide my inexplicability as a sexual partner. Maybe the convergence of the two made me inept at closeness.

What would have happened with Tom if I'd been like other girls with a crush and a fantasy and a sexual pulse, gripped by desire instead of disgusted by it, the mouth and the sweat and the penis of it? What would have happened, had we actually fucked?

Maybe he would have kept it a secret, would've felt he owed me nice. He would've loved my writing. I would have a glowing letter of recommendation and a good reputation and friends from grad school and the degree I wanted. And now, years later, I could revel in feeling wronged along with everyone else; I could be empowered by it.

There was no exclamation I could make, no group I could join, there was only me lost alone in liminal spaces. I was a professor who wasn't a professor. A queer who wasn't that queer. My life had been ruined by a teacher I hadn't even fucked. All I had was bullshit and bureaucracy. And what kind of story is that?

Chapter 12

SCRAPS

Thanksgiving to Christmas was supposed to be the home stretch, but I had hundreds of pages of student papers to grade and a review of a sleep mask to write, and I was desperately emailing department heads asking for classes to teach spring semester, and it wasn't just me who was cracking, the students were cracking, too. It seemed like all of them had gone home for Thanksgiving and realized something horrible, like their parents were getting divorced, or they were seniors and they were in debt and the job market sucked, or, in one case, their sister had been deployed to a war zone, plus those guys had never taken Risky Business and her friends to Assateague. They came to me with their problems, as if I might be capable of offering some solution or solace, but I had worked hard all semester and had less than three hundred dollars in my bank account, and each minute detail of the catastrophic Thanksgiving kept running through my head. *And you, you ridiculous people,* I thought each time a worried student appeared, Denis Johnson echoing in my head, *you expect me to help you.*

I felt sick as I read and reread Gabe's text to me—half apology, half explanation, definitely ending things, well written and astute. I drafted potential responses in the Notes app as I sat on the toilet, my only free time. I couldn't figure out what I was trying to say. The longer I didn't respond, the worse I felt, and the more unanswerable his text became.

Sophie and I were ships passing in the night, the messages between us mostly practical:

out of milk

headed home

insane amount of cheese cubes in donaldson 403

could you double check the stove?

What made me think it was a good idea to put my tongue inside the vagina of my friend whom I lived and worked with? And why was she so fine with it? Was I offended that she wasn't interested in me? Did that mean I was interested in her, or was it just an ego thing?

The freezing rain came, an almost metallic *tink tink tink* on the windows, and I stuffed my dirty puffer into my dissolving raincoat and trudged back and forth to my car at the outreaches of Lewis, dodging the deep, muddy potholes that had been dug out with the plows, the balance on my credit card creeping ever higher than the balance in my bank account.

The adjunct office at Lewis was a recurring nightmare. Damp clothes—coats, scarves, workout leggings—strewn across the tables, hung over chairs, sprawled over printers, causing the papers to print crumpled. Between the wet clothes and the burning printers, the office felt like a sauna, and the windows fogged up. We stripped to undershirts, then froze in the hall on the way to the bathroom, because the heat in the rest of the building was capped at 65 degrees.

I veered off syllabus in the final weeks of The Campus Novel, bringing in some articles about the state of academia, from the rising cost of college to the replacement of tenured faculty with contract labor. But most of the students, safe in the cocoon of Rosedale, had a hard time assimilating the information, seemed threatened by the required shift in point of view.

"I think some people feel really lucky even to go to college," one student insisted, "and are proud to pay for it because they learn the value of grit and hard work along the way."

"So should everyone have to work during college?" I asked.

"It's just a totally different situation for different people."

One of the period's few delights was Subway Sandwich's sudden grasp of punctuation. It was as if a switch had been flicked, but of course it was all the rewiring he had done over the course of the semester. I was surprisingly moved by one of the short-response answers on his final:

> Maybe you were hiking in the woods once and walked by a mushroom and didn't think anything about it. Maybe you actually stepped on it. The point is you didn't notice it. But in the poem "Mushrooms" by the famous confessional poet Sylvia Plath, mushrooms grow powerful because there are just so many of them. They may be "meek" (shy) and hardly need any food or water to survive, but they are actually "Nudgers and shovers" powerfully banging holes through the earth! The poem is all about getting overlooked and being thought of as unimportant. But it is also about the secret strength you may not even realize you have which is all the more powerful when there are "So many of us! So many of us!" There's even

> a line about a "fist" which reminds me of a fist raised in agreement with fighting the power.
>
> Maybe Plath meant the poem as a metaphor for the feminist movement, but the cool thing about poems (and song lyrics too) is they don't have to mean one thing. That's why they don't "make sense" exactly. Poets actually do this on purpose. It's how they make some space for you to figure out what it means to you. So to me this poem could be about gig economy workers who don't get paid enough, something I know about as a delivery driver. We may be "Perfectly voiceless" now—but maybe one day we will "Inherit the earth."

One afternoon at Lewis, stripped to the cami I wore under my blouse, I looked up from placing a handout on the glass of the photocopier to see Sophie in the doorway, eating a bagel.

"Bagels?" I said.

"Oh, shit. I forgot to text you. Want some?" She gestured that she would rip it in half and share.

"Do I dare eat a peach?"

"Do you dare disturb the universe?"

"I don't," I said, waving the bagel away. "My temp will just fall out again."

"Is your temp ever going to become perm?"

"The one-thousand-and-forty-two-dollar question."

A professor—the one who had forced me to relinquish the photocopier midprint during my first week—popped her head in the adjunct office with a look of half-heartedly veiled disgust.

"We're collecting money for Carl," she said.

"For who?" asked Sophie.

"Carl. The custodian. He's retiring."

"How much?"

"Just fifteen dollars."

"Each?" said Sophie.

"Yes, each," she said.

"We're not full-time employees," Sophie said flatly.

The professor—the other professor, we were all professors—glanced around the office like some penthouse dweller coming into public housing and seeing not crisis but moral bankruptcy. "But you work here," she said. "And so the custodial staff washes *your* floors. Takes out *your* garbage. Cleans whatever strain of mess you leave in here."

I saw the sneering curl of Sophie's lip. My last photocopy shot out. We were going over warrants in class, an assumption that connected the grounds of an argument to the claim.

"If we donated to every Girl Scout, GoFundMe, and retiree at every place where we worked," said Sophie, "we'd have even more debt than our student loans." Sophie, I gathered, didn't have student loans, but she was making a point.

"I know your generation thinks work is uncool," the woman said. "But Carl has been a dedicated employee for thirty-five years. Can you imagine?"

Sophie blinked incredulously. Silence hung in the air. I picked up the pile of printed papers, held the warm stack in my hands as anxiety and excitement pulsed through me. I looked from Sophie to the woman. Sophie was so zeroed in that she didn't see me at all. Anger gave her tunnel vision. Frizzy puffs of hair had sprung from the sides of her head. The tiny tremor of her set jaw was not nerves, I knew, but rage.

"Your diagnosis is that my generation thinks work is *uncool*?" said Sophie.

"All your generation ever talks about is how you don't want to work," the woman said, her confidence flagging. "We're just looking for some respect for the custodial staff."

"Respect?" said Sophie, wild-eyed. "Then wipe that look of disdain off your face. This office is shared by twenty adjuncts making less than minimum wage, sweating in the heat of your printers, subsidizing your lifestyle. I'm sure Carl is wonderful. Would you like to contribute by percentage of income? If I give fifteen bucks, you'll have to hand over a hundred. I'm not kidding. Do the math, ma'am."

The math was solid. The hairs on Sophie's arms stood straight up.

~

After work, I found Sophie curled up on the couch—my bed—writing in a notebook. It was unlike her to be still. I thought about the hours of sitting required to finish a PhD. How had she done it? But no, I could picture it after all, the manic flurry of late-night writing, a panicked anger rising inside her. That was the energy she had now. She was still, but she was buzzing.

"You're here," I said, taking off my shoes toe to heel, toe to heel.

"No tasks," said Sophie. The best part of her apartment was the first ten minutes, when you were deluded into believing it was warm. I beelined to the wall to plug in my dead phone, then rummaged in my black garbage bag for fleece pants and a heavy knit sweater. "Did you get invited to the holiday party at Lewis?" she asked.

"The adjuncts are never invited to those. Why, did you?"

"Of course not. We're 'invited' to the orientations, to contribute to the retirement gifts," said Sophie scathingly.

"So unfair," I agreed.

"So unfair? Fucking ridiculous. I don't understand why it doesn't piss you off."

"It *does* piss me off."

"You don't seem angry."

"I *am* angry, obviously."

"Well, you don't *sound* angry," she said. "You don't sound even close to angry enough." She scribbled something in her notebook. "I mean, what would happen if we just showed up at the party?"

"I'm pretty sure you referred to university parties as *bougie hellholes*," I said.

"At Rosedale, yeah. But the point isn't to have fun, it's to show them we exist."

"They don't care that we exist."

"That's my point," she said. "We should go, wear some shit that's festive as fuck, embarrass them into noticing us."

"What? You want *me* to go?" I pointed at myself, then at the black garbage bag. "I don't own any festive shit."

"What about the sequin dress you got with that guy you're dating?"

"We're not dating."

"Hanging out, whatever," she said.

"Everything got fucked up."

"What happened?"

"I don't know," I said. "He applied for Carpenter's job, and I didn't even know it was open. A bunch of stuff."

"Fucking sellout," she said. "Asshole."

I felt bad, backtracked. "I mean, otherwise he was a pretty nice guy."

"I'm starting to think *nice guy* is a contradiction in terms," she said. "This is basically why I don't date men anymore. I don't want to participate in that bullshit."

I didn't love the implication that one was under a moral obligation to reject men just because one's sexuality gave them the capacity. Was it possible to exist without sending a political message? How could you live under that kind of tyranny? How could you buy a shirt? Eat chocolate? Have an iPhone? Watch porn? Fuck someone? Shave your armpits? Not shave your armpits? How could you even move?

"Anyway, you have the dress," she said. "We'll appear, glittering, from the night, mysterious and absurd."

"Absurdity isn't going to win the class war."

Sophie looked at me seriously. "Are you satisfied with your life right now, Sam? We're being treated like crap. Don't you feel *insulted* teaching those classes at Rosedale? You're subbing for a guy who makes at least a hundred and fifty thousand dollars a year. It's fucking ridiculous. It's an insult. Aren't you insulted?"

"I just want to get through the day without feeling like shit."

"What's that going to get you in the long run?" Sophie asked. "*Your* life is happening right now. My life is happening right now. Our lives are going down the drain. That's what I'll say in my toast, along with other things about contract labor, the working class, the extreme hypocrisy of academia in general and political science in particular." She wrote something in her notebook. "Surplus labor," she said. "Disposable as factory workers. Chop off an arm in big machinery, and they'll replace us with someone else. Capitalism 101, since nobody seems to have taken the course."

"You're writing a speech?"

She looked at her paper, then at me. "To be honest, it's getting harder and harder for me to be around people who are sitting there pretending everything is fine."

The people was me. She was scribbling again.

"When's the party?" I asked.

On Friday, I woke up sticky with snot, my throat scratchy, my sinuses rock-hard, my eyes leaden. But my chest loosened with relief: I was too sick to crash a work party in sequins.

I taught my last American Lit II class of the semester, went to Rosedale to give the Campus Novel exam, was in the middle of explaining the test aloud when a coughing fit overtook me and my temporary tooth shot into the wet nook of my sweater. I carefully drew my face away. I picked the tooth out as if it were a piece of lint and put it in my pocket as the students waited for me to continue.

In the bathroom, I was sticking the tooth back in with tooth glue I'd bought at CVS right as one of my students walked in. "Oh my God," she said, taking a step backward. "Did your *tooth* fall out?"

I snapped my mouth shut, and it filled with the astringent taste of glue. I felt less human than sentient robot, some creature that had to keep piecing itself back together. "Yeah," I said.

"Oh." She backed out of the bathroom.

Philip Levine flitted through my head: *and nothing that we made / that night is worth more than me // And in truth I'm not worth a thing . . .*

Back at Lewis, I paged through the blue exam books from the Campus Novel final. Rosedale had dialed back—ever so slightly—its anti-paper stance in response to cheating on open-laptop tests.

Classically, the setting of an enclosed campus is a defining feature of the academic novel genre, began my essay prompt. *In what ways do the major themes we've encountered this semester rely on this conceit? With the changing academic landscape in mind, discuss what might be gained by widening the scope of the campus novel and what might be lost.*

I flipped to the end of one student essay: *I think it's best that the campus novel remains enclosed. While it may not reflect everyone's experience, it reflects the best experience of college and so that is the one we'll get the best themes and literature from.* A lump formed in my sore throat. I had suffered this semester. Had anyone understood what we were doing?

I checked my email on the shared computer, signing in and out of the Lewis system, then in and out of the Rosedale system, then into my personal email, where I had a message from the head of the English Department at Loyola saying that they had already filled their spring adjunct positions. I opened my notebook, etched a dark X next to Loyola, the page now cross-stitched in a line of *nos*. I logged out of Gmail, logged back into the Lewis system, then emailed the American Lit I class to say sorry, thanks for a great semester, but I had to cancel.

Back at Sophie's, I swallowed expired DayQuil and lay on the couch, wondering if I should've taken expired NyQuil. My muscles were sore. Did I have the flu?

I went for a walk to prove that I was fine.

It was a cold, gray day. I dragged myself down Main Street in

Hampden, my mouth still tasting of glue. The traffic lights were strung with garland studded in massive twinkling wreaths. A three-story pink flamingo sculpture, an icon of the neighborhood, wore a tiny Santa hat. The indie bookstore had signed copies of Aliana's and Tom's books displayed in the window. I walked past the beer hall, where Mateo had bought me a round not long after my defense. I walked past a hair salon where cuts went for sixty dollars a pop.

What was I doing on this street? Did I think I was going Christmas shopping at a boutique? Did I think I was going to get a hamburger? A manicure?

I walked on to Miracle on Thirty-Fourth Street, a Baltimore-famous block of row homes decorated to an absurd level of holiday tackiness, festive joy turned manic. The tinny sound of "Santa Claus Is Comin' to Town" wafted from the street. *You better watch out / You better not cry.*

The yards glowed with plastic Santas. Christmas trees were cones of light. Industrial-era trains chugged under porches. Electronic elves hammered happily on repeat. A blinking, smiling Ms. Claus rocked in a chair, hair up in a gray bun. Happy workers, happy wives, happy Christmas. Did other countries do this? Or was it specifically American, this seizure-inducing flash of Christmas?

Sure, we didn't have health insurance that covered anything, but we did have an insane variety of plastic decor. So, so many versions of Santa—cartoonish inflatables; vintage hard plastic, lit from within; realistic, velvet-coated with a curly white beard of synthetic hair—some uncanny essence of Saint Nick always shining through. We didn't have sick days, no, but we had seven-foot Christmas trees made of hubcaps and lobster traps, the detritus of capitalism reworked into a monument to its own excess. It was the holiday version of: Sure, maybe you can't afford to buy a house, maybe rent prices have skyrocketed while wages have stagnated, but couldn't you live in an empty storage container rebranded as a trendy tiny home? What was this, the fucking apocalypse? Beyond me, not a mile from where I stood, street after street of Baltimore row homes stood vacant, save the rats crawling through the walls, as the homeless circled the smokestacks in the harbor's former powerplant, now a Barnes & Noble.

Essence of Sophie had invaded my body.

The song played on repeat, threatening me: *You better watch out / You better not cry.*

I awoke to the noisy rush of the hair dryer coming from the bathroom. My body felt heavy and cold, my face hot and bruised. I'd slept only forty-five minutes, but it felt like three hours.

I pulled the sequined dress out of the hallway closet. It was heavier than I remembered, and stranger. Deep pink, royal blue, and black sequined stripes extended to a zigzagging hem that looked like licking flames. The heels were ridiculous, shoes balanced on daggers. It was exactly what Sophie wanted, wasn't it? For us to stand out? To go down in sparkly flames?

"So you're coming," she said, flying past, her robe swooshing behind her like the cape of a king. Her lips were bright pink, but her eyes weren't done yet, so her face was heavy on mouth.

"I'm a little sick," I said.

"What's new." She squished next to me in the bathroom, so I had to move to the toilet.

"You look great."

"I want to really . . . you know"—she pulled her hand down in a clawing motion at her chest—"sink into character."

"What's your character?"

"Pissed off. But hot."

"So the usual?" I asked. "Can you clarify if this is full career suicide or what?"

"Don't worry, I won't implicate you. You're just my date, basically. I think some sense of queerness could only help the cause at this point."

I shimmied into my dress, asking Sophie to zip the back. "Damn," she said when I turned around. I blushed, but she was already headed into the kitchen to review her speech.

Perhaps a little miffed that she thought I might suddenly, after all her negation of my sexuality, add an instrumental *sense of queerness* to the party, I decided to get it together and shave my legs for the first time in three months.

I did it with bar soap and Bic and my foot on the sink. The electric shock of Thirty-Fourth Street flashed in my mind, the bright, shining blots of white and green and red. I thought of the Cheever story we'd read for The Masculine Voice which started: *I would not want to be one of those writers who begin each morning by exclaiming, "O Gogol, O Chekhov, O Thackeray and Dickens, what would you have made of a bomb shelter ornamented with four plaster-of-Paris ducks, a birdbath, and three composition gnomes with long beards and red mobcaps"?* O Cheever, I thought, what would you have made of a three-story flamingo in a tiny Santa hat and a Christmas tree of hubcaps and lobster traps?

A little email ding from my phone. I hopped a step over, one foot still on the sink, craning my neck to see the alert. The notification flashed the words *pleased* and *long list*.

"Oh my God," I said. My head seemed to inflate like a balloon, like I was high on something. Had I made a long list, the next round? It was unusual to announce a long list.

"Is everything okay?" Sophie called.

"I don't know," I said. "Maybe I got on a long list?" A bud of hope grew, twisted like a knot in my chest. I tried to tame it.

"What?" Sophie appeared in the doorway of the bathroom, her smile so forced, her lipstick so bright, she looked clownish. The skirt of my dress was hiked over my underwear, my foot on the sink. I dragged the razor across the last hairy patch of skin.

"I don't know," I said.

"No, no, congrats! That's so amazing. Where?"

"One sec." I splashed water on my shin, pulled at the skirt of my dress, and picked up my phone to scan the email. "Oh," I said. "Naylor. I heard it's an internal hire." How embarrassing to let myself get excited.

"How do you know that?" she said. "It's weird they would send a long-list email."

"They want to make a big show of doing an external search."

"At the very least, it's a harbinger," she said. "It's amazing. We should celebrate!" She shook her head, as if shaking herself out of a reverie. "Yes, obviously we should celebrate!"

I followed her to the kitchen, where she rummaged through the fridge. My foot was wet; there was soap on my shin. She set two cans of Natty Boh on the table.

"It's okay, I don't need—" I started, but she'd already popped both tabs with a hiss, and so we were clinking cans, tapping them on the table, throwing them back. She guzzled at a competitive rate even though she didn't really like beer.

"Sophie?"

"What?"

"Are you mad?"

"Why would I be mad? Are we not celebrating right now?"

"Okay," I said.

"I'm really happy for you." She got up from the table. "I have to finish getting ready, though."

I followed her into the bedroom, where she opened her jewelry box and began untangling two necklaces.

"You seem upset," I said. "I didn't even get the job."

"I mean, okay," she said, huffing at the necklaces as she tried to work her fingernails through the chains. "But it does feel a bit dishonest, no?"

"What do you mean?"

"I mean, at least I get it now," she said, "why you didn't want to unionize, why you've been so hesitant to go to this party."

"But I *just* got the email!" I said. "I'm not clairvoyant."

"Listen, I told you it was an accomplishment, and it is. What else do you want? But don't pretend you haven't kind of been playing me."

"So it's fine if I apply for kicks and giggles? But not if I might actually get a job? *You've* been applying to jobs, too! Either you're applying and could be in the position I'm in, or you *want* to be adjuncting forever and have already *resigned yourself* to being exploited."

"I'm focusing on public universities," she said. "Not private liberal arts colleges."

She freed the necklaces, flung off the robe, and, in almost one stroke, dove into a nearly backless fuchsia knee-length cocktail dress. A few loose straps crisscrossed the back, just for show, but beneath them, you could see the mechanics of her back, her shoulder blades pulsing as she put on a gold cuff bracelet and a necklace with a pendant that looked like a coin. Her elbows were thrust high above her head as she messed with the fastener. If she'd been lying down, she might have looked like a man trying to relax into a blow job. Her armpits were smooth, and it surprised me that she had shaved them.

"It's stupid to not apply for everything," I said. "Verging on self-destructive. Naylor isn't the fucking University of Phoenix. Is it wrong for me to want teeth that aren't falling out of my mouth? Is it wrong for me to want my own room, not a six-hundred-dollar-a-month couch?"

"I'm sorry that offering you a place to live is an inconvenience," she said. "You make it sound like you're the only person in the world who wants stability. We *all* want that. That's the whole point of unionizing."

"So fucking unionize," I said. "You act like me missing one meeting was a personal assault against you. I was teaching *five* new classes this semester; you'd think if you wanted to be a union leader, you'd have a little sympathy for the plight of the worker. It's collective action. You're not supposed to ostracize people. Besides, pretty much *everyone* in academia is getting totally fucked right now—tenure-track, non-tenure-track, public, private, it's all going to shit. You should want me on your side no matter what position I'm in."

"Listen, if you want to work at a private college, that's your decision."

"You went to a private school!" I said. "Several of them!"

"Yeah, and I think it was fucking stupid."

"Because you come from money." I felt dizzy as I said it, my heart beating wildly. "You've always been rich enough to reject the stuff that someone like me would never dream of rejecting."

"I wasn't rich," she said.

"Right, right: middle class." A category so vast as to be useless. "Do you have student loans?"

"I've always been against student loans," she said.

"That's not an answer," I said. "Your dad was nominated for an *Oscar*."

"For *Documentary Short*."

"Do your parents pay the rent here?"

She looked at me with disgust. "Do you think I have, like, five jobs for fun? Because let's check in on that again when you're the one with a full-time job and health insurance next year."

"Did your parents *offer* to pay the rent?"

"What the fuck, Sam? Do you think I somehow have more money than you right now? Go look in my fucking bank account."

"I don't know if you have more money than me," I said, "but I think you could snap your fingers and have more money than me in an instant. I think you want to pretend we're in the same boat, but it's never going to be true, because you have all that cultural capital you earned in prep school, because your parents already paid hundreds of thousands of dollars for your education." I felt righteous and mean. I dabbed my snotty nose with my wrist. What Sophie didn't understand, what no one like Sophie ever understood, was that the essence of wealth wasn't money, it was the stability of a fallback plan, it was *milieu*. "I don't even think you're really trying to get a job. Deep down, you *like* the misery of adjuncting. But suffering on purpose doesn't make you virtuous. You can try to slum it, but you can't hide who you really are." I waved my hand around. "Oh, I know, I know, you feel more at home in a Tennessee dive bar than at a Hollywood cocktail lounge. That's not fetishization at all."

"Don't pretend like you crawled out of a sewer," Sophie said. "You went to Cornell, Sam. You have a fucking PhD. You act like you grew up in East Baltimore, like you never finished high school, like you were so poor you didn't even own a fucking radio, like you couldn't just switch the dial to NPR."

We were like rats fighting for scraps, then comparing the scraps to see who had it worse, and who had it worse would be the winner, assuming we were still alive.

I watched her in the mirror flicking on mascara with fine, upward wisps of the many-bristled brush. She smeared glimmer on both cheeks, which gave her a statuesque, high-cheekboned look. The dress's deep-cut armholes revealed the fleshy curve of her breasts.

"I can't do this," she said, turning to me. "I can't be friends with norm-core straight people who want everything to stay the same."

My throat and stomach contracted as if I'd been punched. "That's not even close to fair," I said.

She shook her head like I would never get it. "You want to work at a private school, but you'll go corporate if academia doesn't work out. You'll play queer for a few days, but what you really want is a boyfriend to network with at a bougie Thanksgiving dinner."

"You *told* me to go to that dinner. You came on top of me with my finger in your ass."

"Playing gay for a night does not a lesbian make," she said.

"*You're* not even a lesbian!" I shouted. "What's your problem?"

She laughed breathily, dismissively, shaking her head. "You really don't get it, do you? My problem is that, despite everything you've said or implied, it turns out you want to be just like everyone else. My problem is that you're straight as an arrow and all in on the establishment. You're about one inch away from moving to the suburbs with your hubby, buying porcelain dinner service for eight, and having a gender-reveal party for your fetus."

"I don't want any of that shit."

"Just wait," she said. "You will."

Would I?

Through Sophie's window, I watched her car whip backward out of the driveway and into the moonlit night. The wet brown lawn was dotted with hard gray lumps of snow.

A job, a husband, a baby, a house. My stomach turned. It was the boring default, the mainstream, the Rome all roads led to, and yet also: unobtainable, a glimmering mirage.

I wanted to get out of Sophie's house as soon as possible.

I started sorting through my stuff, books in the duffel, clothes in the black garbage bag. Did I really need two copies of my 250-page dissertation? Did I really need my contributor copy of *The Journal of American Literature,* where my first academic article had been published? Did I need my diploma, rolled up in a tube?

Would I ever become an academic? What kind of question was

that? I wasn't going to get this job. Would I ever go to the moon? Would I ever be queen of New Jersey? Shouldn't I use my time to ask better questions, like could I get back half of my December rent if I moved out of Sophie's today? Was I capable of grading a thousand pages in ten days? Was my cold going to get worse before it got better? Would I be employed at all come January? Where the fuck was I going to live? What was a mirage, anyway? It wasn't a pile of gold at the end of a rainbow, it wasn't a buffet or a hot meal, it was *water*. It was the fantasy of basic necessity, born of desperation and hope.

In the kitchen, I gathered the items I'd bought: the nutmeg, the cinnamon. I left the can of coffee, since we'd split the cost. I wanted a clean break. I wanted it to be like I'd never been there at all, like I'd never needed to be there. I took a swig of DayQuil. I tied the fat Infinity pillow around the strap of my dirty duffel, pushed on my heels, pulled my puffer coat over my sequined dress, and left.

I drove to Target, the nice one in Canton, for no reason other than because Targets everywhere have a similar layout and therefore feel like familiar, neutral ground.

I wandered the broad and empty aisles, sniffing the snot back into my throat. The fluorescent lights seemed to flicker above me. My ugly white puffer coat opened to reveal the glittering glory of my thrift-shop sequined dress. Somewhere a cart squeaked.

I touched all the clothes with my dry winter fingers, the soft cashmere-blend sweaters, the sleek silhouette-skimming spandex. On some other timeline—perhaps one where the economy hadn't collapsed as soon as I'd graduated from college—would I have become an advertising agency "creative," an empty corporate shill? If you were better paid, were you necessarily more complicit? Why did you have to go around everywhere apologizing for everything you were and then apologizing again for everything you weren't?

I would never be good enough for Sophie. I would never be queer enough, radical enough, committed enough to the anti-capitalist cause. But so, too, would she never be good enough for me. I refused to give her any leeway. She was a Gatsby in rags, performing pauperdom. Her taste betrayed her. I didn't care if she'd renounced her past. She was an ascetic who could always defect, a get-out-of-jail-free card warm in her pocket.

I also knew that dividing people into hierarchies of suffering was stupid. In the battle of who had it worse, you were lucky not to win. And what did winning get you, anyway? It was a victory you could only celebrate alone, in the dark hole of your own misery.

The empty electronics section made me sad. Why weren't more people Christmas shopping? Was the whole city at a work party? Arnold Schwarzenegger crashed through a table of toys on an enormous flat-screen, on an hour-and-a-half hunt for Turbo Man. Why did I know the plot of a movie I had never seen?

During my brief foray into fiction writing in grad school, it had seemed like a sin to reference fleeting cultural details. But wasn't it pretentious to pretend your psyche wasn't at least as informed by cultural blips—movies, TV shows, commercials—as by the classics you had so studiously read?

Sure, there might be a line of poetry that pierced your skin and sank so deep that your body absorbed it, but what about the particles in the air that you didn't even know you were breathing? What about Turbo Man? Or Felicity's haircut? Or Kim Kardashian's ass, so omnipresent that you simply knew it to exist, knew it to be big, knew it to be rich? What about the feeling of nostalgia you got while drinking Coke from a glass bottle even though you'd never lived in an era when that was a thing? What about the American Dream? What about campus novels? What about the ennui I was promised, the elbow patches, the 401(k)?

I had spent the last decade studying stories, yet I couldn't find my place in the narrative. Not in the story of sexuality or academia or feminism. As a character, I would be weak because a character must want something. "What does she want?" Tom asked again and again, as if he cared.

I wanted, perhaps, to be wanted. I wanted Tom to want me, so I went to his house, I reached for his dick. I wanted the university to want me, so I worked like a dog. I wanted a man to want me, so I got down on my knees. I wanted a woman to want me, but without the construct of the blow job, I didn't know what to do.

I was indispensable to Tom's narrative, which only proved how dispensable I was to him. I was essential to the university but entirely replaceable. And when it might have mattered what I wanted—with Gabe—I was so disconnected from my wanting that he felt unwanted himself.

I checked my phone, hoping Sophie had sent an apology and also knowing she hadn't. What the fuck was the plan here? I felt my chin contract, my lower lip quiver, as I scanned the board games: Monopoly, Risk, the Game of Life. Was I going to sleep in the car? Was there anyone in the whole fucking city I could text? Brianna (no), Aliana (obviously no), Sophie (not a chance), Tom (not a chance in hell), Gabe (no? or yes? no, no, the answer was no).

"Store closing in fifteen minutes," announced the ceiling, omniscient god of Target.

How long had I been here, fondling fabrics and plastics? Had Sophie already made her big speech? Had she clinked a glass, stood up on a chair? I pictured the tiny hairs on her forearms, the way they rose from goose bumps in a delicate fur. My bare legs were freezing, my forehead hot. Was she brave or a fucking idiot? Could I sleep in the adjunct office at Rosedale, just for a night?

HUMILIATION

I awake at dawn, the metal spiral of my wide-ruled notebook poking me in the wrist and several pages of scribble bent up under my hand. My ears feel full—either the building is humming around me, or it is so very quiet that the quiet hums. All week I've listened to people depart in waves: the last of the professors, the last of the students, and now even the custodians have left, turning down the heat on their way out. With my grades officially submitted, I guess that means I'm on vacation.

I pull my coat over my face, as much for warmth as for darkness, but I can still sense the light brightening on the back wall, and after ten or twenty or forty-five minutes, I concede to morning.

The office is awash in a golden light, making the pieces of this book taped on the wall look magical, like they hold secret power. Outside, the sun shoots through an orange-pink sky, the frosty lawn glitters, and the columns of the colonnades flanking the grand library are so brilliantly bathed in light that they look like they could burst into flames. Henri Bowen himself must have stood in this very spot, awed by what he had created, his dream of academia come to life.

I remember stepping onto a campus as a student for the very

first time, some fifteen years ago, how the paved pathways criss-crossed the neoclassical arts quad like an insane geometry problem. I wore a new navy JanSport stuffed full of college-ruled notebooks as if I'd never have back issues, as if wide-ruled lines were a thing of the past, as if, from this point forward, I would slide precise sentences onto narrow rule as I advanced, always, toward something better, or at least not worse.

I often recall the moment I opened the acceptance letter, incredulous and thrilled, the silent processing I did in the yellow-and-brown galley kitchen of the two-bedroom apartment where my mother and I lived. Then I think of Kurt Vonnegut's famous lecture in which he explains the structure of a story as a series of good news and bad news. This generally aligns with what we think of as rising and falling action. Cinderella, for example, or the American Dream: starts low and ends high, ends on very good news. But *Hamlet,* much like life itself, resists this kind of graphing. Is Hamlet's encounter with his father's ghost good news or bad news? *The truth is,* says Vonnegut, *we know so little about life, we don't really know what the good news is and what the bad news is.*

Of course, *Hamlet* is a tragedy. So, ultimately, bad news.

The sun chills out, and my phone reports that clear skies will give way to dark gray clouds and a wintry mix, and that my mom made it to North Carolina, where she'll spend Christmas with her husband's family in his sister's house, which I know from the pictures has a lot of signs that say things like WINED, DINED, & REFINED in wispy cursive.

I log in to my banking app. I have $209 until my final paycheck drops in eleven days. I consider looking at my credit-card bill but decide against it. I work up the courage to text Sophie about getting back some of my December rent, my first contact with her since I walked out a week ago.

I check my email. I've written to all of Baltimore's bookstores to see if they have open positions, as well as to fifteen more department heads at colleges beyond Baltimore, asking if they need coverage for spring classes. But it's just a few days before Christmas, and the lone message in my inbox is a letter from my shitty health insurance company. It has a snowflake graphic, self-care tips, and a discount for a Fitbit.

I drag myself to the bathroom, a white-tiled three-staller with a drain in the middle of the floor. I undress, hanging my clothes over a stall door, my skin sharp with goose bumps.

I set my jaw against the cold and cup my bluish hands under the motion-activated faucet, thrusting them in and out, over and over, wetting the essential parts before lathering up with the almond-scented pump soap. The floor is slimy from suds and grime and slowly draining water. I feel like a block of ice, like if I were hit in the wrong place, or maybe any place, I'd shatter.

For days I have promised myself I'd wash my hair, and for days I have not, but finally I relent because I am having difficulty both avoiding my reflection and assimilating it, and also I have an interview at Chipotle at one.

My hair is so greasy that I look something between feral and high-fashion, as if I have never washed it or have slicked it back purposefully with oil. Nothing else about me could pass as high-fashion, except this dead look around the eyes, both hungry and beyond hunger, like I'm starving but not expecting or even hoping to be fed.

It does turn me on a little to see my gross image in the mirror. Grimy and in a public bathroom, I look extra-naked, completely exposed, like I'm the star of amateur humiliation porn, a category I have never been drawn to, but for a moment it seems inviting, to be exploited in such a visceral and obvious way.

I wet my hair, scrub the soap into my scalp, then begin the cup-and-rinse, my head hanging upside down as I stare at my feet through a puddle, cold and gray as the predicted wintry mix, my teeth clacking.

I thought I had lost all hope earlier in the week, but I must have some reserves, because I seem to believe that the bathroom air dryer, which has not once successfully dried my hands, will somehow dry my hair.

When I step into Chipotle, I'm wearing a hot-pink blazer and vibrating at a low frequency, my wet hair cold as ice on my neck. The beans and rice and chicken smell so good I want to throw up. Sophie's reply pings through: You were here for a half month and also used a half month of utilities and food. I can give you $150. Fair?

Fair? You had to reinvent the universe to get to fair.

A guy who is much younger than I am approaches, shakes my hand. I try to arrange my mouth in a smile that doesn't reveal my missing tooth.

We sit down, and he asks about my aspirations. I can't tell if I'm supposed to have them or not. Do they want a go-getter to work her way up through the ranks? Or an empty vessel, a mere machine to wrap burritos? I straddle the line, try to sell both sides. "Where do you want to be in five years?" he asks.

Liquid gathers in my tear ducts.

He notes that not only have I never worked in food service—the teen years I spent pumping melted cheese onto fries at the county fair don't seem to count—but I'm also overqualified. He is afraid I will leave to find something better. I tell him that the intellectual and bureaucratic challenges of academia have made me want to live a more austere life; also, there are no real jobs in academia anymore, so he shouldn't worry. He wonders aloud if it's a good fit. He says he'll think about it. I ask if he really means it or if he's just saying it, and he stares at me, blinking.

The Barnes & Noble in Baltimore's Inner Harbor is in a former power plant, shot through with massive smokestacks fatter than redwoods. The unhoused come here for warmth. One such person is circling a smokestack as "Rockin' Around the Christmas Tree" plays in the background.

That's not what I'm doing, obviously. My circles are bigger. I'm browsing.

It's four days until Christmas, ten days until my paycheck drops. I wander the aisles, roam the floor, reading synopses and blurbs, reveling in the warmth. On a table of classics, I touch each of the books I've read. *Brave New World, Huckleberry Finn, As I Lay Dying, The Great Gatsby, Song of Solomon, The Catcher in the Rye, Hamlet.*

What do you read, my lord?

Words, words, words.

I sit in the café area and write a few paragraphs about Chipotle in my Notes app, give up, start swiping around on Tinder. I can't say why. I definitely don't want to start dating. It's more like shuffling through trading cards. Plus that one niggling thought: How many of these people would buy me a drink, a meal? Men, mainly, could be convinced.

I go back to browsing the store, opening books to random pages, sniffing the pulpy paper, the fresh ink. Paper used to smell like possibility. I loved it in any form. I loved it blank: in reams, in comp books, in cheap spiral notebooks. I loved it filled: in novels, in magazines, in textbooks. When I was about eight, I borrowed a copy of *Beowulf* in Old English from the library and flipped through it for weeks as if it were an esoteric text, as if it would impart wisdom if only I looked hard enough. And it did, years later, via a copy of the Seamus Heaney translation: *In off the moors, down through the mist bands / God-cursed Grendel came greedily loping.* Who gave a shit about the meaning when something like that could roll off your tongue?

But I shouldn't pretend I'm so smart or so literary. Another line from my youth that got caught in my head: *Guests of* The Oprah Winfrey Show *stay at the all-suite Omni Hotel located in the heart of Chicago's Magnificent Mile.* An announcer said it at the end of each episode of *Oprah,* which I watched every day after school before my mom got home. I often repeated it under my breath, matching the announcer's cadence. The meaning—of an all-suite Omni Hotel, of a Magnificent Mile, of Grendel greedily loping—came eventually, came later, came long after the sounds had left their mark. I liked the *inflections* and the *innuendoes.* I liked *The blackbird whistling,* and I could wait for the after. Language was a gift that you could just keep opening, endless as a hall of mirrors.

But nothing, never mind words, seems that exciting or esoteric anymore. I can see right to the bottom of everything.

I pick up a book with a sleek, pale, nude body strewn across the cover in soft focus. The author bio is only two sentences, the first telling her name, birth year, and alma mater, and the second simply, "This is her first novel." Ten years younger than I am, with a degree from a school that has an excellent reputation and horrible financial aid. It seems so shortsighted to include your birth year, as if your youth stays relevant for long. All this bio says to me is that the writer is rich.

You sensed that you should be following a different path, a more ambitious one, wrote Dostoevsky, *you felt that you were destined for other things but you had no idea how to achieve them and in your misery you began to hate everything around you.*

Which is to say: I am bitter. I am a hater. I am full of jealousy and rage.

I read the first few pages of the novel. It's well written: cheeky and ironic, smart and hostile. She uses words like *scintillating, fetid, juvenescence,* words I couldn't write without feeling like a fraud. I would take artless writhing over majestic backflips any day of the week.

The new paperback release of *Rolex* is on an endcap. I read the opening lines: *We were young. We were smart. We had too much money.* In the front matter, a blurb from Tom that begins, *Women everywhere . . .* Words, words, words. One table down, *Casualty* is prominently displayed. I pick up a copy, examine the author photo: his stupid hair, his serious face, smoothed by Photoshop, in serious black and white.

I don't believe for a second that Tom wrote *Casualty* for himself, with no hope that it would be published. He spent twenty years in a state of artistic ennui, choked by expectation and desperate to prove himself.

We like to think that artistic and academic careers are born of love, of a deep, unquellable desire (*God knows we don't do this for the money*). We write, supposedly, because it's beyond choice, because the craving to create is a constitutional fact (*If you can be anything else, be it*). But for most of us, there is something more fundamental than desire: There is need.

I remember my mom typing up "JCPenney and the Secret Cavern" for me on a boxy gray Dell because I had yet to master the Mavis Beacon typing program and she had been a secretary for many years. The story transformed into six very official-looking single-spaced pages, with double spaces after all the periods. I stapled it down the left side, one two three, so it opened like a book. A single copy, the tiniest print run, lost to time. When I held it in my hands, I thought my heart would burst—but that was nothing compared to the pure, cathartic thrill of writing it.

A few tables down, a man flips through a mass-market paperback of *A Game of Thrones*. It takes me a few seconds to assimilate the fact that this is Gabe. My heart clenches: a sad joy.

He looks better than I've ever seen him. He has a fresh haircut, new black square-framed glasses that are on trend yet not douchey, a warm-looking North Face coat. He glances up. It takes him a few seconds to assimilate me, probably because I, conversely, look worse than he has ever seen me.

"There you are," I say stupidly as we walk toward each other.

"You okay?" he asks. He glows in his beautiful, warm coat, which appears to have both a down and a fleece layer. His cheeks are rosy from the cold.

Good, great, or even *okay* will sound like a lie, so I say, "Still recovering from the end of the semester. You?"

"Okay," he says, but he looks happy. Probably toning it down for my benefit.

He's holiday shopping, though *A Game of Thrones,* he admits, is for himself. He buys me a latte and a cookie in the café with the easy flip of his credit card. I break off a little piece and then another, trying to savor it, talking about the cookie, the latte, the weather, the end of the semester, a student paper that was basically a found poem from Wikipedia. I talk about nothing for so long that he is already taking the plastic lid off his emptied drink to access trapped foam. "Do you want to, like, talk at all?" he says.

"I am talking."

"I mean, *about* . . ." he starts. "You never responded to my last text."

"The breakup text."

"Yes."

"The end of the semester was really busy." Guilt floods through me. "Could we make up for it? Grab a drink?"

"Like beer? Now?"

"Yeah, why not?"

"I can't drink in the middle of the afternoon," he says, and I sense that tone coming through, the tone we left on.

"Maybe we can do dinner one night," I say.

"I'm honestly pretty busy."

I glance over at Tom's book, which I placed on a chair, out of Gabe's line of sight. "I'm sorry," I say, but I don't know what for. Gabe seemed like one of those people I could call if things got really bad, and things are bad, things are getting worse. I feel that irrigation pressure in my nose and eyes, crying's pregame.

"I'm flying out in a few hours," he says, softening.

"For the holidays?"

"Yes, but also for good."

"Did you land something for next year?"

"Postdoc," he says. "Germany."

"Wow, congrats. Auf Wiedersehen." I don't feel jealousy, just an unjustified sense of abandonment.

"Not sure if it's advancement or exile."

"A reprieve, at the least. Berlin?"

"Well, we can't have everything," he says.

"I guess it wouldn't have worked out between us anyway," I say—meanly, like *I told you so.* Like *I wasn't planning on being a faculty wife in Bavaria,* though would that really be worse than my current situation?

"Maybe not," he says.

Outside, a gray mist has descended over the icy inner harbor.

"You would've gone and I would've stayed, so the original point—" I feel angry, like he chose Bavaria over me, even though I never really made myself a choice.

"Can we just say goodbye nicely?"

"Okay," I say. "I really think you'll do well in Germany, Gabe. I hope you like it."

"Thanks. I hope everything works out for you, too."

I watch him descend the escalator. He disappears, then reappears a few minutes later in the window with a plastic bag of purchases, walking through the empty redbrick promenade, over the pedestrian bridge with its guardrails wrapped in garland and cheap red velvet bows that twist in the wind.

Desolation sets in. I will probably never see him again.

I pick up Tom's book and, as casually as possible, slip it in my coat.

I trudge back up Rosedale's stupid driveway, since I don't want to raise suspicions by parking in the empty lot. By the time I'm on campus again, it's dark, and I'm so thoroughly embodying an icicle that I don't notice anything is amiss in the lot, in the building, in the hall as I drag myself toward the adjunct office. It occurs to me that a light is on only when a person materializes in front of me.

We both make the same high-pitched inhale of surprise, then realize we know each other. It's Dr. Brighton. She puts her hand on her chest, feels, I assume, her fast-beating heart.

"What are you doing here?" she asks.

"What are *you* doing here?" I ask.

"*I* forgot a book."

"Same," I say. She glances at the book in my hand and grows suspicious. If I have just arrived, why would I come in carrying a book—Dr. Sternberg's book, no less—while also looking for a book?

"Let's go get it, then," she says, and follows me to the adjunct office. In a movie, this is where the hero develops a plan, but I am not a hero, so I just open the door and turn on the light, revealing the mess: the black garbage bag spilling clothes, the horrific duffel open on the table, surrounded by dirty coffee cups. Most alarming of all, I am sure, is pieces of this very book, the one I've been writing, distributed across the wall like a conspiracy theorist's clues, the wide-ruled pages cut and torn from my notebook and taped up, Post-its scattered throughout, though some have peeled away from the wall, drifted to the dirty linoleum floor. It's certainly an avant-garde editorial method.

Dr. Brighton's chin hangs so low, I wonder if it will disconnect from the rest of her face. She closes her mouth, composing herself, then asks: "What is this?"

"Research," I mumble.

She walks to the wall, inspects the papers. For a moment I imagine her saying something like *You wrote this?* with the upward lilt of awe, but instead she says, "Like mental patients on a field trip?" with the downward lilt of disgust. She turns back around, surveys the office. "Are you living here?"

"Oh, I just needed some peace and quiet to work," I say. Another Post-it drifts to the floor, lies there in a U-shaped curl, legs up like a dead bug.

"You don't work here," she says, walking backward toward the door, eyes on me, as if I'm dangerous. "We're between semesters. And there's no reason you need to work here next semester."

"I'm still on payroll."

"I need you to leave immediately," she says, "or I will call the police."

"Sure, just let me get my book." She nods slowly as I walk toward the wall, but when she realizes that by *book*, I mean the papers taped up everywhere, she says, "No. No. Get out, now. Give me your office keys."

"Okay, okay," I say, putting my hands up in surrender. "But this stuff?" I add, pointing to my desk/table/bed/home. "Just my duffel," I promise. She doesn't nod, but she doesn't shake her head, either, so I shove what I can into the bag.

Then I press the keys into her hand, hard, looking her right in the eyes, trying to explain telepathically that this is her fault, while she is probably thinking about how smart she was to keep the riffraff locked out of her house when I took care of her plants and her pet.

A cloud covers the moon. This fucking driveway again, threading into darkness, contours lost to the grain of night. I strain to see, shivering, arms crossed over my chest. I feel empty and jagged, like a can of food that has been opened, eaten, and is destined for the trash. One foot in front of the other, one step at a time, until one foot slips on a slick patch, and I land hard on my hip. The ice flashes, the vast expanse of road illuminates. Headlights. I scramble off the street into the soggy grass as Dr. Brighton shoots ahead. I feel weak, ghostly, like I'm flickering.

I shiver in the front seat of my car as I write the names of everyone I know in my Notes app. Sophie, Gabe, Aliana, Brianna—all the Baltimore people have gone for Christmas, not that I would want to call them anyway. Do I know anyone else? Mateo is a traitor. Isaac is in Scandinavia. The rest of my grad school cohort left Baltimore; plus, they're under the impression that I ruined Tom's life. I haven't seen a single person from high school in at least a decade.

Maybe you're thinking: Anything is better than sleeping in your car. But why don't you try spending ten years getting a PhD, then Facebook-messaging someone who doesn't even like you, asking to invade their family Christmas, and, oh yeah, send you the cash to get there? You try it. Go ahead.

I find myself swiping on Tinder, wondering if it would really be so bad to talk with one of these guys over a meal, to let him pay, to go home with him. But no, it's ridiculous. I'm not going to do that. I'm wasting battery.

I flick out of the app, embarrassed, and call my mom.

"To what do I owe the pleasure?" she asks, sounding happy. I feel a sudden, overwhelming homesickness. My mother, she used to make me Campbell's soup when I was sick, pour me a glass of sparkling ginger ale. She would tuck me under a pink blanket on our faded floral couch, would push back my hair with her hand, feel my forehead. She would flick the mercury down in our yellow thermometer, place it under my tongue.

"My Christmas plans kind of fell through here," I say.

"Oh, I'm so sorry, sweetie," she says. A pause and then: "We'd love to have you here, of course—*of course*—but it's packed to the gills." I bite my knuckle. I will not cry in the car, on the phone with my mom, as she is explaining the sleeping arrangements in great detail, taking care to note that Don's sons are sleeping separate from their girlfriends, their fiancées, which is why every last room, public and private, is occupied, every last sheet accounted for, every last pillow already behind a head.

I cobble together a night. I'm acutely aware of how useful my whiteness is, how much I can get away with, as long as I stay clean. I drive to the Walmart superstore, use baby wipes and dry shampoo in the bathroom. In the fitting room, I change into a new outfit, ripping out the tags with my good teeth. I put my coat back on, leave my damp and dirty clothes in a neat pile under the dressing room bench. Then I stake out a booth in a twenty-four-hour diner, tell the waitress that my car broke down and I'm waiting for my dad to pick me up. I order a short stack of pancakes and a bottomless coffee for $8.49. When I wear out my welcome at four a.m., I drive to the airport, pretend I'm very early for an early flight. All the while, as night advances toward day, I read Tom's book, trying to stay awake.

—

The Professor has become an outcast. He is holed up in a cozy cabin in Vermont—woodburning stove, inset oak bookshelves, a wine decanter, rugs from a sabbatical in India, wooden carvings from trips to Ghana and South Africa.

When the married Professor was in his forties, he had sex with a graduate student, age twenty-six. Over the course of their relationship, they wrote notes to each other on index cards. He saved hers in a box like a card catalog and sometimes flips through them. They are about his dog, Carver. They are about a box under the bed. On one card, the student describes, in great detail, the items in the box, how hard she came with the vibrator on his bed. But the cards mostly remind him of his own eloquent replies, which were apparently full of profound thoughts on life and literature.

One night they go out for drinks to talk about her work. He opens up about his mother's illness, she about her father's death a few years before, and they go back to his house. They are drunk. She mentions the sex toys. They go upstairs and look at them. She uses the vibrator in front of him, just as she described on the card. But for some reason—guilt, perhaps, or the student's innate inability to be sexy—he's struggling to get hard. She reaches awkwardly for his dick, tugs a little, gives him a blow job, practically insists on it. That does the trick.

He likes her, but he is not in love with her, and regretfully, he has just cheated on his wife. When he breaks it off with the young woman, she thinks it's because she's his student. She quits school so they can be together, becomes enraged when he says they cannot. She starts essentially stalking him: waiting outside his office for hours, showing up at his house in the dead of night, which is how the wife finds out. The young woman is totally losing it and eventually moves away, but the professor's marriage is over. Several years pass, and one day he receives a letter from the young woman in which she apologizes for their catastrophic ending.

So it's a total shock when, decades later, she publicly accuses him of misconduct. She has rewritten the entire experience in light of the cultural climate! The Professor is forced to retire, and for several months, he just goes fishing, drinks whiskey, and wallows.

The book is "genre-bending" insofar as the Professor refers to classic and contemporary literature throughout, the story revealing itself through the books he peruses. The tone ranges from academic to philosophical to faux memoir. He looks at the words his younger self underlined, and he is thrust into reverie. Underline as madeleine.

It is a time of reckoning for the Professor. Despite his early resistance, he begins to understand some of the rudimentary facets of feminism. He begins to feel horrible, just as we begin to feel maybe this former student was kind of overreacting. Isn't she sort of blaming her personal failures on him? Isn't there some path to forgiveness for this guy, who has repented so much via mulling?

A bit about the student: She is attractive in her youthfulness but perhaps attractive only because of her youthfulness. She is smart but uncultured, charming but awkward, talented but not talented enough—she can't put herself aside, can't generate spontaneously. She lives in a houseful of loud roommates where mousetraps snap up newts and cockroaches. No, he did not love her. He took pity on her. He took her under his wing.

Maybe there was a student once who wrote Tom elegant notes on index cards, who talked with him deeply about life, love, literature, and sexuality. Maybe there were many of them. But it was not the eighties, and they were not me. If they were meant to be me—and surely there are elements—he has reimagined it all to his benefit, as if our relationship were more a meeting of minds than cringey text messages. I should be glad she seems sophisticated, but it costs the book what should be its central tension: For as much as the novel constantly insists that the Professor is contending with gray area, the details imply that the Professor and the student are on relatively equal footing, that the area is not all that gray.

I believe none of us is beyond reproach and no one is a single thing. I believe *it was a different time* gets twisted but holds some water, that you have to catch up as the framing shifts, that the lens of discourse is not immutable fact. I believe *good* and *bad* don't often do justice to actual life, that an artist does not have to be good to produce good work. I believe that misogynists can become feminists, and racists can become anti-racists, and homophobes can end up at Pride parades with rainbows painted on their faces. But often the promise of change is a cover, a decoy, a distraction, buying time for people to forget you haven't changed at all.

It was infuriating, that Tom was pretending to take up this noble residence in the no-man's-land of nuance, as if he were interested in dialogue, as if you could take any responsibility for a past you've rewritten.

I am trying to tell you something, not just about my life but about America. About how the fracturing of labor fractures lives, about how I saw that reflected in my relationships, about how I was so sure education would save me, how the PhD was supposed to be a pinnacle, how this is my life, my *one wild and precious life.* I am trying to tell you something about the emptiness of narrative, how I feel ostracized from it, how I have this awful craving for the climax that always alludes me: for some explanation of my sexuality, some childhood memory that clicks it all into place, someone to blame. This is what stories have done to me, made me believe in cause and effect, a karmic line.

All this time I've struggled to make sense of my life within the context of my life—within my own plotline, my own flaws, my own successes—but that's the trick, that's why I'm failing. The narrative is bigger than me, a riptide, a bottom line that doesn't account for me and never will, and so here I am, accounting for myself, the tiniest act of resistance, of protest, the only bit of power I have.

I finish reading Tom's book at Enoch Pratt, Baltimore's main library. Then I spend the rest of the day typing my thoughts, these notes, whatever the fuck this is, in the computer lab, in an email to myself. Right before the library closes at eight p.m., I press send, get a stupid jolt of excitement when the inbox reads 1. After, I walk to the nearby grocery store, buy cheese and crackers, and eat them as I wander the aisles of a windowless CVS.

It's after ten p.m. by the time I park in an inconspicuous spot in my old neighborhood. I choose it simply because I've parked here a thousand times, on this small arc of curb without signs or restrictions, simply because there'll be no streetlight shining directly in my eyes, simply because I won't have to waste precious gas searching for something else.

I curl up in the backseat wearing my coat and the sleep mask I'm supposed to be reviewing, put my forearm under my head, and close my eyes. I drift into a half sleep, a fitful trance. I see the dilating pupils of Sophie's hazel eyes, the flex of her muscles during a rant; I see Gabe walking down the redbrick promenade alone, which is what he was used to being, would be again soon, this time he wouldn't even speak the language; I see my Post-its fluttering from the wall at Rosedale; I see Tom on a hot summer night, looking up and down the street, saying, "Cheever loves you." Saying, "Want to come and say hi?" Saying, "Only if you want."

The knocking at my car window doesn't register at first. I'm awake and not awake. I think it's a dream. But then the knocking gets louder, faster, urgent. Pure panic rises in my throat. I inch up my eye mask.

A gun at the window, aimed directly at me. I seem to rise away from myself. The tangled ball of terror in my chest becomes simple data, 1's and 0's.

Three men wearing balaclavas surround the car. The man with the gun taps on the glass again, says something like "Open the door and let me see your hands. Then there won't be any problems." Or maybe that's a line from a *Law & Order: SVU* episode's cold open. But here, the crime is not the setup for a cozy story of justice but an entirely predictable ending that I stupidly didn't see coming.

I exit the car. "Don't look at me," says the man with the gun forcefully, almost frantically. "Go to the sidewalk. Get on the ground." The other men are in shadow, shifting, nervous, thin as Slender Man, maybe even teenagers. I feel bad for them. But I feel worse for me.

I kneel on the ground with my hands up, realizing I picked the absolute worst place in the world to park, not one apartment window in view. My arms shake. One of the other guys says, "No, bitch, are you stupid?" Another guy laughs. "*Lay* on the ground, facedown."

I lie on the ground, facedown. The ground is cold as ice. The concrete is like sandpaper on my forehead, the tip of my nose. My throat is cement. I can hear my teeth chattering. I can feel my body trembling as a guy pats me down. His hands feel like nothing. Everything is muted, as if happening underwater, in the deep sunless sea among the anglerfish with their dead eyes, their luminescent lures, their horror-movie mouths packed with fangs. He could kill me if he wants. He could pants me right here and rape me. All of them could, one after the other or all at once. I wouldn't even scream, for fear of being shot. I think of Brianna's stupid fucking podcasts, all the DNA that those dead women managed to peel off with their fingernails. How did they do it? I can't even move. Am I an idiot? Have I just calmly acquiesced to my own execution? Is this going to be my last thought?

All these years of abstract concern about the poverty and violence in Baltimore, as if it were a far-off country I sometimes read about in the news. Because that wasn't my Baltimore; that was the other Baltimore. I reassured myself this way, whenever I was hurrying home in the dark: Not over here.

But now I'm over here with my face in the pavement, and maybe somewhere in Hampden or Roland Park or Homeland, a woman with better shoes and better sleeping arrangements is clicking her way home through the dark, reassuring herself, relieved, essentially, that it's my face in the pavement and not hers.

I am not here, I think, the mantra of a person up against a wall, flat against a sidewalk.

Car doors close. An engine rumbles to life. A warm puff of exhaust drifts over my head. Then silence.

I tell myself to get up, but nothing happens. "Move your arm," I tell myself, but my arm will not move. "Move your finger," I tell myself, but my finger will not move.

A noise, and panic sets in all over again, so thoroughly that my entire bladder empties, all that bottled-up fear escaping in a rush of warmth, as if I weren't humiliated enough. Not two feet from me, the glowing eyes of a rat. Is it the tailless rat from my old apartment? The rat I have mangled, shunned, hoped abstractly is still alive? *Here we are,* he says. *You and me.*

I jump to my feet. I can move. I can really move. I sprint to my old apartment building on Preston, as if the rat is chasing me down. I ring the buzzer of my old apartment over and over, but no one answers. If Brianna still lives here, she's certainly home for the holidays. I stand in the doorway, out of breath, the cold piss on my pants stinging my thighs. I assess my remaining belongings: coat on my body, eye mask caught in my hair, phone miraculously in my pocket. I brush the grit from my forehead.

The morning is hard as crystal, the air icy blue. My lungs rattle. The piss on my pants has dried, but even so my legs are cold enough that they seem to blend in with the air. The police were useless, though the guys at the twenty-four-hour convenience store gave me a free sandwich.

I'm walking down Preston when I spy Divine. She is tucked in a narrow alley, so that if you were driving, you might catch only a flash of her, but on foot, you could marvel at the whole damn thing: a three-story mural of the drag queen John Waters made famous, the so-called queen of filth. As a character, Divine was unabashedly everything. Unabashedly fat, always wearing tight, revealing dresses. "Filth are my politics," she said. She reveled in her own anarchy. She celebrated all that one might criticize her for. Her message was this: You can take what everyone believes is worst about you and turn it, extravagantly, into your style. An outcast who stole the show.

The mural is a portrait: a plump face with massive eyelashes, dramatic winged eyeliner, and thin, arched eyebrows. Divine's unruly web of platinum hair wisps out over a bright sky-blue background, extending so dramatically that it becomes a wash of cream, one with the wall. Written in her hair is *I'm So Beautiful*. A platitude that would annoy me coming from the usual suspects—Instagram influencers and makeup models and women paying thirty dollars for a yoga class across the street, less revelation than redundancy. But tangled in the platinum hair of Divine, it feels like an elegant *fuck you.* The words seem to lift off the mural letter by letter, streaming around me in a spiral, as in Disney when magic rains in a swirl of sparkles and Cinderella is transformed.

since feeling is first / who pays any attention / to the syntax of things / will never wholly kiss you, wrote e. e. cummings. *They is, they is, they is,* ends a Tobias Wolff story in which a surly literary critic, in the final moments before his death, is taken back to a simple, lyrical, grammatically incorrect phrase he heard as a kid. "Whether you like it or not is not that interesting," Risky Business and teachers everywhere insist, implying that what you feel is unrelated to anything important you can say about art. But, of course, feeling is the whole point of literature and life, and if a mural of Divine makes me cry, so be it, let the tears freeze on my cheeks.

A car honks and my heart goes ballistic. The spell is broken, the letters evaporate. My cheeks are wet. It's Christmas Eve. I'm all pumpkin and puffer and piss-stained pants.

I go to Starbucks, stare in the bathroom mirror.

In books, first-person narrators look in mirrors as an excuse to describe their own face. In movies, characters go into public bathrooms to give themselves long, hard stares that range from pep-talky to soul-searching. Such characters often look worn and tired in hot, anemic ways. They grip sink edges because they're having a breakdown and need to balance; they splash water on their face to shock themselves awake, literally and metaphorically. Maybe there is some Person Zero who, without pretense, went into a restroom and gripped the sink edges or splashed water on their face. But now such an act always has the tinge of performance.

So, here I am in a book and also a bathroom, gripping the sink edges, overhead lighting such that my undereye circles are particularly pronounced. The largest wrinkle on my forehead is very entrenched. My bottom lip is picked to shreds. My eyes are watery. My hair is greasy again, little strands rising at the crown in shiny arches. I notice one piece of hair, one magical piece of hair, shimmering under the fluorescent light, as if it's glowing from the inside. I lift it delicately between my fingertips.

But no, it's not sparkling. You might call it silver. You might call it gray.

"You have time," older people always insist, envious because they don't. "You have to start somewhere," they say, implying that progress and time are fundamentally linear. So you squander time thinking it's plentiful, then you make decisions thinking you can unmake them, and all the while *you have time* becomes less and less true, and all those decisions are doors closing behind you, and then somehow you're drinking the dregs of someone else's coffee, writing about your trip to the bathroom in the Notes app, swiping desperately on Tinder in an imminently closing Starbucks, your phone charged but for the grace of a barista.

Something akin to homesickness rises inside me. It sits in my chest like a black hole—no, it's more like a magnet, not an empty urge to consume but a desperate reaching. Maybe that's been my mistake all along, a crucial misinterpretation of the subtext. What I thought was emptiness was really longing.

Why didn't I ever put my head on Gabe's chest, listen to his heart, feel the heat of his body? Why didn't I wrap my arms around Sophie, watch *The Kardashians* with her under all those covers, with the glow of the laptop on our faces? Why did I always skip over that part? Was sex an excuse to not really be with people? But this longing for connection, it's not useful now, when I've been ostracized, when I've ostracized myself, when everything's precarious. It's the least useful feeling I could have.

I block it out, shove it down, narrow my focus. What I need right now, tonight, is a meal, a shower, a bed. I swipe right methodically, but it's Christmas Eve, and the few men who respond want to meet after Christmas. The swiping becomes less purposeful, more hopeless, just a distraction as time and the battery drain.

And then: a black-and-white photo, a serious face, a cashmere sweater, too much hair, moody eyes.

Only in literature do you have to earn an ending. In real life, it's the luck of the draw.

The jerk of my thumb, less a decision than a twitch, and it's a match.

Me: You swiped right.

Him: As did you.

Why?

Me: Why not?

What about you?

Him: Same, I guess. Suspense. Why not? Alone on Christmas.

Me: No Aliana?

Him: We needed some distance, to think things over.

And you? Why are you alone?

Me: I just couldn't deal with people this year.

Him: So here you are, among the sad and lonelys.

Me: Here I am, with you.

Him: I have to admit, I'm shocked you swiped, never mind messaged.

Me: I'm shocked you replied.

Him: Are you here to tell me off?

The thing about rock bottom is nothing's a gamble. You can't lose what you already lost.

I imagine Tom's house, the warmth of it: a Christmas tree strung in white lights, a fire roaring in the fireplace, shearling-lined moccasins, Cheever curled up on the carpet, though Cheever has been dead for years.

When I picture Tom, I imagine the original him, the him I first met, the him that is still older than I am now. I make myself conjure the current version: the drooping jowls, the hang of the eyelids. With him and Aliana on the rocks, he has probably been moping and drinking for days, unshaved, a grotesque non-beard. Forget the tree, forget the lights, forget the fire. He is probably playing Mannheim Steamroller on repeat. But the house is heated. There is a bed.

How many nights could I squeeze out of this? How many showers, how many meals? What else could I get? Could I retrieve my book from the wall of Rosedale? Could I have a child? Could I be a spousal hire? Ridiculous. But I understood—suddenly, completely—my mother.

Me: We got along once upon a time, no?

Him: We did.

Me: Then let's call a Christmas truce.

Him: Okay.

Me: This is a hookup app.

Him: It is.

Are you fucking with me here?

Me: I'm not. We're both alone. We're on here because we're horny. We know each other already. Sensuality, sexuality, it's not an insult, you know? Sex between two consenting adults. We both get what we want, we both go our own way.

Him: I feel like you're fucking with me somehow.

Me: You'll know I'm not when your dick is in my mouth.

Him: You want to suck my dick?

Me: I do. I'm coming over.

I order an Uber—fifteen dollars; fifteen-minute wait—then reopen the Notes app. Tom once claimed that, in an ideal ending, a character should begin an action but not finish it, leaving "a tiny sliver of possibility between what could happen next and what will happen next."

For example, the main character runs toward the edge of a cliff, screaming. Or tightens her hand in a fist. Or opens her mouth to say *I do*. Or pinches a match between her forefinger and thumb. In one Nabokov story, the telephone rings again.

Then we close the book, and whatever happens, happens. She trips midsprint or, more likely, she plummets. She loosens her grip or she punches his lights out. She says *I can't* or, more likely, she says *I do* despite everything in her body telling her not to. She answers the phone and the news is catastrophic; she answers the phone and the line is dead. She writes a novel under a desk and somebody, somewhere gives a shit or nobody, nowhere does. The match blows out or she burns it all down.

But this is not that kind of story.

I don't want you to have any doubt about what I am going to do next.

At Tom's house, I'll get down on my knees as quickly as possible—in the kitchen, before he knifes a lime, before he tells me again what a gimlet is. I'll look up at his face with big POV porn eyes and I'll touch his belt buckle and I'll say, "Can I?" And I'll let him say, "Sam, wow, I don't know. Are you sure you're comfortable with this?" I'll let him say, "Only if you want."

"Please," I'll reply. "I want to. This is what I want." Because sometimes faking it *is* the art.

Then I'll lift the cool silver prong out of its hole. I'll slide the smooth leather belt out of its buckle. I'll unbutton. I'll unzip. I'll open wide. I'll unhinge my jaw if I have to. I'll do all of it: the glass dildo, the silicone Rabbit. I'll do whatever he wants with a disconnected silicone cool. Who knows, I might even like it.

I exit the coffee shop to wait for the car outside, bracing myself against the wind, against the fear of being a singular woman in a city deserted of all but the desperate. Sex with Tom will not change the past and probably will not change the future, but as I wait on the icy edges of Baltimore, I convince myself that it might prove something about how I was wronged. It's not as if I have something to lose—not my job, certainly not my dignity. It seems, almost, what I am owed, not the anticlimax of not fucking one's teacher, but the salty reality of his dick in my mouth, the rumor made manifest, years too late.

When I was in my early twenties, fucking Tom had seemed like such a big deal, my disgust that night felt catastrophic. But it won't be any skin off my back now. I separate myself from my body, as I have learned to do through sex, through the machinelike grading of student papers, through cold nights in the adjunct office and tooth pain and a carjacking and pissing my pants and the humiliation of waiting for paychecks and the ends never justifying the means. It has all led me here—not to a place where I know what I want, or what I want even matters, but to a place where I can stomach anything.

My one sad, secret power: I can be unspecific, even to myself.

Works Quoted

THE CAMPUS NOVEL (Chapter 4)

What happens to a dream deferred? "Harlem" by Langston Hughes

The apparition of these faces in the crowd . . . "In a Station of the Metro" by Ezra Pound

EMBODIMENT (Chapter 5)

And I sat among the piles of paper . . . "The Age of Genius" by Bruno Schulz

Something is rotten . . . Hamlet by William Shakespeare

So it goes . . . Poo-tee-weet . . . Slaughterhouse-Five by Kurt Vonnegut

What lips my lips have kissed, and where, and why . . . "Sonnet XLIII" by Edna St. Vincent Millay

with dreams, with drugs, with waking nightmares . . . "Howl" by Allen Ginsberg

so many things seem filled / with the intent to be lost . . . "One Art" by Elizabeth Bishop

the low, humiliating premise of union . . . "Mock Orange" by Louise Glück

TEXTS (Chapter 6)

and in the eyes of the people there is the failure . . . The Grapes of Wrath by John Steinbeck *my dad died (cancer, lung) when I was thirteen . . .* is an intentional mirroring of a line from *Lolita* by Vladimir Nabokov: *My very photogenic mother died in a freak accident (picnic, lightning) when I was three . . .*

Many years later, as he faced the firing squad . . . One Hundred Years of Solitude by Gabriel García Márquez

EMERGENCY (Chapter 7)

Tomorrow, and tomorrow, and tomorrow . . . Macbeth by William Shakespeare

BARELY VISIBLE THINGS (Chapter 9)

O-gape of complete despair . . . "The Moon and the Yew Tree" by Sylvia Plath

Lozenge of love . . . "Sad Steps" by Philip Larkin

Wandering companionless . . . "Art thou pale for weariness" by Percy Bysshe Shelley

Staring from her hood of bone . . . "Edge" by Sylvia Plath

ORAL REPORT (Chapter 10)

His soul swooned slowly . . . "The Dead" by James Joyce

As Freezing persons, recollect the Snow . . . "[After great pain]" (372) by Emily Dickinson

Do I contradict myself? . . . Song of Myself by Walt Whitman

SOMEONE SPECIFIC (Chapter 11)

Have you forgotten what we were like then . . . "Animals" by Frank O'Hara

America I've given you all and now I'm nothing . . . "America" by Allen Ginsberg

SCRAPS (Chapter 12)

And you, you ridiculous people, you expect me to help you . . . "Car Crash While Hitchhiking" by Denis Johnson

So many of us! So many of us! . . . "Mushrooms" by Sylvia Plath

Do I dare to eat a peach? . . . "The Love Song of J. Alfred Prufrock" by T. S. Eliot

and nothing that we made / that night is worth more than me . . . "Sweet Will" by Philip Levine

I would not want to be one of those writers . . . "The Brigadier and the Golf Widow" by John Cheever

HUMILIATION (Chapter 13)

The truth is, we know so little about life . . . "Here is a lesson in creative writing" from *A Man Without a Country* by Kurt Vonnegut

What do you read, my lord? . . . Hamlet by William Shakespeare

In off the moors, down through the mist bands . . . Beowulf translated by Seamus Heaney

inflections . . . innuendoes . . . "Thirteen Ways of Looking at a Blackbird" by Wallace Stevens

You sensed that you should be following a different path . . . Netochka Nezvanova by Fyodor Dostoevsky

one wild and precious life . . . "The Summer Day" by Mary Oliver

since feeling is first . . . "[since feeling is first]" by e. e. cummings

They is, they is, they is . . . "Bullet in the Brain" by Tobias Wolff

Acknowledgments

My editor, Emily Polson at Scribner, understood the book immediately and knew how to make it better. I can't thank her enough for her attention and care while reading many drafts; her insights transformed the novel into what I always hoped it would become. I couldn't have done it without her. Thank you also to the entire team at Scribner for transforming the manuscript into a beautiful book.

Thanks also goes to my agent, Jenni Ferrari-Adler at Aevitas, who provided essential early comments and knew exactly where to send the manuscript once it was ready. And to Colleen Hubbard, the astute and encouraging first reader I desperately needed.

My parents, Karin Hansen and Richard Adelmann, have always celebrated my creativity and accepted me for exactly who I am. My brother, Joe, and his wife, Sarah, gave me the space—literally—to finish writing this book. I could write pages of thank-yous because it is as true as it has ever been: The support and love of my family and friends are what make my life most meaningful. Thank you.

I wrote the chaotic first draft of this book during National Novel Writing Month. It's a challenge to create without self-judgment, but writing at high speed really forces you to get out of your own way. The word-processing program Scrivener made it much easier to sort through the wreckage. And there was no better place to begin that task than in the loving arms of Art Omi, a refuge of time, space, community, and care. Many thanks to all the amazing people who made that magical month a success.

Thank you also to the Baker Artist Awards and the Maryland State Arts Council for their recognition as I started my writing career in Baltimore. I loved living in Baltimore, and my time there made a big impression on me. While the places in the book are a mixture of real and invented, my aim was to represent the spirit of the city as best as I could.

Morgan State University professor Dr. Lawrence Brown describes Baltimore using the terms the *Black Butterfly* and the *White L.* Of Baltimore he says, "The white neighborhoods on the map that form the shape of an 'L' accumulate structured advantages, while Black neighborhoods, shaped in the form of a butterfly, accumulate structured disadvantages. Baltimore's hypersegregation is the root cause of racial inequity, crime, health inequities/disparities, and civil unrest." Marceline White, executive director of Economic Action MD, has put it this way: "I had always described the two Baltimores as part of one body, with the mainly White, wealthy neighborhoods comprising the spine and the predominantly Black neighborhoods as the vital organs, the heart and breath of the city."

At the end of writing this book—and at exactly the right time—I read "The Ballad of Sexual Optimism" from Maggie Nelson's *On Freedom,* which helped give voice to some of my free-floating, unarticulated thoughts about the MeToo movement. Nelson quotes scholar Tanya Serisier, who says that "the enthusiastic consent model . . . proposes that a verbal contract model of sex is the best—or even only—way to have good sex, implicitly devaluing other forms of sexual practice or sexual communication." Nelson's essay helped me navigate my own thoughts on the complexity of female desire.

Finally, and really firstly, and also once again, thank you to my partner, Derek Denman. His support, insights, and edits were integral to this book. He's also the reason the book exists at all.

I met Derek when he was an adjunct professor in Baltimore. He was in the middle of a significant health crisis, which involved two major surgeries. He was also teaching five classes at three different colleges and unable to take time off. The situation was so awful as to be absurd, and one night we joked about all the ways his life would be perfect fodder for a sitcom called *The Adjunct*. The next day, I wrote down ten pages of notes. Five years later—after Derek had worked in three different countries, at five different institutions, in six different departments—I looked back at those notes and began this book. Even as he moved, taught, advised, applied, reapplied, published articles, and wrote his own book, his support for me remained.

Precarious and low-paid intellectual labor is becoming the norm. A 2022 American Federation of Teachers report on adjuncts and contingent faculty—which now make up 68 percent of college faculty—found that a quarter of those surveyed made less than $25,000 a year; 38 percent relied on government assistance; and 75 percent had term-to-term contracts. Meanwhile, according to a 2024 report from the Education Data Initiative, the average cost of college in the U.S. is over $38,000 per student per year.

I was drawn to the plight of the adjunct because it reflected my own experience struggling to make ends meet as a fiction writer with a patchwork of freelance jobs. Even as Derek and I met the professional milestones of our respective fields—now with four published books between us—the question of how we would make money never fully resolved itself thanks to short-term contracts and precarious freelance work.

Society tries to convince us that our individual intelligence, talent, and drive will make us or break us. We're told that artistic and intellectual work is a labor of love, but love doesn't pay for rent, groceries, health care, or student loans. If these kinds of careers are unsustainable without independent wealth, they will always keep out those who can't afford to be in them. This is particularly horrifying in fields that shape our thought and culture.

Across many industries, gig and contract labor is replacing full-time work. The adjunct, the delivery app driver, and the freelance writer have a lot in common. I want the same thing for all of us: wages that create possibility, that reflect our value as workers and as humans; wages that let you, let Derek, let me, live stable, healthy, happy lives.

About the Author

Maria Adelmann is the award-winning author of the story collection *Girls of a Certain Age* and the novel *How to Be Eaten*, an NPR book of the year and Belletrist book club pick. She has written for *The New York Times*, *Tin House*, *n+1*, *Electric Literature*, *McSweeney's*, and many other publications, and her work has been distinguished by The Best American Short Stories. Adelmann has worked variously as a hotel reviewer, product tester, and copywriter, and once sailed around the world while teaching for Semester at Sea. She has lived in Baltimore and Copenhagen and now resides in Philadelphia.